A RIPPLE OF POWER & PROMISE

BOOK I IN THE POWER AND PROMISE SERIES

JORDAN A. DAY

CONTENT WARNING

Please be aware that this book contains the following: Physical assault, misogynistic ideologies, mention of infant death, mention of sexual assault, gruesome and descriptive death, explicit language, excessive drinking, sexual content

Cover Design and illustrations by Laura Shallcrass
Editing by Hillary Sames
Map by Kenneth Day

Dedication

To my late grandmother, Irene Morgan. I didn't become a lawyer like you always wanted, but I *did* write a book with smut, so that's sort of the same thing.

To Booktok for sparking my love of reading once again. And for allowing me the opportunity to meet the most amazing people.

And finally, to *me*. You did it. You wrote a fucking book. Sure there were lots of tears and coffee involved. Not to mention the plethoras of 'what the *fuck* am I even doing?!'... But you did it. Remember that you wrote this story for no one other than yourself. Just to prove that you could. So fuck the haters and be proud of yourself. This is something that you did, and there isn't a single person in this world that can diminish that accomplishment. I'm proud of you, kid.

P.s. Give Taylor her scarf back, Jake.

DISPARYA

TENEBRAE

AGNITIO

VENATOR

ARCANUS

MINISTRO

CAELUM

THE SOUTHERN SEA

KINGDOMS OF DISPARYA

CAELUM
ELEMENTAL MAGIC

UNDA: WATER AND ICE
IGNISIAN: FIRE AND HEAT
AERIAN: WEATHER MANIPULATION

MINISTRO
ANATOMICAL MAGIC

MEDICUS: HEALER
EMPATHI: EMOTION MANIPULATION
IMPERIUM: ANATOMICAL MANIPULATION

AGNITIO
INTELLECTUAL MAGIC

SEER: CLAIRVOYANCE
VERUS: TRUTH TELLER
MAGUSIER: MAGIC AND BOND DETECTION

VENATOR
STEALTH MAGIC

OCULI: PRETERNATURAL VISION
SONOR: PRETERNATURAL HEARING
VENARI: PRETERNATURAL TRACKING

TENEBRAE
DARK MAGIC

TREMO: FEAR INDUCER
SHADOW SHIFTER: DARKNESS MANIPULATION
ILLUSIO: ILLUSIONISTS

PRONUNCIATION GUIDE

AINSLEY: AYNZ - LEE
DASHIELL: DASH - EEL
FELIX: FEE - LICKS
IMOGEN: IH - MUH - GIN
PERCEVAL: PUR - SUH - VL

CAELUM: KAY - LOOM
MINISTRO: MIN - EE - STROW
AGNITIO: AGNEE - SHE - OH
VENATOR: VEN - AH - TOUR
TENEBRAE: TEN - EE - BRAY
DISPARYA: DIS - PAR - YUH

UNDA: OO - N - DA
IGNISIAN: IG - NISS - EE - AN
AERIAN: AIR - EE - AN
MEDICUS: MED - EE - CUSS
EMPATHI: EM - PATH - EE

1.

There was dirt and crushed leaves in all of my crevices. Yes, all of them. Looking up through the forest canopy, I squinted, taking in the blazing light of the scorching summer sun. That's what I wanted to feel, the red-hot flame of burning passion pulsing through my veins, between my legs. Instead, I came to the unfortunate realization that my one escape from the endless boredom of this place had now become just as mundane as everything else. I felt Logan's gaze on me and reluctantly pulled myself back to the familiar movements of redressing.

"Did you, uh..." Logan asked. I looked up from fastening my pants to see his brow raised in question as he raked his gaze over my body.

"Oh yeah," I told him flatly, rolling my eyes as I pulled my shirt over my head, covering the grass still stuck to my sweat-slicked back. My skin felt dirty and itchy in response, but whatever. I'd bathe later.

"Yeah, I thought so. I could tell," he replied triumphantly, leaning back onto the grassy clearing, an arm behind his head and a cocky grin upon his face. Clearly, Logan didn't understand sarcasm. Or the female body, for that matter. Sex with him had always been okay, at times good even. But never great. Being with him was always more about passing the time than anything else. There were no feelings there, no commitments. Neither of us expected anything more than what we had agreed on—just sex. For the past four years, that's all it had been, and I found myself happy that it would soon be over.

"Same time next week?" he asked, rolling onto his side and biting his lip as he stared at me. He opened his legs slightly wider as a reminder—and an invitation.

I couldn't help the snort that came from me. He held himself in too high of a regard.

"Can't," I told him as I tied back my hair, leaves getting caught in the leather strap as I twisted it around my deep golden-brown strands, the shining sun pulling forward the bright hints of copper within them. "I'm leaving tomorrow."

"When will you be back?"

"I won't be," I said, pulling on my boots. "I'm moving to the palace."

"You got a Gift?" he asked incredulously.

A Gift. Magic. *Power*. They were all different words for the same thing. On a person's twenty-first birthday, their body automatically transitions from mere human to immortal, granting them a long lifespan and self-healing properties. If they were lucky, the Gods would bestow upon them one of the three Gifts of magic available in the kingdom they resided in. To receive the magic of a kingdom was rare and often only came to those descended from a powerful bloodline.

"Nope," I told him as I stood, brushing off the leaves from my clothes. Logan had never bothered to get to know me on a personal level, and to be fair, I didn't care to get to know him either, so there would be no way that he would be aware that I was still months away from my twenty-first birthday.

"Then why are you going?" Logan drawled, still making no move to get dressed or cover himself, his legs still spread wide. I suppressed a gag. It was common knowledge that if you were fortunate enough to possess a Gift, you would forgo your current life and move to the palace to be of service to the king and Caelum. The fact that I had no magic yet was still moving to the palace, warranted his surprise.

"I'm marrying the prince," I told him as I stretched out my aching back. I wasn't sore in a good way—that mind-blowing, twisting your body into different positions that you didn't know were possible kind of way. Nope. It was that out of rhythm, being pressed firmly into the ground and trying to ignore the pebbles digging into your back over and over again kind of way.

Logan bellowed with laughter, doubling over himself as he did. Well, at least he was covered now.

"You're joking," he said through the laughter. I shrugged as I grabbed my satchel from the ground, wrapping it over my shoulder. Logan's face grew serious, his eyes wide as the realization hit him. "Tell me you're fucking joking Ainsley." His tone was sharp and cold, and it wasn't from jealousy but rather fear.

"I'm fucking joking Ainsley," I told him, mocking his words. Logan shot to his feet, jumping into his pants as he hastily dressed, pure panic coating his movements.

"You're marrying the *prince*? How long have you known?!" he asked breathlessly, angrily, as he struggled to get his clothes on. I looked to the sky peeking through the canopy of trees high above, letting the heat from the sun wash over my face. Letting the musky, sweet smell of the leaves flood through me. Gods, I'd miss this place. Not what Logan and I always did here, but the location itself. The peacefulness and serenity of it.

"For years," I replied nonchalantly, still not taking my eyes from the world above.

"Fucking Gods, Ainsley! How could you keep that from me?!" The fury with which he spoke commanded my attention. "You can't tell anyone about us. Ever," he seethed. Of course, he'd want to keep it a secret. Screwing the future Princess of Caelum for the past four years wouldn't be a good look for him. Did he think my future husband or father-in-law would call for his death if they had found out?

"Trust me," I said, looking him up and down. "It's not something I'll be bragging about." I turned on my heel and headed out of the clearing, calling over my shoulder as I did. "Have a nice life, Logan."

2.

I took the long way home, wanting to savor the last of my freedom before I was sent off to be the property of the king. Before every decision was determined and made for me. Before, I had little to no choice in anything. Granted, my choices in life were slim to none as it was, but still. I had more freedom now than I would in a mere day—than I would as a future princess.

I had made my feelings on the whole arrangement crystal clear, protesting the betrothal any chance I could, whether it was throwing immature temper tantrums or threatening to run away, though I had no idea where I would go. Maybe somewhere north. Somewhere far away from here. I didn't have any family—or even friends, for that matter—who would take me in if I left. I once even threatened to tell the entire town that I was the prince's intended bride, a secret I was told never to reveal for my own safety. Rather than that working, I was laughed at and told to 'go ahead.' They explained that I would surely be murdered by jealous women or men who wanted their daughter on the throne instead of me. Obviously, I didn't go through with it, save for just revealing the knowledge to Logan moments ago. Nothing I said or did changed my Caregivers' minds; the two women that had cared for me kept me alive since infancy. Since my parents were murdered, leaving me an orphan.

My mother and father had worked out the marriage agreement with the king before I was even born. Apparently, I hailed from a bloodline powerful enough to be worthy of marrying into royalty. How joyous for me. Though I possessed no magic now, due to my lineage, it was assumed that I would. And a lot of it. That's all that mattered to the kingdom, anyway. That's all the royal line looked for when choosing their bride. Not who she was as a person but what she had to offer them.

The royals always tended to pick from the strongest families in the kingdom, choosing women they knew would give them the most during the Entwining Ceremony. The stupid, misogynistic Entwining Ceremony. The time when a woman not only had to swear her commitment to the man in a union of marriage but also had to relinquish part of her magic, part of *her*, to him as well. Women were never to be stronger than men, no matter what, and the Entwining Ceremony ensured that. Her power, her magic, her Gift would lessen. It would dwindle as her husband would take some of it for himself, leaving her with mere scraps of her former self and him even more powerful. The thought made my blood boil and my stomach turn over. I often found myself praying to the Gods that I would be spared of any magic at all so I wouldn't be forced to hand someone part of who I was. Part of me.

The sun began her descent behind the green rolling hills in the distance as I reached the small lake that had always been a marker on my walks. Ten more minutes and I'd arrive home for the final time. I made my way to the shoreline, plopping down on a worn log, the bark damp and dirty, and peeled off my boots, burying my feet beneath the sand. I watched as the grains of sand filtered between my toes, tickling my skin as they shifted. This small lake had always been my place to go when the world seemed to be too much. The place where I could feel what I wanted to without the harsh words or cruel glances from my Caregivers.

My entire life, they had made it no secret just how much they detested me and how much of an inconvenience I was to them. I often wondered why they even bothered taking me in, but then I turned seventeen, and it all made sense. That was the day I found out about my betrothal. The day that my Caregivers told me that the only reason I was still alive was that the king would pay them handsomely once I was delivered to the palace.

"We should demand double the payment for the Hell she has put us through for years," they often said to each other, making sure I heard every word.

I took a deep breath, threw my head back to the sky, and dumped out all the emotions I had bottled up. Letting myself feel. Feel the anxiety, the sadness, the hurt, the solitude, the helplessness, the fear, the anger. Letting myself feel it all as the silent tears streamed down my cheeks like a never-ending river. As soon as I stood and walked away from this lake, the unfeeling mask would have to return. I wouldn't give my Caregivers the satisfaction of seeing me as broken and shattered as a knocked-over vase. As torn and crumbled as a piece of parchment, they tossed into the trash.

"You should be grateful for being chosen," they always told me, their voices like scraping metal in my ears. I should be grateful; grateful that I had no say in my life, that my choice was taken from me, that my freedom had been stripped away. I should be grateful that I was considered someone's property. I wasn't wanted for *me*, but for the possibility of what I had to give. No, not give. 'Give' implies that I would be offering it willingly. This would be taken.

The sun had settled entirely behind the hills, no longer visible, the sky now a medley of soft pink and orange. It was time to head back. I focused on breathing as I forced myself to regain my composure, counting each deep inhale and exhale until I reached ten. I pulled my boots back on and wiped the remaining tears from my face. Another minute to calm down, and then I would leave. Then I would go back to being hard and cold, and ruthless. I'd go back to being unfazed and uncaring. I'd go back to being myself.

I watched as two black birds danced around each other through the clouds, their wings spread wide as they tilted and dove through the air. I could never figure out why, but every time I came here, I always felt oddly comforted as I observed them. Their freedom and their joy kindled something within me. On my walks, I always looked for them in the sky but only ever saw them here at the lake. It was as if this place held an invisible cage, and they couldn't leave. Out of everything I was to give up, leaving them behind felt the hardest.

I finally stood, brushing off the dirt that had transferred onto me from the log as I looked around the lake—my lake— one final time. I smiled at the birds as they disappeared behind the clouds and turned, making my way home.

3.

"Where were you?" asked one of my Caregivers from her seat at the dining table as soon I crossed over the threshold of our house. We lived comfortably, no doubt, thanks to the arrangement with the king. We never went without, always having more than enough food and clothing to get by. Unfortunately, the same couldn't be said for the other families in the village, and I wondered why the king couldn't help them as well. Or maybe *wouldn't* was the correct term.

"Out," I replied, hanging up my satchel and walking into the kitchen. I surveyed the dinner of chicken and bread that had been set out on the table, my mouth watering at the scent, my stomach growling with hunger in response.

"Out doing what," she responded as she took a bite from her plate. A command, not a question. Her light green eyes narrowed at me as she chewed, waiting for my answer. Her disdain for me was present in her voice, in her posture, in her face. I wondered if she had ever felt joy or happiness in her life. Perhaps she had experienced something so terrible to make her such a hateful woman. Or maybe she had always been a miserable shrew since birth.

I piled the food onto a plate and ripped off a piece of my dinner roll, popping it into my mouth before I replied. The bread hit my stomach as I swallowed like a stone dropped into water.

"Screwing Logan." She choked on her chicken, and I smiled wickedly. Logan may not have satisfied me today, but the look on my Caregiver's face more than made up for it. "You asked," I said, shrugging.

"You are such a wretched child!" she exclaimed. I took that as my cue to leave, rolling my eyes as I grabbed my plate from the table and walked away. "Tomorrow can't come soon enough. I've spent years waiting to rid myself of you!" she yelled, her piercing voice traveling down the hall to reach me. The sound was like a cat screeching in the night. My Caregivers had never shared their given names with me, and they hadn't once uttered them aloud to each other. So I was forced to assign them one of my choosing. Names that I kept strictly to myself in fear of the repercussions of them. This Caregiver had continuously spewed such hatred, such nasty, vile words, that I'd bestowed her the name Mouth.

"So you've told me!" I yelled back as I reached my room, slamming the door loudly behind me.

I spent the next hour or so sprawled out on my bed, staring at the ceiling as I picked at my dinner, my plate resting on my stomach. The room had darkened significantly, the night sky now present, the only illumination coming from the stars that shined through the open windows and the small fireplace along the wall opposite my bed. A loud knock at my door sounded through the otherwise silent room, save for the embers that crackled from the fire.

"What?" I called out, annoyed. The door opened, and my second Caregiver entered, dragging a small trunk behind her. Just big enough for a thick blanket or a few sets of clothes. She narrowed her eyes, curling her lips into a sneer as she saw me. She barely ever spoke, but it didn't mean that she was any more friendly than the other. Where I would often receive verbal lashings from Mouth, this Caregiver would give me glances that could kill. I referred to her as Looks. I honestly wouldn't be surprised to learn she imagined my death whenever she beheld me.

She dropped the trunk into the center of the room before turning on her heel and slamming my door as she departed. The message was simple. Pack whatever belongings that I could fit. Easy enough, seeing as I planned to bring absolutely nothing to the palace tomorrow. Partly in defiance, partly because a piece of me had hoped, I would be sent back here. Not because I was happy in my Caregivers' company but because I had some sense of choice and freedom while here. Even if it was a minimal amount, it was still something.

The fire had dwindled to mere embers by the time I decided to finally roll off of my bed and head into the bathing room. I took longer than usual in the tub, letting the hot soapy water soak into my body, hoping it would wash away all of my fears and doubt, along with all traces of sweat, dirt, and reminders of Logan. Hoping that once I emerged, thoroughly scrubbed clean, it would be as if I were an entirely new person. One that didn't hope or care or dream or feel. One that just simply existed, letting the world pass by, unfazed by the brutal reality of it all.

Unlikely.

When I returned to my room, my nightly cup of tea had been set atop the bedside table, the steam from the liquid snaking through the air, indicating that it hadn't been there for long. One of my Caregivers no doubt took advantage of my absence to leave it here without having to see or speak to me. A kindness, honestly.

I paced around my bedroom, the worn wooden floors cold beneath my feet now that the fire was almost nonexistent, barely any heat emitting from the embers. The hot beverage I held between my hands offered the only warmth to my body as the aroma of peppermint and citrus filled the room. I sipped slowly, allowing the hot liquid and familiar, comforting taste of the tea to course through my veins, wrapping me in their delicious notes of relaxation.

With the trek to the palace half a day's journey away, we were to leave before dawn and arrive at our destination before midday. I knew that trying to sleep would have been the smart choice, but my mind was running too wild to hope for such peace. It was filled with thoughts of what my new life would hold and what the king and prince, my future husband, would be like. We didn't often receive news of the happenings at the palace in my small quaint village. If we did hear of such things, it almost entirely consisted of conversations about royals coming from other kingdoms to visit. There was also the time when our entire town—and the entire Kingdom of Caelum, for that matter—was mourning over the queen's passing. I was six at the time, and the only thing that I could recall of the event was my Caregivers complaining the king could have married better, to begin with. Even at that age, I remember thinking they were such spiteful, miserable creatures.

As I thought about it, I didn't even know what the king or his son looked like. With my luck, the prince would be short and stout, his skin covered in red blotches and pimples, his personality dull and nonexistent. If the king had chosen those two women to be my Caregivers, I didn't have much hope for the royal family's temperament either. Maybe the harsh and cruel behavior I received here was just a taste of what would be served at the palace.

After I drained the last of my tea and added another log to the fire, the breeze from the open window creating a slight chill despite the summer heat, I decided to pack my trunk after all. Not with clothing or trinkets, but with books. The books that I had spent years accumulating. Some I swiped from my Caregivers' rooms when they were out or otherwise distracted, though most I had stolen from the shops in the town square. The stories that I had read had become my only comfort, the characters my family. I'd spend hours upon hours laying in the clearing or on the sand near the lake, reading of lives I wished I could live and the adventures I wished I could have. The friends that I wished I could make. And the love that I wished I could find.

Once I was sure I had packed every novel I had hidden away in secret spots behind clothing, under floorboards, and behind furniture, I dragged the trunk through the hall. The weight was so heavy that I could only manage to move the small chest inches at a time. I quietly opened the front door, determined not to wake anyone. Not because I cared about my Caregivers' rest but because I didn't want to get caught. If they knew that I had stolen and smuggled books away for years, some of those belonging to them—or if they knew how much the stories had meant to me and how much I considered them to be my home— they'd never let me bring them to the palace. It would be their one final act of cruelty toward me.

Dragging the chest through the dirt path that led to the stables a short distance from our house was no small feat. The task had taken entirely too long, the black sky of the night now shifting into a deep violet-blue. Dawn was approaching quickly. I heaved the heavy trunk onto the small cart already attached to our single mare and collapsed into the grass nearby, drenched in sweat once again. This exertion of energy was only slightly less enjoyable than the one earlier with Logan.

I laid there for I didn't know how long, listening to the quiet songs of the insects chirping all around me. The tall blades of grass were as soft and comforting as any bed or blanket I could need. I stared up at the night sky, watching as the stars slowly disappeared and the world brightened, the sun making her arrival far too soon as bright shades of lavender and coral dawned in the distance.

The sounds of the house unsettling reached me, my Caregivers, awake and readying themselves for our trip. I wondered if it would be too late to try and run away. I could take the mare, and I'd have my books. What else would I really need? A gentle breeze passed over my body, raising the hair on my arms, and I looked down to see that I was still wearing my bathing robe, never bothering to dress for bed. I sighed deeply at the clear sign that I would not be hijacking the horse and making a great escape. Reluctantly I sat up and pushed myself to my feet before making my way back into the once quiet house, now alive with enthusiastic commotion.

"Good morning, child," Mouth called as I entered through the front door, her tone unusually chipper. She didn't bother to question my attire or where I was, obviously not wanting anything to ruin her mood. Looks watched me as well, a serpentine smile spread wide across her narrow face.

"Good morning," I said flatly, swiping an apple from the bowl in the center of our dining table before stalking for my bedroom.

"We're leaving in five minutes. Don't you dare make us late," Mouth yelled after me, the usual sharpness in her voice finding its way back. I threw my middle finger up over my shoulder as I bit into the fruit, the juice dripping down my chin as I reached the threshold. "Don't you—" she started but was cut off by the sound of my door slamming loudly.

I was dressed and ready in less than two minutes, choosing a simple pair of brown pants, a cream shirt, and my usual pair of boots. I had no desire to wear a dress, to try and look decent or put together. I tied back my hair in my usual half-up, half-down style. Simple. Easy. Not at all what would be expected of a future princess. Perfect. I shut my eyes and fell back onto my bed, the mattress misshapen. I wrapped myself in my quilt, the green fabric so tattered and worn from years of use, and inhaled the familiar scents of my room: cotton, eucalyptus, lavender, peppermint, parchment, and leather. I listened to the familiar sounds one last time of creaking floors and songbirds in the distance. The rustling of curtains blowing in the wind and the pounding on my door. *The pounding on my door.*

"We're leaving now," Mouth said as she pushed into my room. I sat up, and her jaw dropped open as she took in the sight of me. "Change. Right now!" she demanded, spit flying from her disgusting cracked lips as she spoke. I smirked as I slipped from the bed and strode over to her.

"Can't. I wouldn't dare want to make us late," I said viciously as I stepped around her, leaving her alone in my room—my *former* room—and making my way outside. When Looks saw me, her reaction was no better. The disgust was evident on her face as she shook her head, glowering as she watched me climb into the cart and press my back against the trunk opposite where she sat. When Mouth finally appeared, her face was scarlet with rage, but she didn't bother addressing me again as she mounted the mare and we began our journey.

I let my mind wander freely, bouncing from place to place. In hours, my life would be changed. The life I had grown accustomed to was no longer an option, and fear and anxiety began to creep their way into my mind, body, and soul. I felt Looks' gaze upon me, and I twisted to see her features contorted in a vile manner. She wore a sinister smile, and her brown eyes were as cold as the soil after a storm. She was relishing in watching my discomfort. I took a deep breath and rested my head against the wooden rail, closing my eyes. My body swayed with every turn of the cart's wheels on the dirt path that would lead us to the palace. I focused every ounce of energy I had on pleasant thoughts. My mind traveled from sunny clearings speckled with colorful wildflowers to warm lakes with black birds dancing through the clouds overhead.

Before I knew it, hands were pressed against me, shaking and shoving me.

"Wake up, girl!" Looks said as my eyes flew open, and she returned to her seat. I hadn't been aware that I had fallen asleep. "We're here."

4.

I sat up immediately and leaned over the cart railing as I looked forward, my jaw dropping wide as I did.

"Holy Gods," I whispered to myself. I wasn't sure what exactly I had expected, but it certainly wasn't what I beheld as we passed through the massive gate, the wrought iron twisting in every direction shaping the most ornate and elaborate designs. The metal curved and snaked around itself, creating what looked to be the representation of the waves of an ocean. Beyond the gate was a sprawling green lawn, kept in perfect condition and so large that our entire town back home could be set upon it. We continued down the gravel path, the sound of crushing rocks beneath the wheels of the cart filling my ears as I spotted a white building in the far distance.

"Almost there," Mouth said, more to herself than to Looks or me. That must be the palace, the building growing larger and larger as we made our way closer and closer.

"It's... colossal," I said as I swallowed hard, my mouth suddenly going dry.

"It's home to over five thousand people, with plenty of room to spare." Mouth snorted as if she were somehow insulted by that fact. I didn't respond, too busy mesmerized by the sight. I had known that people who possessed magic moved into the palace, but I had no idea it was *that* many people. I had assumed it would be several hundred, not *five thousand*. We were fifty yards from the palace when several people made their way through the front doors and onto the gravel, awaiting our arrival—awaiting their future princess. The women were dressed simply, wearing long plain dresses in varying shades of earth tones. The men appeared to be guards, dawned in shining gold armor with swords sheathed at their sides. I felt the sweat bead on my forehead, my breathing coming in quick short spurts, my anxiety rising to the surface once more. We were feet away now, the mare slowing her pace as the people outside walked forward to meet us. My stomach turned over, and my mouth salivated, the taste sour and unpleasant. Oh, Gods, I was going to be sick. I began breathing heavily through my mouth, swallowing the fresh air; willing it to calm me, to settle the nerves and nausea, but it was no use. A heartbeat later, I vomited over the side of the cart.

In front of everyone. Fucking great.

I locked eyes with a petite woman as she hurried to the back of the cart.

"You imbecile," Looks sneered quietly as I wiped my mouth with the back of my hand. Mouth had dismounted and come to my side. Not to make sure that I was okay, of course, but to scold me as well.

"Do not continue to embarrass us," she demanded harshly. I rolled my eyes as I took a deep breath, trying to calm the nerves that threatened to make me sick again. "I mean it, child."

The petite woman watched the entire exchange, her almond-shaped hazel eyes cold and harsh. It made me wonder what she made of it all. After a moment, she held out her small hand in invitation. I grabbed it as she helped me down. Her rich olive skin was soft and warm, and her grip on my hand was gentle. She handed me a handkerchief from within one of the pockets of her pristinely kept white apron.

"Thank you," I told her softly, just loud enough for only her ears, as I dabbed the corner of my mouth. She held her hands behind her back as she watched me quietly, waiting for me to regain some composure. Or maybe some dignity. I studied her as I cleaned myself up. Her posture was perfectly straight. She was graceful and poised, and her onyx hair was tied into a tight bun atop her head with not a single strand out of place. Her cheekbones were high, and her lips were full. She was beautiful and looked no older than I was, but by the way she held herself, I knew that wasn't the case. At first glance, I thought her eyes to be cold, but observing them now, there was nothing but compassion residing within. Though I was terrified, somehow, I knew that I would be okay as long as I stayed with her. Once I had finished, I took a deep breath and straightened, indicating to her that I was okay and ready. She bowed her head deeply, and I watched as everyone outside followed her lead. Everyone except my Caregivers.

"My lady," she started, eliciting a loud snort from Mouth and Looks. The woman shot them both a pointed glance, her face full of an emotion that I couldn't place. A heartbeat later, her eyes were back on me. "My lady, welcome. My name is Imogen, and I will be your personal maiden." I had no idea what a maiden was. Imogen must have read the confusion on my face. "I'm in charge of seeing that you are well taken care of here in the palace and assisting you in anything that you may need," she explained. Her voice was soft and kind—such a drastic change to what I had grown used to. I nodded my head in understanding, and she turned, giving her attention to Mouth and Looks. "You should say your farewells now. I need to be getting her inside and situated."

Mouth and Looks exchanged glances, their faces contorted in puzzlement as if Imogen had just spoken to them in some ancient language they didn't understand.

"Where is our payment?" Mouth questioned. Imogen raised a brow at my Caregivers before turning her stare to a man at her side, a guard, it seemed. After a moment, she jerked her chin toward them, and the guard tossed a small pouch at their feet. Looks bent down quickly, picking up the pouch and dumping the contents into Mouth's waiting open palms. Large gold coins clinked against each other as they made their way out of the bag. More gold than I had ever seen in my life.

"As I said before. It is time for you to say your farewells," the maiden repeated, her voice still calm and patient.

"This is all we get?!" Mouth screeched in outrage, her voice piercing and unpleasant. I swallowed deeply, unsure of what to do or how to feel. I didn't want to move, let alone breathe, as I listened to the sounds around me. I heard the shuffling of feet shifting uncomfortably on the gravel, the low growls from the guards that flanked me and Imogen, and the gasp of a woman from somewhere far behind me. I looked up at Imogen to see her chest heave slightly as if she were struggling to keep her composure. She raised a brow before taking a slow, deliberate step forward.

"It is the agreed-upon amount. Should you have an issue with it, you may take it up with His Majesty. I'm sure that he would want to hear that his generosity is not enough for you," Imogen said, her voice suddenly as cold as ice.

Looks shook her head, the movement barely noticeable as Mouth met her eyes. A plea to let it go.

"His Majesty has been more than generous in his payment," Mouth ground out, spit flying from her teeth like she had to force the words from between her lips.

"I'm so glad to hear it," Imogen replied sweetly. "This shall be the last time I tell you. Say your farewells and leave this place."

Mouth stared incredulously at the maiden as Looks sneered at her with disgust and hatred.

"She is no longer our responsibility," Mouth replied as she and Looks turned and headed for the mare and cart.

"Very well," Imogen said as she snapped her fingers. The guards moved at the sound, hurrying to the back of the cart to remove my trunk... and dropping it instantly at the unexpected weight, the lid popping open and books spilling onto the ground.

"What in the—" Mouth exclaimed, running over to the mess of novels upon the gravel, no doubt recognizing several of the titles. *Fuck*. "You little thief!" she yelled, arm raised high as she came for me. I turned my cheek and squeezed my eyes shut hard, bracing myself for the strike of Mouth's hand, but nothing came. Just a crunching sound and a loud screech of terror. I looked up to see Imogen standing between Mouth and myself, a trail of crystal ice upon the ground in front of her—a boundary and a warning. Mouth's chest lifted and fell faster and faster, her anger palatable.

"As you said," Imogen spat, the tone of her voice sending a shiver down my spine as cold as the ice that lay upon the ground. "She is no longer your responsibility. She is *mine*." I glanced around the scene to see Looks cowering in fear as she huddled in the corner of the cart. The guards stood in a defensive position, their arms held at their sides, palms up, as if they were ready to summon some sort of magic. I watched as Mouth took in the scene before her—and retreated backward slowly, defeated. She silently mounted the mare and galloped off, towing Looks in the cart behind her. No one spoke a word. No one so much as moved until my former Caregivers were completely out of view.

"Fetch another trunk for the books," Imogen commanded to no one in particular. She smoothed the fabric of her apron, though I couldn't see a single wrinkle, a single thread out of place. She held her hands behind her back once more before turning on her heel and walking past me with her chin held high. "Come along," she said, and I immediately followed, still trying to wrap my head around what I had just witnessed—how everyone had bowed before me, the kindness of this maiden who didn't know me at all, and how ice had just appeared out of nowhere. Being surrounded by magic was something I was clearly going to have to get used to. No one in my village had possessed it, so I had never seen it displayed.

The oversized wooden doors of the palace flung open before us as if done by a phantom wind, revealing a grand foyer. My eyes widened in wonder as I took in my new home. The large space held a massive round table in the center that housed an even grander bouquet of roses in every shade imaginable. The room was flanked on either side by a set of wide and twisting staircases connecting at the top.

"Hurry along," Imogen called, and I looked up to realize I had fallen behind as I caught myself staring at the ornate chandelier overhead. The light from the open windows in the room refracted off the crystal, casting rainbows dancing along the entrance walls. I picked up my pace, hurrying to catch up with my maiden, my reflection catching my eye in the shininess of the marble tiles beneath my feet. "Your room is this way." She turned left down a hall as we reached the top of the stairs.

"I'm not meeting with the king?" I asked, glancing around. The palace was filled with people, most of which were eyeing me curiously as I passed. We stopped outside a wooden door where two women, dressed identically to Imogen, were already standing, waiting patiently. Imogen reached into her pocket, withdrawing a small golden key.

"Not looking like that," she said evenly as she unlocked the door and held it open, gesturing for me to enter first. The room was massive, almost half the size of the house I had lived in for my entire life. "Your bed chamber," Imogen said as if it wasn't already apparent. The room was modest yet elegant and decorated in shades of greens and blues, golds and creams. "Obviously, this is your bed." She gestured to the large canopy bed that sat against the back wall directly in front of us. Its size was big enough to fit at least four people comfortably. "And your bathing room is just through there." Imogen pointed to the closed door in the middle of the wall to my right.

She snapped her fingers twice, and the maidens who had been outside rushed in, stopping before her and waiting for their instructions. Imogen jerked her chin toward the bathing room. The women followed her gaze and understood immediately what she wanted of them. I watched as they entered the adjacent room, the sounds of running water and cabinets opening and closing filling the silence. Imogen walked to the left corner of the room, reaching a large armoire and opening it wide. It was already filled with delicate dresses of silk and chiffon.

"I'm sure your journey was long and tiring," she said, inspecting the dresses that hung. "But you will have to bathe quickly so I can have you dressed and made up." She pulled out a soft gown made of lilac-colored lace, head tilting to the side as she studied it. "Then I will take you down to meet King Perceval." She hung the dress back up, deciding against it, and went back to browsing through the other options. Low whispers and snickering caught my ears, and I turned around to find several ladies huddling together in the hallway, talking closely and pointing at me as they did.

"Can I help you?" I asked them, no pleasantness in my tone. They only snickered louder; no shame to be had.

"Out. All of you, right now. You have better places to be," Imogen said forcefully as she walked past me, shooing away the girls lurking outside my room. She shut and locked the door before heading back to her task. I followed her this time before stopping in front of the large open window next to the armoire, the gentle summer breeze sending in the scent of fresh roses and citrus. "Ignore them," she said. "They often have nothing better to do than to spend their time ogling what they can never have. Or ever hope to be, for that matter." I wished her words helped and made me care less for their opinions, but they didn't.

I turned and looked out the window, surveying the grounds below and the people scattered throughout. Some were huddled together as they conversed, some walked the gardens, and some lounged in chairs reading. Everyone seemed so peaceful, happy, and at ease. My eyes then spotted two men staring up at me, laughing. Both were young, it seemed, though I couldn't be sure. Everyone here looked to be the same age, whether twenty or three hundred and twenty. The taller of the two, only by an inch or so, smirked as he bowed so dramatically, so deeply that I was surprised he didn't topple over. His grin widened even more as he straightened, clearly so pleased with himself. What a prick. I smiled sweetly, throwing my hands over my chest in mock affection before letting my face fall flat and throwing up both of my middle fingers at the men. I didn't bother to stay and watch as amusement filled their faces. Instead, I walked over to the bathing room, the water from the tub cutting off as soon as I reached it. Once again, some sort of palace magic. The two maidens bowed their heads before departing the room, closing the door behind them. I undressed and stepped into the tub, the water warm and soothing.

"Make it quick," Imogen said from the other side of the door. I groaned loudly to myself at the reminder. "I heard that," she replied. Of course, she did. I inhaled deeply, holding my breath as I slid down, bringing my head below the water's surface, where it was dark and quiet. Where I could have just a few seconds of peace. A few seconds alone with the screaming thoughts in my mind. A few seconds to myself before I was to be primped and pampered and prepared for the king.

The last few seconds I had before, my entire life would change forever.

5.

"Your hair is a lovely color," Imogen told me, pinning a loose curl to the back of my head. I had obliged her request for a quick bath and hurried to the vanity as soon as I was finished, where she had stood waiting for me to return. I watched her work, twisting some strands into soft curls and braiding others, securing them all to form an intricate style fit for a princess. She opened the top drawer of the mahogany vanity, removing a delicate comb made of rich gold and sparkling with petite encrusted diamonds, and fixed it above the elegant loose bun she had created at the nape of my neck. "There," she said, meeting my eyes in the reflection of the mirror, "All finished."

I stood, already dressed in the soft green gown she had chosen for me. The neckline of the dress was tasteful and modest, scalloping in the front to resemble the top of a heart and fit snuggly, cinching at my waist before flaring out and flowing to the floor. The loose puffy sleeves of the dress were the same shade of green as the bodice but almost sheer, capping at my wrists and hanging off my shoulders, leaving me feeling bare from the top of my chest up. Exposed. Imogen fastened long earrings that dangled to the middle of my neck and perfectly matched the comb she had secured. She adjusted the few strands of curls she had left out of the bun as the rays of sun caught in the diamond earrings, casting sunspots around the room. Imogen stood back, smiling a little as she took in the work she had just done on me. Completely satisfied, she pulled my arm, leading me across the room to the floor-length mirror that stood tall against the same wall that held the bathing room entrance.

I stopped short as I looked at the girl staring back in the reflection. It was me, but... but different. The hair was the same shade, though now smooth and shiny. The eyes were the same light brown with red flecks but somehow deeper, mysterious. As if they held secrets even I didn't know. The face was somehow brighter, more alive. The makeup the two other maidens had done—Annette and Josephine—I learned, was minuscule. They added just a tiny amount of blush and a light coat of kohl along the base of my lashes, per Imogen's request. The person staring back at me wasn't the woman who arrived here this morning. Out of all the things that I had experienced today—the magic, the laughing, the pointing, the gossiping, the curious looks—out of all of it, that fact scared me the most, and I wasn't sure why.

I hurried through the halls, matching Imogen's brisk pace, my heels clicking loudly against the tile floor as we walked through the winding corridors, the palace already like a maze to me. I wasn't sure I would ever be able to find my way anywhere without the help of a guide. Imogen had given me instructions before we left the comfort of my new room on how I was to present myself to King Perceval. She told me how and when I was supposed to bow, to speak, and when to not. I ran through the directions, reciting them over and over again in my head, praying to the Gods above that I wouldn't forget. Before I could run through her instructions for the seventh time, we halted abruptly, reaching our destination. I shuddered a breath as I worked on composing myself, my hands balling into fists at my side to stop them from shaking.

"Shoulders back and hands placed in front of you while you clasp your fingers lightly. It looks more proper," Imogen said as she looked down at my fists. "And it'll help with the nerves," she added softly. I obliged, bringing my hands forward and resting them against my lower stomach as I held tightly onto my middle and index finger. The world grew quiet around me as we stood in the hall waiting to be called into whatever room lay beyond the large wooden doors we were stationed in front of. I counted my breaths, counted the heartbeats I heard that belonged to Imogen, to the guards with us, and to me. I counted the clinking sounds from my heel upon the marble as my leg bounced nervously in place, the waiting getting to me. My hands began to sweat, and my body ached as I shifted to adjust, shaking out my hands and rolling my neck. Time passed slowly for what felt like hours or even days when in actuality was probably only a few minutes.

"Stop fidgeting and relax," Imogen said sternly. Relax? She had to be kidding. I was a geyser about to erupt.

"Let me get right on that," I shot back, earning a dissatisfied look from her at my sass, making me instantly regret the words. "Sorry," I said softly, no more than a whisper.

"You'll do fine," she replied just as the wooden doors creaked to life, opening before us, my mouth instantly going dry as I faced forward at the sound. "Remember what I told you." We began to walk forward, entering a spacious throne room.

I kept my shoulders back, and chin raised as we advanced, glancing around at the hundreds of faces scattered throughout the room, standing along the walls and at the base of the dais, watching me intently. Some of the faces I recognized from my arrival this morning. The most notable ones were the women who had been gawking at me outside of my room, their faces still unpleasant as they whispered into each others' ears even now. And the two arrogant men I had spied in the garden, now casually leaning against one of the stone pillars. They both had their arms crossed in front of their chest as if they were beyond bored with having to be here. The one that had bowed to me still had a smirk on his face. His shoulder-length silver hair was partly tied back from his warm ivory face, his amber eyes bright against the contrast of it. The other one was smiling as well, though the gesture was softer, his eyes a simple blue. I glared at them, letting the rage building at the reminder of their mocking attitudes replace the fear and anxiety. The silver-haired man smiled wider at my glower and leaned to his side, whispering something to his companion. I tore my gaze from them as the fury built and built, clasping my fingers even tighter to prevent me from flipping them off again. This was clearly not the place for that.

Imogen's pace slowed, and we stopped several feet from the base of the dais, my eyes traveling up the white marble steps to the golden throne, and the person lounged comfortably on it. The king. Imogen moved first, and I quickly followed suit, remembering what she told me as I bent at the knees and bowed my head, not daring to straighten before permission was given. One. Two. Three. I counted my inhales and exhales as I waited.

"Rise," the king commanded. I stood to my full height, lifting my head and taking in the man before me, now rising from his seat and making his way down the steps. "Welcome, my dear." His voice was strong and confident, powerful and sharp. He looked no older than I was, yet the way he moved, spoke and carried himself gave away his age, telling me that he had already been in this world for centuries. He took another step forward, reaching the bottom of the dais and clasping his hands behind his back as he looked at me. A slow grin spread across his face, the gesture anything but comforting. His smile didn't reach his cold dark green eyes as he raked them up and down my body, inspecting his transaction. "Your name," he demanded. Shouldn't he have known it?

"Ains—" I started, my voice cracking as I spoke. A few high-pitched giggles, no doubt from the ogling women, broke out. I cleared my throat, lifting my chin higher. "Ainsley." Imogen shifted at my side, a reminder. "Your Majesty," I added quickly.

"Ainsley," King Perceval repeated slowly as if he were savoring the way it tasted on his tongue. "And how are you finding life here at the palace?" he asked, though there was no curiosity for my answer in his voice.

"I just arrived this morning," I explained. "But I look forward to experiencing all the palace, and its people have to offer, your Majesty." Imogen nodded her head at my response, the movement barely noticeable. She had fed me the answer before we left the room, somehow knowing exactly what King Perceval would ask and precisely what he would want to hear.

"Very good," he said. "And I trust that you have been instructed as to what is expected of you." I felt my blood boil as I remembered the arrangement my parents had made. The arrangement that I had no decision in. The choice that I was never given.

"To give up my life as I had known it and move here. To relinquish part of the magic that I may be given. And to marry your son," I replied flatly. "Did I leave anything out?" I allowed my temper to get the better of me, wishing I could take back the words before they had even left my mouth. What in the Hell was

I thinking? To insult the king was horrible enough, but to insult him in front of hundreds of people from his kingdom? I could only hope for a swift death. Terrified, I met his eyes, and though they burned with fury, there was something else residing within them. Something like intrigue. Something like humor.

"Your Majesty, please forgive her," Imogen cut in immediately. "She isn't—" The king threw his head back, guffawing loudly at the ceiling. The entire room went as quiet as death aside from his roaring, boisterous laugh. My heart pounded, my breathing coming in faster and faster pants as I waited. For what, I didn't know: the strike of his hand, the order of my execution, for him to have any reaction at all other than... this. I didn't know what to make of it. I looked at Imogen, her face gravely pale as she held my stare, just as worried about the outcome as I was. I glanced quickly around the room, everyone watching King Perceval with bated breath. Their hands covered their mouths or clasped their chests at my bravado. Some even shook their head at me with disgust, disdain, with disappointment. Everyone seemed to be completely outraged at my words. Everyone except for the two people leaning against the pillar, quietly laughing to themselves. Probably more than happy to have a front-row seat to my demise.

"Well, aren't you just a little ball of fire, my dear," the king said through the laughter, tears now streaming down his face as he struggled to come down from the high. "Isn't she feisty?" he asked the room, the crowd now erupting with forced laughter, cheers, and applause. I looked to Imogen, desperate for some instruction on what to do. Her eyes widened at me, pleading, and I understood at once what she wanted. I turned my attention back to the king in front of me.

"King Perceval, I am so truly sorry for my words. I spoke out of unwarranted anger," I said, my voice drowned out over the crowd's noise.

"There is nothing to be sorry over, my dear," he said, his tone lighthearted and joyous. He took another step, closing the distance between us as he leaned forward and whispered into my ear. "But I expect it never to happen again," he said flatly, cold. I took the words for what they were intended to be—a threat. A promise. I nodded weakly as he stepped back, a large fake smile returning to his harsh face as he walked back to his throne, the room finally starting to quiet. Imogen put her hand on the small of my back for just a moment, a comforting and reassuring touch, and I knew that she had heard what the king had uttered to me in secret. I swallowed, a lump forming in my throat as I watched him take his seat. "Are there any questions I can answer for you, my dear?" he asked. His voice was friendly and welcoming, but his dark green eyes told me to keep my mouth shut.

"No, your Majesty," I replied, bowing my head again. He smiled, satisfied with my answer, as he nodded.

"Wonderful. My son… your fiancé, that is," he began, a cruel smirk creeping upon his face, "will take you on a tour through the grounds. It's such beautiful weather today, perfect for getting to know one another." He conveniently left out that it was also large enough to allow for every person who wanted to come to watch. By the twinkle in his eyes, I knew that's why he had chosen that location—a final punishment for my outburst. "Dashiell," King Perceval commanded. I glanced around the room at any sign of the prince. There was no one standing near the king. No second throne beside his. Which meant that he had to be somewhere within the crowd.

My heart raced as I met the stares of what felt like every man in the room. No one moved a single inch or even dared to take a breath. Motion out of the corner of my eye caught my attention, and I turned to see the blue-eyed boy from the garden push off the pillar and stride for me, his silver-haired companion grinning with pure glee as he stayed leaning against the stone. The same person I flipped off earlier. I flipped off the Godsdamned Prince of Caelum. *Fuck,* I thought. Judging by the cough Imogen huffed under her breath and how the prince bit his lip as if trying desperately to suppress the urge to laugh, I realized that I must have said the word aloud. Great. This was going so well for me.

Prince Dashiell bowed when he reached me, and I watched as he straightened, refusing to return the gesture. Imogen elbowed me in the side discreetly, and I turned to her as she gave me a look that promised death. Not death by the king, but death by her. I reluctantly turned my attention back to the prince and glowered at him as I gave a small, barely perceptibly dip of my chin. A noise broke out from somewhere within the crowd that sounded like a cross between a laugh and a snort. I leaned around the prince to try and locate the culprit, only to find his friend covering his mouth with his hands. I straightened, my eyes finding

Prince Dashiell's again, only to see him covering his mouth, struggling to contain the laughter I could tell was trying to break free. For fuck's sake, these two were ridiculous. This entire situation seemed to be nothing more than a joke to them, and I was the punchline. I found myself hating them with every fiber of my being. Imogen released a heavy sigh, and I watched as she rolled her eyes, obviously just as fed up as I was.

King Perceval cleared his throat loudly, his patience growing weary. Prince Dashiell stepped closer and extended his arm in invitation. I again refused to move.

"If you do not take his arm, I will kill you myself," Imogen whispered under her breath beside me. I contemplated my choices for a moment, but Imogen pushed me into the prince, forcing me to grab him.

"See. Was it really that difficult?" Prince Dashiell questioned, his voice soft and dripping in amusement.

"You have no idea," I replied through my teeth as he turned us to face his father.

"What a lovely couple," King Perceval declared, the room once again launching into applause. I forced myself to smile as I focused on biting back the gag that threatened to emerge. A loud cheer came from the crowd, and I didn't have to look to know it came from Prince Dashiell's friend. The person I would make it my life's mission to destroy.

"In five days," the king declared, everyone in attendance instantly quieting as his voice boomed through the room, "we will hold a Welcome Celebration in honor of our young Ainsley's arrival to the palace, in celebration of her contribution to Caelum and her union to Prince Dashiell." People smiled and laughed and clapped softly at his declaration. "Now, let us get back to our day." King Perceval clapped his hands loudly twice, dismissing everyone from the room.

Voices rose higher and higher as people conversed amongst themselves excitedly. Some chose to stand against the walls while a few walked up to the dais to speak to the king, and others departed to go about whatever they were doing before being summoned into the throne room.

"Did you want to flip me off now or later?" Prince Dashiell asked over the roaring voices of the people around us.

"Can't I do both?" I snapped back sarcastically, earning a groan from Imogen. The prince smiled widely at me as I saw in my peripheral vision his silver-haired friend rushing forward to meet us.

"Hey there, cupcake," the friend said seductively, dragging his eyes up and down my body.

"Go fuck yourself," I spat back, my blood on fire.

"My lady! That is unacceptable language!" Imogen hissed. The tone in which she spoke was coated in disappointment, and I felt her fingers digging into the arm that hung at my side, her grip firm and unyielding. I refused to look at her. Refused to back down from the friend's stare. He smirked wildly, dimples coming through, and his amber eyes sparkled with wicked delight.

"Oh, I absolutely love you," he said as he winked. Before I could say my retort, the king's voice broke through.

"Felix," King Perceval commanded. Prince Dashiell's friend broke his stare with me to acknowledge his king. "Stay behind for a moment. I need a word."

"I would love nothing more, your Majesty," he replied, bowing his head slowly.

"Suck up," Prince Dashiell said under his breath.

"Prick," Felix replied, shoving the prince and backing away as he laughed. I watched after Felix as he made his way up the dais and halted at the side of the king.

"Take her through the grounds like your father commanded, Prince Dashiell," Imogen said curtly as she ushered us out of the room, hundreds of eyes glancing up from their conversations to watch us depart. I looked back at King Perceval one last time before disappearing through the doors, his cold eyes meeting mine for an instant as a sinister grin slowly played on his lips.

Gods help me.

6.

Imogen chaperoned Prince Dashiell and me through the palace. The three of us remained utterly silent as we walked the halls, heading for our destination. As soon as we reached the gardens at the back of the estate, Imogen bowed before us and headed back inside, leaving us alone. Well, not exactly *alone*. In the company of the hundreds of other people that pretended not to be intently watching our every move. The second Imogen disappeared, I pulled away from Prince Dashiell, crossing my arms against my chest tightly as we walked, causing him to shake his head as he chuckled quietly to himself.

"What," I demanded, already annoyed.

"Nothing," he said, focusing on the sprawling gardens ahead. The aroma of fresh roses wafting through the air surrounded us as I studied him. He was at least a head taller than me and had a lean but muscular build. His cheekbones were sharp and angular beneath his golden skin. He looked at me then, and I noticed I had been entirely wrong about his eyes. They weren't a simple blue. Far from it, actually. The shade was deep and haunting, like the ocean during a storm. His gaze was piercing, and I felt like I couldn't breathe under its pressure. I quickly turned and glanced around, catching the eyes of a girl lounging in a white iron chair, her face twisted in silent rage, her light blue eyes like flames of ice. "What do you think of the palace so far?" Prince Dashiell asked.

I ignored his question, my attention focused entirely on the bright blonde-haired woman that was carving me apart piece by piece with her stare. I raised a brow, and her painted pink lips pulled back into a sneer in response. She could certainly have given Looks a run for her money. Around her, a gaggle of ladies stood, all whispering to each other, nodding their heads at Prince Dashiell, the seated woman smiling widely at him. Ah, so *that* was why she wanted me dead—my proximity to the prince. I glanced over my shoulder as we passed, her bright smile falling flat as she glowered. *Garden Girl* seemed like a perfect placeholder until I could come up with a more appropriate name for her.

"Do you have any hobbies?" Prince Dashiell asked, moving on to his next question. I rolled my neck as we walked, stretching out the muscles that had become sore from the constant bowing. Something that I assumed I would have to get used to. Was I supposed to be bowing to Prince Dashiell? Or was that reserved solely for King Perceval? I *did* have to bow to the prince once, but was that just a formality? I bit my lip as I pondered.

"Try not to be so nervous. I don't bite," Prince Dashiell said smugly. His voice cut through my thoughts, pulling me from my reverie. I stopped our advance as I stared up at him.

"Excuse me? What would possibly make you think that I'm nervous around you?" I didn't hide the bite in my tone. He shrugged, the arrogance dripping off his body like water on a rainy day.

"It's clear that I intimidate you," he said as if it were the most obvious explanation in the world. I felt my jaw drop open at his words. "You seem to be too afraid to answer any of my questions."

"And you seem to be too stupid to realize that maybe I just don't want to," I snapped through gritted teeth. "You may be—" I stopped, remembering at once who I was speaking to as his eyes widened in surprise. I wasn't sure if it was because of my tone or the words I used.

"Oh, please. Do go on," he said, crossing his arms over his chest, waiting for me to continue. The sleeves of his loose cream tunic were pushed back, exposing the toned muscles of his forearms. I clenched my jaw tightly as I looked up at him, wondering if this was some kind of trap. Wondering if the punishment would be worth it if I fell into it. He waved his hand through the air as he tapped his foot as if to showcase his impatience with me. Fine.

"You may be used to everyone giving you what you want, Prince Dashiell, but—"

"It's just Dashiell."

"Whatever. But don't expect the same from me. So you can take the laughing and the staring and the pointing and shove it right up your—"

"Hey there, cupcake," Felix interrupted, coming over to the two of us. "What did I miss?" A crooked grin appeared on Dashiell's face as he looked at his friend.

"My future bride was just about to tell me where to shove something," he explained. Felix chuckled at his words as he placed his hands on his hips.

"The same goes for you, too," I told Felix, raking my eyes up and down his body just as he had done to me earlier. He was only barely taller than the prince, and his body leaner yet just as toned, evident by the outline of his abdominal muscles when his shirt shifted as he took his stance. He approached then, leaving just a small gap between us as he leaned down to whisper.

"Don't tempt me with a good time, cupcake," he said. My chest heaved at the anger I felt, my eyes burning with white-hot rage. My skin felt like it was on fire, and my head swam with fury. I closed my eyes as I tried to count my breaths. I tried to calm down, knowing that word of any obscene outburst here would surely spread to the king's ears. After his threat in the throne room, I knew my days were numbered as it was.

Slowly, and somehow all at once, my heart rate steadied, breathing became easier, and my blood began to cool. My mind became clear and calm. I was still furious but no longer on the edge of destruction. I opened my eyes and stared at the boys before me. At my annoying future husband and his insufferable best friend. I needed to go. I needed to walk away before I said or did something I couldn't take back. Dashiell's face grew curious as he watched me try to compose myself, but Felix's smile only grew wider.

"We're going to be great friends," Felix said. I took that as my cue to leave. Because if I had stayed... If I had stayed, I would have surely stabbed him with the hairpin I had hidden in my sleeve since the moment I left my bed chamber. I immediately turned on my heel and stormed back inside the palace, leaving the two giggling like little girls behind me.

Unsurprisingly, I got lost trying to find the way back to my room. The simple task took so long that less than an hour after I returned, Imogen came to collect me for dinner. I had no desire to set my eyes upon Dashiell or Felix or even the king. I tried to tell her I wasn't hungry, but my stomach growled loudly when I spoke, my body betraying my words and causing Imogen to roll her eyes at my lie. She led me down to the terrace that overlooked the gardens I had been in today, the setting sun washing the white roses in milky shades of reds and oranges. A long rectangular white iron table sat directly in the middle of the space. It had been set for only three but large enough for twelve, with candles scattered down the middle like one long centerpiece. Imogen pulled back the matching iron chair at the head of the table, directing me to sit as I waited.

"Who else is joining us?" I asked. One place setting had been for me, and the other must be for Imogen, but who did the third belong to? She eyed me curiously for a minute as she looked over the table.

"Oh, I'm not staying," she answered as she understood my question.

"But then who—"

"Cupcake. So good to see you again." I felt the blood drain from my face as Felix's voice reached my ears. Imogen raised a brow at me as she held back a smile that I could already see forming.

"Send word when you're finished, and I'll come to retrieve you. No need to get lost for hours again," she said.

"I'm finished," I told her flatly as Felix taking the open seat on my right, echoed in the silence.

"Eat, my lady," Imogen instructed before retreating into the palace. I contemplated running after her, but I knew Felix would enjoy the display of desperation far too much. I took a deep breath before daring to steal a glance at him. When I finally did, he was watching me, elbows planted firmly upon the table, chin resting on his hands.

"So you got lost, huh?" Gods, I fucking hated him. I leaned back in the chair, my back pressed firmly against the metal as I watched him, not deeming to reply. Felix tilted his head, his ever-present smirk causing a dimple to form. I was starting to wonder if his smile was somehow permanently fixed upon his face. "I could show you around if you want." I reached forward, grabbing the golden goblet that sat at the top of my place setting, and brought it to my nose, sniffing once to inspect what lay within. Wine. Perfect. I drank deeply, finishing almost half of the contents, the sweet summer wine traveling smoothly down my throat and filling my empty stomach. I knew it wasn't wise to consume alcohol when you hadn't eaten. The few times I had left me feeling dizzy and out of control. But right now, I needed to get drunk, the consequences of those actions be damned.

"I'd rather get so lost that I end up dying of starvation," I told Felix, the sound of metal hitting metal ringing between us as I set my cup back down on the table. Felix laughed loudly as he sat back, pulling his arms from the table and resting his hands on his lap. There was no malice in his voice, no wicked pleasure. His laugh was joyous and light.

"I simply cannot wait until we're the best of friends." I snorted at his reply. "Go ahead and try to fight it while you can, cupcake. I'll grow on you. Trust me."

"I wouldn't hold your breath," I replied snidely. "Or maybe I would. Why don't you go ahead and try it, and let's see how long it takes?" I said, smiling sweetly at him.

"Now that's something that I'd like to watch." A familiar voice drawled from behind me. I turned to watch Prince Dashiell stride over to the table and take his seat directly on my left. "Felix," he said to his friend before looking at me. "Fiancé," he added sarcastically. I narrowed my eyes at him in response, reaching for my goblet once again and finishing the rest of my wine. As I placed the empty cup back down, I watched as the goblet instantly refilled itself with more wine; the magic of this place made itself useful.

Servants appeared on the terrace, clearly awaiting the prince's arrival before dinner was to be served. They approached, setting down plates full of roasted chicken and vegetables in front of each of us. The smell of the herbs and spices of the meal caused my stomach to growl again. I watched as Dashiell relieved a petite servant of the large platter of bread she carried and placed it on the table, thanking her as he did. It was an odd sight to behold. I never expected the prince to thank those below him, let alone assist them in their work.

"What?" Dashiell asked me. He must have read the curiosity written on my face.

"Nothing," I told him as I stabbed a piece of chicken, the meat so tender it started to fall off my fork before I could bring it to my mouth. "I'm just surprised that you have any manners at all."

"I'm sure many things about me would surprise you." He popped a piece of bread into his mouth.

"It's too bad that I don't care enough to find out," I said flatly, reaching for my wine, desperately needing the sweet escape it promised. One more full glass ought to accomplish it. I drank and drank and drank, emptying the contents and watching the magic cup refill itself again.

"We have the hard stuff if you'd rather have that," Felix said. I looked up to find them both watching me intently. Waiting for me to respond or vomit, I wasn't sure which. I didn't care.

"I'm fine," I told him, going back to my plate and focusing on finishing the food there so that I could have Imogen come and retrieve me. I wanted to escape to the solitude of my room, far away from these two childish men. Though I knew my attitude wasn't much better.

I spent most of the next hour ignoring anything Dashiell or Felix said to me. Instead, I focused on my plate, on my wine. On the fork in my hand and what it would be like to stab Felix in his stupid amber eyes. Or what it would be like smashing the goblet against Dashiell's stupid face. Would it kill either of them? What would it take to kill an immortal, anyway? Would glass through the eye or the heart suffice? Or would I need some fancy magic to do it? Maybe once I received a Gift of my own, I could use it to set them both on fire. Or maybe drown or freeze them. Or maybe... what was the other Gift of Caelum? Water and ice. Fire. And.... What a pathetic excuse for a future princess I was, not even able to remember the powers of her kingdom. Water and ice. Fire. And....

"Weather manipulation." Dashiell's voice cut through my thoughts.

"What?" I asked as I looked up at him, bewildered, the effects of the wine causing his appearance to blur slightly in my vision before becoming clear.

"Water and Ice. Fire. And weather manipulation," he replied. Had I said the words aloud rather than in my head? Maybe drinking heavily around them wasn't the best idea after all.

"You didn't know what they were?" Felix asked, his voice soft and kind. Not at all, like he was making fun of my incompetence. Or maybe that was just another side effect of my inebriation. The inability to detect sarcasm or malice.

"I did too know what they were! I just… didn't remember that I knew what they were," I explained, slurring my words like a drunk fool. I should keep my mouth closed.

"Of course, of course," Felix said, grinning as he winked at me. For some reason, I smiled widely at him, my cheeks feeling flush from drink, my insides feeling light and heavy all at once. I felt calm and at peace, like a cloud drifting along in the sky.

"Which would you want?" Dashiell asked, and I turned my attention to him as he dragged a hand through his short light brown hair. His ocean eyes poured into me as I watched him.

"You have gorgeous eyes," I said, tilting my head to the side as I studied him. The navy and dark teal within both fought for dominance yet married together beautifully. A cocky grin appeared on his face. I shouldn't have said that. Fuck. I had drunk too much. Way, way too much.

"Thank you," he replied, and I nodded eagerly. I had no idea why. It was like my body wasn't my own, so lax, so…. free.

"They're like the ocean. Deep and mysterious," I told him. *Shut the fuck up,* I screamed at myself, but my mouth just kept moving. The words sprang out like songbirds finally flying free after being stuck in a cage their entire lives. "It's like they're trying to drown me." Beside me, I heard the sliding of metal on stone and whirled to find Felix leaning across the entire table to stare into Dashiell's eyes as well.

"They *are* like the ocean!" Felix exclaimed, and I nodded in satisfaction, happy that I wasn't alone in my observation.

"See! I told you! Ocean Eyes," I said to Dashiell, hiccupping on the last word. I reached for my glass again, and the two males watched in intrigue, smiling devilishly as I drained the contents once again.

"Do me next! Do me next!" Felix yelled as he leaned toward me. I met him halfway, staring into his brilliant amber eyes.

"They're like warm dripping honey," I whispered, my face only inches from his. "They're beautiful, too." The words slurred as I spoke.

"Of course, they are, cupcake," he said, planting a quick kiss on my cheek before lowering himself back to his seat. I giggled in response, wiping the memory of his lips from my face as I sat back down. No. I couldn't *laugh* at Felix. I hated him. Hated Dashiell. The wine was messing with my head. With my ability to think clearly. Forget insulting the king. Forget telling the prince to shove it. Drinking in front of Dashiell and Felix had been my biggest mistake yet. I needed to leave before I said or did anything I'd regret.

Before I could make my move to leave, the small petite servant from earlier appeared carrying an entire tray of sweets and setting it on the table, offering a varied selection from cakes to pastries to tartlets to custards. My jaw dropped at the sight, and I felt a small trail of drool drip down my chin. I quickly wiped it away before anyone could notice.

"Are you alright there, cupcake?" Felix asked, and I reluctantly tore my gaze from the tray to look at him. He jerked his chin to my legs which were impatiently bouncing up and down beneath the table. I stopped the motion at once, suddenly self-conscious.

"Which would you like?" Dashiell asked me as he surveyed the sweets, ready to serve me whichever I chose.

"I'm not sure," I answered honestly. "I never—I mean, I wasn't...." I trailed off.

"Have you never had sweets before?" Dashiell asked, genuine curiosity evident in his features. I chewed the inside of my lip as I looked at him.

"Not really, no," I said softly, embarrassed. "I wasn't ever allowed to have them. I stole what I could when my Caregivers weren't watching. But those times were few and rare."

"That's simply criminal and will not do," Felix cut in. "Pile her up, Dash." Dashiell obliged, stacking my plate high with every kind of dessert available. I took another deep drink of my wine as I watched him work, stacking my dish full of more sweets than I had ever seen.

"Here you go, Ainsley," Dashiell said, placing the colorful plate before me. I perked up a little at the sound of my name on his lips, my eyes meeting his. It was the first time I had ever heard him use it. He glanced away quickly as if he had realized it too. I wasn't sure what to make of it as I turned my attention back to my food.

Felix and Dashiell sat back and watched me eat, instructing me on which desserts to try and in what order. After taking a single bite of everything on my plate, I learned that I loved absolutely anything that had chocolate and despised sweet peach cobbler and soaked ladyfingers. The latter, I spit out immediately, much to Dashiell and Felix's amusement. The laughing didn't bother me as much as it had earlier, evidence that the wine was still doing its intended job perfectly.

When the sun had set entirely and the dishes were cleared away, Imogen had appeared to retrieve me, just as promised.

"Hi, Imogen!" I yelled, intoxication clear on my face and in my voice. And the way I shot to my feet, arms raised high, the wine spilling from over the side of my glass and splashing loudly onto the stone terrace. "Oops," I said as I snorted a giggle. Dashiell and Felix laughed wildly from their seats. Imogen stormed towards me, fury in her hazel eyes. I turned around to face the two men. "Uh oh. I think I'm in trouble," I told them softly, laughing as I covered my mouth.

"What did you two do!" Imogen yelled, shoving me behind her as she waved her finger between Dashiell and Felix. The two instantly straightened, throwing their hands up in the air in innocence and biting their lips to suppress their amusement at the situation. I giggled again at their movements, so fluid and so in sync. As if they had been scolded far too often and this was a rehearsed routine that they performed.

"We're completely blameless," Felix said, trying his very best to keep a straight face. A laugh burst from Dashiell's mouth, and I struggled to contain my drunken hysterics at the sight.

"There is never innocence when it comes to either of you!" Imogen snapped back.

"Yeah!" I yelled from behind her as I took another sip of my drink, hearing Dashiell and Felix chuckle as I did. Imogen was on me at once, ripping the goblet from my hands and slamming it loudly onto the table.

"We're leaving. Right now!" she said, her hand gripping my arm tightly as she yanked me away. I stumbled behind her as I followed, struggling to stay upright as the world spun around me.

"Goodnight, cupcake!" I heard Felix yell. I twisted my body to face him, flipping him off before I disappeared back inside the palace, the sound of his and Dashiell's returning laughter reaching me in the halls.

7.

I had made it all of two steps into my chamber before sprinting for the bathing room, Imogen rushing close behind. I threw open the door and ran, my knees slamming hard onto the marble tile floor as I threw myself over the toilet and emptied the entirety of my stomach.

"It serves you right," Imogen said sternly, the way a mother would scold a child when they had done something utterly foolish. She knelt behind me, pulling back the loose strands of hair from my face as I became sick over and over again. The punishment for my senseless decision was completely deserved. The sound of running water nearby caught my attention, and I twisted to look, the sudden movement causing me to become dizzy and another wave of nausea surged. I turned back to the toilet as I vomited again.

"What possessed you to drink so much." Imogen seethed. It wasn't a question but rather a way to express her disappointment. I had known this maiden for less than a day, and already I felt shame at letting her down. She pressed a cool, damp cloth to the back of my neck. That must have been what the running water was for. I savored the feel of the fabric against my skin, the temperature of the water sending a shiver through my body. It wasn't enough to douse the fire coursing through my veins or cure the churning in my stomach. But it helped.

"Have you met Dashiell and Felix?" I asked, focusing on my breathing as I fought another round of sickness. Nausea hit hard like a relentless wave against a rock. "How anyone can deal with them sober, I don't think I'll ever know," I added as I heaved into the bowl again. I could have sworn I heard the quiet pitch of laughter, but I couldn't be sure. My own incompetence drowned out the sound.

"You should have seen them as children," Imogen teased. "Though despite being the grown men they are now, they do still tend to act like toddlers from time to time." At least she agreed with me on the subject of their immaturity. "However, I am curious. You have been here less than a day and already seem to despise them so fiercely. Why is that?" I waited a moment before answering, needing to be sure the only thing that came out of my mouth were words.

"They laughed at me," I told her. When she didn't reply, I continued. "My freedom was stolen from me, and they do nothing but make jokes and mock that fact. How could I not hate them for that?" Before I could say anything more, my drunken mistake climbed up my throat again.

I was content to stay leaning over the toilet for the remainder of the night, the cold tile feeling like paradise against my legs. When nothing was left in my stomach, the vomiting ceased, and the nausea began to subside, yet I was still too afraid to move from my spot on the bathing room floor. Imogen stayed with me, fetching me water, dabbing my face with a cool cloth, and forcing me to eat dry pieces of bread. I protested as much as I could, the mere sight of food making my stomach roll over, but Imogen said that if I didn't eat it willingly, she would shove it down my throat by force.

I didn't argue after that.

When Imogen was sure I was stable enough to leave the bathing room, she led me to my bed, instructing me to change into the nightgown she had left out and then crawl beneath the sheets. I thought about asking if I could sleep there on the floor, but the look on her face told me she wasn't in the mood to be challenged. I quickly changed and climbed into bed, bringing the blankets up high so that they covered me from the nose down. Imogen nodded satisfactorily before placing an empty bucket on the floor beside my bed.

"For if you feel sick and can't get to the toilet," she explained. I bobbed my head in understanding, the furs shifting as I did. "Goodnight, my lady." She turned and departed my room. I closed my eyes, and the world spun again. Oh, Gods. I focused on my breathing. Focused hard on each inhale and exhale until I drifted into a dreamless sleep.

I awoke to the sound of my door slamming loudly against the stone wall as it opened. I shot forward, throwing my hands over my face at the bright light of the morning sun, the rays causing my vision to blur and my head to throb.

"Good morning, my lady!" Imogen exclaimed. Her voice was chipper and entirely too loud. I groaned as I threw myself back down, yanking the blankets high to cover my face. She clapped her hands together, and the sounds of several footsteps moved throughout my bed chamber. I plugged my fingers into my ears, trying to block out the commotion of servants' chatter and the opening and slamming of drawers and cabinets, each vibration of sound like a shock wave to my headache. Imogen knew precisely what she was doing—reminding me of my stupidity.

And thoroughly enjoying it, at that.

"I get it!" I yelled, my voice only slightly muffled by the blankets. "I made a poor decision, and I'm suffering for it." I reached an arm out, grasping at the spare pillow and throwing it over my face, the clinking and banging sounds of the servants readying a bath causing the ache in my head to become more forceful. "Now, please be quiet and let me die in peace."

Imogen ripped the pillow from my hands and smacked me with it before yanking the blankets from my body.

"Stop being so dramatic and get up," she demanded. I stared up in shock for just a moment before rolling over on my side to face away from her. I didn't dare to challenge her last night when I was too sick to move, but today.... Today I was hungover and irritable. Again she struck me with the pillow, smacking it against my ribs, my face, my legs. *Whack, whack, whack.* Over and over. I crawled to the other side of the large bed, fleeing for safety from Imogen's psychotic wrath. I felt the mattress shift behind me, and I twisted to see Imogen on top of the bed, making her way towards me, fury in her eyes and a raised pillow in her arms.

"Fine!" I yelled as I rolled off the bed and fell onto the tile floor, my knees tender and bruised after a night spent over the toilet. I quickly got to my feet and hurried into the bathing room, slamming the door shut behind me.

"You have ten minutes to bathe. Then I expect to see you sitting at the vanity when I return." Imogen instructed as I listened to her footsteps echoing in the adjacent room. I twisted the latch, locking the door as I headed to the tub. Maybe I would just stay in here for the rest of the morning. She had no way of reaching me.

"I hope you don't think locking the door will save you. I have a key," she said as if she could read my thoughts. I groaned loudly as I undressed and sank into the tub, yelping as the ice-cold water covered me, goosebumps forming immediately along every inch of my naked body. "To help with the hangover," Imogen explained before I heard her leave my room. It was as if she had waited to depart until she knew I had gotten into the bath. I didn't know if she was ensuring my obedience or just wanted to hear my panic at the cold temperature. Given her behavior this morning, I'd be willing to bet that she wanted to listen to my suffering.

I seriously considered staying in the tub after Imogen had returned for the sole purpose of getting back at her for rudely beating me with my pillow and then forcing me to take a bath colder than ice, but in the end, I knew she would deliver a punishment somehow crueler than this morning if I stepped even one toe out of line. So I made sure that I was dressed and seated at the vanity several minutes before she was due to return, using the quiet solitude and the surface of the desk to fall back asleep.

Imogen cleared her throat vociferously close to my ear, causing me to jerk awake with such force that I banged my head against the back of the chair as I sat upright. The pain of the blow reverberated through my body. I threw my hands to the back of my head to feel the bump that had instantly formed, the skin red hot and throbbing beneath my fingers. I peered up into the vanity mirror to find Imogen standing casually behind me as if nothing out of the ordinary had happened.

"Was that necessary?!" I yelled at her reflection.

"I'm not sure I know what you are talking about, my lady," Imogen replied coyly as she ran her fingers through my hair, twisting the strands to form a single long braid.

"I know that I messed up last night. I shouldn't have consumed that much wine, but that isn't a good enough reason for you—"

"You think that I'm upset solely about the amount of wine you drank last night?" Imogen interrupted, her voice incredulous. I wasn't sure how to respond. Wasn't that the reason? Imogen walked around the chair to face me and bent down until her hazel eyes were level with mine, her face serious and weary. Furious yet calm.

"My lady," she began, her voice as soft as a whisper but with an edge of concern that told me she was afraid of being overheard. "You insulted King Perceval in front of his court. You told the Crowned Prince to go fuck himself within earshot of his court. You are loose with your tongue and reckless. You seem to have no realization that there are not only consequences but repercussions for your actions. Especially for those around you." I stared at her. Unable to speak, unable to breathe, unable to move. "I can't seem to figure out if your lack of common sense solely lies in your upbringing. If you're too stupid to see the problematic behavior you display, or if you know exactly what you are doing and yet do not care—or if you are just so hurt and so angry and so broken that you are content on destroying yourself anyway that you can."

I wasn't sure that I could give her an answer. That I even *knew* what the answer would be. Her observation that I was hurt and angry rang true. If I was honest with myself, I was probably broken as well. But was I content with destroying myself? Was that the motivation behind my words, behind my actions? I didn't feel like that was the case, but maybe it was. I knew I wanted to walk the edge, but perhaps some part of me hidden deep down didn't care if I fell over and I wrecked myself in the process. I stared down at my hands, unable to hold her gaze any longer as shame, embarrassment, and confusion ran through my body.

"It's my job to take care of you, my lady." Imogen's fingers slid over mine as she squeezed tightly. "That doesn't just include ensuring that you are fed and clothed. This world is new to you, and I'm here to help you navigate it in any way that I can." I looked up to find her eyes soft and reassuring. "I want you to be safe, and if the only way that I can get through to you is by harsh tactics, so be it. I won't stand back and allow you to hurt yourself. I won't watch you purposely lose this fight, my lady."

I felt a tear slide down my cheek, one that I hadn't been aware had even formed. There was something about the tenderness in which she spoke, the softness of her eyes, and the words that she had used. There was no doubt in my mind that she meant everything she said. That she genuinely cared for my well-being more than anyone in my life ever had before. I felt the blood rush to my cheeks as I was filled with shame for my actions. For what I was putting her through.

"I'm sorry," I told her, my voice breaking on the words as I tried to choke down the emotions that threatened to escape. Imogen brought her hand up to cup my cheek.

"I don't need you to be sorry, my lady," she explained. "I need you to think. To be smarter than those around you." I nodded my head. I could do that. I could at least *try* to do that. Imogen patted my hands before straightening and returning to her spot behind me. I watched her work in silence, unsure how to move on from the heaviness of the conversation.

When she was finished, she escorted me out to the terrace where Dashiell and Felix had already been seated, their plates full of untouched food as if they had been waiting to eat until I had arrived. "Remember what I told you," she whispered into my ear before slipping back inside the palace.

I made my way to my seat, the brightness of the sun making my still present headache worse, the smell of the food making my stomach turn over. I sat down, swallowing back the nausea that began to creep up. My hands immediately reached for the cup of hot tea placed to my right, knowing the aroma and taste of the peppermint and lemon would help ease the pain.

"How are you feeling today?" Dashiell asked. I turned my head slowly in his direction as I watched him finally take a bite of his eggs. I narrowed my eyes as I gave him an incredulous look that I knew would convey the stupidity of his question. How the Hell did he *think* I was feeling? Dashiell wisely didn't respond and instead focused back on his breakfast.

"We have a tonic that will help with the hangover, sugar pie," Felix announced as I brought the tea up to my lips, taking one small, tentative sip to test whether I could drink it or whether it would try to claw its way back up my throat. The warmth of the liquid was soothing as it traveled down, staying put in the bottom of my stomach. Thank the Gods.

"I'm fine," I said into my cup, knowing that Felix could hear me. I wasn't fine. Not even a little bit, but I wasn't sure that I could trust anything given by either of these two. Something told me that whatever tonic Felix wanted me to take wouldn't be coming from a Medicus. I would much rather receive help from the magic wielders trained in such exploits.

"What's the plan for today?" Felix asked, directing his question to his friend.

"I figured we could take Ainsley to—"

"I'm not going anywhere," I cut in quickly and watched as Dashiell and Felix looked wearily between each other. They clearly didn't expect me to object, probably thinking that my drunken behavior and informality with them last night indicated that we were friendly. We most definitely were not. I told Imogen I would try to do better, and I knew myself enough to know that nothing good would happen if I were kept in their company for an extended period of time.

"Why?" Dashiell questioned as if he genuinely didn't understand my declaration.

"Because I don't want to," I said plainly.

"Now, sugar pie, how are we to become great friends if you won't spend time with us?" Felix asked, and I looked towards him to find that cocky grin already on his face. Arrogance and smugness radiated from him. I felt my blood heat, and my temper begin to climb.

"What makes you think that I want to be your friend?" I snarled. "Either of yours," I added, looking between them. Felix's smile was gone, his face a mask of neutrality as he listened, but Dashiell's... There was something there. Some emotion or thought that I couldn't place. "Was it when I flipped you both off? Was it the fact that I needed to be drunk just to be around you? Or maybe it was my subtle way of telling you both to shove it." I watched as they stared at each other, neither of them speaking. After a moment, Felix raised a single brow at his friend. Dashiell's response was a slight shake of his head. It was like they had just had an entire conversation without uttering a single word aloud. "Are you speaking mind to mind?" I asked, breaking the silence.

"What?" Dashiell responded, breaking his stare from his friend to bring his deep blue eyes to me. "That's not possible; there is no such magic as that."

"Dash and I have known one another for a long time. We're close enough that we usually know what the other is thinking or planning without him having to say it," Felix explained. I had known nothing about the friendship they shared, but what Felix said surprised me for some reason.

"Listen," I told them. "I just want to leave here. I just want to return home and get back to the life I had to leave behind. It may not have been a fancy palace, and there were no servants to cater to my every need. There was no magic, but...." I turned to Felix, his amber eyes so soft and bright against his warm ivory skin. "But it was *my* life." Felix's face fell slightly, the mask crumbling, and I felt an overwhelming calming sensation. A feeling that maybe he understood exactly what I was trying to express.

I turned back to Dashiell, his expression still unreadable, still mysterious. I found myself annoyed that I was struggling to figure him out. I lowered my chin just barely. It had automatically been raised in defiance towards him. It was like my body wanted to push him far away. To push back against everything he was supposed to be to me. My fiancé and my future king. He symbolized everything that I had lost and still stood to lose.

"So, please. Please release me from this betrothal and let me leave. Let me go back home," I pleaded to Dashiell. His throat bobbed, and he peeled his eyes from mine, focusing his attention back on his plate, though he made no move to eat.

"It's not my choice; it's the king's. There's nothing I can do."

"Bullshit," I said, not bothering to hide the sharp bite in my tone. Dashiell's eyes snapped to mine, flares of what looked to be anger sparking within them. "You are the Crowned Prince of Caelum. This whole arrangement affects you too. Why aren't you doing something to get out of it?" I demanded, and my gaze drifted to the two servants, now looking somewhat uncomfortable as they stood at the far end of the terrace, waiting to be called upon if needed. I shouldn't have raised my voice at the prince. Not with witnesses present, at least. Dashiell looked to the servants and then back at me before addressing them.

"Leave us, please," he commanded. The way he spoke was serene and respectful, more of a request than anything else. It was so unlike how his father had given orders. The women bowed before retreating through the gardens and leaving the three of us alone. Dashiell waited until they had disappeared before turning his attention back to me. "You don't think I tried to get out of this?" he asked as he waved a hand between the two of us. "That when I found out—only one month ago, mind you—that I was to be married to someone I had never met, never so much as *seen* before, all because of some agreement that was made when I was the mere age of two.... You don't think I may have had an issue with that myself?" I hadn't thought about what he was asking. I hadn't cared to. Though I had known my fate for years, and he had only learned of his weeks ago, he still held more power than I did. If anyone could get through to the king, it would be his son. "I tried, Ainsley. I did everything I could think of to get out of this situation. Believe me; I tried my hardest."

"Apparently, it wasn't hard enough," I told him flatly. I knew my words were unfair but so was the entire circumstance. Dashiell clenched his jaw as he tore his eyes from mine and settled them on some fixed point in the distance, his head shaking slightly.

"As I told you, the decision lies with my father." He gritted out the words like it was painful for him to say. "If you have a problem with our marriage arrangement, then I suggest you take it up with him. It seemed to work out so well for you when you tried yesterday," he added, and I felt my heart sink deep beneath my chest as I recalled my outburst in the throne room and the threat that ensued directly afterward. I was living on borrowed time.

"Dash," Felix said gently. A warning and a plea. I watched as Dashiell looked at his friend. His jaw relaxed, and the anger in his eyes subsided at whatever he read on Felix's face. They seemed to be having another one of their private conversations. I realized that there was nothing that Dashiell would or even could do to help me get home. It was a lost cause.

I felt Felix burning a hole into me with his stare as if he was demanding my attention. I reluctantly gave it to him. The red-hot anger and frustration I felt toward Dashiell disappeared the second I tore my eyes away. Just the sight of him caused a storm of rage to billow within me.

"Sugar pie," Felix began, his stare pinning me to the spot. His nickname for me caused the storm to reappear, but it felt different than before. It was smaller, weaker. Far in the distance. I willed it to the surface, but it was as if invisible hands were grasping that rage and forcing it down, not allowing the air it needed to thrive. Felix raised a brow like he was aware of the fight that was happening inside of me. "I know that this is difficult—"

"You don't know anything," I cut in before I could stop myself, fighting those invisible hands with everything that I was. "I don't expect you to understand what it is like to have your entire life ripped away from you. To just be wanted and used for what you have to offer. To not have a choice." I stood as if the height difference now could somehow drive the words deeper into his ears. Dashiell began to speak, but Felix held up a hand, halting his friend. He watched me for another quiet heartbeat before responding.

"So then explain it. Help us to understand," Felix offered, but I didn't want to. I had no one in my life that I trusted enough to bare my heart and soul to. No one that I trusted enough to share the side of me that was scared and lonely. The side that cared and dreamed. The last thing that I wanted to do was to be vulnerable and emotionally exposed to these two. The invisible grasp loosed, and I took the opportunity to attack, forcing the storm to break free.

"No," I ground out as I turned on my heel and headed back inside, wrapping myself in the internal wind and rain and thunder and lightning that was me.

8.

Once again, finding the way back to my room proved difficult. Luckily, Imogen found me wandering the halls on her way down to retrieve me from breakfast. She opened her mouth to speak, but before she could ask what happened, I gave her a look indicating that I was in no mood to discuss. Thankfully, she didn't push me on the subject and instead walked me quietly back to my bed chamber. I spent the rest of the morning in bed, reading my books, allowing my mind to travel and drift away to far-off places and a life that wasn't mine.

Imogen returned at lunchtime and brought me back down to the terrace. I didn't pay any attention to Dashiell or Felix as they spoke at me or to each other. I focused solely on my meal, consuming it as quickly as possible and waiting silently for Imogen to return. After lunch, I returned to my books and waited to be retrieved for dinner. For three days, that's all I did. Meal. Ignore. Read. Repeat. Meal. Ignore. Read. Repeat. An endless drum of monotony.

Imogen had placed a strict wine ban on me after the events of my first night in the palace, so there was absolutely nothing that I could do to dull my senses when forced to be around them. Even after three days of pretending they didn't exist, Felix and Dashiell never once stopped trying to talk to me, trying to include me in their stories and conversation, and asking me questions about my life or my interests. Never quite equating my lack of words to not wanting to speak to them. They treated my silence like nothing more than a game, competing on who could break me first.

On the fourth day, the day of my Welcome Feast, I journeyed to the terrace for breakfast to find only Dashiell there waiting. I glanced at Felix's empty seat as I sat, fighting the urge to ask where he was.

"He's meeting with my father this morning," Dashiell said, answering the unspoken question.

"I don't care," I told him, instantly regretting the words. Not because I actually did care but because I gave him the satisfaction of a response—the first one in four days. I looked at him, hoping there was some slight possibility that he didn't hear me, but he perked up at the sound of my voice.

"Are you excited about the Welcome Feast tonight?" he asked quickly, taking advantage of my slip of restraint. I sipped at my tea, not deeming a reply. "Did you ever have large celebrations in your village?" My head swiveled to the side as I focused all my attention on the palace's gardens in the distance. I watched the purple Angelonia sway in the light breeze and marveled at the vibrant shades of tulips. The late morning light made the maroon, orange, and yellow colors of the flowers come to life. The scene looked more like an artist's rendering than it did reality.

"So we're back to this?" he inquired as he leaned his back against the chair and crossed his arms over his chest.

"Back to what?" I replied, once again forgetting that I wasn't speaking to him.

"Back to you ignoring me."

"I never stopped," I said flatly as I placed my cup back onto the table and met his gaze. His blue eyes poured into me as we stared at each other. His face was unreadable, and more than anything, that pissed me off. Though I refused to engage with either of them throughout each meal, I sat back and observed. I surveyed the way they spoke and the way they held themselves. I noticed how Dashiell's brow would furrow whenever Felix addressed me and I didn't respond. I marked the softness in Felix's eyes as he watched me quietly eat. I studied the looks they constantly gave each other as they had their own silent conversations.

Felix was easy to read. He used humor to try and connect, and though he was annoying as all Hell, something deep within me knew that his character was authentic. He seemed genuinely excited that I was here and sincere in his attempt to become friends. Dashiell, on the other hand, was a completely different story. No matter how long I watched him, I couldn't ever place the emotions he exuded. I couldn't figure out why his forehead creased at times or why he'd rub the back of his neck when he glanced in my direction. His eyes were deep and mysterious, and I found myself tossing and turning at night as I tried to unravel the secrets they contained. It frustrated me beyond anything else that I couldn't figure Dashiell out.

"What is your problem, Ainsley?" he snapped. By the way he straightened in his chair, and how his face fell infinitesimally, I could tell that he didn't mean for the question to come out as forceful and harsh as his tone would suggest.

"Nothing," I replied calmly as my eyes glanced around in uncertainty, looking for any sign of eavesdroppers, wondering to myself if this was a safe space. Dashiell instantly knew what I was doing.

"We're completely alone," he pointed out. "I asked the servants to leave before you got here. It seems to be the only way that you'll speak freely." I leaned forward, resting my forearms on the table, and focused on picking at my nails. I didn't want to have this conversation with him. I desperately wanted Dashiell and Felix to be content with leaving me alone for however long I was to remain here at the palace. Unfortunately for me, it seemed that neither of them was ever going to give up. "So let's hear it," he added when I didn't reply. I took a deep breath before meeting his stare once more, his face still unreadable, his eyes, as always, mesmerizing and haunting. Irrational anger coursed through my veins as I took in the sight of him. If I took his bait and opened my mouth now, I wasn't sure I would ever be able to come back from it; from the things I wanted to voice.

"I don't have anything to say," I told him as I pushed away from the table, rising to my feet to quickly escape. The sound of metal scraping stone loudly echoed in the air between us, and before I even knew what was happening, cool fingers were wrapped around my wrist, halting my retreat. His grip didn't hurt; it wasn't forceful. It was barely anything more than a feather-light touch, but it was still a shock to the senses. As if a bolt of lightning had struck my nervous system, waking me up and bringing me to life. My head turned immediately as my eyes zeroed in on the point of contact. His fingers were delicately curved around my arm just above the wrist in nothing more than a gentle caress. My head veered up, meeting his gaze at the same time he tore his eyes away from his touch on my skin. He swallowed deeply before taking a small step forward, hand still on my wrist.

"Talk to me," he whispered. "Tell me what to do. Tell me why you hate me." I closed my eyes, letting his words wash over me as I considered my next action.

"You are going to be my husband, but I don't want you," I said plainly, opening my eyes to look at him as I spoke. "I hate you because every time I look at you, all I see is what was taken from me, the choice that was stolen. All of it, just to give *you* a better life, to give *you* more power, with absolutely no regard for me." I took a tentative step closer to him, closing the gap between us as I continued. "I hate you because of everything you symbolize to me. There is nothing you can do to fix that, Dashiell. I want nothing to do with you." I let out a long breath as I finished, and Dashiell turned his head, fixing his stare into the distance, his jaw clenched tight.

After what felt like a lifetime, he reluctantly dragged his eyes back to mine, nodding to himself as if he were accepting some conclusion he had come to within his mind. All at once, he released my wrist and stepped around me without so much as a word as he retreated inside the palace. I stared down at my arm, the skin tingling under his phantom touch, before I sank back into my chair.

After a few minutes, Imogen appeared to collect me, but I waved her off, not ready to leave this spot. So I sat. For hours. I stared into the distance, watching a parade of servants hurrying about the grounds, working to make sure everything was perfect for tonight's event. I stared at the tea that had long since gone cold between my hands. I stared at Dashiell's empty chair as I remembered how his face had looked when I told him I wanted nothing to do with him. His eyes held an unending sadness—a hopelessness. And though his features were sullen, there was rage hidden within them as well. My words were harsh, but they needed to be said.

The sun was high, a bright light against a clear blue cloudless sky, when Felix made his way onto the terrace with a book in hand. Once seated, he flipped open to a random page and silently read. The book was worn, the leather cover so aged and loved that the title was no longer decipherable. I squinted my eyes as I moved closer, determined to be as unnoticeable as possible as I attempted to learn which novel he was enjoying and if it was one I had already read myself.

"You could just ask," Felix singsonged. I straightened, embarrassed that I had been caught, and instead focused on the two servants making their way to our table. They placed a small plate of cheese, bread, and a smaller dish of mixed fruits before us. I was seriously regretting not touching my breakfast as my stomach rumbled. Felix threw me a knowing smile before explaining. "The feast starts in a few hours. They want you to save your appetite for tonight. Plus, that's where all the good food is." He dove into his bowl of melon. I looked to my left and noticed nothing had been set out for Dashiell. It seemed he would not be joining us.

"Where is Dashiell?" I asked before I had the good sense to stop myself. To his credit, Felix didn't bat an eye at me suddenly deciding to speak or even at the subject of my question. He placed his fork down and casually dabbed a napkin at the corner of his mouth.

"Dash needed some space," Felix explained as he looked at me. I did not doubt that Dashiell had shared what had transpired between us this morning. I braced myself for a lecture on how I shouldn't have lost my temper at the Prince of Caelum, but Felix didn't say anything more. He simply picked his fork back up and popped another piece of fruit into his mouth as he turned the page of his book. I felt a small amount of gratitude for him at that moment for not pushing the subject further. Maybe that's why I decided to ask.

"What are you reading?"

Felix looked up from his story, and without missing a beat, he answered. "It's a tall tale about the lost Kingdom of Disparya," he explained. "It's pretty interesting. You should read it." He extended the book in invitation between us.

"Maybe I will once you've finished," I replied.

"Oh, I've already read it about five times. It's all yours." I took the book from his hands and gave him a small smile.

"Thank you," I told him as I inspected the novel, flipping through the pages as the intoxicating scent of worn parchment filled my nose. The book felt so brittle and ancient that I was afraid it would break apart in my hands before I ever had the chance to read the words within. "How old is this?"

Felix tilted his head side to side and squinted his eyes as he pondered the question. "I'm not sure exactly, but I can ask the librarian if he has any idea."

"There's a *library here*?" I exclaimed loudly, unable to stop myself. Several servants making their way through the gardens with large floral bouquets in tow eyed me suspiciously, not thrilled at my sudden outburst. Felix clamped his mouth together tightly as he looked around, biting back his laughter.

"Sorry!" he yelled with a wave at the servants. "She's new here." I chewed the inside of my cheek, struggling hard to keep in the smile forming at his joke. Felix turned his attention back to me and winked like he knew just how funny I had found him to be. "There most definitely is a library here."

"Where is it?" I was practically bouncing in my seat. Felix smiled at that.

"I could tell you, but I'm afraid you would die of starvation before ever reaching it." An obvious jab at my declaration that I would rather get lost and die from hunger than have him show me around. I rolled my eyes as he let out a low melodic laugh. Watching him, I bit my lip as I debated with myself. Felix offering me his book was a small act of kindness that I wanted to reciprocate. I reached into the hidden pocket of my dress and slowly pulled forth the novel I had brought. I glided my hand over the cover, feeling the cracked leather under my fingers, before leaning across the table to extend it to him. Felix came forward, meeting me halfway to procure the book from my hands. He quickly glanced over the title.

"I haven't read this one before," he noted as he settled back into his seat and flipped open to the first page.

"It's not as exciting as a story about the lost Kingdom of Disparya, but it's one of my favorites," I told him, suddenly feeling the self-conscious need to explain. Felix smiled empathetically and nodded.

"I love stories of every genre, so I'm sure I'll enjoy this," he replied as he opened the book and began to read. I followed his lead, opening the book he had given me to the first page.

We spent the entire lunch hour lost in the stories we held between our hands. The only sounds that filled the space were those of turning pages and our quiet verbal reactions. A few times, I gasped softly at the words written, my grip tighter on the book as I feared for the character's life. Occasionally, Felix had snickered at his story, and I found myself trying to guess where he was in the tale, wondering if it were the same parts that I had found amusing. Eventually, Felix cleared his throat loudly enough that I looked up. He arched a single brow so high that I swore it was about to retreat into his hairline. I furrowed my brows, not understanding what had brought this about. He cleared his throat once again as he held the book closer to his face.

"*And then he ran his tongue up my—*" he recited.

"Oh, my Gods. I completely forgot about that part." The blood rushed to my face, leaving my skin feeling hot and flush and undoubtedly very red. Felix gave a devilish smile.

"If I knew you read *this* type of literature, sugar pie, I would have brought you something from my personal collection."

"I don't!" I lied. He smiled even wider, seeing straight through the deception. "The story itself is very compelling!" I tried again, but he still wasn't buying it. I clamped my lips hard, but it was of no use. A roar of laughter burst through me.

"You like *dirty* books," Felix singsonged, and I threw my hands over my face as I shook my head, my body quaking with hysterics still. I placed the book down and threw my napkin at his face. He offered a laugh that matched my own. But before either of us could say anything more, Imogen appeared.

"Come along," she instructed. "I need to get you ready for tonight." I obliged, rising from my seat and grabbing my new book from the table.

"Bye, Felix," I said softly before turning to leave with Imogen. He dipped his head in a slight bow and gave me a crooked little grin.

"I'll see you tonight," he said as his eyes returned to his book. "Oh, and make sure you scrub well," Felix added, not meeting my stare. "You look a little dirty."

9.

"Can I ask you a question?" I said to Imogen as she pinned a curl away from my face. She met my stare in the reflection of the mirror and nodded.

"What happens during the Entwining Ceremony?" Imogen secured another strand of hair. The subject had been on my mind more and more lately. If there was no getting out of my marriage to Dashiell, I needed to be prepared for what was to come.

"An Incantis will—"

"An Incantis?" I asked, not familiar with the word.

"They are unique immortals chosen by the Gods to worship them and spread their word. They do not possess any kingdom's Gifts."

"So they don't have magic?"

"It's claimed that their magic is the ability to communicate with the Gods. The Incantis are considered sacred and are protected by Disparya's laws. To harm or even insult one is punishable by death." She gave me a pointed look.

"Why have I never heard of them before?" Though my village was small and my Caregivers didn't concern themselves much with my education, I assumed I would have learned about these omniscient immortals at some point.

"They are rare and reside on private land in Disparya, not belonging to any kingdom known as Arcanus. They only leave their home to perform rituals and ceremonies for royalty throughout the continent," Imogen explained.

"And one will travel here to conduct mine," I commented, trying to follow along.

"Yes. As is tradition, you will have a wedding, and the Entwining Ceremony will take place the following night. During it, an Incantis will perform the act of magically binding you and Prince Dashiell."

"Will it hurt?" I asked cautiously. "When he takes my magic." Imogen stopped her preening at once, no doubt hearing the fear and sadness in my voice. She stepped in front of me and bent to look me directly in the eyes.

"No, Ainsley, it will not hurt," she said reassuringly. I let out a long, slow breath, still hating that I would be subjected to this practice. "I'm all finished. Would you like to see?" Imogen asked. I rose from my seat at the vanity and let her lead me to the twisted gold full-length mirror.

"I look... Beautiful," I told her. On any given day, I was by no means unattractive, but tonight I looked flawless. My skin felt as smooth as silk, and my hair flowed down my back in gentle waves like that of a mighty yet calm river. The light pink rouge that she had applied to my lips made them look soft and supple, and the bronze shadow on my lids made my brown eyes pop. But my looks were nothing compared to what I wore—the gown Imogen had selected was breathtaking. It was modest but hugged me enough to show off my curves. The chiffon was draped along my body in delicate ripples that just barely grazed the floor. I didn't miss the fact that the dress was a deep blue; a gorgeous cross between navy and dark teal—the same shade as Dashiell's eyes. The earrings she chose were tiny diamonds that twisted intricately around each other to form beautiful flowers and dangled so low that they brought attention to my bare shoulders and the thin straps of my gown. I noticed that the flowers hanging from my ears matched the beading that traveled from my neckline down to my waist, wrapping itself around me like leaves of ivy. Imogen crossed her arms and looked at my reflection approvingly.

"You should head down now. The Welcome Feast will be starting shortly."

"I just need a moment," I said, meeting her gaze in the mirror. Imogen nodded and left the room, leaving me to myself. I stared at my reflection for a moment longer, trying to steel my nerves. I had never been to a feast before and hadn't been instructed on what to expect. I probably should have asked Imogen before she departed, but I guess I would have to get through tonight on my own. I took a deep breath and smoothed the front of my gown. "You can do this," I told my reflection out loud before turning for the door.

My jaw physically dropped when I reached the formal dining room. It had been eloquently decorated, dripping in gold and jewels and flowers. There was a long rectangular table positioned in the back of the room. It seemed to be the head table, meant for royalty and the king's most trusted advisors. Four other long tables ran perpendicular to the main one and sat in the center of the room. Each was framed with velvet chairs of the deepest emerald green. The tables were covered in Leatherleaf ferns so bright in color they must have been picked fresh this morning. Scattered between the leaves were several elaborate brass candelabras that matched each place setting and wine goblet. I looked up to discover hundreds of floating candles lighting up the entire room. Despite all the flames, the room felt comfortably cool. Probably due to some form of magic, I realized.

Magic, it occurred to me that I may one day possess. The idea sent flutters through my stomach, and I was surprised at how excited I was. I had never given much thought to the possibility of power running through my veins, but the closer I came to my birthday, the more curious I found myself. The idea became instantly tainted the second I remembered the sole reason I was here: to give up some of that power.

Suddenly, the roar of chatter grew silent, despite the number of guests seated at the tables. I peeled my gaze from the overhead candles to figure out what had caused the murmurs to quiet, only to find everyone's eyes on me. Everyone. Even King Perceval stared at me from his seat at the center of the main table. I felt panic rising, my breath coming quicker and more uneven. I needed to move. I needed to escape their prying eyes, except I *couldn't* move. I was paralyzed, as if everyone's stares were gluing me to the very spot I stood in the doorway.

Fuck. This was not ideal.

Movement on the left side of the room caught my attention, and I turned my head to find Dashiell striding toward me. I swallowed the lump that had formed in my throat as soon as he came into my view. I wasn't sure what I could possibly say to him after our exchange or why he was even coming toward me, for that matter. When he finally reached me, halting just a foot away, he bowed deeply.

I continued to stare at him until he whispered quietly enough that only I could hear, "Bow."

"Excuse me?" I questioned a bit too loudly. I was aware that what I had said this morning wasn't exactly the best way to explain how I felt, but I knew he had not just demanded that I bow before him. I glanced back to the guests, all of them studying me expectantly, some with confused looks on their faces.

Dashiell replied even quieter. "It is customary to return the gesture. Especially in a formal setting." His eyes widened to emphasize our surroundings. "Like this one." At once, understanding washed through me. I inclined my head to him and bent at the knees slightly to bow back. When I straightened, he extended his palm in invitation. "Are you ready?" he asked. His voice was as soft and calm as it usually was. It was like this morning had never happened. My brows furrowed in question as I studied him, trying desperately to read him correctly just once. But Dashiell wore a mask of neutrality.

I gave up on my attempt and instead thought back to his question. *Are you ready?* Not even a little bit, but I would have to be. I nodded and took a deep breath before placing my hand in his, letting him lead me through the room to our table. The bolt of lightning returned once more as my hand rested in his. I looked around the room as we walked, not missing the fact that no one was taking their eyes off of us. At least not until I took my seat between Dashiell and Felix, and the thundering of conversation filled the air once more.

"Way to make quite the entrance, sugarplum," Felix said as he slid my wine goblet toward me. I peeked inside, expecting to see it filled with water, and instead, found wine. I smiled to myself, knowing that Felix had made the switch after seeing that, obviously, I needed it. I took a long sip before responding to him.

"Glad you enjoyed the show. Ass." I narrowed my eyes playfully.

"Always," he said, smiling sarcastically. "Also, can I just say, WOW? That is seriously some dress." Felix lifted his hand up and down as he gestured to my gown. "Dash, doesn't she look fantastic?" He leaned over me, looking at Dashiell expectantly.

"Umm, yes. You look... Nice," he replied, clearly uncomfortable with not only the question but having to address me. From the corner of my eye, I could see

Felix looking up at the ceiling and shaking his head, seemingly frustrated with Dashiell's response.

"Thank you," I told him weakly. His eyes locked on mine as uncertainty flashed over his features. He had no idea how to maneuver around me, and I felt the same. I found myself wishing I had never spoken to him at breakfast. At least things wouldn't be this awkward if I hadn't. The room quieted once again, and King Perceval rose from his chair.

"My lords, my ladies, it is with great joy that we have gathered this evening to honor our newest resident, Lady Ainsley, future Princess of the Kingdom of Caelum." All at once, everyone bowed their heads to me. Remembering what Dashiell had instructed me earlier, I quickly returned the gesture. "In the near future, she and my son, my heir Dashiell, will participate in our most sacred of ceremonies. They will bind themselves together for eternity. The union between them will aid in keeping our glorious kingdom strong and prosperous," King Perceval explained.

I shifted uncomfortably and took another long sip from my goblet. *In the near future.* What does an immortal consider the *near future,* anyway? Weeks? Month? Years? I could only hope the answer was decades.

"And with the grace of the Gods, shortly after solidifying their union, they will produce heirs of their own," the king added. I choked loudly on my wine and began coughing uncontrollably. Felix clamped down on his lips, holding in his laughter as he patted my back hard to end the fit. Looking down, I brought a hand to my forehead to try and shield my face from everyone who I knew, without a shadow of a doubt, was staring at me with bewilderment in their eyes. I glanced sidelong at Dashiell to see him trying and failing miserably to hide his amusement at my misfortune.

My breathing quickened as I ran through the king's words. *Heirs of their own. Heirs of their own. Heirs of their own!* Of all the things I thought about having to do while I was here, creating children was never one of them for some reason. I could not figure out why it hadn't once crossed my mind that I may be expected to reproduce with my husband. Oh. My. Fucking. Gods. I brought the goblet back to my lips and drained the rest of the contents. I sat back, waiting impatiently for the cup to refill itself and saying a silent prayer to the Gods once it did.

King Perceval cleared his throat and started again. "It is true that we have many things as a kingdom to be grateful for. But what I am most appreciative of..." he paused, placing a hand over his heart as he fixed his stare on me. Rage, promise, and excitement billowed in his dark green eyes as he raked his gaze down to my lap and back up, finally setting it upon my eyes. "Is that sweet Ainsley here, is ours." My stomach knotted as his serpentine smile crept up his face. "To Ainsley!" he exclaimed, raising his goblet high in the air.

"To Ainsley!" everyone crowed back, raising their glasses as well.

"Now, let the feast begin!" the king yelled, facing his court once more. He gracefully waved his empty hand, and food magically appeared scattered across the tables.

"Are you okay?" Felix whispered low, and I turned my attention to him. I most certainly wasn't okay. Out of everything that King Perceval had said tonight, the word *ours* was like a knife to my heart. He wanted to ensure that I knew my place and wouldn't ever step out of line again. I shook my head at Felix as I wiped the back of my hands, now slicked with sweat, on the skirt of my gown. Felix casually slid his goblet over to me as he leaned close. "It's stronger than wine." That's all I needed to hear before I grabbed his cup and took a deep drink. I winced as the liquid within burned like wildfire as it traveled down my throat.

"Well, that was awkward," Felix stated, trying to change the subject.

"Just a tad bit," Dashiell responded as he surveyed the food before him.

Gold dishes were filled with beautifully seasoned roasted chicken, pork, and fish, all of which looked so tender and delectable. There were piles of sautéed tomatoes, summer squash, and greens next to heaps of buttery mashed potatoes. I didn't know where to begin, so I gave myself a little bit of everything, distracting myself from my thoughts by filling my mouth so completely that I could barely chew.

"Woah, slow down there, sugarplum," Felix said. "You're going to suffocate yourself." I narrowed my eyes at him since I couldn't offer a retort, but he just winked at me.

Looking out at the guests as I struggled to get my food down, I was met with several people still watching my every movement. I swallowed hard. Was this what my life was going to be like now? I wasn't aware that I had spoken the words aloud until both Dashiell and Felix said "Yup" in perfect unison.

"Splendid," I groaned, taking another sip of Felix's disgusting liquor. The taste wasn't pleasant but based on the tingling warmth that ran through my body, I could assume it was doing its job.

"You'll get used to it," Dashiell said.

"I don't want to get used to it," I quipped, more to myself than to him.

Dashiell turned to me, his eyes cold and unnerving. "Do you ever stop complaining?" he asked. Clearly, he was still mad about our conversation, after all. I couldn't say that I blamed him. My words, though true to how I felt, were unfair. He was bound to be still pissed; however, that wasn't going to stop me from giving him attitude.

"You could just call this whole thing off and let me go home. Then you would never have to deal with me again," I told him flatly.

Dashiell speared a piece of chicken and took a bite as he said, "Trust me, I've tried. And we've been over this already; as far as the matter of *home* is concerned... This is your home now, Ainsley, so I'd suggest you learn to accept it."

"You're a prick."

Dashiell shrugged. "Maybe, but I'm not wrong." My eyes narrowed at him as I grasped my knife tightly, imagining what it would feel like to stab him in his smug face.

"And you wonder why I hate you." I dropped my fork onto the table with a soft thud and glowered at him. Dashiell turned, meeting my eyes. Pain and sorrow and rage and frustration swirled within them, the blue so much deeper than usual. He opened his mouth to retort, but Felix leaned across me again, this time to glare at Dashiell and me.

"As much as I adore dinner with a show, I'd like to remind you both of where we are right now," he told us. "Not to mention *who* we are in the presence of. Perhaps this isn't the best time nor place for this display of the power struggle between you two." He was right. People were watching us now, sensing the visible tension. I returned to my plate, and the three of us consumed our meals in silence.

When seemingly everyone else had also finished eating, the king rose again, holding up his goblet. I braced myself for another unexpected announcement, hoping that I wouldn't be the subject. Everyone stood with him this time, and I followed suit, determined not to give them another reason to judge me.

"To the night the Gods have planned for us," said King Perceval.

"To the Gods!" his subjects repeated back to him. We all drank deeply from our cups as the king flicked his wrist. Instantly, the room transformed.

10.

All around me, everything had changed. Overhead, the magic candles, once illuminating the dining hall, now dimmed to the softest glow, creating a more intimate atmosphere. The long rectangular tables and all of the decor and dishes displayed atop them vanished as if they had never been there in the first place. Several tall round tables, only large enough to fit four or five people around them, were scattered throughout the room. Each table contained glass bowls filled to the brim with water lilies as centerpieces. The six balcony entrances along the eastern wall were delicately draped in blue and white larkspur. I inhaled deeply, drinking in the sweet scent of the flowers. Instantly, music flowed into the room from a source I couldn't pinpoint.

I watched as couples eagerly flocked to the center of the room. The music swept past me like the wind on a fall evening, and I felt the notes in my blood. The instruments married together to create loving and haunting sounds, and I watched in a trance as couples spun slowly across the entirety of the room, taking up every spare inch that the dance floor offered. Their bodies no longer belonged to themselves but instead to the instruments that became their Sirens. The men held their partners close as they twirled around, dresses hissing and swooshing along the ground. The skirts of the gowns were so full whenever they spun that it was as if I were watching flowers bloom before my eyes. I felt joy and longing and sadness all at once while watching their stories unfold, completely transfixed. I could feel both Dashiell and Felix's eyes burning into my skin, and I assumed that I must look insane to them, utterly hypnotized by the dancers before me, but I didn't care. I wasn't about to look away and miss one second of this dance. When the music finally came to an end, soft claps erupted throughout the room.

And with that, the next song played, a much faster and happier melody than the one before. I blinked several times as if I had been released from the hold on me the second the song had ended.

I looked over my shoulder to my right to see Dashiell no longer staring at me but instead glaring at Felix. I glanced over my left shoulder at Felix to see him nodding just barely to Dashiell. I envied their closeness and the ability to converse in a way that only two people who have known each other for years could. I took a deep breath and turned around to face them both, ready to ask what they had been discussing, when Dashiell caught my attention. He looked like he wanted to say something but couldn't quite form the words. After he opened and shut his mouth a few times, he gave Felix an angry look, declared he was getting a drink, and stalked off. I turned my attention to Felix, who was still watching after Dashiell.

"What was that all about?" I demanded, my eyes darting to Felix once Dashiell had disappeared within the crowd.

Still not quite looking at me yet, Felix shook his head and said, "No idea."

"You're lying." This got his attention, and his eyes moved to mine. I knew we weren't friends, and our brief conversation this afternoon was nothing compared to what he and Dashiell had, but I thought it was at least a good starting point. The fact that he wasn't telling me the truth upset me.

"What makes you say that?" he asked, head tilting to the side as he studied my face, and the hurt I was sure was written there.

"I may not know exactly what you two were going on about, but I'm not an idiot. You don't have to lie to me," I said the words as calmly as I could. Felix watched me for another minute before nodding his head, his amber eyes going soft and warm.

"Okay," was all he said as he offered a small smile. Not his usual cocky grin, but one that was reassuring and only for me. A way to tell me that he understood my feelings on the matter. Satisfied with his response, I looked away, scanning the party before me. Against the back wall, I locked eyes with the blonde woman that glowered at me in the garden the day I arrived. Now she was unabashedly glaring at me as if I was something unusual and foreign, her mouth twisting in disgust. So I glared right back. If I was being honest, she was quite attractive. Her skin was fair and soft, with her eyes a clear blue, the color of the sky on a midsummer afternoon. Her blonde hair was piled high in delicate curls and braided into a crown atop her head. She was curvy in all of the places both men and women desired. Her breasts were plump and spilled over the top of her gown, so they heaved whenever she took in air. She knew what she was doing. She gave me one long head-to-toe look over, raised a single well-groomed eyebrow, and smiled coolly as she stalked off, disappearing into the crowd. Dashiell wasn't anywhere near me, so what was her problem with me now?

I looked around the rest of the room to find a group of ladies with their heads turned to the side, all transfixed at some point in the distance. Their gowns were similar to mine in shape but were all a different shade of green, and their hair was all piled high, not a strand out of place. I followed their gaze, interested in what had captured their attention so intently. I found none other than Dashiell walking through the ballroom, raising his goblet of wine and giving a single nod to each person that addressed him in some way as he passed. The women tracked his every movement, his every breath. It was like they were a group of snakes, and he was the prey they so desperately wanted. Their stares turned from longing to envious in an instant.

I shifted my attention back to Dashiell in time to see someone's hand slide up his back and over his right shoulder. He turned his head slightly at her surprising touch, which he seemed not to expect to feel. At least not tonight. Not with me present. Although he may not have expected it, he didn't seem to mind it either. His blue eyes met hers, and he smiled warmly, turning his body around to face her fully. She caressed her wine goblet sensually as if it was a silent and subtle promise of what her plans for him were. Dashiell didn't seem to notice, and if he did, he didn't let on. With her free hand, she delicately dragged a finger across her exposed cleavage, trying to pull his gaze there. I realized at once she was the Garden Girl. She leaned forward on her toes to whisper something into his ear, and I looked away from the intimacy of it. It felt intrusive to watch her seduce him.

Instead, I refocused my attention back on the female group of snakes, wondering if they were disappointed that one of their own had already captured him for the evening.

They were no longer watching Dashiell; instead, their gazes were fixed on me. A few of them held their heads to the side while they studied me curiously, their eyes narrowing. I knew they were probably trying to gauge my feelings about Dashiell and his companion. He was my betrothed, after all. He was supposed to be *mine* in the eyes of this kingdom. Everyone in the palace knew this. The Garden Girl knew this, yet she didn't seem to care. She seemed to be the type of person who would go after what she wanted regardless of any consequences. I admired not only the confidence but also the freedom she had to do so.

I quickly adjusted my features to one of neutrality. Like none of this bothered me. Honestly, it didn't. Not the Garden Girl throwing herself at Dashiell in hopes that he'd bed her tonight. And not him, no doubt indulging her lust. The only thing that kindled a tiny flicker of my anger was that I was *expected* to be bothered by it all. I was expected to throw myself at him and mark him as my own. I was expected to unleash a lethal fury on anyone that approached him. I was expected to care.

I crossed my arms over my chest and extended my goblet of wine high in the air in a blatant gesture to toast them from across the room. I bowed my head, holding their eyes while a smirk formed on my lips. Let them see how unaffected I was. I took a long sip of my sweet wine as I stole another glance in Dashiell's direction, only to find him staring at me. The Garden Girl, still whispering sweet nothings in his ear. His eyes danced with interest as a slow half-smile started taking form. Oh, she was definitely trying to fuck him. He didn't break eye contact with me as he bent down to her ear to whisper his reply. When he pulled back to his normal height, he glanced back at her, his smile growing as he most likely just accepted her obvious invitation. I rolled my eyes and let out an involuntary snort as I took another long sip of my drink and looked back at the dancers before me.

Felix let out a low laugh that scared me half to death. I had completely forgotten that he was standing behind me. "What?" I demanded, the word coming out hard and clipped. I was sick of being everyone's source of entertainment tonight.

"I see that you're acquainted with Dash's fan club." Felix was more observant than I gave him credit for, and I made a mental note to check myself whenever he was in my company.

"If by 'acquainted' you mean being thrown vicious glares all night, then yes. We are well *acquainted*," I said as I widened my eyes to emphasize the last word. He let out another chuckle, and I couldn't help but let a soft laugh of my own escape. Everything that just transpired seemed so utterly ridiculous. I shook my head as if I could clear away the truth of what my life was now like. Elegant balls with frivolous ladies, envious of who I would be to Dashiell, and stopping at nothing to grab hold of his attention.

I turned my head again to glance at Dashiell and found his companion a fraction closer to him than she was before. With the lack of distance between them now, I knew he could feel the warmth of her body. She was looking up at him longingly. Seductively. Her fingers grazed the sleeve of his jacket in long, idle strokes. Her shoulders were held back, and her spine arched to show him all she had to offer. I watched as her cheeks flushed, and she batted her long lashes, looking up at him. But Dashiell wasn't meeting her gaze. Instead, he was watching Felix and me. His features were full of curiosity and wonder and... something else. Something that looked a little bit like frustration. The smile I held on my face from a moment before slowly faded under his piercing gaze. I took another sip of my wine, keeping my eyes locked on his, unable to tear them away.

After a minute, he inhaled deeply, grabbed the Garden Girl's wrist, and kissed the back of her hand, finally peeling his eyes from mine. I turned back to Felix to find him nodding his head and tapping his foot in time to the beat of the music. I inclined my head toward the group of ladies across the room.

"Who are they all anyway?" I asked. I hated that I was curious. More than that, I hated that I didn't know *why* I wanted to know.

"Ex-lovers and women who wish they were. And more than likely, several who wish they were in your position right now," Felix explained as he leaned forward on the balls of his feet and glanced over the top of the crowd, eyes narrowing as he spied someone he seemed to have been searching for.

"If only it were possible to switch with one of them," I said under my breath, but loud enough that I knew Felix would register my words.

I expected him to leave it at that. To leave me here and go set off to find whoever it was he had spotted, when he said, "I know this sucks for you. Being thrown into this world." He waved his hand, gesturing to the scene in front of us. "You've made your feelings about it all clear. And your feelings about Dash are *very* clear." I shrugged nonchalantly as Felix continued, "But you're not the only one in this, Ainsley." I moved my eyes to his at the sound of my name. I'd never heard him say it before—it had always been some insulting pet name with him. I eased a bit at his use of it. As if, for the first time, I was being seen as a person. "Hate him as you may, but Dash has been thrown into this as well. He had a life before you came here, and now he is being forced into one with you. A life he didn't ask for, either."

I stiffened a little at his words. I never thought about what Dashiell might be giving up to carry out his duty of marrying me. Maybe he had someone he already loved. Maybe it was the woman he was with now. Maybe he had plans of his own that never involved marriage to anyone. Perhaps he wanted to be alone... and free. And now, with me in the picture, it hindered the ability for those desires to come to fruition. Perhaps I was and would never be anything more than a burden and reminder of the freedom that was stolen away from him. Shame fluttered within me.

Felix looked down and nudged me with his hip. "Please try to cut Dash a little bit of slack. Maybe keep the thoughts of murdering him down to just a couple of times a day?" I chewed on the inside of my cheek as I pondered. Though I didn't like it, Felix was right. Dashiell had as little control over our betrothal as I did. It was King Perceval's choice, and he seemed all too enthused at our joining to ever allow me to believe he'd call off this arrangement. I knew it was unfair to blame Dashiell for all of this, but hearing Felix say those words aloud made me feel like complete shit over what I told him this morning. I turned my attention back to the couples whirling gracefully across the dance floor like fallen leaves upon the Autumn breeze.

"No promises," I told Felix, giving him a small smile.

It must have been an acceptable answer because he slapped me on the back of my shoulder and said, "Atta girl," way too enthusiastically. I looked in his direction in time to see him backing away from me towards the crowd with a smirk on his face. He threw me a quick wink before turning around and heading in the direction that held his interest before.

His absence made me feel suddenly alone and exposed. I wanted to melt into the crowd and become invisible. More than that, I wanted to slip out and retreat to my chamber, but I would never be able to leave undetected. There were too many eyes on me, watching my every movement with bated breath. I ventured to the dessert table, and my eyes glazed over as I took in the spread. Platters upon platters were covered in the most decadent pastries and cakes. Notes of vanilla and citrus entwined with the scent of cinnamon and cardamom. My mouth immediately watered at the combination. In the center of the table lay an ornate golden fountain. Rich, warm chocolate flowed over its edges, trickling slowly onto exotic fruits of every kind. The berries were deep in color and so plump I was willing to bet that if I plucked one up, its sweet nectar would escape with the barest of pressure from my fingers. The aroma of everything surrounding me was almost satisfying enough. Almost.

I was working on my second chocolate tartlet when Dashiell appeared at the far end of the table to refill his glass of wine under the fountain; a twin to the one that dressed the melons beneath it in a gown of silky chocolate. As usual, he spotted me—right as I bit too deeply into my pastry. He watched with intrigue as I struggled to chew for a good minute, my mouth too full as I cursed myself for not taking smaller bites. I no doubt resembled a squirrel trying to collect nuts for the cruel winter ahead. When he didn't look away, I raised my brows to him as if to ask, *'what do you want?'* Dashiell kept right on staring, and curiosity sparkled in his blue eyes as if he was wondering how this unrefined person was allowed to attend the ball; how she could be meant to be his wife. I wouldn't let myself ask the same question.

Once again, his companion appeared at his side. She was not letting him out of her sight, probably for fear of one of his many other admirers stealing him away. She sure as hell wasn't worried about me. I watched as she grabbed one of the goblets from his hand and offered him a sweet smile. I wasn't aware he had been holding two. He had been here not only to gawk at me but to refill her glass. How chivalrous. She took a small sip and followed Dashiell's gaze to me. To her credit, she didn't startle to see me standing here, watching them. She didn't so much as shy away from me in fear of the reaction I was expected to have. Instead, she linked her arm with his and tilted her head in a small bow to me. As she righted herself, she stroked Dashiell's arm in a territorial way while still holding my eyes. I suppressed a smile. She was trying extremely hard to get a rise out of me. It was a valiant effort, I had to admit, but it was a wasted one, and I didn't have the patience for her games anyway. I inclined a bow toward her to return the gesture, and when I lifted my head, I let a smirk appear on my lips. I popped the last bit of tartlet into my mouth, dusted off my hands loudly, and clasped them behind my back as I turned on my heel and drifted away through the room.

I desperately needed some fresh air. I needed space to breathe and think. As I made my way to the balcony doors, the sheer curtains swaying in the breeze, I spied Felix resting his shoulder against the wall with his back to me. As I passed him, I glanced over my shoulder to see him leaning close to a beautiful man. Too close for it to be anything other than what it was. The man's smooth pale skin and jet-black hair flickered in the light of the candles floating above them. Felix bent closer and whispered into his ear, and I watched as blush coated the man's cheeks as he smiled. Felix bit his lip at the sight. As if he could feel my stare, his eyes looked up to find me watching. He grinned devilishly and wiggled his eyebrows twice, and I felt my lips tug slightly in the corners as he focused his attention back on the person in front of him. It seemed even Felix had found a companion for the night.

When I finally reached the balcony doors, I pushed through the dangling flowers, loose petals falling into my hair, and made my way to the railing. In the quiet dark, the feeling of loneliness flooded through me. I sighed deeply and looked out at the sprawling gardens decorated with hundreds of floating flickering lanterns. A subtle movement alerted me to the corner of the garden next to a large rose bush in full bloom. I remembered it from my first day. Beautiful roses of soft pink, stark white, and deep red covered the bush almost completely, with very little green poking through. But right now, with how dark it was tonight, the flowers all looked black as coal. I squinted in the distance, trying to figure out what the movement could have been. And then I spotted it. The shadows of a couple dancing began to take form. They must be on the other side of the hedge, hidden from view to steal a private moment. I watched as they spun and held one another close enough that I knew they could feel each other's hearts beating beneath their chest. Their love and longing, their desire for one another almost palpable as they danced under the starry summer night. The secret dancers reminded me so much of the black birds that I used to watch at my lake, and my heart swelled as a feeling of tranquility washed over me. It was the closest I had felt to home since arriving. How long I had been watching them, I didn't know. I was entranced by the way they moved so gracefully. Like they were dancing on air.

The sound of a boot scuffing under stone echoed, and I whipped around so fast that I was instantly light-headed my heart racing. A gasp escaped from me as I beheld someone watching from the shadows. I was caught trespassing on a tender moment that wasn't meant for me.

"It's just me," Dashiell said with both hands raised high in innocence.

"My Gods," I said as I clasped my chest, ready to catch my heart before it leaped from my body.

"I didn't mean to startle you. I just—" He glanced over my shoulder. "What are you looking at?"

I turned back around and faced the garden, but as I searched for the shadows once more, they were gone. I assumed they must have moved the dance to their private quarters. My cheeks heated at the thought of the obvious love between them and what that love would surely blossom into when they tangled themselves together in a more intimate type of dance. I didn't want to answer his question. I didn't want him to ruin the feeling I had when I thought back to those dancing lovers. No. I would keep what I witnessed a secret. Just for me.

Instead, I asked over my shoulder, "Where's Garden Girl?" I listened to the sound of his steps coming closer until he was at the balcony's edge as well, though he kept a distance of a couple of feet between us. I threw him a sidelong glance as he leaned over the railing and surveyed the grounds. Probably trying to answer his earlier question for himself. After a moment, he nodded and then looked at me, content with whatever he saw or didn't see below.

"Who?" he drawled, raising a single brow.

"The woman that had been throwing herself at you so hard I thought she was going to break something." His eyes flickered with realization and amusement, most likely reliving those soft sensual touches and whispers of promises in his mind.

"You mean Rosella?" he questioned. I merely shrugged and turned to watch the lanterns float idly by. He moved an infinitesimal amount closer, but I clocked it. I wasn't sure why he was out here with me, especially after our latest exchange over dinner. "Why do you call her *Garden Girl*?"

"What does it matter?" I asked as I looked over at him and tried once again to figure out what was going on within his mind. He shrugged his response, not giving me a verbal answer, and I found myself getting annoyed again. I wanted him to speak. I wanted to try and see if I could detect something within his tone. I wanted to see if I could place what his feelings towards me at that moment were. Although Dashiell annoyed the shit out of me, after speaking with Felix tonight, I felt guilty about what I had said to him at breakfast. I should have handled the situation more delicately, and I was wrong for not considering him before I spoke. I was wrong for not realizing that he had a life before me, and I wanted to convey to him that he didn't have to give that up just because I was here. "She glared at me that first day. When you and I were in the garden," I explained. Dashiell squinted straight ahead as if trying to remember the encounter.

"*Garden Girl*," he mused. "It makes sense."

"So, is she busy warming your bed now?" His eyes snapped back to mine, and a look of surprise flooded his face. "Don't look so shocked. It's evident that she's your lover." I told him as I ran my fingers over the rough metal of the railing.

"She..." he began but trailed off as if he didn't know how to finish that sentence.

"It's fine," I cut in, saving him from having to continue. "I'm not bothered by it at all. You're free to fuck whoever you'd like." He flinched at my crude use of the term. I should have worded that differently. He watched me curiously as if trying to detect some trap I had laid for him. "Really, Dashiell. I give you my complete and utter blessing to pursue anyone and everyone you want."

After a moment, Dashiell withdrew his gaze from me and glared at the horizon. He gripped the railing hard, the whites of his knuckles showing as he said. "Thanks for the permission, but it isn't needed. I'm fully aware that I may fuck whoever I want, whenever I want." It was my turn to flinch now. Each word came out clipped and angrier than the last. I snorted in response which only seemed to make him angrier for some reason. "I would say the same goes for you, but I don't believe you'll find that to be the case."

I looked at him now and raised my brows in question. "Is that so?" I asked, schooling my tone to a perfect balance of boredom and annoyance.

He quickly added, "Oh. Not that you wouldn't be *allowed* to." He stretched out the word for emphasis. "But more of a case of who would even want to?"

"Excuse. *Me*." I twisted my body, so I was now fully facing him. He did the same and moved closer to me, heat radiating from his skin. His scent of sea salt and lemongrass filled the distance between us. My blood boiled with fury as he slowly dragged his eyes over the length of my body once. When his gaze reached mine again, he tilted his head and clicked his tongue.

"You spit more venom than any viper in this realm, Ainsley. You can be so entirely vicious that I don't see how anyone would ever want to go anywhere near you, let alone *touch* you." I could barely hear anything over the sound of my thundering heart as it filled my ears. I felt the familiar prick of angry tears in my eyes. No. No, no no-no-no. I couldn't let him see me cry. I couldn't let him know how deeply his words had cut me. I tried desperately to calm myself as my chest heaved rapidly while I took in small sips of air, willing my body to ease. After a few seconds, I opened my mouth and closed it again, trying to come up with some retort. Something to hurt him the way he had hurt me. But I had nothing. When did this conversation take such a nasty turn? I told Dashiell this morning that I didn't want him. That I wanted nothing to do with him. And tonight, he made it clear that *no one* would want me either.

Minutes, hours, days, or even weeks might have passed as we stared each other down. A roar of laughter and applause filled the ballroom behind us, the noise drifting out onto the balcony. Dashiell looked up toward the sudden sound, his jaw clenched tight. I took that as my opportunity to make a break for it. I quickly and clumsily gathered the skirts of my gown, walked briskly to the open door, and reentered the crowded ballroom. I said a silent prayer of thanks to the Gods for the distraction that aided in my escape. The number of attendees had significantly dwindled since I had last been here, watching Felix seduce the man he had his sights on. I could make a clean getaway to the comfort and safety of my chamber now. I hastily made my way through the crowd, occasionally bumping into innocent bystanders. I whispered quick apologies to them under my breath, but I didn't dare stop.

When I reached the exit, I looked behind me, scanning the room to ensure no one was tracking me. My gaze immediately locked onto Dashiell's. He was standing at the entrance to the balcony, hands curled into fists at his side. He must have read something on my face because he began quickly moving through the room towards me, never once tearing his eyes from mine. I turned back to the exit and hurried through the doors. There was no way I could face him again tonight. I wasn't prepared for another battle. One that I would no doubt lose again.

I ran through the palace halls as fast as I could, passing lovers scattered throughout. Their bodies intertwined as they pressed against the stone walls and shared deep and passionate kisses. I didn't stop running until I had reached my room, locking the door behind me as the tears finally escaped and rolled down my cheeks in full force. I slid to the floor, pulling my knees tight against my chest, and rested my head back against the door. I didn't have it in me to be strong, so I let the tears flow freely. I allowed myself to weep for the first time since I had arrived. I cried for the words Dashiell had spoken and the loneliness I felt. And I wept for both the life I once had and the one I was now to live. I allowed myself to crumble and break into a million little pieces. I knew I would have to rise and pull myself together eventually, but right now... Right now, I would let myself unravel completely, and I wouldn't be ashamed of it. I needed to let myself *feel*.

I sat there for hours, my gown pooled around me like my own little ocean. It wasn't until the faint grey light of dawn crept through the open windows that I finally stood up, wiping away the tears that somehow still poured from my eyes.

I stripped off my gown and left it in a heap of silk and chiffon on the ground, not caring enough to drape it over the chaise on the far side of my room. I never wanted to see it again. I didn't want a reminder of the night I had experienced. I didn't bother to change into the lace nightgown that Imogen had laid on the foot of the bed for me either as I crawled beneath the warm sheets. After a few deep breaths, I willed my eyes to close and prayed the Gods would be kind enough to grant me a dreamless slumber.

11.

All too soon, I awoke to the sound of servants bustling around my room. I opened my eyes to see Imogen riffling through the armoire, searching for a gown for me to wear today. I watched as she settled on a delicate pink dress, the color of a sunset over the ocean. She turned to face me and startled, not expecting to find me staring at her. Concern flickered in her hazel eyes as she took me in, the evidence of last night written all over my appearance. I must have looked like absolute shit. I certainly felt like it, at least.

Imogen was quiet for a moment, looking deep into my eyes as if she could see the entirety of the evening playing out within them. Finally, she said, "Come on, up you go. Bathe quickly so I can do your hair before breakfast. At this rate, you're going to be late."

"I'm not hungry," I countered. I had no desire to go downstairs and have to breathe the same air as Dashiell. Not after last night.

"Then just sit there and drink your tea," she replied sternly. When I made no move to get out of bed, she crossed her arms and glared at me, refusing to back down.

"Fine," I gritted out as I shoved the blankets off and flung myself out of bed. I made my footsteps as loud as possible as I stomped my way over to the adjoining bathing room, slamming the door shut. I could have sworn I heard Imogen's laughter from the other side.

When I emerged, I quickly made my way over to the vanity, my hair soaking wet, leaving a trail of water on the tile floor in my wake. Imogen hurried behind me as I sat down, wrapping a towel around my head to soak up the excess moisture.

"You could have at least dried off properly," she said as she glared at me through the mirror with disappointment on her face. I shrugged and drew my attention to the accessories she had laid on the vanity table. It was the usual display of fine earrings made of pearl and diamonds and dainty silver rings with a single gemstone in the center. But there was one particular piece that stood out from the others. A thin necklace of braided gold sparkled in the rays of sunlight that leaked through the windows, with a peridot gemstone dangling from its center in the shape of a teardrop. It looked so out of place amongst the other pieces that I wondered why she had bothered to pull it out.

Imogen combed through my slightly damp hair. I watched as she pinned small sections of my hair back, leaving down soft strands in the front to frame my face. She reached for a delicate and simple silver comb from within one of the vanity's open drawers, the tiny encrusted diamonds glittering as she fastened it to the back of my head.

"All finished," she informed me, and I looked at my reflection, admiring the job that she and two other servants had done.

While Imogen worked on my hair, Annette and Josephine tried their hardest to fix the disaster that was my face after my long and emotional night. The cream they applied around my eyes had significantly reduced the redness and swelling, the product of crying for hours on end, and the rouge they added to my cheeks and lips made me look more awake. Refreshed. I found myself feeling grateful for them. And incredibly thankful for Imogen, who had fixed my hair in a half-up, half-down style, the same way I wore it every day back home. The same way I had been wearing it when I arrived at the castle and met her for the first time. She seemed to remember, too. My eyes widened as realization and understanding washed through me. She smiled warmly in the mirror as if she knew I needed this small gesture. I smiled back at her and mouthed, 'thank you.' She squeezed my shoulders tightly in answer.

Imogen helped me dress into my gown, the material soft and light, perfect for staying comfortable in the summer sun. She worked on putting away the accessories she had chosen not to use but left out the delicate necklace that I had spotted earlier. She must have noticed the slight change in my mood because she commented, "You don't have to wear this if you don't want to," waving a hand toward the jewelry. It wasn't that I didn't want to. The necklace itself was beautiful, but it didn't seem like the piece made sense with how she had chosen to dress me today.

"I don't want to offend you," I answered honestly. She studied me briefly before picking up the necklace and surveying it.

"I didn't pick this out," she said, twisting the braided gold between her thin fingers. "But I was instructed to deliver it to you."

"A present?" I asked. "A present from who?"

"His Royal Highness," she said casually, avoiding my eyes.

"The king gave me a necklace?" My face twisted with utter confusion. Why would King Perceval send me jewelry? Sending me a death threat, I could understand, but a necklace?

"His Royal Highness.... Prince Dashiell," Imogen said as she threw me a sidelong glance, a single eyebrow raised.

The memories of last night flashed through my mind, and I felt my hands curl into fists, nails digging into my palms hard enough to draw blood. Why would Dashiell ever give me a present like this? Was this his way of saying 'sorry'? Did he think he could buy my forgiveness? Buy *me*?

He was utterly mistaken. Or maybe I was the one who was mistaken. Maybe this wasn't an apology at all. Perhaps it was a reminder. It couldn't have been a coincidence that the gemstone that adorned the necklace was the same color as the vipers that roamed these lands. The sight of the bright green jewel only fueled my fury.

"I'll take that," I said as I strolled over to her. Imogen opened the necklace wide as if to clasp it around my neck. "Oh no. Not to wear. To hold on to," I explained.

Imogen smirked. "As you wish, my lady," she said as she handed the necklace over. I smiled warmly at her and placed it inside one of the hidden pockets of my gown.

"Thank you." I made my way to the door, pausing on the threshold. "Just Ainsley," I called over my shoulder. A beat of silence passed.

"As you wish... Ainsley," Imogen replied, and I could hear the smile in her voice.

Both Felix and Dashiell glanced up at me as I reached the breakfast table. I was indeed late as both of their plates were already half-empty, not bothering to wait for me today. Taking a sharp breath and steeling myself, I pulled out my chair and took a seat. Felix looked like his usual bright and chipper—albeit annoying—self, but Dashiell... He looked exhausted. His eyes seemed dull, and there were purple bags beneath them as if he hadn't gotten much sleep. If I had to guess, it was because Rosella kept him up all night.

"So nice of you to finally join us, buttercup," Felix said, breaking the silence. So we were back to pet names again. Great.

"I overslept," I replied curtly, the anger in my blood almost boiling. A sly smile appeared on his face.

"Did someone have a little too much fun last night?" He threw me a wink and I could see Dashiell out of the corner of my eye stiffen at once.

"Oh yes. It was splendid," the words came out flat and hard, void of anything other than distaste. Dashiell's throat worked, but he said nothing, looking extremely uncomfortable from where he was sitting. I could feel Felix's eyes studying us both, clearly reading the tension and trying to figure out what exactly he had missed. Apparently, Dashiell hadn't informed him of our conversation last night. At least not yet.

Felix cleared his throat and straightened a bit. "Anyway, what are your plans for the day?"

Not taking my eyes off Dashiell, I responded, "I'm not sure. I thought I might just coil up in my room and read a book." Dashiell's eyes widened a fraction at my use of the word 'coil.' After all, he had compared me to a viper, so I might as well embrace it. His eyes softened, and something like pain flickered there.

"Ainsley, I—" Dashiell started but was interrupted as a servant walked over to Felix, handing him a folded piece of paper.

"Thank you, gorgeous," Felix told her, grinning as his fingers grasped the top of her wrist and slid down slowly, caressing her hand before taking the note from her. She blushed and gave him a subtle wink before disappearing inside the palace. Felix watched after her for a moment and then clicked his tongue in utter male approval. I watched as he opened the note to read its contents and thought back to last night and the person Felix had been with. Did I read the situation wrong?

"The man you were with last night... You're not—"

"Exclusive?" Felix asked, and I nodded in response. "Gods no. You can't chain me down."

"So she," I began as I pointed over my shoulder to the path the servant had hurried towards.

"Will be tonight's entertainment," Felix finished as I rolled my eyes. "You can never have too much fun, you know what I mean?" He winked.

My stomach knotted as I remembered my time with Logan. The feel of his body against mine. The way he tasted. The sex wasn't always bad. When it was good, it was really good. I felt my cheeks heat and knew that even the rouge I was wearing couldn't conceal it. Dashiell cut in, interrupting my memories.

"Let's not make Ainsley uncomfortable," he told Felix as he brought his cup to his lips. He took my blushing as a marker of innocence, not desire. *I can't see how anyone would ever want to go anywhere near you. Let alone touch you.* He was under the impression that I had never been with someone. That I had never entangled myself with a lover. That I had never been *touched*. He had no idea how wrong he was. But of course, I had no problem telling him.

"I believe I know exactly what you mean, Felix," I told him breathlessly. Dashiell choked on his tea, but Felix's eyes widened with surprise and interest. They watched me as I bit down on my lip and then slowly caressed my thumb over the hurt. Felix leaned back in his chair and crossed his arms, his grin somehow even wider. I curled my lips into a seductive smile as I stared down at my tea, stirring it slowly.

"Ooh, pray tell," Felix said enthusiastically as he bounced up and down in his seat, desperate for an ounce of sexual gossip.

I gave a noncommittal shrug as I said, "Just someone from my village." I took another sip of tea, the bold and spicy flavor soothing as it traveled down to my stomach.

"What is his name?" Dashiell demanded, sounding less than happy that he had been completely wrong about me. Good. I raised a single brow and looked into his eyes as I answered his question, daring him to push me.

"Logan." I watched him grasp the fork he had been holding with a bit more force than he should have.

"And how long were you and this 'Logan' character an item for?" Felix asked.

I cocked my head and narrowed my eyes toward the sky while I made a dramatic show of counting my fingers as if I was trying hard to remember when it had started between us. Finally, I scrunched my brows together and turned my attention back to Felix. "About four years?" I said, sounding as if I wasn't entirely sure that was the correct answer. In actuality, I knew the exact day that Logan and I had first gotten together. It was my seventeenth birthday, and I had just been informed about my betrothal to Dashiell for the first time. I was less than thrilled and stormed out of the house and straight into the village. Logan was the first age-appropriate man that I spotted when I arrived. I walked up to him, pushed him against the stone wall outside the local pub, and kissed him passionately. He was shocked at first but didn't push me away. And he certainly didn't stop me as I grabbed his hand and led him into the woods, where we had sex for the first time. "But we weren't a couple. The relationship between us was purely *physical*." Dashiell shifted uncomfortably in his seat, but Felix's face lit up with delight.

"Well, well, well. Aren't you just the little minx," Felix said. I bit my lip again and smiled coolly. "And how did that arrangement exactly come about?" he asked, seeming genuinely curious. Dashiell cleared his throat loudly, but I ignored him.

"Well, it originally started because I was trying to figure out a way to get out of this," I waved my hand toward Dashiell. "But when I announced to my Caregivers what I had done, they quickly informed me that it didn't matter. That the king did not care about the status of my *virtue*." I rolled my eyes at the memory and shrugged. Felix raised his brows, quietly begging for me to continue. I dragged my gaze to Dashiell once more as I said, "After that, I slithered into his bed a few times a week for years." Dashiell closed his eyes and shook his head. He opened his mouth as if he wanted to say something, but I turned my attention back to Felix. "It was supposed to be a one-time thing, but I just couldn't stay away because of his... Well, you know," I wiggled my brows twice at him, just like he had done to me last night.

"My Gods, don't I know it," Felix said as he winked at me, and a wide smile spread across my face.

"We're done with this conversation," Dashiell commanded, his tone final. I snapped my eyes in his direction, but he was now glaring at Felix.

"That reminds me, Dashiell," I started. After a few seconds, his eyes released Felix and were now upon me. "I think you may have misplaced this." I took the necklace out of my pocket and tossed it across the table. It landed on his now empty plate with a loud clink. Dashiell stared at the necklace for a moment, his breathing quickening. After a good minute, he snatched it from the table and shoved it into his pocket as his eyes found mine again. I slowly threw up my middle finger at him, and he gripped the arms of his chair so hard I fully expected the bones of his knuckles to break through his golden skin. I may have lost the battle between us last night, but I was determined to win the war.

I crossed my arms over my chest and leaned back against the chair to settle in. I was not running away again. Dashiell and I stared each other down for what felt like a lifetime. Neither of us so much as flinched, determined not to give the other the upper hand. I could hear Felix slurp his tea at an unnecessary decibel. He was enjoying this.

After another minute of shooting eye daggers at each other, Dashiell blew out a long, exasperated breath and rose from his seat. I didn't dare break his gaze. Not yet. His face showed some emotion I couldn't quite place, not that I cared to try to, anyway. With a deep inhale, he looked down and shook his head so slightly that I almost didn't detect the movement. When his eyes met mine again, there was nothing but anger and pain in them. He threw his napkin on the empty plate before him and stormed back into the palace without a single word.

"You're not going to make this easy on any of us, are you?" Felix said as he let out a sigh. I tore my gaze from Dashiell's empty chair and fixed it upon him instead. He was grinning at me. Felix and I had come to some unspoken truce yesterday, but my patience with him was quickly dwindling. I was in no mood for games or humor. "You know, I think I'm starting to really like you, Angsty Ainsley."

"Do *not* call me that," I demanded. Felix merely grinned even harder and gave me a wink. I rolled my eyes, but despite my anger, I could feel myself relax ever so slightly. He annoyed the shit out of me, but I couldn't deny that Felix had a calming presence about him that I desperately needed at this moment.

He nodded to himself before saying, "Get up. Let's go." He rose from his chair and started to head toward the terrace stairs that led down to the gardens.

"Go where?"

"To your death," he replied as he turned to face me, stopping halfway between our table and the stairs.

"*What*?"

"I'm kidding. Will you just come on?" He gestured for me to follow.

"Why can't you just tell me where we are goi—"

"My Gods! Can't you just extend a little trust? I get that you hate this situation that you're in. Believe me, you're not the only one doing something you'd rather not." He placed his hands on his hips, waiting for me to offer a snarky retort. When I didn't respond, he stepped toward me and cocked his head to the side. "You could use a friend right now. But friendship is nothing without a little bit of trust." The playful exterior of Felix was gone. Nothing but a reassuring tone and comforting eyes remained as he observed me, trying to decipher what was on my mind. He looked down at his hands and took a deep breath. I watched him study his palms as if he had a novel tattooed upon his skin. While he stared, I pondered his words. He was right. I could use a friend, but did it *have* to be Felix? Understanding flashed through his features, and I could feel something in my blood lighten at the sight of it. At that moment, he looked back up at me with a crooked smile and said, "So what do you say, Angsty Ainsley? Can you try for me?" I felt myself rising from my chair before I even fully knew that I wanted to go with him.

"Only if you promise never to call me that again."

"No promises," Felix said, and I felt my lips tug up in the corners. "I saw that," he whispered in my ear as I passed him.

"No, you didn't," I said. But it was no use. My smile was fully defined now.

12.

"I want to show you something," Felix explained as he led me across the way to the stables located at the far edge of the palace grounds. I waited outside while he readied our horses, grateful for the several minutes of peace and quiet I had while I processed this morning's encounter with Dashiell. Even though I was still pissed at him, I knew I was being childish and immature. I didn't know why his reaction bothered me so much; why I allowed him to get under my skin in such a way that always made my heart race and blood boil.

Felix came striding out of the stables with a beautiful mare at each side. One with a chestnut coat, and the other... She was a gorgeous creature with a coat so dark that I wasn't sure I could even call it black. It was like a void that sucked you in and refused to let you go.

"Which one do you want?" he asked and it took me a second to realize that he was speaking to me.

"I'm sorry, what?" I blinked looking confused for a moment. Felix followed my gaze to the horse now nibbling on the lush grass to his left. My eyes finally pulled away from the animal and met his. He was studying me curiously like he saw something in my expression other than amazement. Why was he looking at me like that? "What?"

"Nothing." Felix shook his head as if trying to clear some thought. "You can take Nox." He gestured behind him to the mare I had been transfixed on.

"Are you sure? If you want her, I don't mind—"

"—No," Felix cut me off. "I'll take Aura. She's my favorite, anyway." He patted her silken chestnut coat. "We go way back, her and I," he explained as I made my way to Nox, who was still fixated on a patch of grass.

"Oh yeah? How so?" I asked, not caring about the answer. I couldn't pull my focus from Nox. Her head was bowed when I finally reached her, still worried about eating before her trip.

"She's the first horse I've ever ridden," Felix said. "I took the journey from Ministro with her." I was vaguely aware of him settling into his saddle as he spoke.

"Mmmmm," was all I managed to say. I reached out and placed my hand on Nox's forehead. She instantly righted herself, and my hand slid down to her muzzle. Neither of us moved. I wasn't sure I was breathing as I stared into her deep obsidian eyes, somehow even darker than her coat. Her gaze was piercing. It was like she was trying to see into my soul, making me feel empty and whole all at once. My heart was pumping hard in my chest, and I wasn't sure why. I couldn't move, not that I wanted to. I could faintly hear Felix's voice. Was he saying my name? It sounded distant and drowned out like he was underwater. I honestly didn't care. I couldn't focus on anything but her.

Nox, at last, turned her head, and I was free. I blinked a few times to get my bearings and felt my heart return to its normal pace. I shook my head to clear it of whatever just happened and then situated myself into my saddle. I looked over my shoulder once I remembered that Felix was with me. He was ghostly pale and had a look of concern on his face. But before I could murmur a question as to if he was okay, his expression was gone, and he was back to his usual sense of arrogance.

"You ready?" he asked me.

"I guess," I replied, feigning disinterest. I couldn't let him know that I was curious as to where we were going.

"That's the spirit!"

We rode in a comfortable silence that didn't need to be filled with idle chatter. The forest was peaceful and full of life. Birds fluttered next to each other on branches of giant oaks, and flowers swayed gingerly as they danced in the light summer breeze. I stretched my arms above my head, soaking in the summer sun.

"Do you remember your mother and father at all?" Felix asked. Well, that was blunt and straight to the point. I hated when people asked about my parents. It had nothing to do with the questions themselves but more with the fact that I didn't know the answers.

"No. I was a baby when they were killed, and Mouth and Looks never met them." Felix looked confused, and I realized he had no idea who those people were. "My Caregivers," I explained. "I have never met anyone who knew them, but I hoped to meet others when I arrived at the palace. All I know is that I come from a powerful bloodline which is why I was betrothed to Dashiell before I was born." The thought of my mother and father meeting with the king to sign away my freedom before I had ever taken my first breath made my stomach roil. "I don't even know their names. Someone here has to have met them, right?" I was rambling. I never ramble like that. "Are your parents alive?" I asked him, desperately trying to take the spotlight off of myself.

"What makes you think they aren't?" he asked incredulously.

"I- I don't know. Because you asked me, I just assumed." I shrugged. It didn't seem like an odd question to ask at all.

"My mother died in childbirth, and I never knew my father."

"I'm sorry," I said under my breath.

"Nah, don't be. I don't ever think about them, to be honest." It was quiet for a beat. And not in the comfortable silence kind of way, but awkward and unpleasant.

"Have you always lived here at the palace?" I asked, hoping that changing the subject would make things feel more normal.

"Nope."

"Oh. Where did you live before—"   "We're here," he said, cutting me off.

We pushed our way through the last of a tree line, and my jaw dropped. Before me lay the most beautiful and serene place. We strode into an open meadow full of alyssum, zinnia, and red poppy flowers. The sickly sweet scent came rushing towards me as a breeze rolled in. I could melt away right here and now. I glanced at Felix to find him with his usual smirk on his lips, and I couldn't help but return one of my own. He cocked his head and gestured for me to look beyond the meadow. When I did, my heart stopped.

We galloped to the edge of the meadow and dismounted from our mares. I somehow knew Nox would enjoy the location as I watched her and Aura plop down and bathe in the sun. Before us was an endless lake of crystal blue water so clear you could see straight to the bottom in some places. It reminded me of my lake back home. Well, I guess it wasn't my *home* anymore, as Dashiell so lovingly pointed out last night. My lake was nowhere near as magnificent as this, but it felt nice to be reminded of where I was the happiest. I needed to get further. I needed to feel the cool water on my skin. I started removing my shoes when Felix asked, "What are you doing?"

"I'm going in the water?" It seemed obvious to me. Felix shrugged.

"Okay," he replied and started taking off his shoes too.

"What are you doing?"

"I thought we already covered this, Ainsley." He tossed his last shoe over his shoulder, gave me a wink, and ran. I lifted the skirts of my dress and followed after him into the shallow water. Fuck. *Fuck.*

"FUCK!" Felix yelled.

"Owwwww!" I screamed from behind him. "You didn't tell me there were a ton of rocks!"

"Yeah, well, *clearly* I forgot about them," he gritted out as if he were in pain. "I wouldn't willingly ruin my feet. Shit, this hurts."

"No shit," I responded. Felix raised an eyebrow at me and splashed me directly in the face with the crisp water.

"A lady shouldn't talk like that," he laughed. He was right. So instead, I stuck up both middle fingers, and he laughed even harder. "Much better." I couldn't help the laughter that escaped from me.

We slowly shuffled our way through the shallow water and over to a large boulder that could comfortably seat six large people. Felix climbed up first and then helped me as I struggled. We sat side by side while we watched small fish try to nibble on our dangling toes in the lake. Well, *my* dangling toes. Felix was submerged up to his calves. How have I never noticed just how tall he was? I took a deep and long breath as I surveyed the lake. I could feel Felix's smile on me, so I turned to him and raised my brows.

"Do you like it?" he asked, genuine curiosity washing over his features and gleaming within his amber eyes. I shook my head, trying to clear my thoughts. To come up with some way to express how much I liked it. I *loved* it.

"It's…. It's incredible." I couldn't stop the smile that spread across my face. "It's somehow everything I didn't know I wanted or needed. Does that make sense?" He looked away from me and out at the scene in front of us.

"Yes. It makes perfect sense." I could tell he was lost in some memory, and I wondered what he was reliving at this moment. Before I could pry into his mind, he spoke, bringing up the one topic to disrupt the sliver of peace I had found. "So, are you going to tell me what Dash did?" I groaned loudly, throwing my head back to the sky and soaking in the sun's warm rays on my skin.

"He lovingly pointed out how vicious and repulsive I am," I said without tearing my eyes from the world above. When Felix didn't respond, I threw a glance his way to find him side-eyeing me skeptically. He clearly didn't believe his precious best friend would say such a thing. "It's true." His face didn't falter, and I could tell he was waiting for me to elaborate.

For some Gods forsaken reason, I did.

"All night, Garden Girl—sorry, Rosella— was glued to his side, very obvious about her intentions with him," Felix tilted his head and nodded as if he saw it too. "Well, when he approached me on the balcony alone, I gave him my blessing to pursue and sleep with whoever he wanted to. He responded by telling me that I was also free to do the same but because I spit venom like a viper—"

"Ahh, the snake references this morning make sense now. Clever," he said, sounding like he meant it.

"Thank you," I replied, slightly thrown off by the compliment. "Anyway, he said that because I'm so vicious, he couldn't see how anyone would ever want to touch me." I looked out towards the water and gripped the boulder beneath me in an attempt to keep myself grounded. I shouldn't have let Dashiell get under my skin the way he had, and talking about it was bringing up those unwanted feelings.

"He's not wrong, you know," Felix said, and I swiveled my head toward him with anger in my eyes at yet another man telling me that I was untouchable. He threw his hands up in innocence and quickly corrected himself. "I meant about you being allowed to pursue others, not about you being undesirable. Intimacy isn't a stigma. It isn't frowned upon here, which is why your sleeping with Logan didn't get you out of your betrothal. King Perceval wouldn't have been bothered then and still wouldn't be. As long as you fulfill your duty to marry Dash, he won't care if you have other lovers."

I had no idea what to make of Felix's explanation, but it made sense. It would explain why Rosella had no shame in claiming Dashiell while I was present and why he seemed to entertain her interests. But would *I* truly have the same freedom he possesses? Would I be allowed to take a new lover as often as Felix has, or would my chosen partners be too afraid because of my relationship with the prince? I opened my mouth to ask Felix, but he answered before I could.

"Dash wouldn't stop you if you expressed the desire, nor would he prevent anyone from pursuing you if that is what you wished." I chewed on that kernel of knowledge for a moment.

But as I pondered the thought of being able to claim a sliver of my autonomy again, Dashiell's words from last night slithered into the forefront of my mind, and I started to feel self-conscious. Maybe he was right, and no one would want to touch me. It's not exactly like I've made any friends since arriving here, nor have I tried to.

"Trust me, Ainsley," Felix said, and his bright gaze burned into mine. "You are *very* desirable, and several people have expressed their interest since you came here." I swallowed, not expecting to be told I had willing options to choose from. My heart fluttered, and a warm, bright light filled me with excitement for the first time at having prospects. Felix's face shifted, and he eyed me up and down as if seeing me for the first time.

"Is that an invitation?" I asked hesitantly. Felix seemed like someone who definitely knew what he was doing between the sheets, but I felt nothing more than friendship toward him. And even those feelings were sparse. My words broke whatever daze he was in as he threw his head back with a boisterous laugh.

"Oh, buttercup, you couldn't handle me," he said with a cheeky grin, and I bit my lip to stifle a giggle. Ever the humble one. "But if you'd like, I can introduce you to those who'd be more than happy to extend one." I nodded to accept, but then Dashiell's face popped into my mind, turning my mood sour again.

"How did you find this place?" I asked, wanting to change the subject. Felix didn't comment on the sudden switch, and I said a silent prayer of gratitude.

"Dash did, actually. He took me here after...." His eyes went to mine, and I gave him a gentle gaze. A silent request for him to continue. He looked straight ahead again, not quite at the view but like he could see beyond it. Beyond this world. "I grew up in the Kingdom of Ministro. Are you familiar with it?"

I thought back to my history lessons as a child. There were five kingdoms in our realm, and each one possessed three unique powers that were said to be given by the Gods to bless those fortunate. Receiving a power was rare; if you were lucky enough to be blessed, you would possess only one of the Gifts of your kingdom. The only exception to this was the king and their kingdom's heir. Each king had all three powers, and the heir possessed two. Here, in the Kingdom of Caelum, the Gods were said to bestow the power of elemental magic. We had the Unda, those who could manipulate and create water and ice; the Ignisian, those who could manipulate and create flame and heat; and the Aerians, those who could manipulate the weather. I struggled for another minute, trying to remember what exactly the Kingdom of Ministro was known for besides the Medicus—the healers.

"Not much," I admitted, realizing I should have paid more attention to my studies. He gave me a comforting smile to show me that my lack of knowledge of his home kingdom wasn't anything to stress over.

"As I said, my mother died in childbirth, and I had no other relatives. Shortly after I came into this world, I was taken to the palace so the King and Queen of Ministro could decide whether I was worth being cared for or if I was to be... discarded." He couldn't be serious. I tried to wrap my head around the fact that in Ministro, an orphan could be killed simply because the king or queen willed it. I couldn't breathe and felt like I might vomit right here on this boulder.

"Discarded? That's... that's horrible!" I exclaimed, anger quickly replacing nausea. "You were just an innocent child. How could anyone willingly decide to do something like that? It's... it's not right."

"No, it's not," he said, shaking his head. "But Ministro is a cutthroat kingdom fueled on ambition, greed, and bloodlust." He tore his eyes from the horizon to look at me. "But for whatever reason, the king felt generous that day and spared my life." I could feel a gentle wave of relief wash through me. I didn't realize how tense I was until I uncurled the fists that I held in my lap. To decide a child's fate on a whim was cruel and disgusting. "Lucky for me, my powers showed earlier than they do for most. When I was ten years old, the king and queen gifted me to King Perceval to serve him and the Kingdom of Caelum as his own personal Empathi." Felix gave me his famous wink.

An Empathi. Well, that explains the calming presence I'd constantly felt around him, even when I didn't want to. "King Perceval figured that having someone who can feel other's emotions and, in turn, calm those emotions would be quite beneficial to keep close. Especially regarding negotiations with other kingdoms in our Realm. Most kingdoms have at least one Empathi on their king's council." I looked away from him and back at the lake as I tried to process everything.

Felix took in a deep breath before he continued. "When I first came here, I had a hard time adjusting. Don't get me wrong, I was happy to be out of that horrible place, but everything here was so different from anything I had ever known. The only person I knew was Dash, although just barely." Though I wouldn't meet his gaze, not yet, at least, I listened intently. "King Perceval would take him along whenever he'd visit Ministro. Dash was always left with my maiden, and we became fast friends. We'd spend our time play-fighting with wooden swords and sneaking out of our designated rooms after the final bed check so we could steal extra treats from the pastry cart." He laughed softly at the memory, and I found myself doing the same. There was something so sweet and innocent about picturing the two of them as young boys, so carefree and full of life.

When he was quiet for too long, I finally looked up at him. The smile on his face had faded to something that looked like sorrow, and I wanted to look away but couldn't. I held his gaze as he said, "I only saw him a few times a year, so when I came here to live...." He shook his head slightly as if trying to find the right words. "I grew up in one place, and suddenly I was plucked from all I had ever known and placed somewhere completely new. I felt scared and alone." I thought back to our conversation on my second day here. He was empathizing with me, and I lashed out at him. Shame and fury ruptured through me. I was such an ass to him. I felt some small part of me melt, some cold part of me that never wanted to let go of the anger or loneliness because if I did... If I did, that meant I was giving up some of my control when so much of it had already been ripped away from me.

"Anyway, a few weeks after I arrived, Dash found me alone, probably sulking. I did that often. Kind of like someone else I know." He nudged me with his elbow, and I suppressed a smile. "He told me to get up and to come with him. When I didn't move, he looked me in the eyes and told me I needed a friend and to trust him." That sounded familiar. He continued, "So I got up and followed him. He brought me here, and we sat in that meadow behind us for hours. Just staring at the water."

"You didn't go in?" I asked.

"Shit, no! It was winter and cold as balls," he snorted. I stifled a laugh and thought of a much younger Felix and Dashiell sitting in the meadow amongst the hellebore and winter jasmine that would no doubt bloom here. "For the first time in weeks, I felt at peace. Calm. And for the first time in my existence, I didn't feel alone." He smiled at the thought and without realizing it right away, so did I. I felt a trickle of water rush down my cheek and quickly wiped it with the back of my hand before he could see. My heart swelled with the feeling of being understood. We were both orphaned and thrown into a life we never asked for. We had both felt the loneliness and fear, but he had managed to get through the darkness. He had found a friend who had helped him. Could it be the same for me?

"What happened next?" I found myself asking, not wanting the story to end just yet.

"After a while, Dash finally spoke up. He told me how he found this place and what it meant to him." He swallowed deeply as if he was forcing the words back down as they tried to find their way out. Why didn't he want to continue? I knew I shouldn't have pushed him, but I had to know the rest.

"How did he find it?" I stared at him until he looked back at me. Silver was lining his eyes, but I didn't understand why. Felix turned his head from me and closed them. It looked like he was battling with himself on whether he should continue.

We sat in silence for so long that I didn't think he would speak again until he loosed a breath and looked straight at the horizon again. "When Dash was eight years old, his mother died." Immediately I felt terrible. Not just because he lost his mother but because I'd been too busy hating him to ever ask about it. I studied Felix's face, and it was filled with such sadness. It was as if he could feel Dashiell's pain from years ago in this very moment—and maybe he could, as an Empathi. Did the memory of talking in this meadow as children bring up the pain he could feel radiating from Dashiell at that time? I felt my heart break a little bit more. "He and his mother were very close. The way a parent should be with their child. She was his entire world... And then she got sick."

He turned to face me again, and I could feel the tears threatening to escape my eyes. But I didn't look away as I waited patiently for him to continue. "The first time I met Dash, he and King Perceval came to Ministro in search of a Medicus, someone to reverse her ailment."

"But why didn't King Perceval already have a Medicus on his council?" I asked. It seemed like a healer would benefit him more than an Empathi would, no offense to Felix.

"Ah. Well, he did. He had four of them, to be exact. But they all informed him that there was no cure for her." He sucked in a breath. "So he had them all killed. For 'incompetency' as he called it."

"My Gods." My head was suddenly dizzy. He had them murdered because he didn't like their diagnosis.

"Yeah, I know. When they arrived in my old kingdom, the King of Ministro decided to allow King Perceval to take his personal Medicus back home to see what could be done for the queen."

"What happened?" I asked, but something in my bones told me I already knew the answer.

"She died shortly before they made it back to Caelum." My heart sank deep into my chest, and I felt the tears I had been trying hard to keep at bay roll down my cheeks. I no longer cared if he saw me cry. "Dash had to be ripped from her so they could take away her body. It took two maidens and a guard to finally peel him off her. His strength was the first clue of his powers coming through early." A broken sound involuntarily escaped me as I pictured an eight-year-old Dashiell clinging tightly to his mother's corpse. "After that, he ran from the palace straight for the woods. He had no idea where he was going, but he knew he couldn't go back there. At least not for a while. So he just kept running, and running, and running. For hours." He shifted on the boulder and shook his head, the look of disgust creeping onto his face. "His father never noticed that his son was missing. But that's not surprising since his father never paid much attention to him, to begin with. It was his two maidens that finally realized he was gone when they were doing their nightly bed checks. They didn't find him until a day later." I shook my head in disbelief at Felix's words.

"But his father seems to notice him now."

Felix snorted, "King Perceval didn't pay him any mind until his powers started manifesting. It was as if Dash meant nothing to him until that time." With the tone Felix was using, I didn't dare comment on the subject again.

"And he just happened to stumble upon this?" I waved my hand to gesture to our serene location.

Felix looked around. "Well... no, actually." I looked up at him and scrunched my brows together, clearly confused. He met my gaze and said, "He says he *felt* it. That it called to him. I guess another early indicator of his powers." It occurred to me that I didn't know what Dashiell could do. I thought about the Kingdom of Caelum. About the powers that the Unda, Ignisian, and Aerians possessed and wondered which of them also belonged to Dashiell. It occurred to me that I didn't even know if Dashiell possessed two of the Gifts and was truly the Heir of Caelum. I had only read one occurrence in my studies where an heir wasn't an offspring of the king. Instead, it had said that the Gods had chosen someone from a different bloodline altogether. Felix nudged me again. "You know you could just ask him."

I rolled my eyes. "We don't exactly speak. And when we do, it doesn't end well."

"Listen, I know Dash can be a dick. Gods, do I know he can be a dick. But I also know that deep down, he is a good and decent person." I bit my lip as I considered his words. "He's been through some serious shit, and he'll never outright admit it, but you scare the piss out of him. And he's struggling with what to do here," he said, waving a hand to gesture to me.

"What do you mean?"

"Other than you showing him your sunny disposition and shining personality every time you see him?"

"Point taken," I said as I scowled at Felix for a heartbeat and then turned back to the view.

"He doesn't know how to talk to you and—"

"—You can tell him that insulting me isn't the way," I cut in.

Felix just shook his head. "I hate to break it to you, Ainsley, but you *both* are playing that game. And playing it to win, from what I can tell." He wasn't wrong. I hated that he wasn't wrong. I was being an ass just as much as Dashiell was, if not more, at this point.

After a few minutes of us gazing into the distance in silence, he jumped down and stepped in front of me to meet my eyes. His stare was piercing, and it glued me to the spot. "You're here now. This is your life now. You can either sulk about it for the rest of your existence, or you can pull yourself out of the hole you're in. Regardless of your decision, I'll be there with my hand extended to you. When you're ready."

Once again, he was right, and I wanted to hate him for it, but I couldn't. Not on this. I knew with all my being that I couldn't stay this way forever. He was right—this was my life now. I didn't have to like it, but it wouldn't change anytime soon, and it was better to get through this with at least one friend by my side. Oh Gods, was Felix my *friend* now? Without looking, I could feel him smile and knew he could sense the moment I had made my decision.

"Nice pep talk, by the way," I said as I nudged his elbow. He leaned closer to whisper in my ear.

"Thanks. It's the same one Dash gave me."

For a reason I didn't quite understand, my heart fluttered at that.

13.

By the time we reached the palace, the sun was already setting, leaving the sky a mix of apricot and coral pink; the shade matching my dress perfectly. Together, Felix and I strolled through the lawn and up to the table on the terrace. Though dinner wasn't to be served yet, Dashiell was already there waiting. Before we left the sanctuary of the lake, I promised Felix that I would try—honestly try—to get along with Dashiell. Whether I wanted to admit it or not, something cracked within my heart at their story. The least I could do was attempt to be pleasant for the sake of peace between the three of us. However, I did warn him that if Dashiell was being an ass, then I couldn't be held accountable for what I may say or do to him. Felix responded by laughing and declaring he would put his money on me in that fight.

"Did you two have a nice time today?" Dashiell asked by way of greeting.

Felix glanced down at me as he said, "It was a little *rocky* at first, but we managed alright." He nudged me with his elbow, and I let out a laugh. A real, genuine laugh. As unlikely as it was, Felix and I had sparked a friendship. One that contained our very own inside joke. All I wanted was a friend right now, someone to help me navigate this strange new world of mine. He threw his head back, unable to contain his laughter, and Dashiell's deep-sea eyes danced with wonder and amusement as he tried to assess what had transpired to bring out such a change in me.

"Well, that's... good?" He was clearly confused and hoping one of us would clue him in on what exactly he was missing. Felix and I locked eyes and threw ourselves into another fit of hysterics. I hadn't genuinely laughed in so long that

I didn't even recognize the sounds that escaped me. The way it flooded in my ears was foreign but pleasant, and I prayed that it would never leave me again.

Eventually, the laughter eased, but I couldn't erase the wide, toothy smile plastered on my face. "I should go wash up before we eat," I said as I started to make my way into the palace. Before I reached the entrance, I turned around to find their eyes locked on each other. Dashiell's features were curious and urgent, like he was silently begging Felix to divulge the events of this afternoon.

"Thank you for today, Felix," I announced, causing both of their attention to shoot to me. Somehow this person, this *friend* of mine, had gotten through to me when I had been so set in my ways of anger and resentment. I wondered if he would ever know just how much that meant and what exactly he had done for me. "I'll see you at dinner," I said, and Felix nodded in response, his liquid honey eyes soft and warm.

I turned my attention to Dashiell, curiosity covering his face, no doubt waiting for me to leave so he could bombard Felix with questions about our adventure. Maybe it was because of everything Felix had shared with me about him today, but I felt like I was seeing Dashiell for the very first time. He was beautiful, and not just an obvious beauty either, but a mysterious one. Like all those secret stories and experiences, had made him that much more remarkable. Despite myself, I wanted to know more about him. I wanted to learn what made him who he was. I wanted to unravel the truths that he held hidden within.

"Dash," I said, dipping my chin just barely and backing away before turning around and disappearing inside. I didn't miss his eyes widening and amazement flashing over his features. I also didn't miss Felix's slow clapping after me. It was the first time I had ever called him by his nickname. It was a small gesture, but one I had hoped would be enough for now. Baby steps.

I washed my arms and face quickly, eager to return downstairs and stuff my face with delicious food. I decided not to change out of my dress and into the one Imogen had set out for me. The scent of wildflowers and lake breeze still clung tightly to the fabric. I inhaled deeply, not quite ready to let go of the joy I had discovered today.

When I returned to the terrace, Dash was still there, but Felix was nowhere to be found. He stared over the grounds looking a bit uncomfortable and nervous. My heart fluttered at the realization that this was the first time we'd been alone since our argument on the balcony last night. Though I promised to try and make an effort to keep the peace, I wasn't sure exactly where we stood now. If breakfast this morning was any indication, it wasn't on good terms. He heard my approaching steps and snapped his gaze to me, watching as I reached my seat. I pulled out the heavy chair but stopped short of sitting down once I noticed my place setting. A single white rose was draped across my plate. I looked over the table and did a quick inventory of the other two settings, both empty. Scrunching my brows together tightly, I turned my attention back to Dash to find him watching me tentatively.

"For last night," he said softly as if he were worried that the sheer volume in his voice would send me fleeing the terrace. I picked up the long-stemmed rose and studied it, its petals feeling like silk in my hand. Was this another trick of his? Another message like the necklace had been? If so, what could a flower possibly mean? Maybe he thought that I was just as delicate. Soft. Weak. That I would wither and crumble under the smallest amount of pressure. Bracing myself, I looked back at him with wary eyes.

Eyes that widened in pure shock as he said, "I'm sorry, Ainsley. I truly am." Out of all the possible things Dash could have said, an apology was not one I considered. I tried desperately to find the lie, but his face had fallen with shame, and I could see in his mesmerizing eyes that he meant every word. I felt the tension that hung between us begin to dull, and the air somehow became easier to breathe.

"Thank you," was all I could manage to say as I looked back at the rose between my fingers, the flower's flesh so bright and stark in the night that it rivaled the moon.

"I figured it was the safer option seeing your distaste for jewelry," he said shyly, gesturing for me to take my seat, and I obliged.

"I didn't *hate* the necklace, I hated the message behind it." Dash looked at me, puzzled, cocking his head to the side.

"I'm not sure I'm following your meaning," he replied. I felt my palms dampen at the possibility that I had concocted this vendetta of his within my mind. *Oh shit*. I felt a lump forming in my throat, and my cheeks heated with embarrassment as I began slowly realizing my mistake. Dash was trying to apologize with that gift. A gift that I had literally thrown back at him. My Gods, I am such an ass. I looked down at my hands which were now starting to tremble, too mortified to meet his eyes as I decided to share my thoughts.

"The gemstone you selected was a bright green. The same shade of green that adorns the vipers you compared me to last night." The words sprang from my mouth, rushed and all at once, eager to make him understand the reasoning behind my actions. "I thought you were sending me a reminder. I'm so sorry." I bit my lip and looked up at him through my lashes, hoping he could see just how badly I felt about my assumption. How ashamed I was of myself.

After a heartbeat, Dash exploded with laughter, the sound rich and hearty. I couldn't help but laugh with him at my stubborn foolishness. I thought he wasn't capable of compassion and created this whole elaborate story in my head. Which ended up causing me even more pain and anger this morning, and now... Well, now it had caused me complete humiliation.

"Oh, Ainsley, you give me way too much credit," he said between his gasping breaths. He was laughing so hard that I was sure his stomach had to be cramping in pain.

"I'm starting to realize that," I told him as I buried my face in my hands. I was never going to live this down, and I wasn't quite sure that I deserved to, either. It would be far too kind to pretend that this never happened.

"I wouldn't have put it past you to do something like that," I continued, dragging my hands down the sides of my face and interlocking my fingers, my chin resting on the knuckles as I stared at him apologetically.

"I'm honored you think me that clever, and if I'm being completely frank with you, I'm a little disappointed that I didn't think of it myself." I threw the linen napkin that was neatly folded into a swan next to my silverware at him. His booming laugh roared once again, and I found myself lost in the sound of it. In the way, it melodically ebbed and flowed. That is until Felix finally entered the terrace and announced himself.

"I'm here, I'm here! So sorry to keep you both waiting, but I had some business to attend to." Surprise sparkled in his amber eyes as he took in the sight of Dash and me before him. "But it seems that I wasn't entirely missed."

"Are you ever?" I quipped, smiling wickedly. Felix slammed his hand to his chest and dropped his mouth in mock offense, to which I rolled my eyes.

"I'm simply dying to know what brought this about." He waved his hand between Dash and me and sat at the table.

"Ainsley was just enlightening me on what a cunning mastermind she believes me to be," Dash told his friend.

"Okay, the word *mastermind* never escaped from my lips, so that's going a bit too far."

"Fair enough," he said, grinning wildly at me. He then dove straight into the tale of the necklace and my assessment of it to Felix, who snickered loudly as he listened.

"I love how your mind works, buttercup," Felix told me once Dash had finished. "Though I now fear that any gift you bestow upon me may have some evil hidden meaning behind it."

"Perhaps." I shrugged, allowing a little bit of mystery to wash over my features.

Dinner passed in much of the same fashion; easy conversation with bits of amusement sprinkled in. Felix mostly just bragged about himself in every possible sense of the word. From being an expert with a dagger to having multiple suitors beg for his presence in bed. With how Dash threw his head back and rolled his eyes, I was pretty positive that not even half of what Felix was saying could be taken as truth.

"As much as I'm enjoying learning about your harrowing exploits and even more so about your generosity as a lover, it's getting late, so I should probably head to bed," I announced as I rose from my seat. The servants had retired hours prior, and the candles scattered across the table burned low. The only light now was the floating lanterns that lit up the grounds each night with their ever-burning magic.

It had to be well after midnight. Had we gotten lost in conversation for that long? Dash and Felix were far more interesting than I had previously thought, and I had to admit I was having a nice time. I found myself fighting the urge to take back my declaration for fear that if I slept, I would wake tomorrow morning to find this had all been a dream. That this peace and friendship we had all established was nothing more than a fictional occurrence that my mind had created to cure the sting of loneliness.

Before I could announce my change of heart, Dash rose from his chair. "I'll escort you back to your room," he said, causing Felix to through his arms high into the air in protest. "You can't leave too! I haven't even gotten to the good part yet!"

"I'm sure you can hold out for a few minutes," Dash responded flatly, like this was something he dealt with regularly with his friend.

"You are a thief of joy." Felix scoffed, crossing his arms over his chest and staring off into the distance, a slight pout on his beautiful face.

"And you are as needy and temperamental as a child," Dash replied and ushered me back inside the palace. I threw Felix a small wave of goodnight over my shoulder.

I picked at my nails as we walked the halls in silence, feeling uncomfortable. Actually, no, not uncomfortable, but *nervous*. Dash's presence had never made me feel uncomfortable. If anything, being around him tended to leave me curious and intrigued—when I wasn't annoyed. Even when I was busy hating him, I realized I had always found him captivating.

Looking up at his face, it was as though I could physically see the gears in his mind working and twisting around like cogs in a machine. He always seemed to be so deep in his thoughts and observant of everyone and everything around him. The longer the silence between us dragged on, the more intense his features became as he focused intently on some invisible spot straight ahead on our path.

"You don't have to escort me, especially if you want to get back to Felix," I said, making sure my tone was thoughtful and kind. It was considerate of him to offer to walk me back to my room, and the last thing I wanted to do was give him the impression I didn't want him here. Dash blinked a few times as if the sound of my voice released him from whatever trance he was under, and his eyes turned to me.

"Are you kidding me?" he asked. "You're currently saving me from him." I smiled at the thought.

"He's not that bad." It wasn't a lie by any means. I had come to enjoy his company.

"No, he's not. His stories, on the other hand..." he replied, letting out a low laugh. "I've known Felix long enough to know that he likes to take creative liberties with his retellings."

"Nooo. That doesn't sound *anything* like Felix," I drawled sarcastically, giving a sly smile that Dash eagerly returned. "I don't mean to pry, and if this comes off as rude, please know that is completely not my intention at all, and I give you permission to tell me to shut up and mind my own business—"

"Ainsley, just ask your question." Dash cut me off, his tone soft and reassuring.

"I'm sorry, I ramble when I'm nervous."

"I'm starting to realize that," he teased, using my words from earlier this evening against me. I narrowed my eyes at him in mock irritation but continued.

"How are you both such good friends?" Dash looked at me curiously, not quite understanding where I was going with this. "What I mean is, you two are so different, opposites even. Felix is so boisterous, personable, and light-hearted, and well, you're...."

"Not," Dash finished for me, nodding his head in understanding and agreement. He didn't seem offended by my line of questioning but rather as if he often wondered the same himself. He was silent for a few minutes, thoughtful, his blue eyes constantly darting around the space between us as he rolled his neck before finally answering.

"When you're in my position—the heir to a king—who you surround yourself with, but more importantly who you trust, is crucial. It can quite literally mean the difference between life and death." His face became serious once again, eyes as hard as steel. His words were simple but held a dark and horrible undertone, some traumatic experience he had no desire to dredge up. He or someone he was close with had put their trust in the wrong person, and it had cost them.

Dash drew his attention back to the path in front of us, and I noticed our pace had slowed to barely more than a slight shuffle of our feet. Like neither of us was in any hurry to reach our destination.

"Felix told you how we met as children, correct?" I nodded enthusiastically, eager for him to continue. "As I'm sure he mentioned, the first time I ever traveled to Ministro, we were searching for a healer for my mother. She was getting sicker and sicker every day, and I knew in my bones that she didn't have much time left. I wanted nothing more than to stay with my mother at that point. I didn't want her to be alone when she left this world." Dash flexed his fingers at his sides. I could tell he didn't like to talk about this if he could help it.

"I was pissed at my father for taking me away from her, for making me go with him when there was nothing I, at the mere age of eight, could contribute to his mission. I gave him the silent treatment the entire journey to Ministro, not that he even bothered to notice. He barely paid me any attention at that time in my life." His voice was far away and distant. "As soon as we arrived at the palace, I was handed off to a maiden who led me to my room and told me to wash up for dinner. I ignored her. Instead, I crawled into my bed and went to sleep. I was so angry at my father for bringing me there. Angry at the Gods for what was happening to my mother. Angry at myself for not being able to stop any of it."

My heart ached for him. Though I lost both of my parents, it was different for me. I never knew them. I never got to love them. I couldn't pretend to understand the pain that Dash had gone through.

"The maidens didn't bother to wake me that night nor the next morning. When I finally woke, all of the beds in the room were already empty and neatly made. The sun coming through the windows told me that it was already late afternoon which meant I had slept for almost an entire day. My stomach was growling then, but I didn't feel like leaving my room, so instead, I sat on my bed and stared out the window. Children came in and out of the room throughout the day, but I didn't bother to pay them any attention, and they didn't bother to pay any to me. That is, until Felix."

A crooked smile started to take form on his lips.

"I was watching these two red birds fluttering outside the window when suddenly, I was hit in the back of the head with something hard. I remember turning around to see a wooden sword lying behind me on my bed. I looked around to see this scrawny little kid standing in the doorway, holding a matching wooden sword. All he said was, '*There is a Wyvern loose in the palace. Let's go. We need to hunt it down.*' I stared at him for what felt like a good three minutes before turning back to the window and saying nothing. Hoping that he got the hint that I wanted to be left alone."

"Did he go away?" I asked, feeling like I already knew the answer to this one, thanks to my own experiences with Felix. Dash laughed as he shook his head.

"Absolutely not. He responded by throwing a pillow at the back of my head next and told me, '*You don't look like a great fighter, so you'll need this shield too.*' I picked up the pillow, and before I could even yell at this annoying kid, an apple hit me square in the chest. '*It'll be a long journey, and you'll need your strength, so eat that. I've got bread in my pack for us later,*' was his response. I don't know if I was more pissed off that he threw something at me three times or that he insulted me by calling me weak and a shitty fighter, but for whatever reason, I found myself grabbing the items he gave me and following him out of the room.

"At first, I told myself it was just because I wanted the chance to smack him with my sword, but before long, I had forgotten all about what Felix had done to get me out of that room. We spent the rest of the day running and rolling through the halls, dodging imaginary enemies and fighting stone statues. When we were both completely winded, we sat under this big oak tree on the grounds, sharing the cheese and bread Felix had snuck in his pack, and that's when he finally introduced himself. We sat there for hours, talking about our favorite games, what treats we hoped were at dinner, and what creatures we thought we were strong enough to defeat if they presented themselves. For just a little while, Felix allowed me to forget about the pain I was in. He gave me the break I didn't know I needed at the time."

I thought back to my time with Felix over this past week. He never stopped trying to get through to me, no matter what I threw at him. Never stopped caring. I had been so in my head, so angry, that it took me until now to realize it.

"Felix is quite persistent," I told him. "I'm not sure that he understands the word *no.*" Dash shook his head slightly in agreement but offered nothing else. I wasn't ready for this to be over yet. "It must have been welcoming to have such a caring and loyal person in your life when you needed it most."

Dash seemed to ponder that as we rounded the corner to the hallway that led to my room. There was still so much I wanted to know before we ended this night.

"There was this one time in Ministro when Felix and I were punished for Gods knew what— we were always getting ourselves into trouble— but that night, we were sent to our chamber early and without dinner. We were so mad that we came up with this brilliant idea to get back at our maiden," he explained, cocking an eyebrow at me. "So, we snuck out of our room, and Felix led us through the palace. Since he grew up there, he knew all of its secret passages and how to get in and out undetected."

We finally reached my bed chamber, but instead of going inside, I leaned my back against the smooth wood of the door, facing Dash. "What happened next?" I asked, letting him know that I wanted him to finish his story before I was willing to retire for the night. The slight smile he was working hard to hide let me know he was happy about my choice.

"We made our way to this small pond that sat within the grounds and went to work catching as many toads that could fit inside of our pockets and hands."

I gasped and threw my hands over my mouth to stifle the sound that came out, my eyes widening as I shook my head slowly back and forth. "You boys didn't!" Dash nodded slowly as a devious smile stretched ear to ear.

"Oh, we most certainly did! We crept back into the palace, careful to avoid detection, and filled her room with about twenty fat, pustulant toads."

I burst into laughter, barely able to catch my breath. "You two were terrible!" I said, smacking Dash's arm just below his rolled sleeve. His skin was soft, warmer than I imagined, and I could feel the hard muscles beneath it. Dash shrugged as if he was not only already aware of just how awful he was but also as if it was his most proud accomplishment, pure joy beaming on his beautiful face. "Did she know it was you two?"

"Of course!" Dash scoffed. "It didn't help that she found Felix and I in our room still completely dressed and covered head to toe in muck and mud."

"One would think not," I told him mockingly. "How did she punish you this time? Take away breakfast?" I raised my brow at him teasingly, but his face fell, and his features became sullen and serious once more as he focused his gaze off into the distance. I didn't like this sudden change in him. Somehow the air felt cooler around us, and goosebumps quickly covered my arms.

"When the maiden entered our room, I could see the rage on her face, and I knew we had taken our exploits way too far this time. She announced that we were to receive lashings for our misdeeds. Before I could even open my mouth, Felix stepped forward and took full responsibility for the whole ordeal, saying I had no involvement."

"She couldn't have possibly believed that to be true, especially after she caught you *both* covered in filth."

"She never believed it for a second. But as I stepped forward to confess, to not let my best friend take the blame, Felix turned around to face me. He put his hand on my chest to stop me from taking another step and shook his head, silently pleading for me to bite my tongue. So I did. And a maiden wouldn't dare accuse the king's son of something wicked if there was even the faintest possibility she was wrong." Dash shoved his hands in his pockets as he brought his attention back to me. His eyes locked onto mine, and I could see all of the hurt, the regret, the *shame* within them. I felt my heart soften a little at the sight of him and the pain he hadn't been able to let go of.

"Why would he do that?" my voice barely louder than a whisper. Dash cleared his throat loudly, trying to choke down the emotion threatening to escape.

"Felix knew how much was at stake for me. As the king's son, I directly represented him and our kingdom while we were guests in another. The wrath I would endure from my father would far exceed anything the lashings could have hoped to accomplish. If I had embarrassed my father based on a childish prank, death would have been a far kinder punishment compared to what he would have done." Dash rubbed his forehead as if trying to scrub the possibility of what could have happened from his mind. I was too afraid to ask. "From that moment on, I knew with my entire being that Felix would always have my back, no matter what."

"He sounds like a truly valuable friend to have," I told him.

"It's more than that. Felix is the best person I've ever known. In a world with such greed and manipulation... such evil, he is inherently *good*, always doing the right thing."

I nodded my head because I honestly believed that too. I hadn't known Felix for long, but nothing Dash spoke made me doubt his words.

"Back in Ministro, whenever someone was bullied by an older, bigger child, Felix always stepped in to defend them. Most of the time, that resulted in bloody noses and black eyes for him, but he never stopped. Felix didn't care how much older or bigger they were; he'd face them over and over again. He's always been adamant about defending those who can not defend themselves."

"He didn't tell me any of that."

"Of course not," Dash said, shaking his head, "Felix is the first to humblebrag about his good looks and bedroom conquests, but you'll never hear him speak of the things he's done that truly matter."

"But why not?" I asked. Why wouldn't Felix want the world to know the good he's accomplished? Why keep that a secret?

"He says he doesn't need praise for simply doing the right thing. Even more, than I trust Felix—and I trust him with my life—I admire him."

"I can see why." I smiled to myself.

Silence fell between us once more, and the only sound was the flickering candles in the hall as we stared at each other. I watched as his eyes searched mine, trying desperately to read them as if the key to my thoughts lay within. His throat began to work as if he wanted to say more and not let this conversation between us end so soon. If I was completely honest with myself, I didn't want it to end, either. The more I learned about Dash and Felix, the more connected I felt to them. For the first time in my life, thanks to this unlikely duo, I didn't feel so alone. Dash opened and closed his mouth, still struggling to find his words, when I decided to put him out of his misery.

"I should probably head inside," I told him, pointing my thumb over my shoulder at the door.

"Oh, erm, yeah. And I should probably get back to Felix. Gods know what he's gotten into during my absence." I laughed softly at the truth of his words.

"Well, goodnight," I told him, twisting the knob and turning away. Before I made it over the threshold, Dash called out.

"Ainsley?" he asked, sounding almost nervous. I whipped back around and caught him wringing his fingers in front of him. He *was* nervous, but why? My stomach tightened at the thought of what he could say to me. He stared down at his fingers, not making eye contact.

"Can I give you a tour of the palace tomorrow? Unless you've already—"

"I haven't." I interrupted quickly. The eagerness of my tone made his eyes shift to mine. They were soft yet held a slight edge of surprise behind them. "And I'd like that," I told him, giving a small smile.

"Are you sure?" he said playfully. "I thought you would have already seen most of it by now, with often you get lost."

"Prick," I joked as I reached forward, shoving him lightly. "I'm sure."

"Okay, great. Then, I'll see you at breakfast."

"Hey, Dash?"

"Yeah?" he replied, stopping so abruptly that his boots scuffing on the marble floor echoed through the hallway. I suppressed the giggle bubbling within me.

"Try not to be so nervous. I don't bite," I told him, shutting my door before he could respond. That night I dreamt of two small beautiful boys catching toads in the moonlight.

14.

I bathed and dressed before dawn, the excitement of the pending day bubbling over and causing sleep to evade me for most of the night. It was an effort to stay put, but I forced myself to remain in my room until Imogen entered. The presence of her and my servants would indicate that the palace had awoken for the day, and I would be free to move about without causing questions. The second she appeared, I jumped up from the comfort of the velvet armchair I had been lounging in, the book I was too distracted to read falling from my hands and landing on the side table with a soft thud.

"Where are you going in such a hurry?" Imogen questioned as I raced past her, too excited to offer a pleasantry.

"Down to breakfast," I explained, skidding to a halt before I reached the door. She raised a brow in question at my sudden enthusiasm. I had never been eager to leave my room, let alone be in the presence of Dash and Felix, but our newfound friendship had me looking forward to seeing them for a change.

"Mhm," she mused matter-of-factly. I rolled my eyes at her.

"I'm hungry," I said by way of explanation as I waved a hand over my shoulder and quickly exited the room before she had a chance to offer a retort. Her quiet laughter reached me as I briskly walked through the halls. Imogen had taken me to and from the terrace so often that I could finally make the journey on my own without fear of getting lost. I quickened my pace, practically running through the corridors, and my heart began to beat faster with each step. Not from exhaustion but from the anticipation of what the day was to hold. Dash had offered to take me on a tour of the palace, and though I wasn't sure what that would entail, I couldn't deny that I was looking forward to it. During the time we spent together last night, as he walked me to my room, my feelings toward him had started to shift. To change from hatred and resentment to something more like understanding and interest. We weren't exactly friends, not yet at least—but we seemed to be working in that direction.

I was the first to arrive at our table; not even the servants had been down to set it yet. I leaned over the back of the chair, working to catch my breath, when the sound of rushed footsteps caught my attention. I whirled to find Dash as he abruptly halted at the entrance to the terrace. A look of surprise caught in his eyes, and his chest heaved almost as quickly as mine. It was as if he, too, had made haste through the palace.

"Hi," I told him breathlessly.

"Hi," he said back, just as winded as I was. "I passed Imogen in the halls on my way down." He jerked a thumb over his shoulder as he gestured behind from which he came. "She said that you had already left to come here."

"I did," I said, nodding as if that fact weren't already obvious. Dash looked around the space but made no move to come closer like the terrace had been riddled with traps, and he wasn't sure how he could safely maneuver his way through. I didn't blame him for his hesitation.

"Your hair... it's..." he noticed, and there was a twinkle in his eye. After I bathed this morning, I quickly brushed through my wet hair and had the full intention of pulling it back once it dried, styling it like Imogen usually had. However, my thoughts of the pending day consumed me, and I forgot all about my plan. Once Imogen had appeared in my room, the only thing on my mind was getting down to the terrace as quickly as possible.

"Oh. Yeah." I self-consciously pulled on the long locks, bringing them into view. The bright morning sun pulled forth the copper within.

"I like it," Dash said as I dropped the soft strands between my fingers and diverted my full attention back to him. "A lot," he added, smiling, and my heart stuttered. When I didn't respond, he changed the subject. "Why are you down here so early?" He took a small, tentative step, testing the environment.

"I was hungry," I claimed, feeding him the same lie I had Imogen. I wasn't hungry; I just wanted to see him. To see Felix.

"Oh." Was that disappointment coating his words? He began to retreat again. "I'll go fetch you something."

"No!" I interjected, entirely too loud, too forceful, as I threw a hand up in the air. Dash stumbled, his eyes wide with curiosity. "What I meant to say," I said calmly, quickly trying to recover from my outburst, "is that I don't mind waiting for breakfast to be served."

"It's not a problem." He made another move to head back into the palace.

"I'm truly fine to wait."

"I insist." One more step and he'd be entirely inside.

"Dash, will you just shut up and sit down!" I snapped, and he halted immediately. I quietly cleared my throat. "Again, what I meant to say is," the corner of Dash's mouth lifted as I spoke, "Won't you please join me?" I gracefully gestured to the seat at my left.

"Of course." He strolled over to his chair, biting his bottom lip to keep from fully smiling. Once seated, we both gave each other tight smiles before looking away. The silence was deafening, and I needed to fill it. But how? I wracked my brain around the countless questions I had for him, trying to decide which to ask.

"Where are—"

"So how—"

We stepped onto each other's words, and both laughed under our breath. Dash smiled warmly as he extended his palm toward me in a gesture for me to continue first.

"Where are you taking me on our tour? I mean, I know it's of the palace, but what exactly does that entail? What do I get to see?" I asked. Dash smiled widely at my question, like he was happy that I not only remembered but seemed excited about it.

"I'll take you to see anything that you want. The kitchens, the ballrooms, the grounds, the Medicus facility, the—"

"Library?" I interrupted. I had been thinking about the library since Felix had mentioned it days ago and wishing I knew where it was so I could visit.

"You like to read?" Dash asked curiously. Apparently, Felix hadn't told him about our book exchange. Or maybe he had, and Dash was being polite in not betraying what his friend had relayed to him.

"I love to read," I said simply, and Dash nodded.

"The library it is," he replied, just as two servants appeared with platters of eggs, meats, fruits, and pastries in their hands. I watched silently as a third servant entered and placed empty plates in front of Dash and me. She then promptly began to pour a cup of tea from a kettle that seemed to appear out of thin air. Once the spread had been set and the drinks served, the three women disappeared back into the palace after Dash and I offered our gratitude.

"Felix won't be joining us for breakfast?" I asked as I noticed a place for him had not been set.

"No, he had some work to attend to for my father this morning, but he's planning on finding us while we're on the tour," Dash explained as he stabbed his fork into a steaming piece of meat. My heart fell slightly. It wasn't that I didn't want to spend time with Dash, but rather that I had lived a life of solitude for so long that I was eager to get to know both of them.

The entirety of breakfast was spent exchanging small but meaningful conversations, sharing bits about ourselves and what we enjoyed.

"What is your favorite color?" Dash asked, sipping from his cup.

"Blue. Yours?"

"Red," he answered immediately. "But not a bright and cheerful red. More of a dark and bold shade."

"Interesting," I mused. Was I supposed to be as specific as him? "Favorite hobby?"

"Swimming, or just being in the water in general. You?"

"Reading."

"Favorite flower?" he asked. I looked past him at the lush gardens to his back, trying to decide which plant I liked best.

"I'm not sure I have one," I said truthfully. "What about you?"

"White roses," he answered automatically. That made sense, seeing as he left one for me last night at dinner.

"Why?" I asked, but Dash just shook his head, not wanting to answer. It was like there was some hidden reason why he loved them but didn't want to share. I rolled my eyes but didn't push the subject. "Fine. Favorite memory?" Dash shook his head again. "Oh, come on!" Dash smiled at my objection as he rose from his chair and extended his hand to me.

"Ready?" he asked. I sighed loudly in defeat, knowing he wouldn't divulge any more information.

"Fine," I told him as I placed my hand in his and stood. His skin was soft and hot, and mine instantly tingled as lightning shot through my veins. Once on my feet, I withdrew my hand quickly from his touch and brought it down to my side, flexing my fingers at the strangeness I had felt. Dash's brow was furrowed like he had also experienced the odd sensation and couldn't place it. He shook his head as if trying to clear the thoughts from his mind and slid his hands into his pockets for safekeeping.

"Where to?" I asked, wanting to bring our attention back to the subject of the tour.

"Let's begin with the kitchens," he said absentmindedly, his focus still not wholly present.

"Great, I love food." I looped my arm through his, hoping it would be enough to shake him free of his stupor. It seemed to have the desired effect because Dash instinctually glanced down at my barely touched breakfast plate. Throughout our meal, I had only taken a few bites of fruit here and there as we spoke, completely forgetting that I had claimed the only reason I was early was because of hunger. I bit my lip, hoping that Dash wasn't putting together the lie, but the way his lips twisted in a crooked grin as he looked at my dish told me that he had unearthed the truth. I waited for him to call me out on the falsity, but he brought his eyes to mine and tilted his head to the side.

"Well, the kitchens seem to be the perfect place to start, then."

15.

The tour of the palace filled most of the morning. Dash had shown me the kitchens, the stables, three different ballrooms, and the Medicus Facility — though we didn't enter for fear of disturbing recovering patients. He then guided me up a long spiral staircase, and through a part of the palace I had never been to. The structure and decor fit perfectly with the rest of the estate, but something about this space felt different and grander.

"Where are we?" I asked curiously as I eyed a vibrant emerald green and gold tapestry strewn across the stone wall, my fingers grazing over the soft fabric. The scene depicted a man upon a rearing horse, the creature's coat as white as snow in the stark moonlight. He was dressed eloquently, wearing a jacket of glittering gold with silver embroidery. His hand was outstretched toward the heavens with a violent flame twisting around his fingers. The sky around him was a dark storm of spiraling clouds and strikes of lightning. I stepped back from the cloth, and only then did I notice the rest of the scene. A sea of people of all ages were bent over themselves, bowing before the person on the horse, worshiping him. I couldn't place the feeling, but something deep within told me they weren't worshiping out of love but fear. I felt Dash's presence before I heard it and looked up to see him standing next to me, studying the tapestry.

"It's a depiction of Malium, the first King of Caelum, during the First Great War," he explained as he brought his eyes to me. "You don't like it," he said, and it wasn't a question. I chewed on the inside of my cheek as I considered my response. I didn't want to offend him if he appreciated this piece of art, but I also didn't want to be dishonest.

"I don't like the way it makes me feel." I wasn't sure exactly what those feelings were, but I knew enough to recognize that they weren't joyous. Dash smirked as he dipped his head closer to me.

"Neither do I." Surprise flashed across my features, and he smiled as he pulled me along. "Come on." He didn't like the tapestry, and something about that was comforting. Like he could see past the deception of it all. We continued down the hall for a few minutes before he spoke again. "To answer your earlier question, we are in the Royal Wing of the palace. This is where Felix and I reside, as well as the rest of the Royal Advisors."

"Not the king?"

"No, my father's rooms are down the Royal Corridor. That's where he and the rest of the Royal Family stay, where *you* will one day stay. It's also where the royal families of the other kingdoms stay during their visits." I didn't like the idea of moving to this part of the palace. I enjoyed my room on the other side of the estate. It was peaceful and lovely.

"So why don't you reside there? You *are* the only other person who is part of the Royal Family at the moment."

"Because I don't want to." He said it casually as if that were enough of an answer. It wasn't.

"But why not?" Dash's face was blank as he stared straight ahead, and he was quiet for so long that I was sure he wasn't planning on answering.

"I don't want to be in the same hall where my mother died," he said softly. I closed my eyes as I swallowed hard and cursed my foolishness. Our chambers were supposed to be a place of respite and relaxation. Of course, he wouldn't want to be reminded of his deceased mother every time he journeyed to his room. I tugged on his arm, causing his hand to slip from his pocket. I reached down, interlacing our fingers and squeezing tightly as I looked into his eyes. The odd sensation was back, but I didn't pull away. Instead, I welcomed it, letting it wash over me. Eventually, it dulled until nothing was left but hot skin touching hot skin.

"I'm so sorry, Dash. I shouldn't have asked such a mindless question. I didn't mean to resurface old wounds." His eyes were bold and piercing as he stared at me, and I prayed that he could see the sincerity in my face and hear it in my words. He squeezed my hand back as he offered a reassuring smile.

"It wasn't. You didn't. And you have nothing to be sorry for." Though his words were a comfort, I couldn't deny the fact that I still felt shame at my recklessness. At my inability to think before I spoke. Dash seemed to pick up on my discomfort because he stepped in front of me and bent down, so his eyes were level with mine. He brought around his free hand to cover the back of mine. "Ainsley, it's okay, truly. You were rightfully curious and asked a question; there is nothing wrong with that. If I didn't want to answer it, I wouldn't have." I stared at our hands for another moment before mustering enough bravado to look at him again. "Okay?" he asked quietly, his eyes full of concern. I nodded because what else could I do? "Good."

He released his hold on me completely and took several steps backward toward a large mahogany door. "I wouldn't want you to be too distracted to enjoy this." he declared as he turned and threw open the doors to the majestic library that awaited.

"Holy *shit*!" I yelled the second I entered the room. I clasped my hands tightly over my mouth as several people browsing the stacks of books threw angry glances in my direction. A peal of soft laughter came from behind me, and Dash leaned down close to my ear.

"Maybe keep the yelling and profanity down while we're here," he whispered, and the way his warm breath caressed my skin sent a shiver down my spine.

"It wasn't intentional," I aggressively whispered back as I swiveled my head to look up at him. He scrunched his features and nodded his head as if to say, 'sure it wasn't,' a look that had me rolling my eyes. Dash stepped around me and held his arms wide as if he could somehow hold the entire space within them.

"So, what do you think?"

It was truly something to behold. Upon entering, to my left and right were rows and rows of bookcases, all filled. The entrance itself was dimly lit with flickering lanterns upon the walls, the flames reflecting brightly in the white marble tiles of the floor. It made it look like we were walking on fire as we made our way further into the room. Once we passed the initial sets of bookcases, the library opened into a large, cavernous room. The domed ceiling was painted with a beautiful mural of the seven Gods blessing the Kingdom of Caelum, and bright sunlight poured in through the expansive windows that filled the space. Six massive white marble pillars circled the room, each adorned with an ornate chapiter that looked to be made of solid gold.

In the center of the rotunda was a tall stone statue of King Perceval. I walked closer to get a better look. Though the sculptor had seemed to get every detail of the king perfect, his eyes were all wrong. Here in this carving, they were warm and inviting. After my experience with him in the Throne Room, I knew they were truly anything but.

"Dash, this place is incredible," I finally said as I stepped away from the statue, determined to wipe it from my memory. My eyes drifted above to the second-floor balcony. The walls were lined entirely from floor to ceiling with literature, not an inch uncovered. How was it possible that there were this many books in existence? Dash's fingers intertwined with mine once more, the touch pulling me from my bewildered thoughts.

"This way," he said, tilting his head toward a long hallway and tugging me closely behind as he walked. He weaved us through a maze of aisles with eager on-lookers watching curiously, their hushed whispers reaching my ears as we passed. *So uncivilized. Potential to offer so much. King Perceval chose wisely. Beautiful. Curious. Bitch.* That last one gave me pause, the word coming out louder than the rest. I swiveled my head to find none other than Rosella leaning against one of the stacks, arms crossed firmly over her chest and a look that promised my demise. "In here," Dash said, and I turned back towards him as he stopped us in front of a set of dark mahogany double doors.

"What lies beyond the doors?" I asked skeptically.

"Sanctuary." He twisted the golden knob to let us inside.

'Paradise' seemed like more of an appropriate term for the room. The space was large and open, with dark wooden bookcases lining most of the walls. The center of the room held two matching oversized couches in a beautiful shade of emerald green, so wide and deep that they could be mistaken for beds. They faced each other, and between them sat a long rectangular table with books scattered across.

I walked toward the couches and ran my hand over the fabric as I surveyed the rest of the room, the velvet soft and luxurious beneath my fingers. An enormous white marble fireplace was already roaring to life along the back wall. It was so large that I wasn't sure my head would reach the golden mantle if I approached. Natural light poured into the room from three windows along a single wall. Each windowsill had been made into a bench and stuffed with cushions, pillows, and blankets for comfortable reading. The room felt loved and cozy. It felt warm and safe—a Sanctuary indeed.

Why was no one in here?

"How is no one occupying this room? It's quiet and peaceful. It's the perfect place to read," I pointed out, spinning around to face Dash. He was leaning against the door frame in a casual pose, his arms crossed over his chest, his legs crossed at the ankles. His eyes sparkled with wonder as he examined my reaction to this place.

"So you like it?" he asked hopefully. I didn't understand why he cared about my opinion of this room.

"Of course I do. It's amazing!" I made my way over to a large pile of books neatly stacked on one of the benches. I selected the top novel, bringing it to my nose and inhaling deeply, drinking in its musky and sweet scent. "Which is why I don't understand why no one is using this room," I told him, putting the book back down.

"No one is allowed in here," he explained, causing me to raise a brow in skepticism.

"*We're* in here."

"*We* are allowed to be."

"So it's some royal family or future royal family thing, then? Only we're allowed in?" I asked. The room seemed different than what the Royal Wing was like. Everything there was so grand and formal. So extravagant. This space, though elegant and beautiful in its own right, felt like something entirely at odds with everything considered 'royal.' This space felt like *home*.

"Well, no, not exactly." I stared at him then, my brow raised higher as if to say *explain*. "Felix and I claimed this room for ourselves and...." he trailed off, looking toward the fireplace, not meeting my gaze.

"And...?" I pressed.

"And I may have used my title as prince to threaten death upon anyone that entered."

"You did *what*?" Dash pushed off the wall and strolled towards me, his hands raised high in defense.

"First of all, I was ten years old and obviously didn't mean it. I just wanted everyone to leave us alone. Secondly, I didn't bother to take it back because clearly, it worked." He gestured around the empty room.

"Clearly," I scolded as if he were a child caught stealing sweets in the middle of the night. Dash let out a long sigh as he slid his hands into his pocket and bent at the knees as he surveyed the room.

"If you desire it to be so, I will go out there right now and announce that anyone is free to use this room." I narrowed my eyes at his offer. He was serious. He didn't want to do it, but he absolutely would. Dash would give up the room he kept private for thirteen years if I only said the words. I held his gaze for another moment before walking over to the coffee table, plucking a book off its surface, and leaping back onto the plush couch.

"And give up all of this privacy? I think not." Dash smiled widely as he walked over to sit next to me. "Your secret is safe with me, prince," I told him as I flipped open the cover of my book and began to read.

I wasn't sure how much time had passed when the entrance to the room opened, and Felix appeared. His eyes narrowed as he took in the sight of Dash and me, and he slammed the doors shut loudly behind him. He placed his hands firmly on his hips and tapped his boot against the tile floor in a gentle cadence. I caught Dash in my peripheral vision throwing his head back toward the ceiling.

"Here we go," he muttered aloud.

"Wha—" Was all I could manage when Felix cut in.

"You brought her to our special spot without me?! You couldn't leave me ONE place to show her?!" Felix demanded.

"You took her to my lake yesterday," Dash drawled at the ceiling, not bothering to give his friend his full attention.

"Yeah, well…" Felix started as his eyes darted around the room. He was struggling to come up with a defense after that. "You don't even like to read!" he accused.

"What?" I exclaimed in shock. "You don't like to read? How is that even possible?"

"He prefers to *live* life rather than read about it," Felix mocked, and Dash groaned loudly as he brought his focus back to us.

"But your favorite spot in this palace is inside the library. There are literally books lining the walls in this very room. A novel can instantly transport you to a different time and place filled with adventure, mystery, intrigue, and romance!" I said excitedly, addressing Dash.

"I love this room because it's peaceful and private. And if I crave adventure or romance, I'd rather experience them firsthand than read about an encounter that wasn't my own." I found that reasoning to be acceptable. I loved reading because I never had a chance for adventure or even romance. The stories I immersed myself in had provided just that for me. But I guess when you're a prince, the world is open for the taking.

Felix snorted loudly at his response. "You still should have let me be the one to take her here. Sunshine and I share a love of great literature," Felix said. Apparently, I was 'Sunshine' today.

"*You* should have let *me* show her MY lake," Dash retorted. Felix's foot finally stopped tapping on the ground, and his hands dropped to his sides. He knew that there was no way he could win this. He looked at me, and there was mischief in his amber eyes as his lips tugged up in a half-smirk.

"Sunshine here loves to read dirty books," he announced to the room proudly, and my mouth dropped open at the words. That fucker. He was trying to divert the attention off of himself by placing it on me. I would kill him for this. Dash turned his entire body to face me as his eyes lit up, and a giant, open-mouth smile spread across his face.

"Care to explain?" Dash probed. "How does a fine lady like yourself get ahold of such provocative and inappropriate types of literature?" I glowered at him and his smug face.

"Dash was going to open your super special spot for anyone to use," I announced, not breaking Dash's stare. His eyes went wide, and screamed of betrayal.

"You were going to do *what*?!" Felix demanded loudly. It was over then; my composure was completely lost as I burst into a fit of laughter, Dash immediately following suit. "This is a serious matter!" Felix yelled, and Dash and I laughed even harder as we doubled over ourselves. My focus gravitated to the sound of joy that sprung from his lips. The melodic way it filled the room reminded me so much of the music that had swept me off my feet that night at the Welcome Feast. A moment later, when the laughter subsided, Felix squeezed between us on the couch. "I can't stay mad at you two," he said as he reached forward and grabbed a book from the table for himself. I kissed his cheek and gave Dash a wink before I nestled into the soft cushions to read.

We spent the remainder of the day in that room, enthralled in conversation and utterly oblivious to time and the world around us. A gentle rapping at the door caught our attention, and Dash got up to answer. He opened it and nodded once before turning to address us.

"It's time for dinner," he declared, and my eyes slipped to the windows. Sure enough, the soft colors of dusk filled the sky. Felix threw his arm over my shoulder, and Dash came to my other side, offering me a warm smile. As we made our way through the palace, my heart swelled as I thought about the joy and laughter, and genuine friendship I had felt today. For the first time, I could picture spending my life here. And for the first time, I looked forward to it.

16.

The three of us had fallen into our own little routine over the past two weeks or so. Every morning, we'd have breakfast together on the terrace, followed immediately by Dash meeting with his father for his princely duties. When I asked what that entailed, his response was, *'boring shit that I give zero fucks about.'* That would leave Felix and me to ourselves to wander the halls gossiping, or spend time in the library gossiping, or lie around in the gardens... gossiping. We talked about anything and everything. From drama between residents of the palace to our past sexual exploits — which, unsurprisingly enough, happened to be Felix's favorite topic of discussion. Despite my initial opposition, Felix had become my best friend. The one person that I knew I could trust above all others.

By the time lunch rolled around, Dash was free for the rest of the day and would come to join us. Most afternoons, we occupied our room in the library. Despite Dash's lack of love for novels, he always tagged along without opposition. I had even caught him reading a few times, to which I gave a loud 'mmhmm' as if the sound proved the point I had tried to drill into him weeks ago. This, of course, always prompted him to slam the book shut and roll his eyes before walking away—only for me to catch him ten minutes later with the very same story in his hands. We usually stayed there until one of the servants came to retrieve us for dinner.

Our meals were always served outside, and dinner tended to last through the late hours of the night. Imogen had removed my wine ban once I had proven that I wouldn't drink myself silly, though she had no idea Dash and Felix had been sneaking me alcohol ever since the Welcome Feast. Our nights were spent drinking and laughing and sharing stories of our lives. Mostly those stories just consisted of Felix's wild fabrications.

Every evening, when I announced I was ready to call it a night, Dash would excuse himself and walk me to my room. It was the only time of the day when it was just the two of us. After the first few evening strolls, the nerves had subsided enough that the conversation flowed easily. Organically. I found myself looking forward to our exchanges, glad to have this time with just him. He would eventually be my husband whether I wanted him to or not, and our walks together allowed me to get to know him. It gave me the precious time that I needed to try and picture what our life would be like together. We were becoming friends, and that was the most important thing to me.

One morning, as we were finishing breakfast, a servant made her way over to inform us that King Perceval requested that both Dash and Felix be with him today. This meant that I would be by myself until at least lunch. It was odd to journey to the library on my own and to sit in solitude in our special room. Dash and Felix had become a permanent fixture in my life, and their absence left me feeling cold. Like their very presence warmed me and kept me safe and comfortable. I nestled into the pillows of a bench under one of the windows. I told myself that since it was such a beautiful day out, reading under natural light was necessary. It was certainly not because I wanted to constantly check the sun's position in the sky as I waited for lunchtime to roll around. I couldn't focus on the written words I held between my hands as I glanced out the window every ten minutes. I finally decided that I would be better off waiting on the terrace for my friends to arrive, regardless of how long it would take. I dropped the book onto the bench and strode for the door just as it opened. I stumbled backward as I realized who now stood before me. It wasn't Dash or Felix. It was King Perceval.

"Your Majesty," I said as I bowed, quickly recovering from my disconcertment. What was he doing in here? Where were Dash and Felix? Weren't they supposed to be with him this morning?

"Rise, my dear." I straightened nervously. "Have a seat," he said, gesturing to the couch behind me. There was something different about his voice. It didn't hold its usual commanding tone, but for some reason, that made me feel even more uneasy. I followed his instruction and sat quickly upon the cushions, clasping my hands together tightly as I waited for him to speak again. He sat next to me rather than on the couch opposite mine, and I felt the hair on the back of my neck stand up at his proximity. His body was so close that I could feel its warmth and smell his scent of ash and pine. There was nothing pleasant about it and my nose burned as I inhaled.

"Did I do something to displease you, your Majesty?" I asked weakly. Surely that had to be why he found me here, cornering me when he knew I would be alone. Was he here to make good on his promise, his threat?

"No, my dear. I'm afraid that it is *I* who has displeased you."

What?

"No, your Majesty, I—" I began, but King Perceval held up a hand to stop me.

"I fear you and I may have gotten off on the wrong foot. I recognize that I may have come off as harsh and cruel during our first encounter when you arrived at the palace." I shivered as I thought back to that moment, to his serpentine smile and his cold eyes. "You remind me of my late wife. You have a wild and fierce spirit as she did. A fire inside you that burns brightly." He reached forward and twirled a lock of my hair between his fingers, the gesture intimate and wrong. I swallowed my repulsion and held my breath. My heart hammered as he dropped the strand and looked deep into my eyes.

"I often forget how young some of the residents here are. How young *you* are. I forget that young people are so passionate about their thoughts and ideas. I'm so used to instilling such order within the palace and the kingdom that I reacted poorly to your outburst. You were angry, and rightfully so. You were essentially sold to me by your father without a say. I can understand how that would be upsetting to you." His words were meant to be reassuring, but they felt anything but. "I apologize for how I handled that situation on your first day. I should have been more mindful of your feelings and predicament." He brought his hand to his chest, placing it over his heart. "I promise to try and be more considerate should something like that occur again. As long as you promise to try and be more discreet in your displeasure." He smiled then, but it didn't reach his eyes.

"I will, your Majesty," I told him, wanting nothing more than for this conversation to be over. But the king didn't move to leave. He simply sat there, staring at me silently for far too long.

"You are so much like your father," he said finally, and I perked up at the mention of him. I had never spoken to anyone that knew him or my mother. The possibility of having some of my questions finally answered outweighed my current discomfort.

"You knew him personally?" I asked at once. King Perceval laughed under his breath as he nodded his head.

"I did. Your father and I spent a lot of time together and were great friends growing up."

"And my mother?"

"I never had the pleasure of meeting her, but I'm sure that if your father made her his wife, she was extraordinarily gifted." The words brought no pleasure to my ears. I didn't like the idea that my father had chosen my mother based solely on her Gift. I had hoped that they had come together out of love for one another.

"What was my father like?"

"He was strong and powerful," he said without missing a beat. My face fell slightly, and he continued. "He was also humorous and stubborn and kind to a fault. He always tried to see the best in people, which I very much admired about him."

"What was his name?" Emotion flashed across the king's face so quickly that I didn't have time to register what it was.

"Unfortunately, my dear, I cannot tell you that."

"Why not?" I pressed, instantly recognizing the emotion that resided in his eyes this time. Agitation and anger. King Perceval flicked his wrist, and suddenly, we were surrounded by a near-invisible dome. The only indication that something was there was the slight iridescent gleam that shone in the rays of sunlight that leaked through the windows. I straightened as I looked around, my eyes full of panic. I felt trapped. Caged in this magic prison. The king grabbed my wrist, causing me to focus my attention back on him. "What is this?" I demanded.

"Relax, my dear; it's okay. It's just a shield so we may speak freely," he said as he released my wrist. His hold had been firm, and my skin burned from his phantom touch. I wanted to scrub it clean until the skin was red and raw. "There are always ears listening in this palace. No place is safe, even for a king. You'd be wise to remember that." I couldn't tell if his words were a threat or a warning. Perhaps it was both. "Speaking your parents' names aloud is a risk, even with a shield. It could put you in grave danger."

"I don't understand," I admitted.

He studied me for a moment before continuing. Like he was selecting his words with fastidious care. "I'm curious. What do you know of your parents and the night of their death?"

I wasn't expecting that question, nor did I know how to answer it. I wracked my mind around everything I had been told, though it wasn't much. "My mother and father were both gifted with magic, though I'm not sure which powers of Caelum they were granted. They were killed, but I don't know why or what someone could have gained from their deaths."

"And you just somehow happened to survive the attack?" he asked skeptically.

"My Caregivers told me I was hidden," I explained. "When my mother and father's bodies were found, I was heard crying and was discovered under a trap door in our living room. My parents must have known something was about to happen and stashed me away to keep me safe." King Perceval nodded his head as if he were processing the story I had told him. Like he was trying to fit all of the pieces from the puzzle of my life into place.

"That's an interesting tale," he finally said. "And mostly false." I felt the color drain from my face as a sickening feeling sank deep into the pit of my stomach. I felt dizzy, and my head spun with the thought that everything I had ever been told about my mother and father had been a lie. And for what reason? I reached for my glass of water on the table and drank deeply, willing it to calm my senses. It didn't work. I set the cup back down and faced the king again, my eyes begging him to elaborate. He tilted his head to the side as he examined me, probably trying to decide if I were capable enough to hear the truth.

"Parts of your story were correct. Your mother and father were both gifted with magic and incredibly powerful. They were also both killed because of it. Because of *you*." I stopped breathing altogether. "Peace within the five kingdoms had been threatened years ago, just before you were born. The Kingdom of Tenebrae had attacked at our borders, massacring our strongest fighters with their dark magic. So many of our people were slaughtered because of the strength of the Gifts they possessed. Eventually, I was able to work a spy into their ranks and learned of another planned attack. I had ordered everyone who carried magic in their veins to remain inside the palace as I worked out a plan to catch Tenebrae by surprise. I knew they wanted to kill the strongest of my people, but as long as I kept them close, I could spare that tragedy. At that moment, I thought of your father." He looked at me, his emerald eyes slightly glassed over. I wasn't sure what to make of it.

"It occurred to me that he wasn't here in the palace. He and your mother requested to live a quiet and peaceful life in the countryside. Because your father and I were such good friends, I granted him that freedom willingly. At once, I dispatched a group of my strongest people, not caring that I was risking their lives if it meant saving my dearest friend. I kissed my wife and son goodbye and rode off with them to find your parents and bring them to safety. But I was too late." He hung his head as if ashamed of himself. I inhaled and counted to five before exhaling again, preparing myself for the devastation I was about to be told.

"When we found your parents, their blood was still warm. We had only just missed those responsible by mere minutes. It is a sadness I have carried with me for almost twenty-one years and will continue to carry until I leave this world." He took a deep breath before meeting my eyes as he continued. "I noticed that your mother was no longer with child, and there was no sign of you in the house. I knew you had to be close, so I ordered my people to ride into the woods to find and bring you back. Though the assailants had a head start, we knew our lands better. We tracked down three soldiers of Tenebrae and found one of them with you in his arms. You were screaming and looked newly born, not more than a few hours old. I took you from him, holding you close as I interrogated those responsible for my friend's death and your attempted kidnapping. They had told me of their orders to steal you. To bring you to Tenebrae to be enslaved and bred because of your lineage. They planned to mix your power with theirs."

Nausea over his words roiled up within me at the implications. They wanted to kidnap me for breeding as if I were a mere animal to be used for their gain. By doing so, they'd be breaking the most fundamental rule within our lands: no two kingdoms can intermix their magic without penalty. Above all laws in the continent of Disparya, it was the most sacred and most feared. The act of Conjoining was not only illegal—it was an automatic death sentence for everyone involved, including the children resulting from the act. It was no secret to anyone living in these lands that though the Five kingdoms were at peace, there was a distinct divide in which no kingdom fully trusted the others.

Over the past several millennia, two Great Wars had occurred due to power-hungry kings wanting to rule over the others. Wanting absolute power. During the wars, it was said that women who held magic were captured and taken over enemy lines. They were tortured and raped, and impregnated in hopes of creating offspring that possessed Gifts from both the mother and father. The magic wielders known as Magusiers would visit the captives, inspecting their swollen bellies. They had the power to see bonds and what Gifts were coursing through one's veins, even before they were born. If the child possessed only one Gift from only one kingdom, the mothers were murdered immediately, taking their unborn child's life with them. If the child possessed two Gifts, one from each kingdom, they were granted the courtesy of seeing life, though it didn't last for long. When the war ended, every mother that had been captured and child born was slaughtered like animals. Magusiers were executed as punishment for their involvement, and to this day, very few alive have the Gift, making them rare and sought after. The five kingdoms signed a peace treaty that outlawed the act of Conjoining, hoping that it would keep one kingdom from becoming all-powerful. I willed my mind to focus back on King Perceval and not on the implications his confession held for me, if true.

"They admitted to everything just because you asked?" It didn't surprise me that this evil kingdom would try to recreate a heinous practice of the past. But I was surprised that they willingly admitted to it and shared the plans of their king.

"My dear, even the strongest people crack when they are slowly being burned alive from the inside out," he replied. The casualty in which he spoke about such torture sent a wave of revulsion through me. "Once they told me what I wanted to know, I executed them. I knew more soldiers would come looking for you, so I had to devise a plan to keep you safe. We dragged the bodies of the men into the house and made it seem as though they had perished during the fight against your mother and father. A tragic battle that claimed all lives involved."

"But I wasn't in that house. They would surely know that I had somehow survived." I interjected.

"We discovered that a child in the nearby town hadn't survived birth and used her body in place of yours. The mother was more than willing to help if it meant sparing another child's life, and I paid her handsomely for her contribution to the kingdom. Once the scene was set, I smuggled you to a distant village far enough away that it would keep you safe, yet close enough that I would be able to get to you quickly should word of any danger arise."

"Why didn't you just bring me here to the palace? I was always meant to come here to begin with, so why leave me with my Caregivers? Why wait until just before I turned twenty-one?"

"Have you not heeded my warning? I told you, there are always ears in the palace listening. I couldn't very well bring a newborn girl here on the same night I went out to find and rescue your parents. Claiming you had died and then showing up immediately with a baby would have drawn such suspicion. I couldn't risk it, not until enough time had passed that the event was all but forgotten. I stayed with you for the first week of your life, caring for you as if you were my own. Eventually, I had to leave and return to the palace, leaving you with your Caregivers. They only knew what I told them about your existence. The story they had fed you was one of my creations, designed to keep you safe and alive. I shared the same tale with my court, claiming that I had been searching for you and your parents the entire week, only to discover the three of you the day prior. I kept the details of the night the same, only swapping the timeline by a week for your safety. The only people that knew the truth were the handful of soldiers that had accompanied me that night. I'm ashamed to admit it, but I had them all killed shortly after. I couldn't take any chances with your life, my dear." I swallowed back bile. I felt as though I was suffocating and needed to escape this room.

"Thank you for telling me the truth, your Majesty," I told him softly, unsure what else to say.

"What I just shared with you can never leave this room. You can never tell anyone. Not Felix, and especially not Dashiell."

"Why not? They would never tell a soul the truth." I didn't like the idea of keeping secrets from them. King Perceval gave a thin tight smile; his patience was dissipating at having his order questioned.

"I am aware they wouldn't, but their knowing the truth also puts their lives in danger. I don't think you realize just how powerful your mother and father were, my dear. If our enemies find out that you are alive, that your parent's magic still flows through your veins, they will stop at nothing to get to you. That includes hurting the people surrounding you if it would give them a direct path to capturing you. If anyone found out that Dashiell knew who you truly were, he would be tortured and killed for the knowledge he possessed. I know you two haven't gotten along, but I don't think you would wish his death." I wouldn't. The thought of harm coming to Felix or Dash because I shared this information with them made me sick to my stomach. It was enough for me to swear to the king that I would never utter a word of it to either of them.

He nodded his head in acknowledgment, and the shield around us evaporated. I felt like I could finally breathe easier. He rose from his seat next to me, and I thanked the Gods that this conversation was about to end. He made his way over to the entrance and stopped before walking through it.

"I'm looking forward to getting to know you better, my dear. I'm so glad we could have this talk." I nodded, unsure of how to respond. "Don't forget what I warned you about," he said as he pointed to his ears and then to the walls around us.

"Of course not, Your Majesty." I didn't finish getting the last word out before he disappeared back inside the library.

Once I reached my chair at the table, I looked around, unsure how I had gotten to the terrace. I remembered closing our Sanctuary's doors, but not much of anything after that. Muffled voices and blurred silhouettes surfaced at the front of my mind as I tried to piece together my journey down here. My thoughts had been completely consumed by what King Perceval had told me. Everything from the night of my mother and father's death to nowhere being safe enough to speak freely in the palace. And having to keep what I had learned from Dash and Felix, the two people that had come to mean so much to me throughout my time here. I would keep my promise of not divulging what I had been told, but I knew them enough to know they would see the distress on my face no matter how hard I tried to hide it.

"Did you miss us, my little cream puff?" I whirled around at the sound of Felix's voice to see him and Dash making their way toward me.

"I certainly did," I replied cheerfully as I quickly rearranged my features, smiling brightly at them. They slowed their pace and glanced at each other before bringing their eyes back to me.

"What happened?" Dash said discerningly as he and Felix rushed to me.

Well, that didn't take long.

"Nothing, I'm fine," I said as Felix wrapped his arms around me, pinning me against his chest. I inhaled his soothing scent of leather and spice as he held me close, and a wave of comfort rushed through me. I couldn't be sure if it were his magic or the peace and security I always felt in their presence.

"No, you're not," Felix said as he kissed the top of my head. "Tell us what happened."

"I can't," I said as a sob broke through my throat. Dash's hands were on my back then, rubbing in soothing circles as I cried into Felix's shirt, unable to pull myself away from the safety of his embrace.

"Yes, you can, Ainsley," Dash coaxed, and I twisted to look at him. He hooked a loose strand of hair behind my ear before brushing his knuckles over my cheek, catching the tears that had fallen. I shook my head. His face was full of concern and worry, but it was his eyes that broke my heart. He was hurting that I was so upset, but also because I wouldn't share with him the reason as to why. He thought I didn't trust him. That I didn't feel close or safe enough to share what caused my torment.

"It's not that I don't trust you or don't want to share everything with you both," I explained as I pulled away from Felix to look back and forth between them. "I promise, I want to tell you two more than anything, but I can't. Please, just... trust me." They looked at each other for a heartbeat before Dash spoke again.

"Okay, Ainsley, but we're here to listen if you ever change your mind." I offered a small smile, the best I could manage, as I nodded.

"And right now, we're here to comfort you," Felix said, pulling me back into his arms. Dash came around my back and wrapped his arms around Felix, sandwiching me between them.

"Can we get drunk?" I croaked, my voice still thick with emotion.

"Fuck yes," both Dash and Felix said in unison, and I couldn't help the giggle that sprang free through the tears.

17.

The rest of the day was spent incessantly drinking on the terrace. Felix and Dash did their best to take my mind off the misery that plagued me by telling embarrassing stories, trying desperately to humiliate one another. In the end, it was Dash that came out victorious. Not because Felix's recollections of him weren't mortifying, but only because Dash had more examples to give. Their distraction worked for a time, but as night fell, the events of today came back to haunt me.

"I think I'm going to head to bed," I said, standing from my seat at the table. Though we were well into the evening, it was considered early by our usual standards. Servants still mulled about through the palace, and peopled strolled through the gardens, enjoying a moonlit walk. Dash moved to rise, no doubt planning on walking me to my room, as it was our usual routine. "No," I told him, holding out a hand. "Stay here with Felix. Enjoy your conversation." Dash eyed me suspiciously, his hands still clutching the arms of his chair as if he was debating whether to rise or sit. I walked around the back of Felix's seat and threw my arms around his neck, placing my lips on his cheek to kiss him goodnight.

"Sleep tight, cream puff," Felix said as he rubbed the arms that held him. I withdrew and backed away from the table.

"Goodnight," I said to them both and turned to depart. I wanted so much to have Dash walk me to my room, but with the thoughts of King Perceval and our conversation creeping into my mind once more, I wasn't sure I would be strong enough to hold it together in his presence. I wanted to sleep. I *needed* to sleep. I needed to wash my mind clean of this day. I wanted to go back to when I thought my parents were murdered, and I was only spared because I was hidden. I didn't want to live in a world where they were slaughtered because of *me*. In a world where I lived in danger of being enslaved and bred for magic that I wasn't even sure I would one day possess.

Once I made it to the safety of my room, I stripped out of my dress and into the floor-length silk nightgown that Imogen had left out. The navy blue fabric felt luxurious against my skin and the lace detail sewn throughout was exquisite. I climbed beneath the covers and squeezed my eyes shut tight. I tried to recount the stories Dash and Felix had shared, willing my mind to a happy and safe place as I drifted to sleep. But all I saw were cold emerald eyes.

Sunlight poured in from the canopy above, and I wrapped myself in the comforting warmth of it. Songbirds chirped in harmony as they soared through the sky, their beautiful compositions weaving through the trees to meet my ears. Lush bright green blades of grass undulated in a light breeze, carrying the aroma of freesia and.... Snow? What an odd scent when it was so clearly the summer months.

"Are you coming, Ainsley?" I looked up to find Dash and Felix at the edge of a winding path. They wore matching loose gray tunics rolled up to their elbows to expose their forearms and simple black pants. Their feet were bare and filthy from the dirt of the woods. I looked down at my own attire to see that I was still wearing the blue nightgown I had changed into when I returned to my room. The fabric clung to my body, showing every curve of my hips, my breasts. I crossed my arms over my chest feeling raw and exposed. Dash and Felix turned then and continued on their walk.

"Where are you going?" I called out, but they didn't stop. "Hey, answer me!"

"Come find out." I wasn't sure which one of them said it. The voice sounded familiar but foreign at the same time. Dash and Felix disappeared around a bend, and I moved my feet to quickly follow, not wanting to be left here alone. But when I reached the corner, I stood before a fork. I scoured the start of the two paths, but there

were no footprints on the ground, no trace that they had been here at all. It was like they simply vanished.

"Dash? Felix?" I yelled, hoping for a response, but all I was met with was silence. I had no way of knowing which path they had chosen, and the fear and anxiety of being lost and alone rushed through me like water bursting through a dam. I would have to rely on instinct and luck. I studied my options carefully, though the two trails looked identical.

Sight wouldn't help, so I would have to depend on other senses. I inhaled deeply, praying that I could detect a trace of lemongrass, leather, sea salt, or spice, but there was nothing but the fragrance of snow, flowers, grass, and dirt. I sighed loudly, frustrated with my lack of progress. I closed my eyes and focused on the noises that surrounded me. The rustling of leaves, the twittering of birds, the buzzing of insects and... water. There was a distinct whooshing sound as if there were a nearby river. Dash. He loved the water. That's where he had to be. I concentrated intently, willing the cacophony of sounds to dwindle to only one as I tried to determine from which way the source came. Left. I would go left.

I hurried down the path, needing to reach Dash and Felix as soon as possible, when I encountered a man looking at me curiously as he walked in the other direction. I offered a tight but warm smile, not wanting to strike up a conversation with the stranger but also not desiring to be rude.

"Can I help you with something, my lady?" Though I did not recognize him, the way he addressed me indicated that he resided within the palace.

"I'm alright," I told him as I passed.

"Is there something I can do for you, my lady? Someone I can retrieve for you?" His questions had me halting my trek. Maybe he knew where Dash and Felix were. Though I felt confident they had taken this route, I wasn't sure how far they had traveled. They may have cut through the woods rather than stayed on the trail. I turned to face the stranger. His features were kind, and his eyes were compassionate and unique. One a rich brown and the other a seafoam green. I was entranced by the rarity and beauty of it.

"My lady?" he asked, breaking me from my daze.

"I'm sorry," I said quickly, feeling guilty for my intrusive stare. He smiled brightly, flashing his white teeth. The gesture was friendly and forgiving, making me feel more at ease in his presence.

"Do you know where I can find Lord Felix and Prince Dashiell?" I asked. He tilted his head as he pondered my words as if he weren't sure whether he wanted to divulge the information he had. I began to feel restless under his watch.

"I can go retrieve and bring them to you, my lady," he reasoned, not wanting to answer my question fully. I started to get annoyed.

"No, I would like to go to them myself, but thank you for the kind offer." Though my words were gentle, my tone was final. I was in no mood to be challenged, and he was keeping me from getting to Dash and Felix. "Do you know where they are?" I questioned again. The man shook his head from side to side.

"I do not know where they are now, but I last heard them not long ago. Just down there," he explained as he pointed down the path I was currently on. Not long ago. I had to be close then.

"Thank you," I told the stranger as I made to continue on my journey.

"My lady," he said as he came up behind me. "Please, take this." He slipped off the jacket he had been wearing and draped it over my shoulders. Despite it being daytime in the summer, the air was frigid and crisp.

"Thank you," I told him as I offered a genuine smile of gratitude. "Your kindness is much appreciated." He bowed his head and continued on his way.

I proceeded down the path once again with a renewed sense of hope that I would soon find my friends. My heart began to beat faster, and I had the peculiar sense that I was being followed. I whirled around, but no one was there. There was nothing out of the ordinary, just a dirt path lined with massive oak trees and... a shadow. Like an enormous puff of onyx smoke snaking and twisting around itself. I retreated, not breaking my stare, but it didn't follow. It stayed watching, waiting. Terror shot through me, and I sprinted.

The ground was cold and rough under my bare feet, with sharp rocks digging into my flesh with each step. I didn't care, didn't let myself feel the pain as I ran. The further I went, the brighter the sun grew through the trees and the colder the air became. I was thankful for the warmth of the stranger's jacket around my arms.

Finally, the path opened to a clearing, and I halted as I reached it, catching my breath from my escape. I turned to check, but the shadow was gone.

I let out a long sigh of relief as I surveyed my surroundings. The clearing was filled with wildflowers in vibrant shades of the rainbow. The sound of Dash and Felix's voices reached my ears. They were muffled and distant but close. I hurried to the edge of the expanse to discover a cliff at the end. I leaned over carefully and spotted Dash and Felix in the water, waving up at me. Beckoning me to join them. I looked around the space, searching for a way down. For a way to reach them, but there was nothing. How did they get down there? They couldn't possibly have jumped. The distance was too high. It would be like jumping from the roof of the palace. I cupped my hands around my mouth, hoping it would help my voice travel.

"How do I get to you?" I yelled.

"You jump," they told me, though they couldn't be serious. Their voices were hushed over the roaring of the plunging waterfall to my left, certainly causing me to mishear them. There was no way they would be suggesting that.

"What?" I yelled again and moved as far away from the waterfall as I could.

"You have to jump!" they said again, and this time, I knew it was no misunderstanding. My eyes widened in shock, and I shook my head back and forth. They laughed at that. "Don't be scared, Ainsley! You'll be fine!" I knew Dash and Felix would never willingly put me in harm's way. They would never allow me to get hurt under their watch. It still didn't change the fact that I was scared shitless to jump from this great height.

"You can do it!" they encouraged, from the safety of the lake below, the turquoise water so clear that I could see straight to the bottom, even from this distance. I took a deep breath in and out as I nodded my head. I could do this. I could do this. I could do this.

"How?" I asked, and they pointed in unison to an enormous log along the cliff's edge. The dead tree trunk was nearly half my height on its side, and I wasn't sure I would be able to climb atop it. "Can't I just jump from here?" They shook their heads.

"There are rocks in the water below where you stand now. The only place to jump is from there," they said. Fucking great. I made my way over to the tree trunk and

leaped, my hands digging into the bark to find a hold. The wood was so hard and rough that it felt like stone beneath my fingers. I was going to kill them for this. I pulled myself up and onto the log, standing on shaky legs. The wind gusted wildly from up here, whipping my hair across my face in painful strikes. An eeriness crept over me, and I swiveled my head to see the darkness once again. Tendrils of smoke billowed in the wind at the entrance to the clearing. My heart pounded in my chest, and I nearly slipped off my perch and into the watery depths below. I extended my arms out on either side, trying to maintain my balance, though the fear of height and darkness made it hard to focus against the strength of the unyielding wind.

My entire body began to shake forcefully as I watched the shadow slink across the clearing slowly. It wanted to reach me. To take me.

"Ainsley," a voice beyond the darkness called. The tone was urgent and desperate, and terrifying. I needed to get to Dash and Felix. They would keep me safe. I focused my attention on my friends below, my legs trembling as I prepared to jump. I squeezed my eyes shut as I squatted deep and sprung myself into the air just as the darkness reached me. It wrapped its shadowy claws around my body, holding me tightly in its grasp. I screamed and kicked and fought to release myself. Droplets of water sprayed my face, so cold it might as well have been ice. Did I make it? Did I reach the lake and take the shadow demon with me? I wasn't submerged in water, that much I could tell. Maybe I was still falling, and the mist was coming from the waterfall. That had to be it. I continued to fight, scratching the force that restrained me as I screamed until my voice gave out.

"Open your eyes," a muffled voice said. No. I didn't want to see the demon. I didn't want to see the lake come closer and closer into view as I fell. No, I would keep my eyes shut until I hit the water. "Open your eyes!" the voice said again, this time more forceful and clear. But I couldn't, wouldn't obey. Not until I knew I was safe with my friends.

"AINSLEY, OPEN YOUR EYES!" Felix bellowed, and at the sound of his voice, my eyes flew open and sheer terror ripped through me as I screamed in panic.

"You have to calm down! I have you!" he yelled over the roaring wind, over my screams, over the sound of crashing waves. I stood on the parapet of the roof. No,

I *was* standing on the parapet, but right now, nothing was beneath me but air and a massive wall of water, there to break my fall should it come to that. Felix's hold on me was all that prevented me from free-falling. My heart was bursting out of my chest, and I couldn't control the sobs and shrieks that broke out of me. Not even Felix's powerful magic could calm the feelings of horror that coursed through my body.

"Ainsley, you have to breathe; you have to focus. I won't let you go, but I can't pull you to safety unless you calm down. You're going to be okay, but you have to let me help you." I was past the point of being able to calm down. I begged and pleaded with my body to be silent and still, but nothing happened. I was going to die here. "Dash, do it!" he yelled, and all at once, the massive wall of water shot straight up, the force of it so powerful it was like a stone wall had been slammed into me at a terrifying speed, knocking all the air from my lungs.

18.

I was falling. No, not falling. I had been shoved backward through the air with Felix's arms tightly wrapped around me. My back collided with his chest as we hit some barrier that abruptly stopped our momentum, causing us to fall forward onto the roof. My knees slammed into the stone so hard that I cried out immediately at the pain. A second later, Felix had me in his arms again, scooping me up from the ground and carrying me back inside. My body shook violently as he held me close. Partly from being thoroughly drenched, the water so cold it felt like I was wrapped in ice, and partly because I had just jumped off the fucking roof.

"What happened?" I asked Felix weakly as I coughed up water that had made its way down my throat.

"I don't know," he said worriedly. "I think you were having a nightmare." Just then, Dash appeared, running straight for us through the hall. Felix lowered me slightly as Dash reached us, throwing a warm blanket I hadn't noticed him carrying across my body. "She's okay," he explained to the prince, but Dash's eyes stayed on me, examining every inch of my face like he didn't believe his friend's assessment.

"I'm okay," I told him, coughing once again.

"Stand her up," Dash commanded, and Felix placed me down gently. My legs trembled beneath me, and I wasn't sure I could stand on my own. Luckily, I didn't have to find out because Dash wrapped his hand around my waist and threw my arm over his shoulder as he supported my weight. Felix rubbed my back, and Dash held my hair as I vomited water into the corridor. I should have been mortified with them seeing me like this, but instead, I felt oddly comforted that I didn't have to hide any weaknesses. "What happened, Ainsley?" Dash asked once I wiped my mouth and straightened.

"I don't know. I went to bed and woke up hanging over the roof with a tidal wave beneath my feet," I told them, the words coming out short and clipped. "I must have been sleepwalking."

"What was the dream about?" Felix chimed in.

"I don't know. I was in the woods, and you two were there, but you left me. I couldn't find you for a while, but once I finally did, you were in a lake and wanted me to jump off a cliff to get to you. And then there was this dark, creepy shadow that kept following me, and I leaped from the cliff to escape it. That's when I woke up. Everything felt so real." They nodded their head at my words but didn't offer any opinions.

"It was just a bad dream and an unfortunate case of sleepwalking," Felix said, smoothing my wet hair. "I guess we'll have to lock you in your room at night from now on." I offered a polite breathy laugh at his joke, though I wondered if that wouldn't be the safest option.

"Let's get you to bed," Dash said as he led me through the halls. We walked in silence back to my room as I tried to wrap my mind around the day. First, the conversation with the king, and now this. Maybe the palace wasn't such a safe place for me after all.

"Are you okay, my lady?" an onlooker asked. Great, more witnesses to my humiliation.

"Yes, I'm—" I stopped. That voice. I knew that voice. I looked up to see the man from my dream—the one who so kindly offered me his jacket. The jacket, I realized, that I was still currently wearing. "You. You were there," I said, trying to put the pieces together. "This is *your* jacket."

"Yes, my lady. You are wearing—" He gestured a hand to me, and I looked down at my nightgown. The soaked fabric clung even tighter to me, giving a full outline of the naked body underneath. I pulled the blanket tighter around me, covering my front as the stranger diverted his eyes away. "You looked cold."

"You told me where to find them. You led me to the roof," I bit out angrily. He had pointed me toward the staircase that brought me to danger. The path that had led me to jump. Felix and Dash straightened beside me, becoming tense and suspicious of this stranger.

"No, my lady, no! I would never!" He took a step forward, reaching for me, his eyes pleading with innocence. Dash released me, stepping between us, and I wobbled at the loss of his support. Felix quickly replaced him, wrapping his arm around my middle to steady me.

"Explain yourself," Dash demanded, and I stilled at his tone. It didn't just sound like the voice of a prince; there was a protectiveness weaved within it as well. The man looked genuinely terrified as he brought his attention to his ruler.

"I ran into my lady in the corridor just over there," he said as he pointed from where we had just come. "She looked..." He glanced at me as he struggled to find the words to explain what he saw. "Confused. Like she was searching for something. I stopped her and asked how I could assist. That's when she told me she was trying to find you, Your Highness. I offered to retrieve you and bring you to her. I didn't think she should wander the halls in her nightgown, but she insisted she go to you herself." Dash's eyes found mine, and there was a question written within. I nodded my head once to confirm his story. He focused on the stranger again, giving him a curt nod to instruct him to continue.

"My lady asked if I knew where you were, and I informed her that I was unaware of your current whereabouts. I did, however, point her in the direction where I had last heard you and Lord Felix speaking."

"Yes, and you sent me to the roof!" I exclaimed. The stranger's eyes went wide with disbelief.

"No, my lady! I told you they had been over there," he said defensively as he gestured down a long hallway to our right. I eyed him skeptically, not believing his tale. There was no reason why Dash or Felix would travel down that corridor, at least not at this hour. It housed nothing but formal meeting spaces and King Perceval's War Room. Dash and Felix exchanged a wary look before the prince spoke again.

"And then what happened?" Dash demanded.

"After I gave her my jacket to cover herself, I offered to escort her, but she turned and walked in that direction," he said, gesturing to where we had come from. "I called after her, but she paid me no mind, and I assumed my lady had dismissed me. She seemed content and determined, like she knew where she was going. Like she was being led somewhere though no one was present, Your Highness."

"There was a shadow on the path," I whispered to myself, my brow furrowing as I thought back to the massive dark form. I met Dash's eyes. "In my dream, it wouldn't stop watching me, so I ran."

"It's okay, my lady," the man said reassuringly, "It was only an illusion of your nightmare. You are safe now." He seemed to put together what had happened, undoubtedly relieved that he would no longer be suspected of sending me into harm's way. I offered him an apologetic smile, ashamed that I returned his gesture of kindness with one of accusation. I glanced up at Dash to find him as still and ashen as one of the stone statues in the courtyard. His blue eyes were locked onto Felix, and I swiveled my head to see him with the same look of terror on his face. What was happening?

"Leave us," Dash said, cutting through the silence. The stranger bowed and backed away, but before he could fully turn and retreat, Dash called out, "What is your name?"

"Pecus, Your Highness."

"Pecus," Dash repeated, his voice deadly calm. "If I learn your story to be false, if I find out that you intended to hurt her," he said, taking a calculated step closer. Pecus swallowed loudly, and his hands trembled at his sides as he was approached. "I will end you," Dash growled. Pecus bowed again and quickly made his way through the palace, determined to get as far away as possible from his prince. I didn't know what to make of Dash's promise. His threat was cold and violent. And by the way his eyes darkened as he faced me, I knew he had meant every word.

"Tenebrae?" Felix whispered from behind me, and I stiffened at the name of the kingdom that only hours ago I learned was responsible for my parent's death. The kingdom that would enslave me if they knew of my survival. Dash shook his head, his jaw clenched tight as he walked over and rubbed my arms, creating friction that sent warmth pulsing through my body. I was shivering, but I knew it wasn't from the cold.

"They think she's dead. Not to mention, they'd have to be close to cast an illusion on her. Don't you think we would have discovered someone within the palace that possessed that magic by now?" he replied. *What*? How did he know they thought I was dead? King Perceval made me swear not to share what I learned with him or Felix.

"What... How do you...." I couldn't finish my train of thought, too afraid to voice it aloud.

"There is only one person in this palace that can strike that much fear into someone," Dash explained. "When you retired for the night, I sought out my father and demanded that he tell me what happened between the two of you."

"And he did so willingly?" I asked. After the way the king had expressed concern over the danger his son would be in if he ever uncovered the truth, I didn't see that as a possibility.

"I wouldn't say *willingly*, but I was told nonetheless." He took a step closer, placing his hands on either side of my face. My skin seared under his touch and the protective gaze of his eyes. "Ainsley, I'm so sorry. You shouldn't have had to go through learning about your parents all alone."

"I'm just happy you know, and I don't have to keep it from either of you anymore." Felix pressed his chest into my back, wrapping his arms around my shoulders and resting his chin on top of my head.

"You don't ever have to. Anything we say to one another stays between the three of us. We don't keep secrets from each other, Ainsley," Felix explained as he tightened his grip around me. My chest ached at the words. I blinked through the tears that began to form as Felix spoke again. "And you're sure it couldn't be Tenebrae?" I felt his chin lift from my hair and knew he was now focusing on Dash.

"As I said before, they think she's dead, and you know how meticulous and careful my father is. He would have taken great measures to keep her survival a secret." I was about to object to speaking about the matter in the middle of the hall where anyone could hear when I noticed a faint iridescent glow in the candlelight.

How long had we been under a shield? "Right now, I don't see how they would have found out."

"There are always ears listening in this palace. No place is safe, even for a king. That is what your father told me this morning. Someone had to have figured out the truth and smuggled out the information. Think about it," I started as I stepped away from both Dash and Felix to look into their eyes as I spoke. I needed to see their reactions to my words. I needed to know that they were taking me seriously. "I had been safely hidden for almost twenty-one years, and then I was almost killed only weeks after my arrival at the palace. I have never once had a nightmare *that* vivid, nor have I ever experienced a case of sleepwalking. You're now marrying a random orphan when you had previously been betrothed as a child to someone who supposedly died only a week after I was born. That fact alone is suspicious enough. Maybe someone has started to put the pieces together." Dash crossed his arms over his chest, and his eyes narrowed in a way that told me he was turning the information over in his mind—inspecting it for validity and defects.

"Your betrothal to me before your birth wasn't common knowledge. The only people that knew of it were my parents and yours, and three of those members took the secret to their graves. Our betrothal was announced to the kingdom only a few weeks before you arrived, and the details of when the arrangement was made were never shared with anyone but myself. The only other soul that knows the undiluted truth is Felix, of course."

"Of course," Felix parroted like that fact went without saying.

"Not to mention, we would have noticed someone living in the palace with dark magic like that over the years. And you're the only new resident we've had for some time," Dash continued. I closed my eyes, twisting his words around in my mind. I knew him enough to know that the points he made weren't because he didn't believe me. He was simply trying to be as thorough as possible, thinking through every scenario and possible motive. I straightened, and my face lit up with realization.

"You said someone from Tenebrae would have to be close to cast an illusion on me. You also said that if someone residing in the palace had that Gift, then you would have learned about it by now, right?"

"They'd have to be relatively close, but yes. You're right," Dash answered, his eyes full of intrigue as he watched me build my case, his lips curling up in the corner.

"Well, what if they don't *live* in the palace?" Dash and Felix looked at each other for a moment and then back at me. "You told me yourself that you and Felix used to sneak through the palace in Ministro undetected because you knew the secret passageways. Why couldn't the same be done here? If someone has figured out who I am, they could be acting as a spy for Tenebrae. Feeding them information and sneaking them in and out of the palace. Is that a possibility?" Dash moved so quickly that he was a blur in my vision. He pressed his lips to my forehead and took off down the hall.

"Get her to her room now," he commanded, but Felix had already swept me into his arms and was running through the corridor to my room. Holy Gods, was I actually right?

As soon as we reached my chamber, Felix went straight into the bathing room and drew a bath for me, dumping in contents of bottles that had the room smelling like lavender. He instructed me to get in, leaving me in private to undress as he gathered a change of nightclothes.

"Where did Dash go?" I asked as he returned to the bathing room with a dry nightgown and sat on the bench next to the tub. In true Felix fashion, he sat up straighter trying to take a peek inside but was met with a barricade of bubbles. I splashed him with the warm soapy water for his boldness, and he laughed.

"He went to tell the king of our suspicions," he explained, drying his face off with the light green towel draped over the side of the tub. "He'll come here as soon as he's done."

"What if it turns out to be nothing? What if it was just a nightmare?"

"That's the outcome we're hoping for, cream puff."

"I can't believe you managed to get to me in time." I shivered at the possibility of what would have happened if they had been just a minute later.

"Yeah, well, imagine our surprise when we're sitting on the terrace enjoying our evening and look up to see you walking along the parapet. I don't think I've ever sprinted up the stairs so fast."

An hour later, Dash knocked on my door, a set of guards standing behind him. The three of us sat together on my bed as he shared what had transpired between him and his father. The king was apprehensive but didn't want to cause panic within his court, telling Dash that they would find a way to handle this discreetly. I couldn't say I blamed him for that. For now, the king would investigate the matter in secret, and I was to have a set of guards stationed outside my door overnight as a precaution for my 'sleepwalking.'

Eventually, I told Dash and Felix that I wanted to try and sleep. Though they both offered to stay with me, I felt like enough of a burden after tonight. I knew they were genuine in their offer, but I couldn't bring myself to accept. My heart broke as I thought back to the terror I witnessed on both of their faces this evening. The pain and fear within their eyes at not only what happened but also the realization that it may not be over.

19.

The hour had to be the middle of the night, if not drawing close to early morning, and though I was exhausted, I couldn't bear to close my eyes. My mind flooded with thoughts as I watched the moonlight dance upon the tiles across my bedroom floor. If what I had experienced wasn't a nightmare, if Tenebrae did somehow send an illusion into my mind—an illusion that nearly cost me my life—what's to stop them from doing it again? Though I now had two guards stationed outside my door, something as innocent as sleep no longer felt safe.

I tossed and turned for another hour before finally deciding to leave my room, hoping a simple walk would calm the clutter within my mind. Was this pure coincidence and not an attack at all? Was this just a case of a nightmare and sleep-walking and my paranoia wanted me to believe otherwise? My head throbbed from all of the unanswered questions and possibilities.

I slipped out from beneath the heavy blankets, the cold tiles nipping at my skin as I pressed my feet onto the ground. I hurried over to my slippers and grabbed the long deep green velvet robe that hung from my armoire. Securing it tightly around myself, I unlocked my door and headed into the hall, stopping as the guards stationed outside tensed in surprise, their hands sliding to the weapons at their sides.

I held my hands up in surrender. "It's okay," I told them. "I'm awake. No night-mare, no illusion, truly." The guards glanced at each other, unsure of whether to believe me. "I'm just going to go down to the kitchen to grab something to eat."

"We can call down for food to be brought up to you, my lady," one of the guards said.

"I'd rather go myself."

The guard nodded, and as I made my way into the hall, they both fell in step behind me. I stopped and turned on my heel to face them with my arms folded across my chest and annoyance written all over my face. "I don't need an escort," I said sharply. "I am wide awake and lucid, so there is no need to monitor my every movement within these walls."

"We were given orders to make sure you are kept safe throughout the night. Unfortunately, that does mean following wherever you choose to go," the first guard said. "I'm sorry, my lady." By the softening of his eyes, it seemed that he meant it. I exhaled through my nose before turning and making my way through the dimly lit halls, heading to the kitchen, the sound of the guards' following footsteps intensifying my headache.

I finally reached my destination, the smell of fresh bread and spices wafting through the air when I stopped abruptly. Dash was leaning over the large wooden kitchen bench, a dessert in front of him and a silver fork in his hand. His eyes shot to mine, and he dropped his fork, a soft thud reverberating through the room, concern flashing over his face.

"Are you okay? Did something happen?" he asked, straightening himself and making to move around the bench. I held out a hand to stop his advance.

"I'm fine, just hungry." I strolled to the space across from him and eyed the spread of sweets displayed atop the bench, clearly leftover from earlier this evening. The sound of boots on stone approaching close behind had me closing my eyes and inhaling deeply. Trying desperately to reign in that irritation I felt bubbling within once again.

"Leave us," Dash said, and I glanced up to find him watching me.

"Your Highness, we were given orders to—"

"And I'm pretty sure I just gave you a new order," Dash said, interrupting the guard, his piercing gaze now on them. His voice was laced with command.

"Of course, Your Highness," the guard replied at once, the sound of them retreating from the room echoing between us. Dash watched after them, and when his eyes slid back to me. I knew we were now alone.

"Thank you," I said, giving him a small grateful smile. Dash's blue eyes warmed as he nodded his head, picking his fork back up from the table. I chewed on my lip as I scanned the array of choices before us, not quite finding exactly what I wanted when I spotted the chocolate tartlet Dash had claimed for himself. I set my elbows on the bench, placing my chin in my hands as I pouted at him. I wasn't beneath begging when it came to sweets. His lips curved in a crooked smile as he slowly shook his head at me, denying my very obvious request. I crossed my arms over my chest and glowered at him, determined not to back down. This seemed only to amuse him more.

"It's the last one," he said very matter of fact, hand still gripping his fork with the uneaten bite upon it.

"And if you were chivalrous," I countered, with a pointed look, "you would let me have it."

"I think you mean if I was *stupid*." He popped the bite of tartlet into his mouth, chewing slowly, never breaking our stare. He swallowed deeply before replying. "I just want you to know, Ainsley, that this tastes *so* good."

Before I could help myself, I lunged across the table, reaching for Dash's plate. He was far too quick, sliding it back just out of my reach. His mouth dropped open in shock as he shook his head slowly at me in such a display of disappointment.

"Such unladylike behavior, beautiful." My eyes widened just a fraction at the endearment. By the quick flash of panic across his face, it seemed as though he had never meant for it to slip. "I'll tell you what," he said quickly, trying to recover from his stumble of words, "I will split this with you *if* you allow me to improve on the recipe."

I thought about his proposition for a moment, trying to detect any trap within his meaning, but came up empty.

"Deal," I told him, pushing back from the bench and following him to the counter next to the stove. I watched silently as he gathered cooking utensils and ingredients, wondering what he could be doing or how he even had any knowledge of what to do in a kitchen. Surely it wasn't a requirement that a prince should know how to cook.

Dash surveyed everything he had collected before nodding to himself in satisfaction.

"Ready?"

"Yes?" I replied, leaning my back against the stone countertop. Dash laughed softly under his breath and stepped closer to me, his hands coming down to rest on the sides of my waist. My heart quickened at this touch—at the proximity. His lemongrass and sea salt scent filled my senses. Before I could ask what he was doing, Dash lifted me in one smooth, quick motion, setting me down on the counter before turning back to his workstation. I shifted, trying to regain my bearings from his hands on me.

"So, how do you even know how to do all this?" I asked, trying desperately to break the tension as I observed Dash finely chop a small bundle of what seemed to be mint. He discarded the leaves into a small pot of boiling water, adding sugar to the mix before he finally spoke.

"My mother," he said softly, stirring the mixture that was now coming to a gentle simmer. "Her parents had owned a little bakery in one of the nearby towns. That's how she learned."

"And then she taught you," I deduced. Dash smiled slightly, but it didn't reach his eyes. Seeing the hurt and sadness that resided within them broke my heart. He put down the spoon, stepped away from the hot pot, and grabbed a large mixing bowl. He began pouring different ingredients in as he spoke.

"Her mother and father both died during the Second Great War, and she took over the bakery immediately following. One day, my father stopped inside during one of his visits to the town, and he fell in love with her on the spot. He told her he wanted to make her his queen, so she closed the bakery and moved here to the palace the next day." I would have believed the story to be a romantic dream come true if it wasn't for the sorrow in his voice. If it weren't for this gut feeling that told me Dash believed his mother would have been better off far away from this place.

"She didn't possess magic?" I asked, and Dash knitted his brows. "It's just that you said she ran a bakery. I assumed that since she didn't live in the palace, she didn't have a Gift."

"Ah," Dash said in understanding. "She did, actually. Back then, it wasn't a requirement to move to the palace if you had magic. That didn't go into effect until decades later during the attacks from Tenebrae."

"Was she happy here?" I asked. He inhaled deeply and bobbed his head back and forth—a noncommittal answer. I didn't push.

"Even though she was now the Queen of Caelum," he continued, "keeping her from the kitchen was impossible. She was always in here cooking or baking something. She once told me it was her favorite place to be. The one place where she truly felt alive." Dash removed the pot from the heat and poured its contents over a small strainer, separating the syrup from the mint leaves. He then went back to his large bowl, new utensil in hand. I watched in amazement as he whisked together the contents, forming stiff peaks of whipped cream. My mouth began to water. A smile spread wide across his face as he gently tapped the whisk against the side of the bowl, removing the excess before handing the utensil to me for tasting.

"Thank you," I told him before immediately shoving the whisk into my mouth, the flavor of the whipped cream so sweet and delectable.

"When I was a child, I used to come down here with her and sit right where you are now." He jerked his chin to my spot on the counter. "I'd watch her for hours, just mesmerized by how she moved so effortlessly through the kitchen and was able to make such beautiful dishes. She was truly an artist when it came to food, and I would beg for her to teach me all that she knew." He spoke with such a fondness for his mother that I was truly sad that I never got to meet her. "And, of course, being her official taster was a perk of all of the free labor I provided," he said with a wink.

"Of course," I replied, smiling widely at him as I waved around my now clean whisk.

Dash grabbed the now-cooled syrup and gently poured it little by little into the bowl, folding the whipped cream over each drizzle to ensure everything was blending smoothly. Once finished, he stepped closer to me and held out his hand in invitation. I took it, squeezing tightly as I hopped off the counter and strode to the far end of the kitchen. I returned with a small bowl of raspberries and sat them between us.

"You contributed, so I figured I should as well," I explained, shrugging.

"Well, raspberries are certainly an acceptable contribution," Dash said as he transferred my half of the chocolate tartlet onto a new plate and slid it across the bench to me. I bounced from foot to foot as I eagerly waited for him to dish out the whipped cream. "You're so impatient," he laughed as he dolloped a spoonful onto my pastry. I didn't move. I merely looked at him with a raised brow as if to say *that's it?* He narrowed his eyes but offered another spoonful. I sighed loudly as I strummed my fingers along the wooden table. He shook his head, laughing softly under his breath as he added more to my tartlet. Three extra dollops later, I pulled my plate away, satisfied with the amount.

"Thank you," I told him smugly as I sprinkled several raspberries on top of my dessert before leaning over the table and adding a handful to his.

"You're welcome," he replied. "And thank *you*."

"Anytime," I forced out, my mouth already full of pastry. "Holy Gods..." I raised my hand to cover my packed mouth as I struggled to chew. "This is fucking incredible, Dash."

"I know," he said confidently, grinning like a fool as he took a much less significant bite than myself. I rolled my eyes at his arrogance as I swallowed my food, unable to keep the smile from my face.

I grabbed another handful of raspberries and sprinkled them on his portion.

"You did a good job, so you get extra," I explained.

"What an honor," he teased.

"It is. And we can both agree that the real star of this dish is the raspberries anyway," I declared, popping another small bite into my mouth. Dash narrowed his eyes at me as if he wasn't sure he wanted to agree. "Please? Just give me this win," I joked. We both knew my addition to the dessert was nothing compared to the culinary masterpiece he had just whipped up.

"Just this once."

"I'll take it," I told him as I played with the whipped cream on my plate. I glanced up to find Dash watching me intently, as if something was on his mind, his ocean eyes pouring into me. He set his fork down before he addressed me.

"Can I ask you a question?"

"You just did," I said, and he rolled his eyes at my sarcasm. "Go ahead," I continued.

"You were raised by Caregivers?"

"Yes, but..." I chewed on my bottom lip as I placed my fork on the table, struggling to find the words I wanted to say. "I wouldn't exactly say that they *raised* me. It was more like they kept me alive until I was sent here. They made it abundantly clear my entire life that I was more of an inconvenience than anything else to them."

Dash's face fell, and his eyes went soft. "Were there any good times? Maybe holidays or birthdays?"

Unfortunately, I knew that there were none to be found. A subtle shake of my head, barely even noticeable, had Dash shifting in his seat, aggravation evident in every movement he made. Not at all directed at me, I realized, but at what he was being told. I glanced back down at my half-eaten dessert, unable to meet his stare as I said in a voice no louder than a whisper, "I've never celebrated my birthday before."

"What?" His tone contained surprise and maybe something like anger as well. "Are you kidding me?" Yup. That was definitely anger.

I ran my fingers along the table nervously, the wood hard but smooth. I wasn't going to continue but something about opening up to someone—to him—felt good. I took another bite of the tartlet before speaking again, the chocolate and mint dancing in merriment on my tongue.

"My Caregivers didn't believe in celebrating birthdays," I explained. "The only reason I ever knew it *was* my birthday was that on the same day every year, they would always tell each other 'one year closer,' and I knew what it meant. They were one year closer to being rid of me."

"Ainsley, that's...." he trailed off, shaking his head. "I'm so sorry that was your life."

I shrugged as I took the last bite of my dessert and rolled my neck. I didn't want to talk about this anymore. That life was behind me now, and at this moment, I couldn't remember why I even wanted to return to it. I looked up at Dash to find his hands flat on the surface, leaning over the table and watching me closely. The gears of his mind seemed to turn at every passing second.

"What?" I asked, but Dash was quiet. He tilted his head as he studied me before finally speaking.

"Can I take you somewhere tomorrow?"

I mimicked his movements, setting my palms flat and leaning closer, meeting him halfway. My face was only a foot from his now.

"That depends. Where will you be taking me?"

"Say yes, and you'll find out," he replied, mischief swirling in his brilliant eyes as a slow, devilish smirk crept up his face. Gods, he was handsome. I leaned farther across the table, closing the distance between us to mere inches.

"Fine," I told him as I held his stare and swiftly extended my arm just a little farther, grabbing the last of his chocolate tartlet and withdrawing quickly from the bench.

"You little—" Dash leaped onto the table to get to me, not wasting the time it would have taken to run around the bench. I squealed as I sprinted away, Dash's arms quickly wrapping around me. I shoved the remaining bite of tartlet into my mouth. Dash spun me around to face him, my cheeks full and bulging. He threw his head back in laughter at the sight as I struggled to chew and swallow. He brought his hand to my face, wiping a small amount of whipped cream from the corner of my mouth and smearing it on my nose. I swatted his hand away as I swallowed hard, finally finishing what I had stolen.

"I'm going to get you back for that," he said, and I was suddenly aware of his arm still wrapped around me, pressed into my lower back. His eyes flickered to my lips for just a second, and I wasn't sure why but I felt a shiver throughout my body. Did I even want him to kiss me?

"Maybe you will, maybe you won't," I said sweetly as I stepped out of his embrace and headed over to the kettle to boil water for tea. Dash appeared next to me, spinning the handle of two teacups around his fingers before setting them down on the counter.

"There is one memory I have of my Caregivers that wasn't so horrible," I told him as I set the full kettle over the small flame on the stove. Dash hopped onto the counter and sat in my previous spot as he listened. "When I was eleven, something happened to me. For about a week straight, I was in excruciating pain, and my Caregivers couldn't figure out why. Several Medicus had come to inspect me but found no trace of what was causing my agony. I hadn't fallen and hit my head or broken a bone. Nothing was physically wrong with me, but the pain continued in relentless waves. They kept instructing me to explain what it felt like, but I couldn't describe it properly. It was like an overwhelming sense of grief and anguish. It was heartache and loss and despair and fire. This raging fire that burned and burned night and day without ever dulling." The kettle released a high-pitched whistle, and I removed it from the heat, pouring the boiling water over the tea leaves. I let them steep as I continued. "I overheard my Caregivers explain to one of the Medicus that a similar event had occurred when I was around two years old. For three days, I screamed and screamed and couldn't be comforted despite their attempts."

"What happened?"

"The first time, when I was two, it suddenly stopped. My Caregivers said it was like it had never happened. The Medicus assumed that the episode I was experiencing directly correlated to what occurred when I was a toddler. He explained that due to my lineage, it was probably an early manifestation of my powers. Based on my description of the pain, he said it was most likely fire magic that ran through my body, and it was trying to find a way out." I strained the finished tea into the cups he had provided. Dash watched quietly as I worked, just as I had done with him earlier. "The Medicus announced that because it was my own magic, I would have to let it run its course. He provided herbs and tonics to help the pain, but they didn't do much. Both of my Caregivers never left my side for that week, bringing me a cup of hot tea every night. It was the only time I had ever felt cared for in their presence."

I handed him a full cup, and he offered me a small smile of thanks before blowing gently, the steam whirling through the air like flower petals in a breeze, the smell of jasmine and peppermint filling the space between us. I leaned back against the counter, basking in the soothing scents and warmth from the cup between my hands. "Though looking back at it now, they probably only stayed to ensure that I survived the night in fear of the king's wrath should something have happened to me." I stared down at my drink, tilting my head as a thought occurred to me. "Maybe that's why I drink it every night. It's soothing and comforting and reminds me of the one time in my life I felt like I meant something. Gods, that sounds so depressing to say aloud." I laughed nervously under my breath.

I looked up at Dash, hoping he would see my desire to change the subject. He watched me carefully as he took a small sip of his drink. I raised a brow in his direction, urging him to say what thoughts were haunting him.

"How are you feeling about everything that happened earlier?" he asked, now staring at his cup as if he were wondering if that were an appropriate thing to ask me.

"You mean about the nightmare that very well might not have been a nightmare at all?" I replied nonchalantly. Dash nodded his head in confirmation, his fingers circling the rim of his cup as he waited for my response. "Honestly," I said quietly, "I'm terrified." His eyes shot to mine, the worry and concern that shone within them was overwhelming, and it made my heart skip a beat at the thought that he cared so much. "It's not only that I can't fall asleep. It's that I'm too afraid to. It just doesn't feel safe," I confessed. "And I know that is utterly stupid, especially because of the guards that now live outside of my door, but—"

"It's not stupid, Ainsley," Dash interrupted. "It's not stupid at all to feel that way. You went through something traumatic and terrifying. You're entitled to feel the way you do." He reached over, tucking a loose strand of hair behind my ear. I had to look away, a lump catching in my throat as I tried to fight the tears that threatened to line my eyes. It felt like such a weight lifted to be able to express my thoughts. A weight that I hadn't been aware I was holding. And to hear Dash validate those fears... To hear those words from him meant so much.

I closed my eyes as I took a deep breath, counting to three before exhaling and turning my attention to Dash.

"I should head back," I told him, running a hand through my unbound hair. He nodded his head once before handing me a single white rose. I brought the flower to my nose, inhaling deeply. "Thank you," I told him. "Where did this come from? I didn't even see you grab it."

Dash threw a wink. "I'm sneaky like that," he said, hopping down from the counter and extending his arm in a gesture for me to lead the way. "I'll walk you back."

We spent most of the way to my room in a comforting silence as we sipped on what was left of our drinks. Just the presence of him near had made me feel better, and I found myself questioning why. We had spent the past couple of weeks laying the foundation for the friendship that had blossomed between us. But was it turning into something more than that? I couldn't deny the happiness I felt whenever he was near or even the spark that shot through me whenever we touched. But did I even want something *more*? We were finally getting to a good place in our friendship, and I wasn't sure I wanted that to change.

After a few minutes, we reached my room, the guards already waiting at their posts. I sighed deeply as I turned the knob and pushed the door open, the moonlight leaking through the windows, the only source of light across the room. A twinge of panic coursed through me, and I tried to shove it back down deep—yelling at myself within my head that I was safe and that nothing was going to hurt me. I twisted the stem of the rose between my trembling fingers as I turned back around to face Dash, his eyes narrowing at me.

"Do you..." he started. He seemed to be battling with himself as to whether to continue. I waited patiently as he decided. "Do you want me to stay with you? At least until you fall asleep," he finished.

"Really?" I asked, my voice sounding entirely too desperate.

"Of course. I want you to get some sleep, but more than that, I want you to feel safe, Ainsley." His voice was so soft, so caring.

"Thank you, Dash," I told him, even though *thank you* didn't seem fitting enough for the gratitude I felt for him at this moment. "And yes, I would very much like that." I extended my arm for him to lead the way into my room.

20.

I closed the door, securing the lock as Dash made his way to the center of the dim room and surveyed his surroundings. I knew he could see everything clearly in the dark; just one of the many things being an immortal came with. I, however, was still a month away from being one, so I walked to the dresser and lit a single candle. As my mortal eyes adjusted, I found Dash watching me. He smiled, and with a slight flick of his wrist, every candle in the room illuminated. Not with fire. No, it was some sort of magic emitting a soft flickering light throughout my bed chamber. I reached for one of the candles in amazement, my fingers slipping through the luster, feeling nothing but air upon my hand. This must be the same magic used within the lanterns that floated along the grounds night after night.

"Show off," I said as I pulled back my hand and walked over to the bed. Dash shrugged in response, his playful arrogance rolling off him like water droplets after a storm. I unfastened my robe, hanging it up inside my armoire, and kicked off my slippers, the tile painfully cold under my feet once again.

"Can't you use your fancy magic and make it warmer in here?" I asked as I crawled onto the mattress and underneath the heavy blankets.

"I could if I had the powers of an Ignisian, but alas, I do not. At least not yet," Dash replied, settling into the oversized armchair across the room, the blue of the fabric bringing out the color of his eyes. So no fire magic, then.

"So you're an Unda?" Though I already knew he possessed water magic due to the wave that slammed into me tonight.

"An Aerian as well, though I don't use those powers often." So weather manipulation too. He possessed two Gifts from Caelum, making him the true heir to the kingdom. Should his father ever die, Dash would receive the third Gift—fire magic—making him king.

"Felix mentioned your powers came through early."

"They did," he admitted.

"Is that common?"

"Yes and no. Heirs to a kingdom tend to receive both of their Gifts a few months before their twenty-first birthday. It's rare for someone not from a royal bloodline to receive magic early, and it's even rarer for it to happen to anyone a year or more before their birthday. I became an Unda not long after my mother died, but my Gifts as an Aerian didn't manifest until I was sixteen. Because I didn't receive both at once, for years, I thought I wouldn't be named Heir to Caelum—hoped, actually." My brows rose at his confession. I hadn't witnessed any indication that Dash wasn't happy with his role in the kingdom, save for how he felt when he first learned of our betrothal.

"You don't want to be a prince—to be king one day? Do you not think you will be a good ruler?" He was silent for a long while, and I wondered if this was a truth he regretted admitting.

"I hope that I will be a fair and just king. I love my people, and it's not the responsibility of ruling that deter me, but the expectations of the role." Dash dragged a hand through his hair and looked around the room like he could discover the words he wanted to say, hiding in a shadowed corner. "There are difficult decisions that must be made, harsh punishments to dwell out, and oftentimes I find myself leaning towards paths my father and his advisors stray from. Caelum has been a peaceful and prosperous kingdom for years. What if the decisions I make ruin that?"

"I don't think they would," I told him honestly. He didn't respond, and I could tell this wasn't a conversation he wanted to have. "I wonder what power I'll be given," I said, changing the subject. I placed my head on the pillow and pulled the blankets higher, seeking the promise of heat. "I hope I'll be an Ignisian. It would be fun to be able to set things on fire. Or to just not be freezing right now." Dash laughed softly as he interlaced his fingers, resting them on his chest. His shirt was tight enough that I could tell how toned his body was, and I was mesmerized by the outline of his muscles beneath the thin grey fabric.

"My mother was one," he explained. "My father always said it had suited her because of her fiery personality and temperament."

"I think I would have gotten along with her quite well." Dash lifted his head, and his face fell as he looked at me. His eyes softened, and I could have sworn they gleamed slightly in the light, making me instantly regret my words. Dash broke my stare, looking down at his fingers, sorrow covering his features. I rolled onto my back, staring at the ceiling and wishing I hadn't said anything at all. It was quiet for a few minutes before he finally spoke, breaking the silence.

"I think you would have, too." It was barely more than a whisper. An aching in my chest began at his confession. His voice held such a haunting sadness whenever he spoke of his mother. I wanted to go to him, to comfort him. To tell him that I was so sorry that he had experienced such a devastating tragedy, but instead, I didn't move.

Instead, I changed the subject once again.

"Why were you in the kitchen so late?" I asked.

"I couldn't sleep either. Tonight was... a lot," he explained, and I knew exactly what he meant. I was mortified at what had happened. Mortified at the fact that my mind wasn't strong enough to fight off an attack. Mortified to know it may not have even been an attack, and I let a simple nightmare almost get me killed. But most of all, mortified that by morning the entire palace would know what transpired here tonight, and I would never live it down.

"I'm sorry," I said, even though I wasn't sure why I was apologizing.

"There isn't anything for you to be sorry for, Ainsley." He was right, but it still didn't stop the distressing feelings that ran through my veins. I felt like I had become more trouble than I was worth. "Unless, of course, you're apologizing for stealing the last of my tartlet because you should be extremely sorry over that," he said light-heartedly. It was as if he could sense the slight shift in my thoughts and wanted to banish them. A small laugh bubbled to the surface.

"I will never be sorry for that," I told him. "And I just want you to know, Dash, that last bite tasted *so* good." His answering laugh boomed through the room, the sound like a symphony in my ears. He looked so happy and at peace, so young and carefree. Like he wasn't the Crowned Prince set to inherit an entire kingdom. I liked this side of him. More than I probably should have.

When the sound of the laughter settled to nothing more than a comforting silence, Dash spoke again.

"Lights on or off?" he asked, his hand held up, fingers lazily suspended.

"On," I replied and watched as Dash slowly brought down two of his fingers in a long, slow movement as if stroking the air itself. The lights around us dimmed, creating a more soothing and relaxing ambiance.

"Goodnight, Dash."

"Goodnight, Ainsley."

I closed my eyes, no longer feeling the terror and hopelessness I had hours prior. I felt warm and comforted and safe, and I knew in my bones that nothing bad could ever reach me as long as he was here. I let the exhaustion sweep in and take me away.

"Rise and shine!" Imogen exclaimed, yanking the blankets from my body. I squinted my eyes, the sun's brightness flooding my vision and causing me to throw a hand up to guard them against the light.

"What time is it?" I asked. Only then did I remember my night with Dash, my gaze shooting over to the now-empty armchair.

"It's midmorning." Her eyes followed my stare. I couldn't help but wonder if he had stayed through the night or retreated to his room once I was finally asleep.

As if Imogen could read my thoughts, she said, "I woke Prince Dashiell shortly after sunrise, and he asked me to allow you to sleep for a few more hours before I came back." Her voice became soft and uncertain as she continued. "I heard about last night." My gaze drifted to her, concern prominent in her face and posture. "How are you feeling?"

"If I'm being completely honest, I'm scared but also confused," I said as I worked through my thoughts. "I just want answers. I want to know if it was deliberate or if it was just some fucked—"

"Language," Imogen interrupted sternly.

"Sorry. Some messed up nightmare." I exhaled loudly through my nose and threw my head back against the soft pillow.

"I just fluffed that," Imogen said through her teeth. I ignored her as I pulled the blankets over my head, not content to leave the comfort of my mattress quite yet.

"Well, if you refuse to get out of bed, then I shall refuse to give you the message Prince Dashiell has asked me to relay once you are awake." I pulled the blankets down a little, peeking a single eye out to find Imogen with her hands on her hips and head tilted in annoyance over my antics. She stared me down for another moment before I fully lowered the furs, revealing my face completely. "He told me to tell you that once you have dressed, to meet him on the terrace. He said something about taking you somewhere."

I leaped out of bed and sprinted into the bathing room, grabbing the light blue dress Imogen had set out on my way in. I had never bathed and dressed so quickly in my life, running out of the room as soon as I finished, my hair still damp. I decided to walk hastily through the halls rather than sprint like my life depended on it. I didn't need the extra stares in my direction, especially after the whole roof incident.

When I reached the terrace, there was no sign of Dash anywhere; however, there was Felix. Standing against the far end of the table with a servant's face between his hands and his tongue no doubt down her throat. She moaned as she pressed her delicate body into him, and I cleared my throat loudly, not wanting to witness whatever was about to happen between them. The woman jumped back, shocked that they were no longer alone, but Felix just looked up and smiled wickedly at me.

"Excuse me, my lady," she said before bowing and scurrying away, not even a glance in Felix's direction as she raced back inside the palace, obviously embarrassed that they were caught. I watched after her until she disappeared within the halls and then turned back to Felix, unable to stop the smile that spread across my face as I shook my head at him.

"Really, Felix? Outside. In the middle of the day. Where anyone can see you. Have you no shame?"

"You were taking forever. I needed something to do to pass the time," he claimed, shrugging innocently.

"I think you mean *someone*."

"Well, you had to go and interrupt the possibility of that, didn't you? You need to work on your timing, sweet pea," he said. I rolled my eyes as I walked over to him.

"I was told to meet Dash here. Have you seen him?"

"Yes, he's running a little behind, so I have been instructed to bring you to him. You've been given the honor of being in my company on our little walk rather than having to deal with Dash."

"Are you ever not full of yourself?" I asked. He looped my elbow through his and led the way onto the dirt path that mazed through the gardens and into the woods.

"It's too hard not to be when you're as spectacular as I am, you know?" he declared as he playfully bumped me with his hip—causing me to trip over myself, twisting my ankle as I hit the ground below.

"Fuck! Ainsley, I'm so sorry," he said, falling to the ground next to me, worry thick in his voice. I don't know what I expected my reaction to be, but it wasn't to burst out in a rolling fit of laughter like I did. Felix's eyes held nothing but confusion as he let out a small laugh of his own. Probably from relief that I seemed to be okay.

"I'm okay, really," I told him through the giggles. "I hurt my ankle, though. I'm not sure I can walk." Felix gently lifted my foot as he assessed the damage. Though the pain was minuscule, my ankle had already swollen to nearly double the size, and the skin was reddening.

"The good news is that it doesn't seem to be broken." I let out a long sigh of relief. "We'll get a Medicus to evaluate it once we get back to the palace, but they should be able to heal you enough that you'll be back on it in a couple of days.

But until then...." Felix bent down, scooping me up and throwing me over his shoulder.

"Is this really necessary?" I said as he tightened his grip on the back of my legs.

"Well, seeing as you can't walk, I'd say so."

"I'm positive there is a much more dignified way of being carried." I protested as I banged my fists against his back.

"I'm sure there is, but this view is the better one," he explained as he smacked my ass. I reached my dangling arms around to push my fingers into the sides of his ribs, finding the ticklish spot I had accidentally discovered the other day in the library when Felix held the book I wanted high above his head, knowing that I couldn't reach.

Felix squealed as I hit the spot again. "Fine, fine, fine!" he yelled, pulling me back in front of him and placing me down carefully onto a log in the path. "I hate you," he said as he turned his back to me and knelt. "Hold on tight."

I obliged, wrapping my arms around his neck from behind and swinging my legs to his front as I crossed them over his stomach. Felix looped his arms under my thighs as he carried me on his back.

"No, you don't," I told him as I leaned forward and planted a kiss against his cheek.

"No, I don't," he agreed, the smile evident in his voice. We walked in silence for a few moments, nothing but the sound of leaves rustling in the breeze and songbirds chirping their melodies.

"Where are we going?" I asked, my curiosity getting to me now.

"I have been given strict orders not to tell you anything."

"That's stupid," I said as I removed my arm from his neck, bringing it down to touch his ribs again. Felix slid his hand from beneath my leg, catching my wrist in time.

"Don't you even think about it," he warned, and I pouted as I brought my arm back to his neck. "Take it up with your fiancé." My body went rigid in his arms. Yes, Dash was technically my fiancé, but I was just getting used to calling him my friend. Felix detected the change within me, whether from my posture or his powers as an Empathi. "Dash really wants it to be a surprise," he continued. "Just another minute longer. It's right through those trees up ahead."

I felt my heart quicken at the anticipation and then slow again into long steady beats. A calmness coursed through my body as if I was floating on air. I leaned around Felix's neck and shot him a pointed look as I raised a brow.

"Sorry," he said, "It's a habit." The sensation eased.

"Do you do that to everyone?" I asked, genuinely curious. Felix pondered the question for a minute as he looked ahead. We were quickly approaching the trees that marked our destination.

"Not to everyone. But when I feel heightened emotions, it's like an automatic reflex. It's been my role for so long that half the time, I don't even realize that I'm doing it anymore." I often forgot just how powerful Felix was. That he was a trusted advisor to King Perceval for a reason. "I'll try to be more mindful of my magic around you."

"Thank you." Sometimes Felix's Gift was welcome, but other times I just wanted to experience my feelings undiluted and without manipulation.

"Besides, this is something you should feel excited over," he explained as he pushed through the trees, and my heart stopped as I took in the view.

21.

In the center of a meadow bounteous with purple and blue wildflowers stood Dash, a smile on his face and his arms outstretched wide. Beside him, upon the lush green grass, lay a beige blanket so large that it could cover ten people comfortably. Spread across the blanket were a display of bread, meats, cheeses, fruits, and wine. It was an entire picnic feast for us. My mouth began to water as the scent of the food hit me.

"What is all of this?" I asked as Felix set me down gently, holding my arm steady just below my shoulder as I balanced on one foot. Concern filled Dash's face immediately, and he jogged over to meet us, his hands coming up as if to touch me. They suspended in the air for a moment, reaching, but then Dash dropped them to his sides. He roved his eyes over me instead, checking to make sure that I was completely intact. His eyes dipped to the lower half of my body, finally focusing on my foot that hovered over the ground.

"Are you okay? What happened?" he asked quickly.

"Nothing serious," I said, shrugging. "Felix tried to kill me, but I survived."

Dash directed him a look.

"She twisted her ankle when she tripped," Felix said, rolling his eyes, and I glowered at him and the crucial detail he chose to leave out.

"When…" I pressed, crossing my arms over my chest, Felix's grip still holding me steady.

"When… I pushed her." He looked away and rubbed the back of his neck.

"You did *what*?" Dash questioned.

"It was a joke, and I didn't realize my own strength," he explained, obviously remorseful, but it didn't change the fact that I still wanted to make him squirm just a little bit.

"I don't know, Dash. He seemed pretty set on trying to murder me," I said, meeting Dash's gaze as a sly smile formed on my face. "I think he deserves some sort of punishment for such behavior," Dash smirked as he stepped closer, taking the bait.

"It was an accident!" Felix exclaimed, arms raised defensively as he retreated backward a few steps, the absence of his grip causing me to wobble as I worked to regain my balance.

"The lady demands retribution. What kind of prince would I be if I did not avenge her?" Dash replied, his hands drawing up to his chest, fingers splayed around the air as if he were holding an invisible ball.

"Yeah, Felix, what kind of prince?" I chimed in, happy to instigate.

Felix glared as he pointed at me, marking me for his revenge, his eyes silently telling me to stay out of this. The look he gave me only made me smile wider. "The merciful kind!" Felix bellowed. He took a few steps closer to Dash, his arms slowly lowering to his sides, his voice becoming soft and pleading as he spoke. "Dash, we've been friends for almost our entire lives. Think of all that we've been through. Think of all that we've overcome. We're family. Brothers, even." Oh, give me a break.

Dash relaxed slightly, letting the weight of Felix's words wash over him as he lowered his hands and turned his attention back to me.

"We *have* been friends for an awfully long time," he said by way of reasoning. You have got to be kidding me. I looked to Felix, who was now grinning like a cat, so triumphant in the success of his ploy to get Dash onto his side. He was reveling in his victory, knowing that Dash had chosen him, but I still had one card left to play. One that I was sure would seal Felix's fate. I tipped my chin high as I turned to look at Dash, his blue eyes now on me.

"Felix smacked my ass," I told him. Dash's eyes grew wide, and I knew at that moment I had won. He turned from me and set his sights on my competitor, my rival, for this moment. Felix's mouth dropped open, and he held up a finger as if he were about to object. As if he were about to explain, yet no words emitted from his mouth. He had no defense, and he knew it. Dash raised a single eyebrow, and Felix lowered his hand in defeat.

"Fuck." That was all Felix managed to say before a giant ball of water the size of a boulder hit him square in the chest, sending him sliding through the meadow fifty feet back at a speed I did not dare want to know. I nodded my head in satisfaction at the punishment Dash had dealt as Felix finally halted, throwing his middle finger high into the air. I didn't bother to hide the small laugh that broke through.

Dash stepped closer to me, his hands lightly grabbing my wrists, and he guided them around his neck. The delicate brush of his knuckles along my arm sent a tingle down my spine. He smiled as he leaned down and lifted me into his arms, one hand beneath my back, the other under my legs as he carried me over to our picnic. I rested my head against the crook of his neck and shoulder, basking in the smell of him, in the warmth there.

Dash set me down carefully on the blanket as Felix made his way over, completely drenched and dripping from head to toe. I surveyed everything around us, from the food and the display of candles and flowers laid out with such care and detail, to the two small packages wrapped in brightly colored paper. I looked back to Dash to find him watching me intently with wonder in his eyes. He studied my every movement as if he would find the answer to some unspoken question that plagued his mind.

"You never answered me before. What is all of this?" I asked him. Dash bit his lip as if he were embarrassed. Or maybe he just wasn't sure he wanted to tell me. I was still learning how to read him but found that just asking him questions directly seemed to be the best route.

"You told me last night that you've never celebrated your birthday, so..." he trailed off as he gestured around us. "I wanted to give that to you."

"Dash, this is...." I struggled to find the words to describe the way I felt. The way my heart was bursting inside of my chest. "Thank you." It was all I could manage as I looked deep into his eyes, hoping the gratitude I had for him was shining in my own.

"If you think this is great, just wait until you see what we have planned for tomorrow's event," Felix said as he finally reached us, plopping himself down on the blanket and wringing the excess water out of the shirt he had removed. The muscles beneath his warm ivory skin flexed as he did. "Although, given her injury, maybe we should switch day two's events with day eight's. She doesn't need to walk for that one." Dash nodded along as he agreed with Felix.

Tomorrow. Day two. Day eight. What in the world were they even talking about? I eyed them both suspiciously, glancing back and forth between the two.

"What do you mean?" I asked, desperately needing one of them to clue me in on the information I was so clearly missing.

Felix looked at me confused, tilting his head as he spoke. "You didn't think that this was it, did you?" he questioned, waving around his index finger at the picnic set up around us. I turned to look at Dash as he leaned back, bracing himself on his palms, his legs crossed in front of him, making himself more comfortable.

"We have years and years of birthdays to make up for, Ainsley," Dash said.

"Each day for the next nineteen will be a new celebration," Felix continued.

I shook my head, fighting the tears I felt beginning to line my eyes, my heart tightening at each word they uttered. This was too much. They were doing too much.

"Why would you—" I began but quickly stopped, unable to find the words to continue, my focus now solely on not crying. Not letting the pure emotion I felt creep up in such an embarrassing way. I had never celebrated my birthday before, and I had never let it bother me. At least, I didn't think it bothered me until now. Until Dash and Felix, whom I had only known for such a short time, had made it their mission to make me feel appreciated and seen.

"You're one of us now," Dash said gently, as if he could sense just how delicate I was at this moment. As if I were made of glass that would shatter and the lightest touch.

"And we will not stand for such injustice done to one of our own," Felix added in the same manner. I knew he could feel everything happening within me at this very second, but he kept good on his word of being more mindful of his magic around me, allowing me to feel everything on my own.

I truly had no words. My mind was flooded with thoughts of gratitude and appreciation. Of love and friendship. But nothing I could ever hope to say would come anywhere close to what I wanted to express to them. My mouth opened and closed several times as I struggled to come up with something, but even a simple thank you didn't seem like enough. I felt a tear stream down my cheek, quickly followed by Dash's thumb brushing it away, his hand hot against my face. He gave a small and comforting smile as he nodded his head, letting me know that he could read the thoughts and emotions in my eyes. Silently telling me that words were not needed.

"Happy first birthday, sweet pea!" Felix exclaimed, handing each of us a glass of wine and then extending his in the air in a toast.

"You've grown so quickly, right before our very eyes," Dash added, sitting up and raising his glass.

"You're talking and walking…. Well, maybe not so much that last one." Felix said sarcastically. From the corner of my eye, I saw Dash flick his wrist with delicate ease, barely a movement at all. Another sphere of water, much smaller in size than the last, hit Felix once again, sending him flying back just a few feet.

"Okay. Too soon. Got it," Felix said, his back flat against the ground. I snickered at the sight before looking back to Dash.

"Happy birthday," he said, clinking his glass against mine before we both drank deeply, the wine as sweet as a summer's day, the notes of berry and spice going down smoothly, yet burning once it hit my empty stomach. I realized that I hadn't eaten today, and my insides grumbled in response. I twisted to grab a piece of bread, completely forgetting about my injury, the sudden movement making me hiss in pain.

"May I?" Dash asked, his hands hovering over my foot. I nodded my permission, and he grabbed my ankle with such gentleness. He rested my foot on his open palm, his other hand covering the top of my ankle. Instantly, a cold sensation swept over my limb, frosty smoke snaking free from beneath his grip as soft ice coated his fingers. "It'll help with the swelling," he explained. "The numbness from the cold should also help with the pain until we can get you to the Medicus."

"Thank you," I told him as I watched him work.

"I shouldn't be having to do this at all," he said, raising his voice louder to ensure the subject of his rant could hear him.

"I said I was sorry!" Felix yelled back, making his way to us for the second time. Dash rolled his eyes as he carefully lowered my foot, setting it down upon a pillow he placed in his lap. His cool fingers continued to caress my swollen ankle, and I felt my breathing hitch at each pass of his touch. I popped a piece of bread into my mouth and focused on chewing. Focused on the clouds that shifted shapes in the sky. Focused on anything but the stroke of Dash's fingers on my skin.

"I know how I can make up for earlier," Felix announced, sitting back down and grabbing one of the small packages I had spied earlier. "With presents." He handed me a rectangular box wrapped in bright green paper and tied with a white ribbon.

"What is it?" I asked him as I turned it over in my hands.

"That's not how presents work, sweet pea," Felix said, rolling his eyes. "You're supposed to open it to find out."

"Oh, I know," I told him as I brought the package to my eyes and examined it closely. "I just wanted to make sure it wasn't going to explode or anything when I did. You know... Since your earlier attempt to kill me failed," I said sweetly, winking at him.

"Har har har," Felix added sarcastically as Dash laughed next to us. I beamed in self-satisfaction at my joke as I untied the ribbon, letting it fall to the ground. I ripped off the paper to reveal a book. "It's my favorite story. I thought you might like it too." I ran my hand over the leather-bound cover, and brought the book up to my face, the intoxicating scent of worn paper and cracked leather filling my nose.

"It's perfect, thank you," I told him as I extended my arms wide to embrace him. Felix leaned forward, wrapping his arms tightly around me.

"Happy birthday," Felix whispered into my ear. "And I am truly sorry about earlier. The push, not the ass smacking. I stand by that decision."

I huffed a laugh against him as I heard a low growl come from Dash. "You are completely forgiven," I told him. "But just know I'll never let you live it down."

"I'd expect nothing less from you, my angsty Ainsley." He pulled back, grabbing the other unopened box wrapped in purple paper, a small white rosebud attached to the top instead of a ribbon. He handed it to me, and I peeled off the flower bringing it to my nose and inhaling deeply, the crisp floral scent automatically triggering the memories of the times Dash and I spent together. I shook the box slightly, the sounds of rattling coming from inside.

"I wouldn't do that," Dash explained. I unwrapped the package with more care than I had the previous, not wanting to accidentally break whatever the gift was that was hidden inside. I opened the box and removed a small stained-glass orb. Dash held up a dark blue blanket, gesturing for me to look at the sphere under the cover. I crawled beneath and watched in amazement as the magic light within the glass cast shades of blues and greens, and yellows in the darkness. My thoughts drifted back to our conversation last night about my fear of the night after what had happened and my request for him to keep the lights on as he settled into the chair in my room. My chest ached at the thoughtful gift. After a moment, I reemerged from beneath the blanket, my eyes taking a second to adjust to the sudden brightness of the sun.

"I love it," I said, reaching out my arms for him. Dash leaned forward to hug me, and I threw myself around his neck, my fingers automatically finding their way into his silken hair as I held him close. "Thank you," I said against him. "It means more than you know." Dash's grip around me tightened in answer.

"I don't get it," Felix stated as he took the orb from my hands and eyed it suspiciously.

"Well, then it's a good thing it isn't for you," Dash replied as he released me and leaned forward to survey the spread in front of us. "Felix…" he drawled with annoyance. "Did you forget the cake?"

"Shit," Felix said, placing my gift down beside him. "I had to attend to some delicate matters before I brought sweet pea here to the festivities. It completely slipped my mind."

"*Delicate matters,*" I mused. "Was that the name of the servant whose throat you had your tongue down when I found you this morning?" Felix gave me a death glare, and I answered him with a satisfactory smile that spread ear to ear.

"Of course," Dash replied flatly as he shifted from beneath my legs, setting the pillow upon his now empty seat with my foot atop it. "I'll be back shortly." He stood, and I stared after him as he walked across the meadow and through the small break in the trees that sat along the border. Felix scooted closer, wrapping an arm around my shoulder and pulling me close. I leaned into his embrace, resting my head against him.

"How did you like your surprise?" he asked, planting a kiss on my hair.

"I'm still trying to find the words," I told him honestly. "But I'm somewhere between wonderstruck and incredulous." Though everything was displayed directly in front of me, it still felt like a part of me didn't want to believe what I was seeing. That there was no way, they would have planned *twenty days'* worth of elaborate surprises simply because I mentioned that I had never celebrated my birthday. It seemed so surreal and over the top. "How were you able to do all of this so quickly? And also, how in the world were you able to come up with weeks' worth of plans in just a few short hours? I only just mentioned it to Dash last night."

"Oh, I had nothing to do with any of it." I leaned away from him to meet his eyes. "This was all Dash." Felix and I had spent nearly all day every day together for the past couple of weeks, so naturally, we had grown close. I would have assumed he would have come up with this, not Dash. Dash and I... We were still building a foundation, still learning how to navigate what we were. We were becoming friends, but we were also engaged. The dynamic between us was so much different than the one between Felix and me.

"You mean he—" I didn't finish that thought. I couldn't wrap my head around the fact that Dash would go so far above and beyond over something I had mentioned briefly.

"The prick barged into my room just after dawn, throwing clothes at me as he demanded that I get my ass up and follow him to the kitchens," Felix explained. "On our way there, he told me about your conversation late last night and the atrocity of not ever commemorating your birthday. Which, by the way, makes me incredibly angry, and it usually takes a lot to get me to that point," he said, looking down at me as he spoke. My heart tightened in response to his words. I found it endearing; not that he was angry, but that he cared enough about me that any pain I may have experienced in the past hurt him in some way too.

"So he took you to the kitchens and told you his idea for today?"

"He took me to the kitchens and shoved a stack of scribbled-on parchment into my hands," Felix said, looking around the space, presumably to make sure Dash hadn't reappeared unnoticed. "The paper was completely marked up with his ideas. He had planned out all twenty days down to every last detail." My breathing hitched as my heart hammered within my chest, threatening to explode at his words. Dash had done this. Had planned *all* of it. I shook my head back and forth as if the motion could somehow untangle the thoughts and feelings within my mind.

"I don't understand. Why would he... This is all so..." The kindness was almost unbearable. I didn't deserve any of it. Not after the way I had treated him for the better half of a week when I had gotten here. Not after the things I had said to him so many times out of anger.

"We told you. You're one of us now," Felix said, scanning the meadow once more before bringing his eyes to mine. "And Dash really is trying. You already know you mean something to me, but you also mean something to him too. This is his way of trying to show you that." Before I could fully digest his words, Dash appeared, stepping through the trees, a small basket swinging in his hand.

"Thank the Gods. I'm fucking starving," Felix whined. I quickly turned away, blinking back the tears that began to form without my permission. Felix's grip around my shoulders tightened with a small reassuring squeeze. "It took you long enough," he added, and I knew in my bones that he did it to trigger a reply from Dash; giving me a few extra moments to try and pull myself together before facing him.

"I gave you one task this morning," Dash replied.

"Two." Felix corrected as I took a deep breath and turned back around to see Dash approach. "To bring the cake and to bring Ainsley. Both are high-value items that you should have never entrusted me with."

"I'm starting to realize that," Dash said flatly as he dropped his head to give a pointed look at my hurt ankle. I bit my lip to suppress my grin as Dash made his way back over to me, lifting the pillow my foot had been resting on and placing it back in his lap; his cool fingers stroking my injury again. I was amazed at how even the slightest touch from him set my blood on fire.

Felix reached behind himself, grabbed a large platter of delicately arranged meat, cheese, and fruit, and placed it between the three of us. My stomach audibly rumbled in response as Felix handed each of us a small silver plate as he spoke.

"Can we just eat and pretend like nothing happened this morning?" Felix begged. I turned to Dash to find that his eyes were already on me. A single brow raised as if to say *it's up to you.* I clamped my lips together tightly to keep from smiling as I turned back to Felix, squinting as I studied him. "Please?" he said, jutting out his bottom lip in an adorable pout.

"Fine," I said, and Felix leaned over, giving me an appreciative kiss on the cheek. I glanced between Dash and Felix, taking in the sight of the two people who had welcomed me; who had made me feel appreciated and important. Who were quickly starting to feel like home.

"Let's eat."

The food had been consumed, the cake had been destroyed, and the wine bottles completely emptied. The morning had faded into afternoon, which had then transformed into dusk, the sky now a beautiful ombre of orange and pink as the sun lowered beyond the hills. We spent the entire day lounging in the meadow as we ate, drank, and laughed deeply. At some point in time, when I was completely unaware, my walls started to crumble, giving Dash and Felix a clear path to reach me. I didn't want to build those walls back up, to lock myself away again. Not after I had let them in. I didn't want to be alone anymore.

"Are you both ready to head back?" Dash asked as he stood, stretching his arms high above his head and rolling his neck from side to side.

"I think so," I replied as Felix helped me stand. It was as if time had slowed for a moment as I took in my surroundings. Felix was before me, arms outstretched, ready to carry me back to the palace. I looked at my own hands, already reaching for him. Dash had turned away as if he had expected me to go with Felix; as if he expected me not to choose him. The thought fractured my heart just a little bit. I knew the reason Dash had expected me to choose Felix wasn't because of the close friendship he and I had built. It was because I had made my feelings about Dash known to everyone, including him. And though we were starting to become friends, I didn't know if those words from the past still haunted him.

I looked up at Felix, hoping he could read the thoughts and emotions written on my face. His eyes flickered to Dash, and he smiled in understanding as he dropped his arms to his side. I took one small wobbly step towards Dash, and he whirled, grabbing my arm to steady me.

"Ready?" I asked him as I brought my arms up and around his neck. His brows pinched in confusion but then smoothed once the realization hit him. A muscle on the side of his mouth twitched as he lifted me into his arms. He took a few steps and then stopped, turning towards Felix, who was packing away the remnants of our picnic.

"Are you coming?" Dash asked.

"I'm going to clean up here, and then I'll meet you both at home."

"We'll be in the library," Dash told his friend as he turned away to carry me through the meadow. I looked over Dash's shoulder at Felix, who was now wiggling his eyebrows at me in a suggestive way. I threw up the middle finger he seemed to love so much, and he responded by puckering his lips to make several kissing gestures. I squinted my eyes at him as I mouthed *fuck you* before facing forward again. Felix, our self-appointed matchmaker, didn't understand the word subtle.

There was still this part of me that wanted to keep my distance from Dash and what I was expected to be—what I was expected to give to him. The other part of me craved his presence. I wanted to hear his voice, to see his deep blue eyes staring back at me. And now I wasn't sure there would ever be a moment I wasn't yearning to feel his touch on my skin. I felt my blood rise and my cheeks heat as

I suddenly became aware of his hands on me now. One arm wrapped around the middle of my back, fingers splayed wide along my ribs, the other gripping me just above my knees. His thumb gently stroked back and forth over the exposed skin from my dress shifting as he carried me. The touch of his fingers was like kerosene to the fire that had kindled inside. Mustering enough bravado, I leaned closer and pressed a light kiss upon his cheek. He stumbled a step as his eyes shifted to mine, wide with shock and awe. His mouth dropped open just barely and then quickly closed again, unable to form a sentence.

"Thank you," I told him, though I knew it wasn't enough. "For today. For last night. For everything, Dash. Thank you." He was at a complete loss for words, but his eyes shone with pleasant surprise. After a heartbeat, he nodded his acknowledgment, never able to come up with a verbal response. I turned forward once again and rested my head in the crook of his neck. Today was the first time I had ever been in his arms, and I found myself wishing that it would not be the last.

22.

Over the next two weeks, Dash and Felix made good on their promise of a new celebration every day. They had taken me horseback riding through the woods, stargazing on a cliff that overlooked the deep valleys of Caelum, and even dancing. One evening, I came down to the terrace to find a chocolate tartlet at least a foot wide with swirls of whipped cream adorning the top of the pastry in the shape of rosebuds. Like his mother had been, Dash was truly an artist in the kitchen.

"And because I know you...." he said as he placed an entire mixing bowl full of whipped cream next to my dessert, and my face broke into a smile just for him.

Another night, I found our dinner table elegantly decorated with several vases, each a different shade of blue and holding a single white rose.

"What is all of this?" I asked as I waved a hand over the space, studying the blue vases and trying to figure out why there were so many.

"You said your favorite color was blue." It seemed like such a trivial piece of information to keep tucked away. Though I also remembered his favorite color. Red. Dark and bold, not bright and cheery. "But you never told me what shade of blue you liked best, so..." He waved a hand over the variety. Dash had collected nearly every shade of blue I knew to exist. My heart constricted, and I swallowed thickly.

Felix shifted in his seat, grinning from ear to ear, no doubt feeling the heightened sense of emotion and desire I had for Dash. I kicked him under the table, but rather than wince in pain, he laughed and then cleared his throat to cover it up. At that moment, I hated his Gift.

I reached across the table, selecting a deep blue vase—the color of the ocean during a storm.

Dash and I had been getting so much closer over the weeks, and it had been slowly starting to feel like more than just friendship. I loved spending time with Felix, but I *missed* Dash each morning after breakfast. I missed hearing his voice, his laugh. I missed seeing his wide smile whenever I said something he found amusing. Though we were apart for only a few hours each day, even that was starting to feel like too much. Saying goodbye outside my door after our evening walk back to my room was getting harder and harder. Every night I lay awake thinking about the instances when his fingers grazed mine, or his hand brushed my back in passing. I'd be lying to myself if I said I didn't think about being in his arms or what it would feel like to have his lips on mine.

When I came down for lunch the following day, all of us deciding to sleep through breakfast, there was a folded note next to my plate. I took a sip of tea as I surveyed the table, noticing there wasn't a setting for Dash and Felix. Would they not be joining me? Had they already eaten? I flipped open the parchment and read.

Once you've finished eating, meet us on the east side of the grounds. We'll be in the training ring.

-Dash

P.S. Tea does not count as lunch.

I rolled my eyes. Dash knew me well enough to know I would want to meet them as soon as possible, foregoing food altogether. Further down the paper was another scribbled line. The handwriting was sloppy, as if the author was trying to rush through it.

And hurry up. Kicking Dash's ass is boring.

-Fel

I could only make out the first three letters of Felix's name; the rest were just slants and dots. No doubt the result of Dash ripping the note away from him before he could finish. I laughed to myself as I pictured the encounter. I quickly drained my cup of tea, grabbed an apple from the table, and made my way over to the training ring.

The east side of the grounds wasn't somewhere we ventured often. This was mainly because it was a favored location for most of the palace residents, and the three of us enjoyed our privacy. Sure enough, as I rounded the corner, hundreds of people were in attendance. Some were lying in the grass, staring up at the passing clouds, some were reading in the shade of the giant oak trees along the edge of the grounds, and others were playing lawn games. I watched as they tossed their palm-sized heavy balls across the grass, hoping to make it the closest to the small white sphere on the other end. Felix had tried to teach me how to play once, but I was terrible, never making it anywhere close to my target. I swore off the game, stomping away and calling it a stupid waste of time. Felix had given me the name Pouty Pants for three days straight after that.

I strolled past the players, and as I reached the outskirts of the training ring, I spotted a large gathering of people. Close to a hundred of them were seated in the grass. Women had their backs arched, so their chests were on full display, and all of their stares were transfixed on the middle of the ring. I followed their gaze and immediately knew why. Dash and Felix were sparring.

Without their shirts on.

I swallowed hard as I took in their perfectly sculpted bodies, sweat gleaming and dripping off them. I watched them lunge and parry. Strike and evade. Each movement caused their hard muscles to flex beneath their skin, making my heart race and heat flood to my cheeks. They looked strong. Perfect. God-like. Felix and Dash clashed their swords, and the vibrating sound of steel on steel roared in the space. They pushed back from each other, laughing as they began to circle the ring. Eyes locked on one another. Dash's back was facing me as he passed, and I noticed for the first time that he had a tattoo. One that covered nearly his entire back, creeping over the side of his shoulders. Before I could determine what it was, he twisted again, walking sideways and pointing his sword at Felix.

"Are we sparring or dancing?" he asked sarcastically.

Felix shrugged. "I'm better at both, so it's up to you." He was in front of me now with his back turned, and I saw that he, too, had a tattoo, though smaller than Dash's. Felix's was much easier to make out. Along his spine was one straight arrow pointing up, with another arrow twisting around it like a vine as it pointed in the opposite direction. It was simple but beautiful, and I wanted to know its meaning. I pushed myself through the crowd, stepping over the heaps of onlookers huddled on the ground. No one bothered to move out of my way, but they all managed to throw dirty looks and loud annoyed sighs as I passed.

"At this rate, I think the two of you are terrible at both," I told them once I finally reached the edge of the ring, my hands planted firmly on my hips as I spoke. Dash's eyes found me instantly. It was as if the sound of my voice had called to him, pulling his attention from the task at hand.

"Good morning, pumpkin," Felix said without looking at me. He lunged for Dash, taking advantage of the distraction, but Dash was quick. He deflected and clicked his tongue, scolding Felix for the lousy sportsmanship. Felix laughed and shrugged as if to say *you can't blame me for trying.*

The two continued their sparring, eliciting cheers and applause from the crowd swooning over them. They were fighting with actual swords, and though I knew they weren't in any real danger, I didn't like the idea of one of them getting hurt. Dash charged, but Felix was too fast, avoiding the strike, causing Dash to slash at the air and skid to a halt to my right. The two best friends let out a fit of laughter, and my heart warmed at seeing them like this.

"A wonderful attempt, Your Highness," a seductive voice yelled above the soft clapping from the crowd. I rolled my eyes, not having to look to know the voice belonged to Rosella. Dash straightened and walked the few feet to me, leaning down and placing a kiss on my forehead, my skin searing beneath the feel of his lips.

"Good morning," he said, his blue eyes full of joy.

"Good afternoon," I corrected with a smile. "Why don't you two come down here more often? You seem to enjoy this." Dash smiled, and Felix laughed from across the ring.

"We spar every morning at dawn while your lazy ass is asleep," Felix yelled, tossing the hilt of his sword back and forth between his hands. "It's our ritual, and you are currently interrupting my certain victory over Dash." I rolled my eyes at Felix's dramatics, and Dash ignored him entirely as he spoke.

"How'd you sleep?" he asked, wiping the beading sweat from his forehead with the back of his hand and causing his wet hair to fall forward. I reached up, brushing it out of his face.

"I slept alright. You?" An annoyed and exasperated sound came from across the ring as Felix became more restless. Dash shook his head at me as if to apologize for our best friend's temper tantrum. "Will you teach me?" I asked, changing the subject. Dash straightened just slightly, the move barely noticeable, and I was vaguely aware of hushed whispers and soft gasps of surprise coming from the women in the grass.

"Can't," Dash said, backing away, his face becoming serious. "You know the rules." He turned and faced Felix, going back to their fight.

The stupid rules. Women weren't allowed to fight. We weren't allowed to have an edge over any man. We weren't allowed to be strong and capable on our own. We were put in this world for the sole purpose of existing quietly and providing means to make men stronger. My chest heaved with anger as I felt my blood begin to heat, the dormant fire within roaring to life once more.

"Sorry, pumpkin. There's nothing we can do," Felix said, not sounding sorry in the least bit. I was well aware of the rules, but I had hoped that Dash and Felix wouldn't care about them. Apparently, I was wrong. Out of the corner of my eye, I could see Rosella with a sinister smile on her face, clearly basking in the exchange she had just witnessed, as the rest of the crowd giggled under their breath at my misfortune. I wanted to go back inside the palace and get as far away from these people as I could. I wanted to get away from Dash and Felix. I was pissed at their refusal to teach me how to fight, despite it being against the rules. Before I could move, Felix's voice boomed across the ring.

"Solstice?" he asked.

"Absolutely not," Dash replied.

"But it's my turn, and you don't need it anymore," Felix whined as he lunged at Dash, their swords clashing loudly. What the Hell were they talking about?

"We have somewhere to be," he replied, pushing away from Felix.

"And Solstice will help with that. Think about it." Dash bobbed his head back and forth as if contemplating Felix's request. Finally, he nodded.

"Fine, but make it fast, and it stays *here*," Dash commanded, pointing his sword at the ground as if instructing him not to leave the safety of the ring. Felix sighed but agreed to the terms, and they began their fight again, but something had changed. They were relentless with their attacks, each thrust of their swords coming faster and faster. They were out of breath but didn't stop. They kept lunging and striking, barely evading the blades' sharp edges, until....

"Ahh, *fuck*!" Felix bellowed. He dropped his sword and fell to his knees as his hands pressed into his side, dark red blood spilling through his fingers.

"It's just a scratch," Dash replied like he was annoyed at Felix's pain. I made to rush to Felix, but Dash grabbed my wrist, halting my advance. "He's fine." He did not look fine. A hoard of concerned spectators ran for Felix, kneeling before him as they fussed over his injury.

"It hurts, but I think I'll be okay," he told them dramatically, not bothering to stand or push the worrying people away from him. He grunted in pain as he tried to move. They shushed him and stroked his hair as they pressed a cloth to his cut, soaking up the leaking blood.

He was enjoying this.

"Come with me," Dash said quietly as his hand grazed mine. I pulled away from his touch, still angry with him.

"I don't want to," I protested. Dash stepped in front of me and bent down to meet my eyes. "I'm mad at you." Dash clamped down on his lips to keep from smiling, and it only added kindling to the fire. I turned on my heel to stomp away, but Dash was in front of me once again, stopping my advance. Gods, he was so quick.

"I know," he said, his lips twitching in the corner. He found my pain and frustration amusing, and I wanted to punch him for it. Punch him hard in his gorgeous smug face. He stepped closer, reaching for my hand and interlacing our fingers. I didn't stop him this time. All thoughts vanished from my mind at his touch. "Trust me," he pleaded. I swiveled my head to find Felix lying on the ground, his head resting firmly in a random woman's lap as someone else held his hand tightly. I rolled my eyes at the sight before focusing back on Dash.

"Fine," I told him flatly, the annoyance I still felt evident in my voice. Dash leaned forward, pressing his lips to my cheek, and I felt my body melt against the feel of his kiss.

"Good," he said as he pulled away. "We have to hurry." There was mischief in his words and eyes as he tugged me to the far edge of the ring and grabbed a large leather satchel sitting in the dirt. He reached into the pack and pulled out a white shirt, throwing it over his head and pushing back the sleeves to reveal his toned forearms. He looked around the space, ensuring no one was watching us too closely, and ran into the woods, pulling me behind him.

"Where are we going?" I asked once we were safely under cover of the trees, the songbirds chirping loudly overheard.

"To the lake. This is a shortcut."

The entire walk to the lake, Dash didn't address me, and I was grateful. I was still angry with him and knew that if he tried to talk to me, I would most likely snap, ruining our day. That was probably the reason for his silence. He knew me well.

Once we stepped into the meadow, Dash dropped the satchel and stretched his arms high above his head, rolling his neck. He turned to face me and crossed his arms over his chest, a crooked smile forming on his lips. I planted my feet into the soft grass and mimicked his stance, bringing my arms tightly over my chest. He raised a single brow in response and took a deep breath. He was waiting—letting me know he wasn't going to make the first move. If I wanted to be mad and silent, he'd let me. It was true that I was mad, but my desire to talk to him was starting to outweigh my anger. I paced back and forth as the war within me raged, and I watched with bated breath as my fury and desire fought against each other. Each emotion, wanting to be the victor. Eventually, my need for him was triumphant.

"What's Solstice?" I asked, breaking the deafening silence between us.

"It's a holiday—"

"I know it's a holiday, Dash," I interrupted, and he tilted his head at my outburst. "Sorry. Continue."

"It's a holiday and a codeword," he explained. "We held a large Solstice celebration one year, and many visitors from other kingdoms were staying here at the palace. Felix and I were about sixteen years old and sparring in the training ring, trying to impress the guests who had been watching." I rolled my eyes, and Dash grinned. "We weren't as experienced with swordplay as we are now, so we were sloppy and careless. Felix had lunged, but I was too slow, and his blade sliced along my side. The cut was superficial and barely drew blood, but our onlookers rushed for me. They coddled and cooed as they tended my wound, and Felix and I basked in their attention. I pretended it hurt worse than it did, and Felix acted guilt-stricken so the strangers would soothe him." I shook my head at his story, disappointment flashing over my features. "So throughout the years, we implemented 'Solstice' whenever we wanted to be fawned over, trading off who would have to be the one to get hurt."

"You two are pathetic," I quipped.

"We were young and liked the attention," Dash countered.

"And when was the last time you used the codeword?" Dash opened his mouth to speak, but I interjected. "Before today." He closed his mouth and narrowed his eyes as if I had just prevented him from giving the response he wanted.

"I don't remember," he lied. I uncrossed my arms and walked toward him, stopping just a foot away as I looked into his eyes.

"Yes, you do," I told him, and his throat bobbed. "Felix said it was his turn, meaning it was last used for your advantage. When?"

"I don't want to answer that." He was being stubborn, so I closed the distance between us. Dash uncrossed his arms and reached for my hands, his fingers intertwining with mine as he held them at his side. The heat from his body radiated off of him, and I breathed in his scent, mixed with sweat. I wanted to push my body against him and wrap myself in him.

"I don't care," I replied, closing my eyes as he leaned down and rested his forehead against mine. "I want to know." Dash sighed in defeat, knowing I wasn't going to give up.

"The day before you arrived," he said quietly, the heat from his breath tickling my skin and smelling of mint. Irrational anger and jealousy spread through me like wildfire at his confession. The thought of someone holding him, touching his bare skin, and caressing him... I swallowed the lump of emotion that caught in my throat and stepped back, releasing his hands. I had no right to be upset with Dash, and I wasn't, but I hated the thought of him being with anyone else. I didn't like feeling this way.

"Ainsley—" Dash started.

"What's in the satchel?" I asked, wanting desperately to change the subject. Dash knitted his brows together as he looked at me, his features falling slightly. He nodded to himself as if accepting that I didn't want to discuss the matter further. He walked over to the bag and pulled out three wooden objects, tossing one at my feet. I bent down to pick it up.

"What? But you said...." I trailed off as I inspected the wooden sword in my hands.

"You didn't very well think that we gave a shit about the rules," Felix said, announcing his arrival as he pushed through the tree line, now fully clothed. "Of course we were going to teach you, pumpkin," he explained as Dash lobbed the third sword over to him.

"We were always planning on it. That's part of the reason why we wanted you to meet us in the training ring. We wanted to share that part of us with you," Dash added. I closed my eyes as I hung my head, exhaling through my nose. Of course, they were going to show me. Dash's scent wrapped around me as soft fingers slid beneath my chin, tilting my face up. "I'm sorry we had to lie to you about it. Because it's against the rules, we couldn't afford to answer truthfully in front of witnesses."

"I'm sorry I was an ass and didn't give you the benefit of the doubt," I confessed.

"You can make it up to me by holding your sword properly," he said, rearranging my hands, so I was grasping the hilt instead of the blade. "Now, widen your stance and bend your knees a little." I obliged. "You'll want to stay on the balls of your feet for balance and better mobility." I bounced up and down, getting used to the stance. "Good." Dash came behind me then, wrapping his strong arms around me and placing his hands over mine. Together, our fingers curled over the hilt as he leaned close and instructed me on fundamental movements. Felix came over and stood in front of me with his sword, acting as my attacker as Dash showed me different ways to evade and parry his assaults.

After about an hour of swordplay, we dropped our weapons, and the two instructed me on how to throw a punch and defend myself from an attack.

"How do you do this every day?" I asked breathlessly as I rested my hands on my knees, sweat rolling off my face and falling into the green grass of the meadow. My legs shook from exhaustion, and I felt like I was going to collapse onto the ground at any second. Dash had disappeared about half an hour ago, leaving me to train with Felix.

"Not everyone can be as incredibly fit as me," Felix said, winking. He removed his shirt once we switched from swords to fists, and I marveled at his tattoo.

"What does it mean?" I asked, pointing to his back.

"It's the symbol of an Empathi." Felix turned so I could see it clearly. "The straight arrow represents a person, and the twisted arrow represents our ability to weave through their emotions. Once a person receives their Gift, they tattoo a symbol for it somewhere on their body to commemorate." Dash appeared just then and made his way over to us.

"Ready for your celebration?" he asked, taking my hand in his as he led us across the meadow.

"This wasn't it?"

"Nope," Dash said as we pushed through a thicket of trees that opened to a small clearing. "That is." He pointed to the hill before us, and my mouth dropped open in shock.

23.

From the top of the mound, down to the base, ran a long trail of shimmering ice. The path was no more than a few feet wide and curved up at the bottom, creating what looked to be a ramp. I sprinted for the slide, curiosity outweighing my exhaustion, and ran my hand over the frozen water once I reached it. The ice was frigid and solid despite being the middle of summer. Even the heat from the brightest star in the sky was no match for Dash's magic.

"This is incredible," I said as soon as I felt Dash's presence behind me.

"I'm glad you like it," he replied as he pressed his hand into my lower back to guide me up the hill. My breathing hitched as I sank into his touch, and I wasn't sure I'd ever get used to the feeling of his hands on me. I wasn't sure I ever wanted to. I heard the shudder of his breathing as he slid his hand across my back to wrap around my waist, his grip firm but gentle as we walked. Once we reached the top of the hill, I surveyed the slide. The path to the bottom seemed so much longer and higher from up here, and I felt my heart leap into my throat.

"What happens once we reach the bottom?" I asked frantically, realizing there was nothing there to slow or stop our descent before the lake.

"Guess you'll have to find out," Felix said as he wrapped his arms around me and threw us onto the slide.

"*Felix*!" I yelled as we plunged down the slope together, the slickness of the ice causing us to travel faster and faster as we raced toward the bottom. Panic roared in my ears as the ramp grew closer by the second. Felix laughed from behind but squeezed me tighter against him as a reminder that I was safe. My heart stopped altogether as we hit the ramp, the angle propelling us high into the air. With a deep breath, I quickly filled my lungs and then expelled all the air from within, screaming as Felix and I flipped and twisted in our free fall. Somehow, it had felt like both a whole lifetime and only a second had passed when we finally were submerged in the lake below. The water was calm and warm as we plunged into it, and I kicked and swam hard for the surface, breaching it just in time to watch Dash launch from the ramp. He twisted and dove into the water effortlessly, the movement and form like a rehearsed dance.

"What did you think?" Felix asked, his body swaying with the gentle waves as he trod water.

"I think I want to kill you."

"That much I know, but what did you think of the slide?" he said with a laugh. I looked toward Dash's creation, the surface glittering in the sun's light.

"Once I got over the fear of dying, it was fun," I admitted as my chin dipped below the surface. My arms and legs were aching from our sparring lesson earlier, and it was a struggle to keep my head above water. An arm wrapped around my stomach, and I was pressed into a firm chest.

"Take a break. You're exhausted," Dash said as he held me. My heart hammered at his closeness, at the intimacy of his touch. "Relax your body. I won't let you drown." I halted my limbs at his words, instantly feeling the relief of rest. I leaned my head back against him and focused on my breathing as I tried to muster up my strength. "We can go down again when you're ready, but take your time. You exerted a lot of energy today." His voice was soothing, and I noticed the water surrounding us had become so calm that the surface looked as smooth as glass, not a ripple to be found. I marveled at the use of his magic; at the current I felt coursing beneath us, keeping us afloat without Dash having to so much as move. I looked over to find Felix had made his way to shore and was now lying in the grass as he waited for us.

"How are you doing all of this?" I asked as the rush of water under us tickled my feet.

"Magic."

"Okay, smartass," I rolled my eyes, and Dash spun me around to face him, guiding my arms to brace his shoulders for support. "But seriously, how? It's summer, and there is a massive slide of solid ice that doesn't seem to be melting, and I am also quite literally standing on water right now."

During my time here, I witnessed only subtle hints of magic from the residents. Ice spidering across a cup to keep a drink cold, or a snap of someone's fingers to light a candle in the library as the sun dipped below the mountains. Occasionally, a faint shimmer of a silencing shield would catch my eye, and I'd find two people having an intimate conversation. Not one display had come close to the amount of magic and control Dash was garnering here and now.

"I possess a lot of magic," he explained simply. "And I've spent years learning how to wield it properly."

"Is it difficult?"

"Not anymore, but it was when I wasn't fully trained. I struggled for a while with maintaining control while expelling it and understanding my limits."

"Limits? Like what you can do?" I asked.

"Like how far I can push myself. There is a threshold everyone has when it comes to their power level. It's what we call a Baseline. If you use too much of your magic and dip below your Baseline, you risk your magic not replenishing itself." Dash explained.

"So you could lose your Gift if you use it too much?"

"If you use too much of it at one time, yes. It's quite rare, but it has happened before. Your Baseline is one of the first things you will learn how to discover when your magic manifests."

"And are you close to that threshold now?" I questioned, concerned he was pushing his limits for me.

"Not even a little bit," he replied, and a smug grin formed on his face. "But when we're finished here, I'll refrain from using magic for the rest of the day to allow mine to replenish fully." I nodded, happy he would be taking it easy later on. My gaze wandered to my present once more, and I sighed. "What is it?" Dash asked.

"I feel like saying 'thank you' isn't enough," I confessed, tilting my head to look up at him. His brows were furrowed as he met my eyes, and confusion washed over his features. "The two of you have done so much for me, and I haven't given anything in return."

"But you have, Ainsley," he said at once, his voice pleading and urgent. "Every day, you give more and more of yourself. You've given us your friendship and trust, and that means everything to Felix and me. Like I told you before, you're one of us now. You're part of our family, and we would do anything for you." My eyes burned, and my vision clouded with tears. I had never had a real family. I had never had people who loved and cherished me like Dash and Felix. The overwhelming emotions of gratitude and adoration surged to the surface, causing the tears to overflow. Dash wiped them away with the featherlight touch of his knuckles.

"I feel like I don't deserve you two."

"Yes, you do," he replied, pulling me against his muscled chest and kissing the top of my wet hair. We stayed like that until Felix groaned loudly from his place on the shore.

"Are you done yet? I want to go on the slide!" he whined, and Dash let out an annoyed sigh at his friend's interruption. I shook my head and laughed under my breath.

"Come on," I said, pushing back from Dash.

"Are you sure you want to go down again?"

"Only if I get to go with you this time. Felix enjoyed my terror far too much." Dash smiled widely, and genuine joy swirled in his eyes.

"Deal."

We traveled down the slide a handful of times before the three of us decided that we were too exhausted to continue making the trek up the hill. Instead, we returned to the meadow and sprawled onto the grass, letting the sun dry our damp clothes as we basked in its warmth in comforting silence. Eventually, the sounds of Felix's soft snoring filled the space. I twisted to see if Dash had also fallen asleep but found him watching me. I rolled onto my side to face him, and he did the same.

"What is your tattoo of?" I whispered, not wanting to wake Felix. Without a word, Dash sat up, pulled his shirt over his head, and turned his back to me. I pushed off my side and onto my knees as I scooted closer to inspect the art. His tattoo was exquisite and beautifully designed, the dark black ink stark against his golden skin. Between his shoulder blades, no bigger than the palm of my hand was an intricate design of a sun. Within the sphere were several delicate whorls that I imagined were a depiction of the wind. Around the circle were straight lines that showcased the rays of the sun. This must be the tattoo that represented his Gift as an Aerian. The rest of his back was filled with a sprawling design that I knew illustrated water. The pattern spread out in all directions, forming a small curve of a wave at the end of each swirling line. I brought my fingers to his skin, and Dash shivered as I traced the lines of his tattoo.

"This is beautiful, Dash," I told him as I reached the end of one of the swirls that peeked over his shoulder. I glided my finger back down, and his hard muscles flexed beneath my touch. His breathing hitched as I reached the side of his ribs, where another wave ended, and he grabbed my hand, twisting to face me. He held my gaze for a moment, uncertainty flashing in his eyes as if he were debating some thought in his mind.

"Thank you," he said as he released my hand and pulled his shirt on. I watched as he laid back down and looked up at the sky. I suddenly felt confused and self-conscious. Had I overstepped? Had I crossed a line by trailing my fingers along him like that? Dash was usually the first to initiate touch between us. He constantly interlaced our fingers or placed his hand along my back. And he always chose to remain close, opting to sit next to me or stand by my side. But had I misread those signs? The same could also be said for Felix. Most days, I could be found curled up against him in the library or with his arm around my shoulders as we strolled through the palace, and I knew that Felix didn't have feelings that were more than friendship for me. Why did I think it would be any different when it came to Dash? For a while now, my feelings for him had been growing, evolving from hatred to interest to friendship to... Something more. I knew what I now felt for him, but it was presumptuous and wrong of me to assume that he reciprocated those feelings. We had never talked about it.

I laid back down on my side, tucking an arm under my head to act as a pillow as I picked at the soft blades of grass with my free hand. Closing my eyes, I took a deep breath and then let it out slowly in a long, quiet sigh. I wanted the insecurities I felt to expel from my body and drift along with the wind. Fingers curled around mine, and I opened my eyes to find Dash watching me.

"Are you okay?" he whispered.

"Yes," I told him as I gracefully pulled away from his touch, squeezing my hand into a fist, and bringing it against my chest. I wanted to sink into myself. To curl into the tightest ball possible. To protect myself from rejection. I didn't want things to be uncomfortable or awkward with Dash, and they wouldn't be. I just needed a little bit of time to come to terms with the fact that he might want to be strictly friends and nothing more. I could do that, but I needed a moment. "I'm just tired," I added, hoping it would be enough of an explanation for my distance from him. I kept my eyes closed and eventually fell asleep.

When I woke, Dash and Felix were up and packing the wooden swords back into the satchel, whispering to each other across the meadow. I sat up, stretching my arms above my head, my pale green dress now completely dry. I stood and walked over to them though something in the air between us felt off.

"Ready to head back?" Felix asked, throwing his arms around my waist and squeezing tightly as he lifted me off the ground. I squealed and squirmed against him until he lowered me back onto my feet.

"Was that necessary?" I said as I hugged him back.

"Absolutely. Happy birthday." He kissed my cheek and draped his arm over my shoulder as we walked. Dash hadn't waited for us, already halfway across the meadow. He hadn't so much as looked at me since I had woken up, and I began to fear that I had made him uncomfortable when inspecting the tattoo. We were almost to the palace when Felix asked, "What happened?" He jerked his chin toward Dash, now breaking through the trees that opened to the garden grounds.

"I'm not sure. Aren't you his best friend? Shouldn't you have some sort of idea?"

"Why do you think I'm asking you?" he countered, insinuating correctly. I seemed to be the cause of his sudden change in mood.

"I think I crossed a line I shouldn't have," I confessed. "It was unintentional, of course, but he seems upset about it." Felix raised a brow, and his amber eyes begged for an elaboration. "He showed me his back, and I outlined his tattoo with my finger. I didn't think anything of it, but he grabbed my hand to stop me and pulled away, clearly uncomfortable."

"I don't think that was the case," he said, his brows knitting together as he stared into the distance. Voices from the palace residents medlied together as we reached the lawn. I followed Felix's line of sight to find Dash stopped before a small group of ladies, Rosella on his right. Once again, that irrational anger and jealousy bubbled to the surface.

"Well then, maybe you should ask her. You'd probably have a better chance of finding out that way," I mumbled, the words clipped and annoyed.

"Ainsley—" Felix began.

"Lord Felix," someone interrupted. "A quick word, please." Felix bent down and kissed my cheek before striding over to the person that beckoned him. I stood there watching the group giggle and bat their lashes as Dash charmed them with his gorgeous smile. Rosella clutched his arm tightly as she let out a sound of seductive laughter, her body pushed against him and her breasts heaving with the movements. My heart sank, and as if Dash could feel it, he twisted his head to find me watching. I quickly averted my gaze and hurried across the lawn toward the palace entrance. A moment later, Dash caught up with me.

"Where are you going?" he asked as if he hadn't ignored me for the past hour.

"To the library," I gritted out.

"Okay. I'll come with you," he said, causing me to stop my advance and whirl around to face him.

"No, Dash. It's fine." Surprise flooded his face. "You're busy with other things," I told him, and my gaze automatically drifted to the circle of women now watching us with piqued interest. Dash followed my stare before turning his attention back to me. "As I told you that night on the balcony, you're free to fuck whoever you want." The words tasted like poison as they left my mouth, and Dash flinched as I spat them. His eyes were wide with shock, as if he hadn't expected me to act this way. To be honest, neither had I. "You don't need to halt your plans to babysit me. I'll meet up with you and Felix later." Dash's chest rose and fell quicker and quicker as we stood there, staring at one another. The anger raging through him was evident in his face, and I felt my heart crack. I couldn't look at him any longer. I turned to go inside the palace but only made it a few steps before Dash's hand was on my wrist, spinning me around to look at him. Gone was the anger, replaced by hurt and devastation.

"What is going on?" he demanded, as his blue eyes searched my face for any clue as to what led to this.

"I was just reminding you that you're free to—"

"No," he ground out. "Don't give me that bullshit, Ainsley. You and I... We're past that, and you know it." Movement caught in the corner of my eye, and I didn't have to break Dash's stare to know who it was.

"Are we?" I said coldly as a delicate ivory hand curved up and over Dash's shoulder.

"Your Highness," Rosella started, but Dash cut her off as his eyes stayed locked on mine.

"Not now."

"Of course," she replied sweetly, "I just wanted to confirm our plans this evening. It's been too long since we've last been alone together." My chest heaved quicker at each word she uttered. "The last time was weeks ago when I cared for you after your injury in the training ring. We have a lot of time to make up for, and I have a few ideas on how we can." He clenched his jaw at her words. Fucking *Solstice*. Of course, it was Rosella that he let come to his aid the day before I arrived. I laughed without humor as I shook my head at Dash.

"Of course," I whispered under my breath, but I knew Dash had heard it. The pain of heartbreak flooded through me, and I felt the tears prick in my eyes. I wanted to find comfort in the fact that she admitted they hadn't been together since I had arrived at the palace, but the only words that plagued my mind were her checking to *make sure* they would be together tonight. Had he extended the invitation when they had spoken moments ago?

"Get the fuck away from me right now, Rosella," he growled, taking a step towards me.

"My apologies, Your Highness. My lady," she added, and I heard the smile in her voice as she walked away, satisfied with what had transpired. Dash brought a hand up to cup my cheek, but I turned away, breaking his stare. He took another step, closing the distance between us. His index finger and thumb gripped my chin as he directed my face back to his. I swallowed, begging the tears to retreat as my chest ached.

"There is only one person that I'm pursuing," he said, and his eyes poured into mine, drowning me again and again. "There is only one person that I want and—"

A blood-curdling scream erupted from within the palace.

24.

Dash, Felix, and I sprinted through the halls, trying to locate the source of the terror. A woman screamed over and over again, horror and fear in her voice. We rounded a corner on the third floor to discover a small group of residents standing in a circle, their focus on the ground in front of them. The person screaming had her back against the stone wall as two people tried desperately to soothe her, but to no avail. Dash and Felix pushed through the crowd, and I followed close behind. Dash reached the edge first as I struggled to get past several large men standing in my way.

"Find and alert my father immediately," Dash commanded, urgency in his voice. He spun when I reached him and blocked my view, trying to shield me from whatever was in the center of the circle. "Ainsley, no. Don't look." I ducked below his arm, dodging him as I shoved my way to the edge to see what had happened.

My hands clasped over my mouth, and my knees began to buckle as nausea rushed through me. In the center of the circle lay a body twisted and deformed. The skin of the deceased man was pale gray and stretched taut over his bones as if he had been starved for a lifetime. The corpse's hands were held up into the air as if trying to shield themself from the attack, his fingers curved and twisted at unnatural angles. His legs were bent at the knees but in the wrong direction like he had been brutally tortured. The worst was his face. His skin was wrinkled and stretched so thin it was as if he could tear as easily as parchment. His cheeks were sunken, and his lips were cracked and bloody. His mouth was stuck open as if he had died screaming. And his eyes.... His eyes were rolled into the back of his head, showing primarily white except for a tiny sliver of the irises. One brown and one seafoam green.

Pecus.

A hand grabbed my arm below the shoulder and began pulling me through the crowd. I twisted to see that it was a guard that held me, most likely an order given by his prince. Once we squeezed through the last of the onlookers, I found Dash and Felix standing next to the servant that had once been screaming. Felix clutched her hands, using his Gift to calm her as she whispered to Dash. I had almost reached them when another guard appeared from down the hall and leaned close to speak to his prince.

"Another body has been found, Your Highness. A maiden, right outside Lady Ainsley's chamber door." Panic crashed through me like a tidal wave. Imogen. I pulled out of the guard's grasp and raced through the corridor. Dash yelled my name, but it was muffled by the roaring in my ears. It couldn't be Imogen. My heart pounded faster and faster with each stride of my legs. I couldn't breathe—couldn't think. I just had to get to my room. I had to make sure Imogen hadn't suffered the same fate as Pecus. I turned down the hallway where I resided and stumbled to a stop as I saw two guards kneeling beside the maiden on the floor. I couldn't see her face from this distance. I could only make out her emerald dress and crisp white apron, her long black hair sprawled across the ground.

Time slowed, and I felt like I was suspended in air as my legs moved on their own, taking me to the body. I held my breath, and once I reached her, I crumpled to my knees, wailing as I wrapped my arms around myself. I was a shattered vase trying to keep the pieces together. All at once, I was being scooped up and pressed against Dash's warm chest as he carried me away from the corpse.

"It's not her," I said, sobbing into his shirt as relief and shame washed over me. Relief that Imogen had been spared and shame that though Josephine had died, I found solace in knowing it hadn't been Imogen who had suffered.

"I know," Dash said as his lips pressed into my hair. "I'm sorry you had to see that." His voice trembled, and his hold on me grew tighter.

"What happened to them?" I asked, pulling back from his chest to meet his eyes. Dash shook his head slowly. Not because he didn't know the truth but because it wasn't safe to talk about it here. I remained silent as he carried me into the War Room, Felix already there and waiting. Dash set me on my feet once inside and shut the door behind us.

"Your father is on his way. He's speaking with Tristia first." Felix must have read the confusion on my face. "The woman that discovered the first body," he explained as he walked over, bringing me into his embrace the second he reached me. I inhaled deeply, comforted in his leather and spice scent that always felt like home.

"Can you both please explain what the fuck is going on?" I said, my voice breaking on the words.

"They were murdered," Felix said. That much I figured out on my own. "And..."

"And..." I replied when he didn't continue.

"And it looks like it was Tenebrae," Dash finished.

"How can you possibly tell that? Did Tristia see the assailant?" I questioned.

"You already know one of Tenebrae's Gifts is the ability to cast illusions." I thought back to my nightmare and how real it seemed. The night I met Pecus. "Another Gift is fear-inducing magic. They can create such terror within someone's mind that their bodies wither and their organs shut down, killing even an immortal." I felt like I was going to be sick.

"And they attacked outside of your bedroom," a cold voice called from the door. King Perceval. He held a folded piece of parchment in his hands as he made his way over to the three of us. "Correspondence that came this afternoon." He dropped the note onto the large marble table that was a model of Caelum. He paced the room as Dash picked up the paper and read.

"Tenebrae attacked Ministro?" Dash said as he skimmed the letter. The king nodded, looking visibly angry as he raked his hands through his brown hair so that it fell over his forehead and into his eyes.

"They found three bodies last night, exactly as ours appeared today. The king's daughter was taken but, by the grace of the Gods, was found before the kidnappers made it over the border with her," Dash's father explained.

"Is Cordelia okay?" Felix asked worriedly. I had forgotten that he had lived in the palace of Ministro for the first ten years of his life. Was he close with her? He nodded, and Felix sighed in relief. The king stopped and rested his hands flat on the table as his chest heaved with fury.

"Father," Dash said, taking a tentative step towards him. The king reached his hand out, grabbing a glass goblet full of dark amber liquor. He brought it to his lips, draining the contents before throwing the cup across the room. The glass shattered loudly as it hit the stone wall and shards dispersed in every direction like snowflakes during a blizzard. I jumped back at the sound, and Felix shoved me behind him.

"After I received that letter, I sent guards to retrieve you two," he said coldly, and I knew he was referring to Dash and me. "But they said you had slipped away after a sparring session in the training ring." His hands settled back onto the table, and his fingers gripped the edge so hard that the whites of his knuckles showed. "Dashiell, I was so angry with you for leaving without a guard." He took a deep breath before facing his son. "But more than that, I was terrified that I was about to lose you." I looked at Dash. His eyes were wide, and his face softened as if he didn't think his father had cared for him before now. The king laughed under his breath. "You defying my rules is what kept you from this horror. Had you been here just an hour earlier, it could have been you." He turned to face Felix and me, taking a step in our direction. "It could have been all three of you. Dashiell, I've never been so grateful for your disobedience." He wiped his eyes and cleared his throat before turning away.

"We're all okay, father," Dash said, and the king nodded, his back still turned as he worked on composing himself. After a few minutes, King Perceval finally spoke again.

"The day after Ainsley's birthday celebration, I'm journeying to Ministro to discuss what actions to take against Tenebrae." He turned around to face us, and gone was the emotion he had displayed a moment prior. There was nothing but the face of a cold king defending his land and his people. "While I'm away, Caelum is yours to rule Dashiell. You know the day-to-day basics, but should any problems arise, I trust your judgment." Dash bowed his head to his father. "Remain within the palace walls at night, and the three of you do not leave the grounds under any circumstances." He pivoted to face Felix and me. "As the sovereign in my stead, Dashiell will have guards with him at all times, but I will also be assigning two to each of you. That is not up for discussion. Is that understood?"

"Yes, your Majesty," Felix and I replied as we dipped our heads.

"Good." King Perceval exhaled and walked over to the exit. "Keep her safe, Dashiell," he instructed before retreating from the room, though I didn't know if he was referring to Caelum or me. Felix let out a low whistle, and I stepped out from behind him.

"Well, that was intense," he said. "Thank the fucking Gods about Cordelia."

"I know," Dash replied as he came over to us. "She must have been scared shitless."

"You know her too?" I asked, and Dash nodded, a smile forming on his face.

"Cordelia was head over heels in love with Felix when we were kids," he explained. "She always got mad when I visited because he would rather play with me than with her. Even when we got older, and she would come to visit Caelum with her father, she always hated that Felix and I were inseparable."

"Cordelia is a sweetheart but not used to being told 'no.' She's used to getting what she wants when she wants it. And, of course she'd want this," Felix said, gesturing a hand over his body. I rolled my eyes at his arrogance.

"So what does this mean? It was truly Tenebrae that sent the illusion that almost killed me?" Dash exhaled through his nose and nodded his head, his face somber. My blood went cold at the news. "So they know I'm alive," I said into the silence.

"I don't think they do," Felix chimed in, his fingers caressing his chin as if deep in thought. "They attacked Cordelia too. She is the Princess of Ministro, and you will be the Princess of Caelum. Their attacks seemed targeted based on power and proximity to the Crown. I believe they tried to get to you based on who you will be, not who you truly are." Dash bobbed his head as he processed Felix's theory.

"I think Felix is right," Dash finally said. "I don't think they know of your history—just your future with Caelum and me. And now that we know they aren't just after you, we'll have a better chance at convincing the other kingdoms to come together and take them out." I shivered at his words, and Dash moved closer, rubbing his hands down my arms, willing warmth back into my body. "We'll keep you safe. I promise." He placed a kiss on my forehead. I felt comfort in his oath.

"So what now?" I asked, changing the subject. I wasn't sure what we were supposed to do anymore. Dash and Felix exchanged worried looks. "What is it?" Felix nodded his head at Dash. "Tell her," he instructed, and Dash exhaled loudly as he closed his eyes.

Tell me what? What was going on? Dash opened his eyes again and placed his hands on my waist, holding me steady as his face grew serious. Anxiety flowed to the surface, and my breathing began to get heavy as I waited for him to speak.

"We...." he began, but looked to Felix and shook his head, unable to continue. Felix placed a hand on his friend's shoulder and nodded, encouraging him to go on. I swallowed the bile that crept up my throat, terrified of what Dash was about to share with me. He turned his head, finding my eyes once more. He took a deep breath and nodded to himself as if he had accepted that he had to divulge this information, even if he didn't want to. My heart raced faster, and my hands began to tremble at my sides. "We... Get fucked up," Dash said, clamping his lips together to stop from smiling as Felix chuckled from behind him.

"I hate you both!" I yelled as I smacked the two of them in the chest repeatedly. My assault did absolutely nothing but cause them to laugh even harder.

"To the library!" Felix announced as he picked me up and threw me over his shoulder. I knew they were pretending they hadn't a care in the world for my benefit. I'd heard the worry thick in Felix's voice when he asked about Cordelia. I saw the look in Dash's eyes when he realized how terrified his father was. They were scared. All of them. Their display of nonchalance and immature fun was all an act to mask the fear they each held. Although I had more questions, I couldn't bear to bring up the feelings they were trying so hard to hide. If trying to keep me unafraid brought them comfort, I wouldn't be the one to take it away.

25.

We spent that night in the library, drinking away our worries and fears, comforted by knowing we were together—that as long as the three of us had each other, we would be okay. Sunlight stretched across my face, pulling me from my slumber. I opened my eyes to find that I had never made it back to my room last night. I lifted my head from where it had been resting across Dash's lap, the hand he had planted on my back shifting with the movement, and twisted to see Dash and Felix sound asleep from where they sat on the couch. Felix was snoring softly against Dash's shoulder, and Dash's cheek pressed into the top of Felix's head. They looked so peaceful and so young. I couldn't help but picture them as small boys, fast asleep in the library together after wreaking havoc upon the palace. They were brothers, not by blood, but by choice. I moved closer and curled into Dash, resting my head on his other shoulder. Fingers began to stroke along my back, and I looked up to see his sleepy, bright eyes shining down at me.

"Good morning," he whispered.

"Good morning," I replied. "I didn't mean to wake you."

"You didn't. Felix's snoring did." I laughed under my breath. "How are you feeling today?" I hadn't let myself think about the bodies that had been discovered yesterday or the fact that Tenebrae wanted me because of who I'd be to Dash. What if, despite their failed attempts to kidnap both Cordelia and me, they didn't stop? How far would they go? I could only hope that King Perceval's trip would result in a plan to stop the attacks before someone else got hurt.

"I'm worried," I admitted. "I don't want something to happen to either of you because of your proximity to me. What happened to Pecus and Josephine yesterday... It could have been you and Felix instead." Dash pulled me closer to him, and I fisted his shirt, needing to know that he was real. That he was okay.

"My priority is keeping you safe, Ainsley. I don't care about the risks to my health. I only care about ensuring no one harms you, and I know Felix feels the same." I found no comfort in his words. I didn't like the fact that they prioritized me over themselves. "I know it's not what you wanted to hear, but it's the truth, and I won't apologize for it." A gentle knock sounded at the door, ending our conversation. Dash rose to answer, causing Felix to jolt awake from his sudden absence.

"Your Highness," a guard said, standing over the threshold. "Your father would like to see you and Lord Felix immediately. I will escort Lady Ainsley to breakfast, where two guards are already stationed, waiting for her."

"We'll be out in just a moment," Dash responded, dismissing the guard to wait on the other side of the door. "Ready for the fun to begin, Felix? Today should only be a few hours."

"Can't wait," Felix said dully, stretching his arms over his head as he stood.

"What do you mean?" I asked.

"My father wants to meet with us to go over what is to be done in his stead. He wants to ensure I know what I'm doing as the ruler of Caelum. Felix is not only one of his trusted advisors, but he's also my number two," I looked to Felix to find him grinning proudly, "making him second in command over the kingdom. This lesson is for both of us."

"That sounds riveting," I responded sarcastically.

"You have no idea," Dash said flatly as he rolled his eyes, stepping closer and planting his hands on my waist. "But it does, unfortunately, mean that Felix and I will have to be in meetings for most of the day while my father is out of the kingdom." I groaned. I hated being away from them. "I'm sorry."

"Will I at least see you both at dinner during that time?" Dash smiled like he enjoyed my not wanting to be separated from him.

"We wouldn't miss it," he answered as he stepped away. Felix kissed my cheek before following his friend out of the room.

"Follow me, Lady Ainsley," the guard said, appearing again.

He took me down to the terrace where breakfast had been set and waiting as promised. I nibbled on pieces of fruit and opened the book I had snagged before departing the library. Soon my days would be spent reading as much as possible to fill the emptiness caused by being apart from my friends. I had finished my breakfast and was nearly halfway through my book when the guards on the terrace straightened, going still as statues. I turned to see what had brought about the change to find King Perceval striding toward me. I stood, bowing my head, as he stopped before me.

"May I?" he asked, pointing to the open seat on my right.

"Of course, your Majesty." He didn't wait for me to finish answering before he sat and gestured for me to do the same. I swallowed nervously, and the late morning sun beat down, causing sweat to bead on the back of my neck. The only solace I felt was that we weren't completely alone. Four guards were now stationed around the dining space, bearing witness to this conversation.

"Leave us," the king commanded.

Fuck.

I interlaced my fingers together, gripping tightly as I held them in my lap. What more could he possibly have to say to me? And why did he always feel the need to make sure I was alone? "How are you feeling, my dear?" he asked, though something in his voice made me feel like the question was more of a formality than one of genuine interest.

"I'm fine, your Majesty." He gave a pointed look, calling me out on the lie. "I'm scared," I corrected. He nodded, and his eyes grew thoughtful and endearing. An emotion I had never seen him display.

"I'm sorry about everything that has happened. I promised your father when he agreed to you marrying Dashiell that I would keep you safe. It's not easy to admit that I have failed him." He dragged his hand through his brown hair, looking uncomfortable. I wasn't sure what to say, so I said nothing. King Perceval waved his hand, and a tea kettle, along with two cups, appeared on the table. He poured the beverage into each of the mugs and handed me one. The aroma of peppermint and citrus wafted, steam snaking into the open air. He wrapped his hands around his cup, gripping harder than he should have. "I almost lost my son yesterday," he announced as if he had only just realized.

"I know," I told him softly. I didn't want to think about Dash suffering the same fate as Pecus. I blew on my drink before taking a sip, the beverage hot and soothing as it traveled down my throat. I winced at the flavor as I swallowed.

"Too strong?" he asked with a smile. I nodded shyly, not wanting to offend. He flicked his wrist, and a small bowl of sugar cubes appeared. He plopped two into my tea, adding a small stirring spoon as well. I dipped my head in gratitude, and he smiled warmly. "My late wife liked her tea weak too. With far too much sugar, I might add." A soft laugh under his breath. "It's hard missing her every day. But when I look at Dashiell, I'm reminded of her. Same eyes, same hair, same stubbornness." I laughed, enjoying hearing about how similar Dash and his mother were.

"Has he told you about her?" I shook my head. Telling the king about the few facts Dash *had* shared with me about his mother seemed like an invasion of privacy—a breach of trust we had built. King Perceval took a deep breath as he caressed the lip of his mug in slow circles. "It was torturous for me when she died. I had lost a part of myself, and I wasn't sure I would ever come back from that. In my grief, I did the one thing I regret most in my life: I rejected my son. I couldn't hear his voice or even look at him without seeing her, and it broke me. When it happened, he was only nine years old, and I pushed him away when he needed me the most. I don't blame him for resenting me." His voice caught in his throat.

"I don't think he does, your Majesty," I added, reassuring him. His emerald eyes found mine. They were cold and hard and glazed over like he was swallowing down an emotion that threatened to escape. "I think he knows that you care for him."

"I hope you're right, my dear. There are so many things I have to make up for with him. Ignored birthdays, sparring lessons, missed trips to the orchard...." He looked to the distance as if remembering everything he had missed out on when it came to his son.

"The orchard?" I hadn't discovered one during my walks through the grounds, and Dash and Felix had never mentioned such a place. The king's face lit up at the question, his eyes shining bright like the gemstone they resembled.

"Yes, the orchard. Dash hasn't spoken of it?" I shook my head, and the king's face fell with sadness. "I guess that makes sense. It was a place that his mother and I would take him to every weekend. It's a short walk through the line of trees on the south side of the estate," he explained, pointing his finger in the general direction. "Dash's mother once owned a bakery where I first met her." I thought back to the story Dash had shared with me weeks ago of his parents' meeting. "She loved to bake apple tarts, so I created an orchard for her when she came to the palace. Its magic keeps the fruit perfect year-round. We used to have picnics under the apple trees every weekend, watching Dashiell run through the trees, collecting the fruit that had fallen. It was his mother's favorite place in the world.

"After she passed, I still went every weekend, like we always had, but Dashiell refused to go. He refused ever to step foot there again. It breaks my heart to know that the place that had brought our family such peace and happiness was now the source of his turmoil. I'd like him to revisit the orchard. I still hold on to the hope that if he sees it, he'll be reminded of the beautiful memories that we created there. Maybe *those* memories will overpower the bad ones. I know his mother would want him to remember her happy and thriving. She wouldn't want him to be scared and hurt whenever he thought of her." I took another sip of my tea, the sugar now drowning the strong flavor of the peppermint. I wasn't sure how to respond to the king. I wasn't sure why he was confessing any of this to me. He seemed to realize this as well. "I'm sorry, my dear. I shouldn't have put my frustrations on you."

"It's okay, your Majesty."

"I think it's because you remind me so much of your father. He was a kind friend and always willing to lend an ear and give advice." I smiled as I thought of the type of person my father had been. It warmed my heart to know he was so admired and respected. I took a deep breath and looked into the king's eyes, wanting to offer him the same thing my father would have.

"Give him time," I told King Perceval. "I have gotten to know your son well throughout my stay here, and the one thing I have learned above all others is that Dash is loyal and caring. He is kind and loving. And he will come around when he's ready." He reached over and squeezed my hand, his skin rough and his touch cold. So different from that of his son.

"I hope you're right." He gave a weak smile. "And I hope you're with him when he finally decides to go. I hope he shares those beautiful memories with you." I broke his stare, glancing down at my half-empty teacup. "You're good for him, my dear. You bring out a side of Dashiell that I have never seen." I felt my cheeks heat at his words. I wasn't aware that he had been watching closely enough to notice a change in Dash—a change he was convinced I had brought about. "It's a side that I pray I get to keep seeing." He tightened his grip on my hand, forcing me to meet his gaze again. "I know Dashiell will keep you safe while I'm away, but I'm asking you, not as king, but as his father: please keep him safe. I lost my wife. I cannot lose my son too."

I wasn't strong or a skilled warrior, and I had no magic yet. There was nothing I could do to keep Dash safe that the palace guards weren't capable of doing themselves. My heart hurt knowing that I couldn't protect him—that I couldn't do the only thing the king asked of me. But rather than protest or tell him that I had nothing to offer, I nodded. He released his hold, patting my hand twice before pulling away and turning his attention toward the terrace doors.

"Your Majesty," a shrill voice called, the sound like shattering glass. I swallowed back the bile in my throat as I listened to the sound of Rosella's approach. "May we?" she asked, pulling back a chair. Dash's chair. Irrational anger coursed through me.

"Please do," the king responded, smiling warmly at Rosella and the other ladies in her company as they sat around the table.

"My father asked me to relay a message to you, your Majesty. He said that your travel arrangements have been set," Rosella said.

"Wonderful. Thank your father for me." King Perceval rose from his chair. He held out his hands, halting us as we moved to do the same. "It was lovely to see you, ladies," he said, acknowledging Rosella and her friends. "My dear, as I am leaving the day after your birthday, I have moved your Primum Celebration to take place when I return. I hope you understand." The Primum Celebration was a tradition held for the palace residents. The twenty-first birthday celebration was thrown to honor the length of time one had been in the world, whereas the Primum Celebration marked the start of a new beginning; An immortal existence.

"Of course, Your Majesty," I replied, not caring one bit.

"Thank you for listening, my dear." He smiled down at me, and I returned the gesture. "And for the advice." I dipped my head as he turned to face Rosella once more. "Prince Dashiell and Lord Felix will be busy while I'm away. Make sure you ladies keep Ainsley company in their absence." I bit back the sound of my groan.

"We'd be happy to, your Majesty," Rosella replied, a vicious smile on her face. With that, the king turned on his heel and departed back inside the palace, the guards returning to the terrace once he disappeared. Rosella cleared her throat, and I closed my eyes as I worked to keep my composure. "So sorry to hear about your poor maiden," she said, not sounding apologetic at all. I offered a tight smile rather than a retort. "When I was with Prince Dashiell last night, he mentioned that it was Tenebrae that issued the attack." My blood went cold, and my heart stilled. Dash had been with Rosella last night? I swallowed and tilted my chin higher as if I wasn't bothered, but I knew my eyes betrayed me. Rosella's smile grew as she spoke. "Oh, you didn't know? The hour was so late he probably didn't want to wake you."

The ladies around the table snickered, and my chest caved in at her words. Dash went to her after I had fallen asleep. Despite the fresh open air, I felt as though I were suffocating. I don't know why I was surprised at her confession. Yesterday she had approached him to confirm their plans for that evening, but I had hoped it wasn't true. *There is only one person that I'm pursuing. There is only one person that I want and—.* He had never finished that sentence.

And what? And it was Rosella? Were those the words he was planning to say? I hated feeling this insecure. I had to ask him. I had to know one way or the other.

I wasn't going to sit and let her worm her way into my mind. I would get the answers I wanted from Dash himself. I pushed away from the table loudly, not caring what they thought of my abrupt departure.

"Where are you going, Ainsley?" Rosella asked snidely. I stopped as I stared into her cold, ice-blue eyes.

"It's *my lady*," I shot back. "And to find my fiancé," I called over my shoulder as two guards followed behind.

26.

I hurried my way through the halls as I searched for Dash. It had been hours since we had last seen each other, and the fact that King Perceval was just on the terrace told me that he and Felix were no longer needed. I checked our Sanctuary, but they weren't there, nor were they in the sparring ring or the kitchens. I knocked on their bedroom doors but no answer. I was running out of places to look and started to get frustrated. The longer I searched, the more Rosella's words festered in my mind. I quickly turned down an open corridor, but when whispered words reached my ears, I slowed. Two women were pressed against the stone wall up ahead, their bodies close together as they spoke.

"Tell me what else you found out," a dark-haired woman said to her servant companion.

"People have been going missing over the past several weeks only for their bodies to be discovered days later, nothing more than grey husks. But there's more," the servant replied, and I felt the blood from my face drain. I pulled out the book I always kept in my pocket and pretended to be lost in the pages as I inched towards the women. "Men with the Gift of shadows have been spotted in taverns in a nearby village. One of the working girls who serviced him said he had been asking strange questions about the palace."

"What sort of questions?"

"How many people reside within, what type of magic is present, and if she knew anything about *her*," the servant whispered the last word, and I could feel their burning stares on me like a brand. I gripped my book harder to steady my shaking hands and focused entirely on my breathing as I continued my pace. The women waited until I passed them to continue, but I could still make out their words.

"What did she tell him?" the woman asked with worry in her voice.

"That she didn't know anything. She came straight to the palace this morning and requested an audience with King Perceval just after dawn. That's all I know."

"See what else you can find out and tell no one but me," the woman commanded, and with that, rushed footsteps echoed off the walls in the opposite direction.

I gritted my teeth as I continued with my snaillike speed, determined not to draw attention to myself though my lungs burned with fear and my insides knotted. Someone had been asking about me. Someone who wanted to hurt me. Was that why Dash and Felix had been called away this morning? If I mention what I heard, would they tell me everything they learned or only confirm what I already knew?

I rounded a corner sharply and collided with a strong, muscled chest.

"There you are!" Dash said breathlessly. "I've been looking all over for you. Come on. We have to hurry." He grabbed my arm, pulling me into a sprint behind him.

"Dash, I need to talk to you," I said as we ran down the hall, suddenly remembering I had been searching for him regarding Rosella.

"Okay, but I need to show you something first." He brought us to a small balcony that overlooked the courtyard fountain.

"What are we doing here?" I asked as I surveyed the view. The marble fountain depicting King Perceval stood tall in the center of the courtyard as streams of water flowed up from all directions, twisting and wrapping around the statue. Around the base were rows and rows of stark white oleander and vibrant aconitum, the purple shade so vibrant beneath the rays of sunlight. The flowers twisted in intricate spirals along the grounds, with a pathway of lush grass leading from the fountain to the palace's entrance. Dash held a finger to his lips and tilted his head over the balcony, instructing me to look below. I walked closer and leaned over the edge, finding Felix with his hands intertwined in some random person's long red hair and his tongue down his throat.

"Consider this your birthday present," he whispered, and I gave him an inquisitive look.

"How is watching Felix kiss someone a suitable birthday present?"

"It's not. But this is." He came behind me, pressing his chest to my back as he dragged his hands down my arms. His hands held the back of mine as he guided my palms to form a cup. "Are you ready?" he whispered, his cheek pressed against mine. His warm skin and fresh scent made every thought in my mind disappear. Every insecurity and worry I had about him, and Rosella dissolved as I basked in the feel of him against me. I nodded. Suddenly, my skin tingled, and my blood sang as Dash pushed his power through me, letting me be the one to hold his magic. I watched as a ball of water formed in my hands.

"Dash," I whispered, my voice so full of wonder at the magic I held. I felt him smile against my cheek, and I twisted to look at him. I held a ripple of power in my hands. Magic. *His* magic.

"You haven't even gotten to see the best part," he responded. I furrowed my brows. How could anything possibly be better than this? He guided my hands forward and over the balcony. "One. Two. *Three.*" He separated my hands, letting the ball of water fall right onto Felix's head, soaking him and his companion. Their eyes flew open as both of them succumbed to fits of coughing. Felix's stare shot to us, and fury flooded over his features.

"I'm going to kill you both," he yelled, pushing away from his companion and making his way for the palace entrance. I laughed, thinking back to the look on his face as the ball of water hit him.

"Run!" Dash yelled as he grabbed my hand and pulled me through the halls again, our laughter following us like echoes through an empty room. "Hurry, in here." He pulled back a silver and gold tapestry, revealing a hidden alcove, the area so small we had to press against each other to fit. When the tapestry fell into place once more, darkness enveloped the space, and there was nothing but the sounds of our rushed breathing. I pressed my forehead against his chest to quiet the sound as Dash's hands glided down my back, stopping at my waist. "What did you need to talk to me about?"

"We don't have to discuss it now. It can wait." I tilted my head back and squinted as I tried to make out his features. I couldn't, but I knew he could see me clearly.

"We may be hiding here for a while," he whispered. "If something is on your mind, Ainsley, I want to know." His hands found mine, and he lifted my arms, guiding them around his neck. Our bodies were now chest to chest with nothing but the sound of our beating hearts filling the space. He pressed his forehead against mine, and I closed my eyes as I swallowed. "Please," he added softly. I exhaled through my nose as I nodded. I would keep what I learned moments ago to myself and instead question him about his late-night excursion.

"Rosella found me earlier and felt the need to share that the two of you were together late last night." He stiffened against me. "So it's true then."

"Yes, but—" I began to remove my arms from around his neck, but he stopped my retreat. "I don't know what she insinuated, but I have a guess, and I'm telling you, nothing happened between us." His voice was rushed and urgent, like he needed me to believe him more than he needed air.

"So then tell me what happened. Tell me why the two of you were together last night," I whispered. Dash had always been honest with me, so I had no reason to believe he'd lie about his encounter with her.

"You and Felix had fallen asleep, but I couldn't quiet my mind. I kept picturing what happened to Pecus and Josephine and the fact that Tenebrae was targeting you because of your relationship with me. I decided to go for a walk to try and clear my head. That's when I ran into Rosella outside of my bedroom door." A low growl rumbled in the base of my throat, a sound I had never heard myself make. The noise was both primal and possessive. "As soon as I saw her, I rushed to her, thinking something terrible had happened, and she came to inform me. It wasn't until she explained nothing was wrong—until I had sent her away with guards—that I realized why she had been there. Looking back, it should have been my first thought, but with the hour being so late, my only concern was for her safety and the safety of my people." Relief flowed through me, dissolving the unwanted thoughts of Rosella and Dash together intimately last night.

"When she interrupted us, she did so to confirm your plans for the evening," I pointed out.

"We never had plans, Ainsley, I swear to you. Rosella doesn't like rejection and thrives off the ability to have what others want. She will say anything to get a rise out of you."

"So the two of you aren't...."

"No," he whispered, bringing his hand around to cup my jaw. "We're not." His lips hovered just out of reach, his breath mixing with mine. My fingers sprawled across the back of his neck and in his hair as he pressed on my lower back, pushing me firmly against him. I was encased in heat, darkness, and desire as I felt his lips inch closer and closer. I held my breath as I waited for him to close the distance entirely and press his mouth to mine.

"I can feel your fucking hearts beating out of your chest," Felix announced from somewhere in the hall. "And you should be scared because I'm going to destroy you both." I bit my lip as I stifled my laugh.

"To be continued," Dash said, planting a kiss on my cheek before righting himself to his full height. "On my mark, I want you to run to the library. Don't look behind you, don't wait for me, just run. I'll hold him off." I nodded my acknowledgment, and Dash released his hold on me as he sucked in a deep breath. Droplets of water misted my skin as a faint bubbling sound hung in the air. "*Now!*" he yelled, ripping back the tapestry. We leaped into the hall, and my eyes landed on Felix.

His hair was now tied back completely, and he donned a large shield on his left arm. The fingers on his right hand bent as if he were squeezing an invisible object. A wave of calm burst through me, and I felt my body slow with exhaustion so strong it was as though I had spent the entire day running uphill. Dash thrust his hands forward, releasing the ball of water that had formed, but Felix was ready. That's what the shield had been for. He had anticipated his best friend's attack before it even happened. Felix's hand dropped as he focused his energy on blocking Dash's assault. The wave of calm disappeared immediately, replaced with feelings of joy and excitement.

"Hurry, Ainsley!" Dash yelled, and I realized that his attack wasn't meant to defeat Felix. It was meant to stall him so I could safely get away. Dash knew his friend would come prepared, and he knew I had no means of getting away untouched on my own. I took off down the hall and didn't stop until I had reached our Sanctuary.

Ten minutes later, Dash and Felix arrived, their arms draped over each other's shoulders, dripping wet and laughing. Felix's eyes narrowed as he strode over, pinning me down on the couch and wringing out his soaking shirt over me. I squealed and squirmed as I tried to get away to no avail. When he was done with his torture, he kissed my cheek before pulling away and plopping himself down on one of the window benches, a book in hand.

"What do you want to do on our last day of freedom? Once we all have guards following us, it'll be a bitch to try and shake them," Dash asked as he sat down next to me, resting his head against the top of the couch. I laid down, using his lap as a pillow, and looked up at him.

"I just want us to all be together," I replied as I closed my eyes and took a nap.

27.

Though we were stuck in the palace, they never let it get in the way of my birthday celebrations. They had to improvise and be creative, but they made it work. A scavenger hunt through the rooms of the palace, a picnic in the library that had been filled with floating lanterns, and a feast of desserts that we had consumed under a giant tent constructed of mismatched sheets and blankets. Finally, the day of my final birthday celebration arrived.

Dash headed down to the kitchens to retrieve dinner for the three of us as Felix walked me to our special room, with guards following close behind. They wanted to move dinner from our usual spot on the terrace to our Sanctuary, hoping it would be the one place where we wouldn't be interrupted. Dash made it abundantly clear that the guards were never to step foot within the Sanctuary walls without expressed permission.

"Why didn't you tell me about your newest conquest?" I asked as Felix, and I settled into the soft velvet couch in our room. I had discovered him entangled with the same woman twice now, and he hadn't shared the information with me on his own. "You're not one to keep things from me, especially when it has to do with someone who *wants* you." I winked.

"Are you worried about a little competition, pumpkin? There's plenty of me to go around." I wiggled my fingers against his ribs, and Felix let out a high-pitched squeal as he restrained my wrist. "I will destroy you if you do it again," Felix promised, and challenge shone in my eyes. I brought up my other hand and began tickling again. He laughed and squirmed beneath my touch before leaning forward and flipping me onto my back against the couch cushions as he hovered over me. The door swung open, and we focused our attention on the other side of the room. Dash stood frozen on the threshold, his head tilted to the side as he took in the two of us. Without saying a word, he walked over, placing the basket of food he carried onto the table. He stepped back and crossed his arms over his chest as he waited for an explanation. "*She* came on to *me*," Felix said with a shrug, and Dash nodded as he came closer.

"That sounds about right," he replied as Felix climbed off me.

I sat up, adjusting my dress and smoothing out my hair, the strands now tangled and knotted from writhing against the couch. Dash sat next to me and shoved a wine goblet into my hand as he leaned over and kissed my cheek.

"To pumpkin and her growing lust for me," Felix said, raising his glass high. Dash hit his arm with a pillow causing the wine to splash onto his face, drenching him completely.

"Happy birthday," Dash said, and I smiled.

"Your present is seeing my beautiful body again," Felix announced as he removed his shirt. "Not Dash defending your honor. Try not to let your fantasies run away from you too much."

"Felix," I said softly, seductively. "You wouldn't know what to do with me if given the chance."

"Oh, trust me, I definitely would," he replied.

"Oh yeah? Why don't you explain? What would you do?" I leaned across Dash to address him. Felix opened his mouth but then closed it as his eyes shifted back and forth between Dash and me.

"I...." he started but then quickly stopped again, frustration washing over his features. It wasn't because he didn't have some witty comeback or explicitly detailed ideas running through his mind. It was because he wouldn't dare say them in front of the man sitting next to me. It was one thing to flirt shamelessly with me while Dash listened, but it was another to describe every intimate thing he would do to me in detail. I had him and he knew it. Felix looked between his friend and me, debating on what to do.

"Continue, Felix. What exactly would you do to my Ainsley?" Dash probed, wrapping an arm around my waist to pull me into him. '*My* Ainsley.' The small word sent a thrill through my veins. I rested my hand on his thigh, feeling his toned muscles beneath. Felix scrunched his face, wanting nothing more than to relay his quip. I felt an immense amount of joy at watching his internal struggle unfold before me. I arched my back slightly, just as I'd seen the women swooning over Dash do so many times. I gathered my hair to the side and twisted a strand between my fingers directly over my breasts, trying desperately to draw Felix's eyes there.

"Why don't you go ahead and tell Dash every little detail of what you would do to me." I smiled a devious grin as Felix glowered at me. Finally, he stood and stomped away to a nearby bookshelf.

"I hate you both," he called over his shoulder.

"No, you don't," I responded as Dash and I clinked our glasses together to celebrate our victory.

"No, I don't." Felix reluctantly said under his breath.

Felix stewed in his misery for only fifteen minutes before he wanted attention again and made his way back to us. Dash and I had already finished two cups of wine by the time Felix reached for his first, downing the full goblet in seconds. He then turned and grabbed three crystal glasses, pouring a generous dark amber liquid into each. Without a word, he distributed the drinks, and in unison, we tapped our glasses onto the table before draining the alcohol in a single swallow. It tasted of smoke and cherries and burned on the way down. I coughed immediately and reached for my other drink, begging the sweet flavor of the wine to overpower the bitterness of whatever it was Felix had given us.

"That was disgusting," I complained, taking another sip of my wine.

"It doesn't have to taste good. It just has to get the job done," Felix explained as he refilled the empty lowball glasses. "We need to be good and drunk for this game. Cheers." I winced and looked to Dash for help, but he was already draining

Felix's two-finger pour of alcohol. I groaned as I picked up the cup, squeezing my eyes shut tight as I forced the liquid down my throat for the second time. Felix poured again, but this time, we didn't drink. "The game is Wyvern Pit, but with a twist," he announced, walking around the room and strategically moving the furniture about. "The theme tonight will be drunken trivia."

"I don't know the game," I admitted as I stood and finished the rest of my wine, eagerly waiting for it to magically refill. Firm hands rested on my waist as Dash leaned in from behind and pressed a kiss to my cheek, his breath smelling of sweet wine and cherries.

"We'll teach you," he whispered against my skin and then pulled away to grab the crystal glass on the table. I felt instantly nauseous at the thought of having to drink any more of that revolting liquor. I reached for my glass, but Dash stopped my advance and shook his head as he swallowed his drink. I watched as he poured himself another and drained it effortlessly. "You're done with this for now." He set his glass back down and refilled it for the third time. "Our immortal bodies burn off alcohol quicker than you do. We have to drink more to be on the same level." I hadn't thought about that. Of course, their immortal healing would be working to counteract the effects of the liquor. I wondered how long it would take for it to be entirely out of their system. "As long as Felix and I keep drinking through the night, we'll stay decently intoxicated."

Dash walked over to the basket of food and pulled out a dinner roll, ripping off a small portion and bringing it to me. It looked as though the room was shaking with each step he took, and I realized at once that the alcohol I had consumed had begun to take effect. I placed my hands against my cheeks, feeling the skin flush and warm beneath my fingers. Dash stopped in front of me, pressing the roll to my lips.

"You need to eat, or you'll be sick," he said, playfully tapping the bread against my mouth until I opened it and took a bite. I chewed and swallowed though my mouth felt numb, and the food had no taste. "Good." Dash placed the rest of the roll into my hand before striding to Felix to help him set up.

"The rules are simple—" Felix announced, hopping down from a side table he had been standing on.

"And yet complicated," Dash added, straddling the arms of a chair across the room like he was testing its durability. They began listing off various instructions and rules, all of which made little to no sense. Ultimately, I learned that the main goal was to get from one point to the other without touching the ground and that drinking would somehow be involved.

"So if I touch the ground, then I lose?" I asked.

"If you touch the ground, then you are devoured by Wyverns," Dash clarified. "To get back into the game, you must finish your drink." He jerked his chin to the three crystal glasses that sat around a liquor decanter on the table. "Ready?" I wracked my brain around the countless rules they had explained, still unsure how to play, and shook my head. I most certainly was not ready.

"You'll figure it out along the way," Felix said as he and Dash leaped onto the coffee table, extending their hands out to help me up. They stood with their backs to each other, and I followed suit. "One. Two. Three," Felix said, and they both brought their goblets to their lips and chugged. I quickly did the same, finishing just a few seconds behind them. Once the drink was gone, they jumped from the table in different directions to a piece of furniture around the room. Dash landed nimbly on the back of an armchair, and Felix was now perched on a small desk. I hopped from the table to the closest object, which happened to be the couch only a foot away, causing Dash and Felix to roll their eyes at my choice of an easy target.

Felix hadn't been wrong. Though the game made absolutely no sense, it was easy to figure out. The hardest part was answering trivia questions about each other. For each question that was answered wrong, a sip of wine had to be taken. Anytime a cup became empty, as punishment, that person had to drain the contents completely once it replenished itself. Dash was nice enough to enforce a rule that I was to be given multiple-choice answers, seeing as I was the new member of our trio. Even with the extra assistance, I still got nearly every question wrong, and a new rule had to be implemented: all mortals present had to drink after they answered three questions incorrectly. Though I tried to protest the special treatment, Dash had claimed that finding a new fiancé after I died of too much alcohol consumption was a tedious task he didn't feel like dealing with.

After two hours of leaping across the room and nearly falling off every object, Felix was declared the winner for reasons I didn't understand. This prompted him to jump up and down in celebration on the small side table he had been standing on. The poor piece of furniture was no match for the momentum of his weight and came crashing down into a pile of wood beneath him. The sound of splintering oak boomed through the room with a crack similar to the roar of thunder. Once I learned that Felix hadn't suffered death by impalement, I doubled over myself in laughter at his stupidity, Dash joining in beside me.

"I'm glad I can amuse you two," Felix said flatly as he rolled off the broken table.

"It serves you right," I told him, reaching for another piece of bread. Dash had been right to suggest eating to fight off pending nausea. *'It'll also help soak up the alcohol as we play,'* he added during the game. Thanks to his advice, I drifted along the lines of sober and pleasantly buzzed.

"You're just being a Pouty Pants because you lost another game," he threw back at me, and I flipped him off. He knew I hated losing and wanted to rub it in my face. "And my reward for winning is that I get to choose the next game." He dusted off his pants and climbed onto the couch across from the one Dash, and I sat on. "And I pick Sharing is Caring."

"I hate that game," Dash groaned loudly, throwing his head back in a display of dramatics.

"Well, if you didn't sacrifice yourself for Pouty Pants here, then maybe you would have won and got to choose. But you didn't, so shut up and share," Felix quipped. Dash rolled his eyes, but my heart warmed to know he had given up his victory to save me. I hopped onto the desk Felix first occupied but slipped on my dress as I hit the wood. Before I fell to the ground, Dash caught me in his arms and helped me back up. He then walked over to the table and drained his liquor before climbing back onto the chair he was previously on. I hadn't realized that decision had cost him the game. I gave Dash a small apologetic look, but he merely shook his head as if to say, *'don't worry about it.'*

"Is this game simple yet complicated too?" I asked, turning my attention back to Felix.

"Very simple and not at all complicated," he admitted. "We pick a topic, and all share our stories regarding it. After everyone has told their tale, we vote on who has to finish their drink. Sometimes it's the person with the best story, and sometimes it's the one with the worst." That did sound simple. "Since I won our last game, I'll pick the topic first."

"Brace yourself," Dash whispered into my ear. I twisted to look at him, knitting my brows in confusion.

"I want to hear about everyone's first sexual encounter," he declared with a wink. "In detail." A mischievous smile crept up his face. "Once again, as the winner, I'll go first." Why did I have the feeling that he chose this topic just to brag about himself? "I was sixteen, and it was with a servant from the kitchens. She had been eyeing me for a while, as one usually does," I rolled my eyes, "and propositioned me to meet her by the horses one afternoon. Obviously, I accepted, and we made sweet, sweet love against the stable door. I was forever changed." He placed a hand over his heart as if he were fond of the memory.

"What a beautiful story," I said sarcastically.

"Oh, he's not done," Dash added back, the sarcasm just as thick in his voice.

"We heard someone creeping around the corner and were caught by one of the stable hands. Because I am so thoughtful and considerate, I invited him to stay and fucked him too," Felix said triumphantly.

"Now he's done," Dash announced. I shook my head at Felix's cocky grin, obviously pleased with himself.

"To Felix's poor lovers," Dash said, raising his glass high. We parroted the words and took a small sip.

"Your turn, pumpkin," Felix said.

"You already know mine was with Logan," I said, shrugging. Our first time was nothing special, or even good, for that matter.

"Details," Felix countered, and I sighed in defeat.

"Fine. It was the day I turned seventeen, and right after I had been informed about my betrothal. I walked straight to the village and found this boy leaning against the wall of a tavern. I told myself, *'he'll do,'* and kissed him. He didn't stop me, so I led him into the woods. We did it against a tree, and that was that. The next time we met up, I learned his name."

"And did he make you..." Felix probed.

"Come? No. But that wasn't unusual when it came to Logan. Leaving unsatisfied was the case more often than not." I shrugged. It was the truth, and I felt more than comfortable sharing that with the two of them.

"To pumpkin's orgasm," Felix announced, raising his glass high. Dash and I repeated the words, but I didn't drink. Instead, I waited for them to bring the cups to their lips.

"I do it better on my own, anyway," I remarked and watched as Felix and Dash choked on their wine. Mission accomplished. "It's your turn, Dash."

"Oh, I'm not playing," he said nonchalantly. "I know exactly why he picked this game and the topic, and I refuse to indulge in his antics." I looked at Felix to find him smiling from ear to ear, so happy with his plan.

"Then indulge *me*. I want to know," I whined as I shoved him, his firm muscles like a rock under my touch.

"Yeah, Dash, she wants to know," Felix instigated.

"First of all, fuck you," he told Felix. "Second of all, I *really* don't want to." He stuck his bottom lip out in a pout.

"It's my final birthday celebration, so consider this your gift to me," I reasoned. Dash rolled his eyes and groaned but sat straighter as he stared at his wine goblet.

"I was sixteen years old, and it was during the Solstice celebration that I told you about. One of the ladies that came to comfort me during our sparring session had expressed her desire to...." He looked up and bobbed his head from side to side as if trying to find the correct words. "...had expressed her *interest* in me."

"Nice save, Dash," Felix chimed in. Dash glowered at his friend but continued.

"So I met her in the Throne Room that night, and we had sex against one of the pillars. The end."

"That doesn't seem like such a bad story," I asked, sounding confused. His tale was mild compared to both Felix's and mine.

"Tell her how long it lasted," Felix said, biting his lip to keep from laughing. My eyes widened, and I looked at Dash, but he was glaring at Felix with a face that promised death.

"I fucking hate you," Dash said coldly.

"How long did it last?" I asked sweetly, desperately wanting to hear him say it. He shook his head. "It's in the rules of the game. You have to tell me."

"Sharing is caring, Dash," Felix added. Gods, I loved my best friend right then.

"One minute," he gritted out. Felix and I burst with booming laughter, and I clasped my hands over my mouth as I tried to muffle the sound.

"It was Felix's fault! He got me shitfaced drunk knowing exactly what would happen!!" Dash yelled, trying to get his point across over the sound of our hysterics. "He knew I wouldn't last long under those circumstances!" he continued, trying to defend himself, but Felix and I paid no attention, too engulfed in our amusement at Dash's misfortune. "And just to be clear, it was a one-time thing."

"So you're up to two minutes now?" I asked, sending Felix howling.

"Go fuck yourself," Dash replied as he shook his head, but a small smile formed on his lips despite his protests.

"Apparently, she already does," Felix added as he clinked his glass with mine.

"Someone has to," I replied and took a sip from my wine as Dash shifted next to me. "And we established earlier that Felix wouldn't know what to do with me." Felix's face fell at the reminder that he couldn't say what he so desperately wanted to with Dash present. With a huff of frustration, he raised his glass high.

"To Speedy Dash!" Felix exclaimed. We recited the words back, and all finished our drinks, declaring no one to be the loser. "I think it's time for presents."

28.

Felix claimed he needed a minute to go and retrieve his gift, leaving the two of us to ourselves as we waited. Dash got up from his seat and headed to the window bench, only to return with a blanket. He sat back down, extending his arm up in invitation for me to squeeze next to him. I obliged, curling into his warmth as he covered us. The feel of the cashmere was soft and luxurious. He draped his arm around me, and his fingers drew idle strokes along my skin. I pressed into him further, and his head dipped against mine. My heart raced, and my breathing quickened as his nose grazed the shell of my ear.

"So, only one minute, huh?" I said softly, my voice shaking. "That's an image I'm not going to be able to get out of my head." I had hoped he would ac- knowledge my joke. Hoped he would say anything to help douse the fire that was beginning to build within me.

"So you satisfy yourself, huh?" he whispered into my ear. My face burned with lust and desire. "And likewise," he added. I swallowed hard as I pressed my thighs together.

"Fine," I said breathlessly. "New topic. We're not talking about either of these."

"But I have so many questions," he said, sweeping my hair from my neck.

"I don't care," I whispered as I pulled away, leaning against the couch and getting comfortable as I flipped open to the page I had left off on in my book. After consuming only one paragraph, I could feel his burning stare upon me. I closed my novel, placed it on my lap, and twisted up to look at him, finding a curious glint in his eyes.

"What?" I said, and he smiled at my playful tone, knowing that he had gotten exactly what he wanted–my attention once again.

"Nothing," he answered, and I reached forward, grabbing my wine from the table as I waited for him to continue. "I just can't believe that you find my company so dull that you would rather read a book than talk to me." I took a sip from my cup as I rolled my eyes. By the cocky smirk he was proudly displaying, I knew that he didn't mean a single word. He was fishing for compliments. And staying true to our relationship, I was determined to give him none.

"Well, I don't think you can compete with the main character in my story. He's far more deserving of my time."

Dash raised an eyebrow, not buying my response. "I doubt that's true."

"Oh, it is." I sat up straighter as I lifted the book once again and flipped through the worn pages. "You see, the hero in this novel is a charming and fearless prince." I waved a hand towards him as I continued, "And you... well..." I shrugged and offered an apologetic look as if I had just delivered him a terrible bit of news. His face fell in mock offense. Dash grabbed the goblet from my hand and placed it back on the table before leaning closer to me.

"I'll have you know that I am *very* charming," I widened my eyes and gave him an exaggerated nod of encouragement, "*and* a prince."

"Of course, of course," I said, indulging him, unable to hide the grin that was breaking free. Dash pressed his tongue against the inside of his cheek as he looked away, trying desperately not to give in to his laughter. After less than a heartbeat of time, he turned back to me, index finger raised as if to offer another point.

"And I am fearless." I couldn't help but snort at his response and quickly reached for my glass to drain the rest of its contents. "I am!" he exclaimed through a huff of laughter.

I swallowed the rest of my wine before offering a retort. "Says the one who has been too terrified to kiss me." The words were out before I even knew what was happening. *Oh, Gods.* I did not just say that. The amount of wine we had consumed this evening was no doubt the cause for my brazenness. My cheeks instantly heated. Not from drink but pure humiliation. The words I spoke were the truth of my mind, but they were thoughts I certainly was not planning on sharing with him. My fingers stilled on the stem of the empty wine goblet in my hands as I tentatively looked up at Dash. His face was full of astonishment, and his mouth had dropped open. He shook his head back and forth in disbelief as he gave me an enormous opened mouth smile.

"Is that so?" he quipped, shifting his body even closer to mine. His eyes flickered to my mouth, and I knew he was reveling in my embarrassment. That simply would not do. I averted my eyes back to the words written on the paper. Showing him that I wasn't the least bit bothered by my confession.

"Just merely an observation... *Prince*," I scoffed, emphasizing the last word. Before I could so much as blink, Dash dipped his head, planting a soft kiss against my throat. The sudden gesture caused me to drop my book on the rug beneath our feet.

"There," he said matter-of-factly. "Fearless."

"That is not what I meant, and you know it." I was all too aware that Dash had not lifted his head. His mouth hovered over my throat, the heat of his breath causing my head to swim and every thought within it to drown. He lifted his hand, slowly gliding it up the side of my neck as if he were meticulously inspecting it. Like an artist marveling at the fine details of his work. My skin tingled beneath his touch, every nerve in my body awakening. He cupped my jaw and tilted my head just barely, giving himself better access. He was a predator ready to sink teeth into his prey.

"Is that what you want?" he asked as he grazed his full lips along the length of my exposed throat. I swallowed as I tried to focus on his words and not on what his mouth was doing, but that was useless.

"What?" I asked, forgetting his question entirely. Dash pressed his lips against me once more, this time adding a whisper of his tongue flicking over my skin as he kissed me again. I squeezed my eyes shut as heat and desire for him coursed through my veins, filling every crevice of my being.

"Do you want me to kiss you... *Princess*?" Dash twined his fingers through my hair as he spoke. With one hand holding my face, the other gripping the back of my head, and his mouth on my neck, I was completely in his grasp. There was no escaping the physical or emotional hold he had on me. And I thanked the Gods for that fact. I didn't miss his use of my future title. The title he knew I would hate just as I knew he hated his. But at this moment... with Dash's hands and mouth on me, I didn't have a care in the world about it. I shifted closer, and Dash let out a low growl as I pressed my body against his, the sound vibrating against my throat. I wanted and needed more. So much more.

"I'm not a princess yet," I said breathlessly as he kissed me again, this time closer to my jaw. This time with even more tongue. I wrapped my arms around his neck and ran my fingers through the back of his hair. Every thought had eddied from my mind. The only thing I knew was that I wanted him. He dragged his nose up and down my throat as if savoring every inch of skin there. As if he were inhaling my scent and committing it to memory.

"Not yet," he said, his voice low and guttural. Nothing in it but primal need and desire. The desire for me. My blood was a raging fire that burned like an unyielding force, and I felt slickness pool between my legs. Dash's hand released the back of my head and slid down my body, tracing the length of my thigh as he hoisted my legs from the ground to lay across his lap. "But you will be," he said as he found my waist, his fingers digging into my side. He held me firmly to him as he opened his mouth wider and licked up the column of my neck before pressing his lips to my skin. I arched my back as a breathy moan escaped from my lips. I felt his hardness beneath me, and I pressed my thighs tightly together to halt the pressure I felt building in my core.

My heart pounded inside my chest, and the sound roared in my ears like a mighty war drum, preparing me for battle. The feral need was written within his spoken words and his territorial grasp. *But you will be.* I would be *his* princess. Making him *mine*. I tugged his hair gently at the thought of him belonging wholly to me. The idea sent a tingling burst of pleasure through me. As much as I had fought it, as much as I was initially against it, I *wanted* to be his. I wanted his touch in every possible form. My mind drifted with lust as he feverishly licked and kissed his way across my neck, my jawline, and beneath my ear. I wondered what it would feel like to have his mouth on other parts of me.

"You didn't answer my question," Dash said, pulling me from my fantasies.

"Hmmm?" I could only make sounds now. No words would form, and I didn't bother trying. He pulled away, and I whimpered at the loss of his lips on me. He lifted his head and his eyes, glazed over with lust, finally met mine. The blue within them was now like the sea at midnight, so dark it could be mistaken for black. There was a hunger that swirled deep within. I shifted as a throbbing between my legs began the second I realized that hunger was for me. He held my stare for just a second more before leaning in and grazing his mouth along my lower lip, taunting me. Teasing me. I was going to explode if he kept this up for much longer.

"Do you want me to kiss you, Ainsley?" Yes. Yes. *Gods, yes.*

"Meh," I told him breathlessly as I shrugged. *Wait, what?!* Of all the times to be sarcastic. Of all the times to make a joke, this... *this* was the time that my brain thought was appropriate? Dash laughed softly under his breath, clearly expecting nothing less from me.

"I see." He began to pull back, clearly not wanting to pressure me, even if he didn't believe my tone. No, no, no, no! I clawed through my mind trying to find the ability to speak. To stop him from retreating.

"Do *you* want to kiss me?" I blurted out, finally able to find the words. Dash halted his movements, eyes darting up to mine as he smiled just a little bit. My heart hammered loudly in my chest as I awaited his answer. Everything I had seen from him screamed that it would be *yes*, but I couldn't be sure until he uttered the word. His hand grazed along my jawline, and his thumb brushed softly over my bottom lip as he stared at me. He dipped his mouth, now hovering just above mine as he spoke, still maintaining his piercing stare on my eyes.

"Meh," he said softly, and I felt a smile spread across my face.

"I see," I told him as I pressed into the back of the couch again. This time, with my arms still locked around his neck, I brought him with me. His gaze flickered back and forth between my mouth and my eyes as if he couldn't decide which held his attention more. I lifted my chin higher, desperate to lose the few inches that separated his lips from mine. Every sensation in my body sang against him. He smiled as he removed his hand from my waist and brought it up to cup the other side of my jaw. He held my face between his hands for what felt like an eternity. Like he wasn't sure if this was really about to happen. As if he wasn't sure if this was what *I* wanted to happen. I looked at him, my eyes pleading, begging him to just put me out of this torture. To just finally kiss me. His grip on me tightened as he leaned in, and my lips automatically parted, open and ready for him. The heat of his breath smelled of wine and mint, and I needed to know precisely what he would taste like. He stared into my eyes, the need and desire I felt in this moment mirrored in his own. He shifted, and my eyes fluttered closed, savoring this final moment. Where we would go from this beautiful foundation of a friendship we had built to something more. Something I was now ready for.

The door to the library creaked open.

29.

"You're going to love this, pumpkin," Felix declared as he stared down at a piece of parchment he had been clutching and made his way into the room. He had the absolute worst timing. Dash groaned his frustration as he pulled away, throwing his head against the back of the couch.

"To be continued, yet again," he muttered, and I laughed softly under my breath, interlacing my fingers with his and resting my head against his shoulder. "I *will* kiss you," he whispered as he pressed his lips to my hair.

"Meh," I replied, and Dash's body shook with gentle, quiet laughter.

"Pay attention," Felix demanded. He leaped onto the coffee table and cleared his throat loudly, dramatically. "I'll have you know that I wrote this from the heart." He held the paper high in front of him. "An ode to Ainsley."

"Ainsley, you are as sweet as sugar
And as sharp as a spice
As beautiful as a flower
With an ass that is oh so nice.
You are fierce with your words
And sarcastic with your looks
And your face is so adorable
When you read your dirty books.
When we first met you hated me
Thinking I was crude and absurd
But I promised we'd be best friends
And I've made good on my word.

And now you think of me often
While lying alone in your bed
You should be envisioning that time with Dash
But you're wishing it were me instead.
You have to marry the prince
And I know that must suck
So how about you leave him
And you and I can just go— "

Felix was tackled to the ground by Dash before the last line was finished. The two rolled around, wrestling, as they crashed into bookcases and tables, knocking stacks of novels and vases to the ground. Felix's laugh was boisterous as he hooked his legs around his friend and moved in a sweeping motion, causing Dash's back to slam onto the ground.

"It says 'Try our luck'! Get away from me with your filthy thoughts!" Felix yelled through his laughter, shoving Dash before rising to his feet. I couldn't help the smile I had plastered on my face from watching their playful attacks. Felix smoothed out his hair before coming to kiss my cheek. "Happy Twentieth Birthday."

"Thank you," I told him, wrapping my arms around his neck as I pulled him into a tight embrace. "The poem was beautifully written."

"Of course it was." He walked over to Dash and extended his hand to help pull him to his feet. "Sadly, I must now leave you both. I ran into Martim on my way to retrieve your poem, and he expressed a certain interest in me," Felix said with a wink. I rolled my eyes.

"Because you gave me such a wonderful present, I will allow the early departure from my celebration," I concluded.

"You're too good to me, lemon drop. Try not to have too much fun without me," he said as he headed for the exit. "Oh, and Dash," he called before stepping over the threshold, "I lied. The last word was *fuck*." Felix slammed the door shut just as ice splintered over the wood, spidering in all directions. I bellowed with laughter as Dash whirled on me.

"Do not encourage him," he said, jumping onto the couch and pulling me onto his lap. I snuggled against him, burying myself in his warmth. "I still have to give you your present."

"You already did," I said, tilting my face to place a soft kiss against his throat. He shivered under my lips, and I reveled in the small physical changes I brought out in him. "When you told me about Speedy Dash." He groaned and rolled his eyes as he threw his head back against the top of the couch.

"I'm never going to live that down, am I?" I shook my head, and he smiled. "Well..." he said, reaching into his pocket. "I'd much rather *this* be your present." He pulled out a small white square box the size of his palm and placed it in my hand. I inspected the package and the neatly tied deep blue satin ribbon it was wrapped in. "Don't shake it," Dash said, seeming to anticipate my actions.

I bit my lip and unraveled the ribbon, the fabric rippling like the gentle waves of a stream. I let the tie fall to my lap, and soon after it, the lid to the box. My mouth dropped as I marveled at the present in my hands. Inside the box was a delicate bracelet with a braided chain that was dainty and golden. Upon it was a single spessartite garnet gemstone cut in the shape of an inverted pear. At first, I thought it was a representation of Dash's Gift. The design was similar to a water droplet, but the stone's deep orange and red hue suggested otherwise. Dash lifted the bracelet, unclasping the hook with a single hand as he reached for me. I watched as he secured it.

"You told me once that you hoped to be an Ignisian, and your Gift would be that of fire," he explained, twisting the bracelet so that the small gemstone dangled from the base of my hand. "Even if that isn't the power you are given, even if that is not the magic you were chosen to wield... You have a spirit as bright, passionate, and fierce as flame. You are wild and unyielding and strong, Ainsley. Every time you see this, I hope it reminds you of that." He held up my hand, and I watched as the gemstone reflected the flickering lights of the room, making it look as though flame danced upon my wrist.

My heart swelled and emotion caught in my throat as I stared into his brilliant eyes. The eyes of the person who had begun to feel like home. The person I had been falling in love with for weeks now. It was the first time I had come to that realization. The feelings I had for him were no longer that of solely friendship. No longer that of solely interest and intrigue. What I felt for him was so much deeper. It was real and strong and filled and consumed me completely. I could only pray he felt the same. I struggled to speak, wanting to say so much, but not knowing how. How could I ever thank him for this? He wiped away a tear that I hadn't realized had fallen.

"Dash, this is...." Struggling to find the words, I pressed a hand to his cheek as we locked eyes, hoping he could read every emotion held within mine. Everything I wanted to say. The present itself was beautiful, but the meaning behind it, the reason he had chosen it, meant the world. I released his face and grazed my fingers over the delicate gemstone hanging from my wrist. His forehead creased slightly, and his stare grew wide in anticipation. Like he was waiting with bated breath for me to finish. "This means everything to me," I whispered. He exhaled a shuddering breath, and his lips formed into a smile. I threw my arms around him and buried my face in the crook of his neck, content to stay that way forever.

"Happy twentieth birthday, beautiful," he said softly.

Dash held me like that for hours. Until finally, I drifted to sleep in his arms.

30.

"Are you ready for your history lesson, lemon drop?" Felix asked as he entered the Sanctuary with a breakfast tray, waking Dash and me. With everyone still on high alert after the bodies of Pecus and Josephine were discovered and the possibility of my nightmare being an illusion placed on me, I had expressed my desire to learn more about Tenebrae. Felix and Dash were more than happy to educate me on the matter.

"I'm ready," I said enthusiastically, reaching my arms high above my head as I stretched out my stiff limbs. Leaning forward, I grabbed the cup of tea Felix had poured for me, the aroma of peppermint waking my senses. The cushions shifted with Dash's movements as he scooted closer from his spot on the opposite end of the couch. His fingers caressed me as he swept away the hair draped over my shoulder to press a tender kiss upon my skin. I swallowed the lump in my throat and willed my beating heart to settle.

"Good luck. He's a terrible teacher," Dash said against me, sending a shiver down my spine. Gods, I wanted him. By the delight that sparkled in his eyes and the cocky grin upon his face, he knew it, too.

"I'm a fantastic teacher," Felix barked back. "You're just an idiot." Dash flipped him off before helping himself to one of the pastries Felix had brought up. "Anyway," Felix said, now directing his attention to me as he waved around a long, thin stick he had found and brought with him for some Gods forsaken reason. "Tell us what you know of Disparya." I took a small sip of my tea, still too hot to fully enjoy, before placing the cup onto the table and answering.

"Disparya consists of five kingdoms that—" I started.

"Wrong!" Felix bellowed, bringing down the stick in a swift motion, smacking it hard against the table, the sound like a cracking whip. I flinched at the unexpected action. Ah, so that's why he had it. Always the need for dramatics with him. "There is a myth of a sixth kingdom that was lost during the First Great War." He spun the stick like a baton between his hands. "But because there is no proof, that theory isn't relevant."

"So what the Hell was the point of yelling and whipping the stick?" I demanded, my ears still ringing from the loud noise.

"Oh," Felix said, inspecting his new toy with love and devotion in his eyes, "I just wanted to hear what it sounded like." Before anything else could be said, a stream of glistening ice darted out from beside me, hitting the piece of wood Felix held. He startled at once, the wood slipping between his fingers. It was as if time had slowed as we all watched the frozen stick hit the hard tile floor, shattering into tiny shards of ice crystals. Felix's shoulders slumped forward as he beheld his beloved teaching device in pieces. "That was my stick," he said sadly, his face crumpling as if his entire world had been taken before his very eyes.

"Maybe try not to be so insufferable next time," Dash advised. Felix narrowed his eyes at him before reaching behind his back and pulling out a second stick, bringing it to his chest before Dash could destroy that one too. Of course, he'd brought a backup.

"If I promise not to smack it as loudly, can I keep it?" Felix asked quickly, holding one hand out to stop the assault. Dash straightened, ice coating his hands as he got ready to destroy the defenseless piece of wood.

"Three smacks total, and that's it," I cut in, knowing that Felix was better off bargaining with me than his oldest friend.

"Deal!" he said, smirking victoriously as Dash lowered his hands to his side, his magic disappearing. I cleared my throat, ready to start again.

"Disparya consists of five kingdoms, each with their own set of Gifts," I answered.

"And what are the names of the kingdoms?" Felix probed as he paced back and forth, the picture of professionalism.

"Well, Caelum is where we live." Felix slow-clapped sarcastically, and I tossed a chocolate croissant at him, instantly regretting it as I realized it was the last one. Dash followed my gaze, laughing softly to himself as he walked across the room to pick it up and set it on my lap, kissing my forehead as he did. I popped a small piece into my mouth before continuing. "Tenebrae is the kingdom that wants to either breed me or kill me." A low growl rumbled in Dash's throat. "And Ministro is where you were born," I said, looking back at Felix.

"And the other two?" Felix coaxed, spinning his stick around, just waiting for the right opportunity to use his newfound authority.

"Exist...?" I replied quietly. From the corner of my eye, I saw Dash's head cock to the side.

"Were you not taught this?" he asked thoughtfully.

"Yes and no," I admitted, slightly embarrassed. "My Caregivers were only concerned that I knew how to read and write. Once I could do both, they provided me with texts on history to teach myself. As a child, I had no interest in the subject, and as I got older, I refused to learn out of spite. Though now I realize I only hurt myself with that decision."

"Agnitio and Venator are the other two," Dash explained, taking my hand into his, interlacing our fingers together as he leaned his back against the couch. I made a mental note of the names, hoping I wouldn't instantly forget them once our lesson was over.

"And what powers do they all have?" Felix questioned.

"Felix," I said flatly. "I didn't know the names of five kingdoms—what makes you think I'd know all fifteen powers of Disparya?" I felt irritated with myself for my ignorance. For not paying attention and taking my education more seriously. As a future princess, I should know my continent and the magic of its people.

"Valid point." Felix paced back and forth, slicing his stick through the air like a sword. "Can't you just guess?" he whined, and I looked at him, confused. "I really want to smack it." He stuck out his bottom lip in a pout, and I rolled my eyes.

"I'm going to smack YOU with the stick." Dash retorted. "She knows what Caelum has to offer. Teach her about Tenebrae. That's the one she needs to know most."

"Okay, fine." Felix agreed. "Tenebrae is the Kingdom of Dark Magic. The magic wielders there are known as Shadow Shifters—those that can manipulate darkness itself, creating weapons, creatures, and just about anything else you can think of." I swallowed deeply as I listened. "Illusio—those that can create physical and mental illusions. They are quite rare but extremely powerful." A shudder rocked my body as I remembered how real my nightmare had felt, still not knowing if it was an illusion. Dash sat forward, shifting closer to me, his hand squeezing tighter on mine. "And Tremo—those with a power to induce pure fear and terror within one's mind. A terror so great that it can push the body into overdrive, causing the heart to give out and end an immortal life. It also leaves rather grotesque results." Pecus and Josephine's pale, distorted bodies flashed into focus.

"Is that all?" I said through uneasy laughter, trying to make light of the serious conversation. Dash placed a finger under my chin, tugging gently for me to look at him.

"We will not let anything happen to you, Ainsley," he promised, and I felt the truth in his words. "Come on," Dash said, kissing my forehead, "enough of the heavy. Let's focus on having fun today. Anything you want, it's yours." I looked between them as I pondered.

"Anything I want?" I asked.

"Anything," Dash confirmed.

"So if I said I wanted to see you two kiss...." Felix lunged across the table. He grabbed Dash's face before he could protest and planted a quick peck on his lips before his friend could push him away. Dash wiped his mouth with the back of his hand, and Felix simply shrugged in response.

"I didn't actually tell you to do it," I said.

"Honestly, I wish I could say that was the first time it happened," Dash explained. I narrowed my eyes as I wondered when it had occurred before.

"It was during a game of Truth or Dare," Felix offered, reading the question on my face. "And you know you liked it," he said, winking at Dash.

"Absolutely not. I know we aren't blood-related, but it still feels a bit incestuous, no?"

"Sometimes incest is the best," Felix declared.

"Gross!" Dash exclaimed.

"That's disgusting!" I added.

"I know," Felix said at once. "Even *I* think I went too far on that one." I laughed at my best friend before rolling my eyes and moving my attention back to Dash.

"I know what I want," I told him.

"As long as it doesn't involve kissing my brother again, it's yours," he teased.

"I want to see magic. I rarely see it used unless it's the two of you wielding it. My birthday is in a week, and after our lesson this morning, I want to know what I may have the potential to do." Dash and Felix both grinned at my request, no doubt happy they could also show off.

"As you wish," Dash replied and pulled me to my feet.

"Residents of Caelum," Dash announced, his voice loud and commanding. He had gathered as many people in the garden as he could find. "Your future princess would like to see your abilities. Let's give her a show, shall we?" The crowd roared with cheers and applause as everyone gathered toward the terrace, waiting their turn to be put on display. "What would you like to see first, beautiful?" Dash whispered in my ear. His proximity and the feel of his breath curling around my neck sent goosebumps over my arms. I sighed as I leaned back into him and his hands rested firmly on my waist. For a moment, I wondered if it was too late to change my mind and demand that I wanted time with him alone instead.

"I can't decide. I want to see it all," I breathed once my mind cleared from the spell I was under. Gods, I wanted him.

"Very well," he replied. "Everyone, show the princess what you can do." Flames flickered, water sprayed, ice shone, and the wind howled as everyone used their Gifts all at once. Children rushed the terrace steps, hoisting themselves on top of the wall to get a better look at the scene playing out. I watched as tiny hands climbed up both Dash and Felix, trying to get higher. They lifted the children onto their shoulders while other little bodies clung to their stomachs and legs. Dash's smile was dazzling as he held the kids, pointing out people in the crowd using their magic. The children laughed and clapped along, content to be in the presence of their prince. A prince who obviously loved them dearly. Their interactions had my heartstrings tugging, and I couldn't help but smile.

After a few more minutes of observing Dash and Felix entertain their tiny guests, I decided to make my way into the crowd, curious to see the Gifts unfold around me. Thunderous applause grasped my attention first, and I followed the sound to a circle of Ignesians letting their fire blaze brightly. Their flames roared in the center, spinning around faster and faster until a tornado of fire was formed. I watched in amazement as it lifted from the ground and suspended midair. The group then outstretched their arms and pushed the flames higher into the sky. At once, the tornado burst apart, sending embers raining over the residents. Instinctually, I covered my head, but as the sparks reached my skin, their heat was nonexistent. They simply looked like millions of fireflies swarming all around. Gods, I wished I would be granted this Gift.

I thanked the Ignesians for their display and walked over to the beckoning Undas on the other side of the garden. They eagerly pulled me into their gathering, and several held balls of water in their hands.

"Name a creature, my lady," a woman said. "Any creature and we can make it."

I stood thoughtfully for a moment before selecting a sea dragon.

"Is that okay? I can pick something else if it is too difficult," I offered, but she scoffed at the suggestion.

"Nonsense. We will show you why we are the most skilled of the magic wielders in Caelum," she announced, and an Ignesian standing next to me snorted before strolling away. They worked in pairs, each tasked with a different part of the creature's body. In less than ten minutes, a Sea Dragon had been sculpted. Not only that, its features seemed to come to life. A long tongue of water slithered, and its scales rippled as it moved.

"This is incredible!" I exclaimed, reaching a hand out to touch it. The woman halted my advance and shook her head before giving me a playful wink. Four more

Unda stepped forward, putting their hands on the sea dragon. My jaw dropped as the water transformed into clear glistening ice, setting the creature into a solid work of art. She released my arm, and I leaned forward, sliding my fingers along the beautiful ice sculpture.

"What do you think?" Dash's voice came from behind, and I whirled to find him watching me with a child still high upon his shoulders.

"I'm awestruck," I admitted turning back to the statue.

"It's your turn, Your Highness. What will you do?" the child asked.

"I'm not sure, Gideon. Do you have any suggestions?" he said playfully. Gideon leaned forward and whispered something in Dash's ear. "Do you think that will be enough to impress my fiancé?" The child nodded his head eagerly. Dash removed Gideon from his shoulders, setting the child back to the ground before crouching low. "Do you think you can keep her company for me while I do this?"

"Yes, Your Highness! It would be my honor," he said as he ran for me, wrapping his small arms around my legs. Dash gave me a flirtatious wink before closing his eyes in concentration.

The crowd quieted as they watched their prince with curious anticipation. A rumble echoed in the distance, and soon dark grey clouds formed overhead, blocking out the morning sun completely. It was late summer, but the temperature began to plummet, and soon I could see my breath in the air. I wrapped my arms around myself as my body began to shake from the cold when tiny, soft droplets landed on my skin. I looked down as more and more white flakes reached me. Snow. It was snowing in the summer. I brought my stare to Dash. His arms were raised high, and his palms faced up as if he were holding the world itself above him. How could anyone possibly be *that* powerful? Dash's eyes fluttered open, and he lowered his arms back to his sides, a tired smile on his face.

"You made it snow," I said as I strode for him.

"Gideon thought you would like it. Was he correct?"

"He was," I told him, wrapping my arms around his neck. Dash's grin grew as he slid his hands around my waist, pulling me tighter against him. "Do you know all of the residents by name?" Over five thousand people lived within the palace, so the idea seemed unlikely, but I was curious nonetheless. Maybe it was a requirement of being a prince.

"Not even close," Dash said, laughing to himself. "But I do know all of the children. I like to spend my time with them as they tend to be more honest and better company than their parents. Not to mention there aren't many of them here, so memorizing their names is far easier."

"Why are there so few children?" I asked, and Dash shrugged.

"When you're immortal, you have all the time in the world to have children. There isn't a need to rush."

"Maybe you should explain that to your father," I said pointedly, recalling his toast at my Welcome Feast. Dash nodded as he laughed and rubbed his hands over my cold arms.

"You're freezing," he observed, and my teeth began chattering on cue.

"Once again, you made it snow," I pointed out. Of course, I was freezing. I wasn't dressed for this sudden extreme weather, though I wasn't going to complain. I got to witness Dash do something marvelous, and I wouldn't have changed a thing. Dash closed his eyes again, and a moment later, the clouds dissipated as the sun shone bright again.

"What's next?" he asked. I thought about it for a minute, debating if there were something fun and adventurous I wanted to try. But the reality was, all I wanted to do was curl up with him somewhere safe and warm.

"The Sanctuary."

31.

"As much as I would love to grace you both with my presence all night, I have other matters to attend to," Felix announced, rising from the armchair he had been lounging in. After the magic fun this morning, we occupied the Sanctuary for the rest of the day. Dash and Felix took turns pampering me. They retrieved whatever food or beverage I required, read aloud whatever book I requested, and played whatever game I wanted. It was the perfect day.

"Who is it tonight?" I asked, looking up from my book.

"Tonight is Felicity," he said with a wink. I sat up, removing my legs from across Dash's lap, and plopped my book down next to me. She was always rude and cruel to not only me but everyone she deemed lesser than her. Unsurprisingly enough, she and Rosella were best friends.

"Felix, I thought you had better taste in lovers," I ground out, disappointment evident in my tone. He shrugged, stretching his arms above his head and twisting his back, probably trying to limber himself up for his much-anticipated exploits this evening.

"I'm looking for a good time, and from what I've heard, Felicity is quite experienced in that area."

"Let him have his fun," Dash added, grabbing my legs to set them back across his lap.

"No!" I said, glowering as I pulled away from him once again. "Felicity is a terrible person and constantly makes the servants and other ladies cry."

"I'm pretty sure there's only one thing he cares about her mouth doing, and it has nothing to do with speaking," Dash replied. My mouth dropped open as his words filled me with abhorrence. I looked to Felix for some sign that this wasn't true, but he smiled proudly. I shot to my feet, anger rising in me at his poor choice of company and at the fact that Dash was supportive of it.

"Fine. Then you and Felicity, " I turned my stare to Dash, "and you and Rosella can have a double date. I'm sure you four would have a fantastic time together," I said, stomping away to the wall of bookcases across the room. Dash and Felix's chuckles at my temper tantrum only pissed me off more.

"Is someone jealous?" Felix asked smugly.

"I believe she is," Dash added, a stupid cocky grin on his face. I wanted to punch him.

"I am not!" I exclaimed, far louder than I should have. Dash bit his lip in a desperate attempt to suppress his rising laughter.

"My apologies. I must have read the situation wrong," he remarked.

"Yeah. You must have." I snapped.

"My beautiful sunflower, you'll always be our number one girl," Felix said sweetly as he made his way to the exit. "But they put out." I whirled around, throwing a book as hard as I could at him. It hit the door with a loud bang at the exact moment he closed it, safely escaping my wrath. Dash laughed under his breath, and I twisted to face him, another book in my hands, ready to propel it at his face.

"He said it, not me." Dash defended, throwing his hands up in innocence. I lowered my weapon and turned back around, directing my focus on the bookcase, not wanting to look at him anymore. How could he encourage Felix to sleep with someone so hateful? I shuddered at the thought of Felix, Felicity, Dash, and Rosella together. Drinking wine and exchanging stories and laughing until they took each other to bed. Arms wrapped around my middle, and I instinctively tilted my head back, resting it against Dash's warm, muscled chest as his scent cocooned me.

"Don't be mad at me," he whispered as he swept my hair from my shoulder and planted a soft kiss in the crook of my neck. The irritation I felt melted away like hot butter the second his lips touched my skin. "I was just trying to get him out of here because I want you to myself." He tightened his embrace as he grazed his lips along my neck. "Come on." He led me back to the couch and pulled my legs over him once more as he handed me a book. I held it as he traced idle circles along my thighs. There was absolutely no way I could concentrate on written words with him this close. I tossed the novel onto the coffee table, narrowly missing a goblet full of wine, and turned my focus to Dash.

"I don't want to read," I told him. He nodded his head as he waited for me to make another suggestion. "I want to play Sharing is Caring." Dash groaned.

"You know I hate that game. Let's play Ten Questions instead."

"What's that?"

"It's similar to Sharing is Caring, but we don't tell stories. Each person gets to ask ten questions, and we go back and forth, answering them honestly. No question is off-limits and must be answered," he explained.

"Okay, let's play." I was intrigued by the idea. I knew that I could ask him questions under normal circumstances, but something about this being a game made me feel brave with my inquiries. "First question, who were you with that first time on Solstice?" I had wanted to ask him that when he first told the story, but the possibility of it being Rosella made my blood boil. The thought had haunted me ever since, and now I needed to know one way or the other.

"Easy. I don't know," he replied. I gave him a flat look. "Really, I don't know. All I remember was that she was from Ministro. She wasn't a royal, but the fact that she was here and seemed to be friends with the other visiting ladies tells me that she lived in the Ministro palace. A couple of years later, I saw her again during another visit, but we didn't exchange words." I nodded my head, content with his answer. "It's my turn now," he said, handing me my wine and taking a sip from his own before addressing me again. "Since we're bringing up Wyvern Pit night, I have a few questions of my own in mind."

I straightened, giving him my full attention. "Go ahead. I'm an open book when it comes to Logan." I had nothing to hide and would gladly answer anything about him.

"Oh, my Ainsley. I don't want to know about Logan." A devilish smile formed on his lips, and wickedness swirled in his eyes. I thought back to that night and the stories we each had told as I attempted to figure out what he would ask. After a heartbeat, the realization hit me, and my eyes widened. Dash's smile grew as he watched me put the pieces together. "I seem to recall you mentioning rarely being satisfied with Logan," oh dear Gods no, "and doing a particular activity better on your own." He bit his lip as he watched the dread on my face play out. "I want to know more about that." I had discussed sexual topics openly with just Felix before and even Dash in a group setting, but never one-on-one. With only the two of us here and how I felt about him, it seemed more personal now. More intimate than anything else. I drained my goblet before facing him.

"Fine. Ask your stupid question."

Dash sat up straighter and began drumming on my legs as he contemplated which question to ask. His smile was self-satisfying, and his face so full of glee that I wanted to smack him across it with the book that was now just out of reach.

"There are just so many things I want to know. What to ask first?" he mused happily, bobbing his head from side to side. "Okay, I know my first one. What do you imagine while you're doing it?" I narrowed my stare as I thought about how to answer.

"What do you mean? Like what location I picture myself in?" I asked, wanting to understand. It wasn't the question I thought he would ask first.

"Yes, but more so, do you picture yourself with someone? Are you the one doing it, or do you envision someone else's fingers inside you?" I swallowed hard. I hadn't expected Dash to be that bold in his questioning, but it thrilled me. A part of me wanted him to ask, and an even bigger part wanted to tell him everything he desired to know.

"Ummm..." I closed my eyes as I thought back to when I was alone in bed and the fantasies I had created in my mind. Twisting, shaping, and bringing my wildest desires to life with such detail and color like an artist with a brush and palate before a blank canvas. "I picture someone else doing it," I answered, my eyes fluttering open.

"Who?" Dash asked. I smiled as I shook my head back and forth.

"You already asked your question. It's my turn." I took a sip from my wine, debating on what I wanted to know next. If he wanted to know intimate details, so did I. "What do you imagine when *you* do it?" Dash wasted no time answering, like he had already prepared for this question.

"Sometimes someone else's hands or mouth. But most of the time, I picture my fingers inside her or my head between her thighs." My breathing hitched at his response, and I shivered. He took another sip of his drink before leaning forward to place it on the table. "Sometimes I also imagine that I'm buried deep between her legs," he added as if it were an afterthought.

"Oh," I said, almost breathless. "How often do you picture that?"

"Lately? Every day," he said without hesitation. My heart hammered beneath my chest, the blood pounding in my ears. I shifted in my seat, surprised at how much his confession had affected me.

"Who do you—"

"It's my turn now. And I answered two, so you have to as well." He placed his arm along the top of the couch, curling at the elbow, and rested his cheek against his fist while he studied me. His gaze was burning, and I felt the pressure build in my chest and my core under the heat of it. "Have you ever tasted Logan?"

"I thought you didn't want to know about him," I countered.

"I want to know about this."

"Yes," I answered, watching as Dash took a deep breath like he hated that fact.

"Has Logan ever tasted you?"

"No."

"You never wanted him to?" he asked, confused.

"No, it's not that. It's just that he never...." I trailed off, shrugging. Dash's eyes narrowed, and his brows knitted together as if he couldn't believe my answer.

"Would you have wanted him to?"

"It's not your turn anymore," I told him. "Have you ever used your magic with someone?"

"You mean while with a lover?"

"Yes. For uses of pleasure."

"No, never," he said immediately. I arched a brow, not quite believing his words. "It's true."

"But why wouldn't you? I know I don't have any magic of my own, but I would imagine the addition of it could enhance the experience for the better."

"I'm sure that's true, but I never wanted to." I gave him a look that silently begged him to elaborate. "My Gift isn't some party trick to show off. It's part of who I am, part of me. Using it in that way with someone had always felt too intimate, and it wasn't something I wanted to share." I had never thought of that. Dash had a vulnerability about him, and I could understand why he wanted to keep that side of him hidden, especially while with someone in an intimate way. "My turn?" I nodded, still processing his explanation. "Would you have wanted him to?" he asked, repeating his previous question.

"Yes."

"Is Logan who you picture?" he said, shifting closer.

"No." My voice was barely more than a whisper.

"Then who?"

I shook my head at him. "That was two."

I took one last sip of my wine before setting the cup down. Dash's throat bobbed as I licked my lips, trapping the last remnants of the sweet drink. I took a deep breath as I prepared to ask the one question I wasn't sure I wanted to know. "Is Rosella who you think of?"

"No. Not at all," he said before I could fully get the question out. I exhaled the breath I had been holding, and the tightness around my heart lessened at his answer.

"You said that you fantasize about it every day lately?" Dash nodded his confirmation, and his eyes encouraged me to continue. "And you don't picture Rosella," I stated more to myself than to him, but he shook his head nonetheless. "Do you picture a different person each time?"

"No. It's the same person every time." I felt comfort in knowing that.

"What do you imagine?"

"I already answered that," he said, reaching over and interlacing my fingers with his, his touch igniting something hot and bold in my blood.

"What I mean is, can you share an example? A specific memory you think of when you do it."

"I don't think of a memory," he said, and there was a seductive edge to his voice that sent goosebumps over my skin.

"Then tell me something that you've thought of." I wanted to know the extent of his imagination. I wanted to know exactly what he pictured and in detail.

"Okay," Dash said after a moment of consideration. "There is this one particular fantasy that I keep going back to. It starts with her straddling me." His eyes narrowed marginally as if a thought had just occurred to him. As if a decision had been made in his mind. "Like this," he said, pulling my hand and guiding me over his lap. I willingly placed my legs on either side of him and then rested my hands on his shoulders. He lifted my dress slightly and placed his hands just above my knees. My breathing caught at his searing touch, and I watched as Dash's chest began to rise and fall faster. It was as though he was working hard to stay calm; to restrain himself. "And then I'd work my way up, savoring the feel of her bare skin." His hands slid slowly up my thighs. I gasped softly and dug my fingers into his shoulders for support. "Is this okay?" he whispered. I nodded eagerly, wanting more. Wanting him to advance higher and higher. He continued upward, and as his hands grazed further under my dress and over my hipbone, he stilled. His eyes shot to mine, and surprise flashed over his features. "And then I'd find that she wasn't wearing any underwear?" I bit my lip at his discovery and gave him a sly smile as I shrugged.

"Sometimes I'm not." Dash's eyes darkened with hunger and glazed over with lust. He leaned forward, resting his head against my stomach as his chest heaved and his grip on me tightened. "Is that a problem?" I asked coyly.

"No. But I just learned that you have been completely naked under your dresses. I need a minute." I smiled as I impatiently waited for him to garner control of himself. After what I felt was enough time—ten seconds, give or take—I raked my hand through his silken hair and tugged gently, pulling his head back to look at me.

"Your minute is up. Finish your story," I commanded. He bit his lip, and his hands traveled to my backside, squeezing tightly. I groaned at his touch, and Dash let out a low growl of approval as he brought his hands back to my front.

"Sorry to keep you waiting," he said, dragging his hands back down to my knees and then moving to the insides of my thighs. His fingers slowly began their ascent once more, but this time, along the sensitive part of my inner legs. I began to tremble beneath him as he climbed higher and higher, so close to the spot that I wanted him to touch. "Finally, I'd be close enough to feel her warmth," he said breathlessly. I leaned forward, gripping his shoulders hard as I closed my eyes and worked to catch my breath. If his hands traveled just an inch higher, he would feel the evidence of how much my body craved his touch. How much I wanted him. I shifted my hips forward, begging him to continue his advance, but he halted and withdrew. I pulled back a little to meet his eyes, my face full of confusion and worry.

"Why did you stop?" I whimpered and a crooked smile formed on Dash's face. His eyes were bright, and his stare was longing as he looked up at me.

"Are you sure you want me to continue?"

I nodded eagerly as I gripped him harder. "I was the one who asked the question. I want to hear your answer," I said, my voice laced with desire, my breath almost escaping me completely. "I want to know what you do to her." I leaned down, my face now close enough to feel his breath on my skin. Dash's eyes slipped to my mouth and then back to my stare as he slowly shook his head. No?

"Not *her*. You. It's what I think about doing to *you* every day." I stopped breathing at his confession. "And it starts with me doing this." He dragged a finger through my center, and I fell forward, moaning at his touch. Dash sucked in a breath as he felt how soaked I was. How ready I was for him. "Gods Ainsley, are you always this wet?" he said, his voice pained as his grip on my waist tightened. A territorial need that let me know just how hard he was struggling to restrain himself. I leaned back to meet his eyes. They were wide and so dark they looked nearly black. His breathing quickened as he drew his fingers back and forth over me again in slow, torturous strokes. My head swam with pleasure, and I wanted more. I needed more. I needed everything he had to offer. He said it was me that he fantasized about each day, and I rejoiced in that confession. I took his face between my hands as I bent down, resting my forehead against his, inhaling his scent. His breath smelled of sweet wine and mint.

"Yes," I whispered. "Every time I imagine, it's your fingers inside of me instead of my own." Dash groaned, and his thumb traveled up, rubbing delicious circles around my most sensitive part. My fingers twisted in his hair, pulling tightly as I held on, the pressure in my core building and building.

"You think of me?" he asked, moving his fingers to my entrance. I squeezed my eyes shut in anticipation, ready to savor the feel of him.

"Yes. Every time I touch myself, I think of you. Only you," I told him. As soon as the words escaped from my lips, Dash plunged a finger inside. I gasped as he groaned in pleasure.

"Fuck, Ainsley," he growled as he slipped in a second finger, pumping in and out of me slowly, deliberately. I pressed my forehead harder against his as I moaned with each thrust he gave.

"What are you thinking right now?" I said, exasperated, needing a distraction. Needing something to take me away from the edge I was about to fall off.

"How fucking good you feel," he replied without a thought. "You feel so much better than I ever imagined." His thumb worked in time with his fingers, and I knew I wouldn't last much longer. The heat and pressure now coursed through my body, and I felt a tingle build down my spine. "You?"

"That I don't want you to stop," I said breathlessly and moved on him, my hips rocking forward as I rode his hand. He gripped my waist, guiding me back and forth with his free hand, pushing me deeper and deeper. "Dash," I whined and covered my mouth to quiet the sound I knew was about to break free. He pulled my hand away from my lips at once.

"No. I want to hear every sound you make," he demanded. His thumb swirled faster, and I moved to match his tempo, feeling my inner muscles clench around him. I was teetering on the edge of ecstasy. "That's it, Ainsley." He bent forward, dragging this tongue up the column of my throat, fire burning through me in his wake. Fucking Gods. He released my waist, bringing his hand up to hold the back of my head, his face close to mine. I leaned into his mouth, taking his bottom lip between my teeth and tugging gently as I pulled away. Dash groaned, and I gasped for breath moving faster and faster on him. My body was so close to falling over the cliff I had been holding on to. "Come for me," he coaxed as he pressed his lips to my open mouth, our breath mingling and mixing in raw, undiluted passion.

I unraveled at his words, splintering into a million pieces. I screamed his name as I climaxed, holding him so tight it was as if he, not gravity, held me to this world. Dash slipped in his tongue, flicking it against the roof of my mouth like he was tasting the sound of his name as I yelled it. His fingers continued their work, pumping in and out, drawing out every last ounce of pleasure, draining me completely. I trembled above him as the final wave rocked through me, leaving me panting and weak.

I opened my eyes in time to see Dash withdraw his fingers and bring them to his lips, sucking them clean. I felt the pressure build again at that sight alone and pressed my thighs together, feeling the slickness that had pooled. He brought his hands up, brushing back the strands of sweat-slicked hair from my face as I struggled to catch my breath and pressed a soft kiss to my forehead as he cupped my flushed cheeks.

"That is what I've thought about doing to you every single day," he said, and a shiver went down my spine. "Making you whimper. Making you scream." His lips traveled down, grazing my jawline as he spoke. "But the next time I make you come, Ainsley...." He leaned back to look at me, his eyes alert despite the haze of lust within them. He wanted to ensure he had my full attention, "It will be on my tongue." I sucked in a breath at his promise, my hands fisting in his shirt. "And when I finally come," he said, his stare dark with hunger, "I want to be buried deep inside you."

My mouth went dry as a throbbing between my thighs began to form. Gods, I wanted him. His chest heaved faster as his eyes dropped to my mouth like he was thinking the same thing. I lowered myself onto his lap, feeling him hard as granite beneath me. Instinctively, my hips rocked forward, grinding against him. Dash groaned as he gripped my waist so hard that I knew I would bruise. I needed to feel more. I needed to feel him inside of me.

"So what's stopping you?" I challenged. His blue eyes widened with feral need. They were the words he was waiting for—the permission he needed to hear. Dash lifted me and sat me next to him on the couch, pressing me firmly against the back cushions. He leaned over, claiming my neck with his mouth, kissing and licking his way across it. "I want you, Dash," I breathed, reaching for him, wanting to stroke him. But he pulled back and moved in front of me as if getting ready to kneel. He leaned forward, kissing my cheek as he spoke.

"I want to taste you first," he whispered. A soft moan escaped from my throat at his words just as the door to our Sanctuary banged open with a sound as loud as thunder.

32.

I twisted my face away from Dash on instinct, as if I were caught doing something wrong. But it didn't *feel* wrong. It felt so, so right. Dash pressed his forehead against the side of my face as he sighed. We were *so* close.

"You two simply would not believe what just happened to me," Felix announced. I pivoted back around to face forward and found Felix entering the library with his back to us, pulling a dessert cart with him. I dragged my hand through my hair and choked back the laugh that threatened to bubble over at his less-than-impeccable timing. I threw a sidelong glance at Dash to find him staring up at the ceiling, shaking his head and muttering something about how he was going to murder his best friend and then hide the body so it would never be found. I laughed softly then, causing Dash to snap his eyes to mine. He curled his lips into the most adorable pout as he exhaled loudly through his nose and plopped himself back onto the couch.

Felix had been divulging the story of his evening as he tended to his cart of desserts, fixing each of us a plate. Unfortunately for him, neither Dash nor I had been paying any attention. We were too transfixed on each other and what almost just occurred between us. Dash glanced at my mouth, and I immediately felt the familiar drum of desire within my blood as my mind traveled back to moments before being interrupted. My breathing hitched and a lump formed in my throat as I remembered how good it felt when his fingers were moving inside of me. Blood rushed to my cheeks, and I tore my gaze from Dash, forcing myself to watch Felix instead as I worked to control my breathing. As I worked to control the delicious thoughts that were plaguing my mind.

"Right? You know what I mean?" Felix asked as he set a plate full of raspberry pastries on the table and then worked on filling the second dish.

"Mhm. Of course," I told him absentmindedly. I hadn't the slightest idea what he was talking about but agreeing with him always seemed like the safest choice. The cushion next to me shifted as if a weight had been applied, and I glanced over to see that Dash had moved closer at the same time his arm wrapped around my shoulder. He was staring straight ahead and nodding as if he were fully engrossed in Felix's story. As if he wasn't gently stroking my arm with his fingers that had been inside me moments before. I shuddered. His touch was like lightning through my body. Pure energy paving its way through and becoming part of me. My eyes fluttered closed as I focused on his touch.

"That's true," Dash told Felix, sounding confident in his response. Like he had been paying attention this entire time. My eyes fluttered open as warm breath tickled my ear.

"Just so we're clear," he whispered close enough that I knew Felix had no chance of hearing. Our friend was still talking, completely enthralled in his tale as he worked on pouring wine into three fresh glasses. "I desperately want to taste you." I wasn't breathing. I bit my lip to keep from gasping. From moaning. From verbally giving away any clues as to what his words were doing to me. His thumb brushed over my bottom lip, pulling it out from between my teeth. "And that—" he said as I brought my stare to him, his eyes fixated on my mouth, "isn't helping." His chest heaved nearly as quickly as mine. The need for each other was near palpable.

"Are you guys even listening?!" Felix demanded.

"No," we said in unison, eyes locked on one another.

"Okay, well, start now. Because this is truly a great story," Felix explained as he shoved a full glass of wine in one of my hands and a plate of chocolate tartlets in the other. Reluctantly, Dash and I settled into the couch and faced forward, giving Felix our full attention as he dove into his story from the very beginning.

33.

The following day, I awoke in my bed, unsure how I'd gotten there. Dash must have carried me to my room at some point during the night. I sat up, still in the dress I had worn yesterday, to find Imogen entering from the bathing room, her onyx hair in its neatly piled bun atop her head and a welcoming smile across her face.

"Good morning, Ainsley," she said as she headed to the armoire to pick out my attire for the day. "It's nice to see you in your room for once." Some nights I had fallen asleep in the library, too exhausted to walk across the entire palace to get back to my chamber. Other nights, Felix had carried me to his bedroom down the hall, complaining that *he* was too exhausted to walk across the entire palace to take me back to my chamber. And on rare occasions, Dash had walked me back to my room, taking up his usual seat in the armchair by the window until I had fallen asleep. "What is the point of setting out nightclothes for you if you refuse to wear them?" she asked, waving a hand over my current ensemble.

"I don't even remember making it back here last night," I confessed, dragging a hand through my hair. She strode over and handed me a folded piece of paper before returning to her task of rifling through dresses. *'My Fierce Flame'* was written in Dash's hand on the front. Grinning like a fool, I hopped out of bed and walked to the open window to read my letter. The sunlight shining through was warm against my skin, and the scent of roses and citrus swirled along a gentle breeze. I rested my head against the frame as I flipped open Dash's letter.

"Dinner tonight... Just you and I? Please select from the following options below: Yes. No. Meh.

p.s. You're beautiful

p.s.s. Please save me from these meetings because they are terrible and keep me from seeing you.

p.s.s.s. I miss you."

I laughed under my breath, my heart squeezing tight as I read the note over and over again. I twisted, searching the vanity directly to my right for a pen. I found one, out and waiting, next to a single fresh white rose. I beamed ear to ear as I brought the flower to my nose and inhaled its sweet scent.

"Which option are you going to choose?" Imogen asked, pulling a pastel blue dress off its hanger.

"You read the letter?" I scolded, not surprised in the least by her actions.

"Of course I read it," she scoffed, striding towards me with my attire for the day in her hands. I rolled my eyes at her confession, and she shrugged as if she had no shame. "Niall!" she yelled, and a guard entered the room. "Take this to His Highness immediately." She jerked her chin to the paper in my hands. I quickly circled '*Meh.*' before adding a little note of my own.

'Only if you promise there will be a chocolate tartlet in attendance.'

I folded the paper and handed it to Niall, offering him a quick 'thank you' before he bowed his head and retreated from the room. Imogen reached for my hand, unclasping the bracelet and placing it on the vanity. My wrist now felt bare and cold. I didn't like having it off.

"Go and quickly bathe. You're going to miss breakfast." I took the dress from her outstretched hands and headed into the bathing room. As I sank into the tub, the hot soapy water lapped over my body, and the smell of lavender from the oils Imogen had added filled the room. I closed my eyes as I soaked, letting my mind wander to thoughts of last night. To falling asleep in Dash's arms as he held me close, and to Felix's ridiculous story. To the memory of Dash's lips on my skin and how my fingers felt as I ran them through his hair. To the thoughts of my body pressed tightly against his and how his hands trailed up my thighs beneath my dress. A knock on the door jolted me upright, causing water to spill over the side of the tub as I worked to quiet the fantasies in my mind. "You are taking too long," Imogen called from the other side of the door.

"I'm getting out now," I announced, annoyed at the interruption. When I entered my room once more, Imogen was staring out the window, surveying something below. I headed for her and was met with the sound of Rosella's shrill laughter. I groaned as I leaned over the opening, spying her and her friends gathered around the table on the terrace. My appetite disappeared in response. I would have to find somewhere else to go today as I had zero desire to be in Rosella's company. I could head to our Sanctuary, but it was beautiful out. The weather was warm but not hot, and fluffy white clouds floated gingerly across the sky. It would be a shame to waste the day inside.

"I heard there is an orchard on the grounds," I said, still watching Rosella lounge arrogantly in Dash's chair as if it were her very own throne.

"There is," Imogen said softly. A sadness in her voice that I didn't understand pulled my attention from the scene below. "Did prince Dashiell tell you about it?" I shook my head, and she nodded before gesturing for me to sit at the vanity. I obeyed, and she came behind me, working a comb through my damp tangles. "King Perceval had the orchard built for his queen as a wedding present. It became a tradition for them to have an afternoon picnic there every weekend. It was something prince Dashiell very much looked forward to when he was younger." Her hazel eyes met mine in the mirror as she spoke again. "As far as I know, he hasn't been there since she died. The only people that ever enter the orchard are the kitchen servants who collect the fruit for meals." She set down the comb, my hair now free of knots. I stood from the chair and faced her.

"Do you think he'll ever go back?"

She offered a tight smile and reached for the bracelet to secure around my wrist once more. "I think that is something only he will be able to answer." I nodded as I processed her words. I wanted to know how Dash felt about it, but I was too afraid to ask. I hated the thought of bringing up any memories that would cause him pain, but I was curious about this orchard and why it had meant so much to his family. The sound of a throat clearing caught our attention.

"My lady," Niall said, returning with the paper from Dash. I opened it at once to find a new note scrawled along the bottom.

"There most definitely will be. But you never said I had to promise to share. I can't wait to see you tonight.

- Dash"

I smiled at the response before scribbling the word 'Speedy' in front of his name and handing the parchment back to Niall to deliver one final time. I could picture his cocky smile and hear his beautiful laughter in my head when he saw my correction.

"Felix came by while you were in the tub," Imogen said as if only just remembering this fact. "He said he was just finishing up with King Perceval, and he'll meet you in front of a room."

"In front of which room?" I asked, but Imogen shrugged.

"To be completely honest, I don't pay attention to half of what that boy says. All I know is that he is probably waiting somewhere for you now."

My guards—Aleczander and Dementri—fell in step as I headed straight for the Sanctuary, assuming it was Felix's chosen location. It made the most sense as that was where we spent every day, but he wasn't there when I arrived. I waited for ten minutes, fifteen, twenty, before finally leaving. I guess I was wrong. Maybe he meant *his* room. I walked the short distance to Felix's bed chamber, but he wasn't there either. What the Hell? Maybe I was supposed to wait for him in my room? Perhaps I had just missed him earlier. Once I reached my room, I noticed the door was slightly ajar, and I sighed in relief to know I had finally located Felix. I plopped myself on my bed as the sound of running water filled the space.

"You should be more specific next time you want to meet somewhere. I've been walking around the palace for the last half hour trying to find you," I whined over the splashing sound. "Why did you want to meet in my room, anyway?" He didn't answer. "Felix?" I called louder this time. Still no answer.

Cautiously, I slid from the bed and made my way over to the door. "Felix, can you hear me?" I asked, knocking on the door. Nothing. "Okay, I'm coming in. I swear to the Gods, Felix, if your dick is out...." I warned as I jiggled the handle. It wasn't locked. "One. Two. Three." I flung the door open and water pooled at my feet. The entire bathing room floor was flooded, and every faucet was on. What the fuck? I hurried over to the sinks, turning each nozzle to stop the relentless stream, before running over to the bath that was now overflowing. As I shut off the water, something unusual caught my eye. I leaned closer and found Annette's deformed, grey, and lifeless body at the bottom of the tub.

I opened my mouth to scream, but nothing came out. I was too paralyzed with fear and shock to do anything, completely rooted to the spot. The hair along my arms rose, and a sickening dread and alarm filled every vein in my body. Someone else was here, or at least they were about to be. My instincts took over, and I rushed to a tall cabinet with towels and other supplies. I pushed them to the side and cramped myself into the tight space, closing the door behind me. My stomach rolled over, and my heart pounded loudly in my chest as the sounds of quiet footsteps approached. I clasped a hand over my mouth to limit the sounds of my breathing as the room began to fill with darkness.

Peeking through the tiny crack in the door, I could see swirls of shadow ink out from a dark silhouette and coil around his arm. The tendrils spun and morphed until it was clear that one hand held a rope and the other a blade. The stranger could sense I was here in the same way I could sense him. Had he been waiting here for me to show up after he made his first kill? I screwed my eyes shut and prayed to the Gods that someone would find this murderer before they found me. Their footfalls grew louder, and I could feel their presence inching closer to my hiding place. Any second now, they would find me. I prayed harder. Laughter echoed loudly in the hall, and I could feel the murderer's focus slip at the sound, their steps retreating and unsure. The room grew quiet but still heavy. I couldn't garner the bravado to open my eyes as I waited for my capture. Suddenly the cabinet door opened, and arms wrapped around me, pulling me from the cabinet and dragging me away from the bathing room as I fought to free myself. I wouldn't go without a fight.

"Ainsley, it's okay! It's me!" Felix's voice cut through my panicked fog, and my body slowly calmed without my permission. "I'm sorry, I know you hate when I use my magic, but you must calm down. We need to know what happened." We? I glanced up to find Dash speaking quickly to a guard, but his eyes were firmly locked on me.

"I was looking for you," I told Felix weakly, finally able to find my voice thanks to his Gift. Dash ran over the second I started speaking.

"Are you okay?" he demanded as he pulled me to his chest. I nodded and buried my face against him, never feeling safer than I did in his arms. "What happened?"

"I couldn't find Felix, so I returned to my room, and that's when I found Annette," I explained. "Where were you?" I asked Felix.

"The Sanctuary," he answered. "I was waiting for you there, but then King Perceval needed my assistance with something. I assumed you would have waited for me until I got back."

"Did you see anyone near your room?" Dash asked me.

"No one. When I arrived, there wasn't anyone in the hall, and the door was left open. I thought it was Felix inside the bathing room. I had no idea that...." Tears began to spring from my eyes, and Dash held me tighter. "And then my instincts started screaming that I wasn't alone, so I hid in the cabinet. Someone from Tenebrae came in the room shortly after that," Dash's face paled, and his blue eyes widened as he nodded for me to continue. "Dash, they used their shadow magic to form a rope and blade. They were looking for me," I said, my shaky voice breaking on the words.

"But they didn't find you," Felix reassured.

"Only because there were voices outside my room that scared them off," I snapped back. Tenebrae was getting too close.

"I need to inform my father what has happened," Dash announced. "Felix, have the guards keep this corridor clear. I don't want anyone coming in and out until we can move the body. Then, take Ainsley to the Sanctuary." Felix dipped his head, accepting the order from his prince. Dash turned to me next. "I know you're going to hate this, but I'll be assigning two more guards to stay with you at all times unless you are with Felix or me. That includes being stationed *in* your room at night while you sleep." I didn't bother trying to object as I knew he would do anything to ensure my safety. He leaned forward and kissed my forehead before letting me go. "I'll try to be as quick as possible with my father, but it may take a while. I'll see you tonight, though?" he asked hopefully, and I smiled.

"Will I still get a tartlet?" I teased, trying to bring a sense of normalcy back to my shaking body as if I wasn't just hiding in a freaking cabinet and scared to death.

"I will bring as many chocolate tartlets as you want, beautiful," he said and then backed away through the corridor.

34.

I averted my eyes as I walked, avoiding the curious glances and hushed whispers that followed me through the palace. The two new guards following so closely that one of them had tripped me twice on the short walk weren't helping matters. I let out a long sigh the moment I reached the terrace, seeing Felix's bright eyes and smiling face as I approached.

"Did you enjoy your beauty rest?" he asked, closing the book he had brought with him. The moment we reached the library, he demanded I take a nap, telling me that I looked like absolute shit and he wouldn't be caught dead next to someone in that state. My best friend, ladies and gentlemen.

"I would have rather you had woken me," I replied, narrowing my eyes as I tried to read the title. Felix shook his head as he tossed the novel between us, the iron table vibrating with a thud.

"It's just okay," he said as I picked up the book. "Not as dirty as we like." I rolled my eyes and then looked around, noticing a place setting had not been set for Dash. "He's with his father," Felix explained, reading my thoughts before I could voice them.

"Still?" I asked. I knew he said it could take a while, but it had been hours since we parted. I had hoped he would have been done by now so we could have our private dinner together. The fact that it was taking this long had my stomach knotted with worry. This was the third body that had been found since I arrived at the palace, and each attack was getting closer and closer to me. At this rate, it wouldn't be much longer until Tenebrae succeeded in their attempts to—

"Is my company not enough anymore?" Felix asked in mock outrage, interrupting my morbid thoughts. He pressed his hand against his heart as if trying to keep it from breaking into tiny pieces.

"Of course it is, and you know it," I said as two servants appeared with our dinner of fish and vegetables, my stomach audibly rumbling at the sight. I wasted no time digging in, piling the flaky salmon on my fork and taking a bite entirely too big for my mouth. I tried to focus on eating and not on the idea that if I had been in my room minutes earlier, it would have been me at the bottom of that tub. Or worse, kidnapped and taken away to be bred for the magic I may possess.

Felix sighed, but I ignored him, spearing a green bean and popping it into my mouth next. Another sigh, this time noticeably louder. I sipped from my wine cup as I swallowed and stared at the plate in front of me. Once again, another sigh, loud and exaggerated, only now it was accompanied by silverware clinking against ceramic dishes. I reluctantly looked up, finding Felix stabbing a small potato so hard that the plate beneath made a piercing sound as the fork made contact. He glared at me, eyes narrowed with annoyance. What the Hell was his problem?

"What?" I said, setting my fork down to give him my undivided attention; nothing less would be acceptable to him.

"I was just wondering when we stopped being best friends," he said, puncturing a single green bean beneath the potato.

"I wasn't aware that we had stopped," I countered, crossing my arms and settling in for Felix's display of dramatics.

"Best friends tell each other things," he said, setting his fork, still filled with untouched food, onto his dish.

"Okay?" I said, dragging out the word, not understanding what he was getting at. "I do tell you things. Everything, actually."

"Sure you do."

"Okay, can we cut it out with the temper tantrum, and you just tell me what you're mad about?" Today was rough enough, and I was quickly becoming annoyed with his antics.

"You didn't tell me about you and Dash in the Sanctuary last night," he said, and his arms tightened across his chest, the muscles in his forearms flexing with the movement. "You know sexual gossip is my favorite."

"I thought he would have told you." To be honest, I assumed Dash would have mentioned it to Felix immediately, as they'd shared every detail of their lives with one other for years.

"Well, he didn't, and he won't tell me anything," he whined. "I already tried to get it out of him." I laughed as Felix stuck out his bottom lip in a pout. He truly hated being left out of anything.

"Since when does Dash *not* tell you of his exploits?" I picked my fork back up and took another bite of food now that Felix seemed to calm down.

"Since they have to do with you," he answered, grabbing his own utensil. I swallowed hard. Why wouldn't Dash share what happened between us? Was he ashamed? Did he want to keep it secret? My appetite started to dissipate at the unwanted thoughts. "Relax," Felix said. "It's because he doesn't want to make you uncomfortable by sharing the details with me." I let out a small sigh of relief under my breath. "And also because he wants to keep you to himself. Which is stupid."

"I like that Dash wants to keep the intimacy of our relationship just between us. But more than that...." I whispered, leaning across the table and looking left and right as if checking to ensure no one could overhear our conversation. Felix's eyes widened with intrigue as he bent forward, closing the distance between us. "I like knowing something you don't," I admitted, tapping my finger against the tip of his nose. He threw himself back into his chair as he let out a loud and frustrated groan causing me to bellow with laughter at his tantrum.

Felix pouted for another five minutes, picking at his food before I decided to finally put him out of his misery. I had always planned on telling him, but he deserved to squirm after interrupting us last night.

"We played Ten Questions," I said, breaking the silence. Felix's eyes shot to mine. He was practically bouncing in his seat as he realized I was willing to divulge the information he so desperately wanted to know. "During the game, we asked questions about what we picture while we...." I trailed off, allowing him to make the connection. He slid his plate away and set his elbows on the table, resting his chin in his hands as he listened intently. "I told him about things I've done to Logan and things Logan never did to me."

"Like?" Felix interrupted. I debated how to eloquently explain it without sounding crude or vulgar, though I knew he wouldn't care.

"Let's just say Logan used his mouth for talking and nothing else." Felix's jaw dropped in shock.

"What a fucking douche noodle," he said, the words dripping in disgust. "So no one's ever traveled to the border? Ate from the honey pot? Learned a new language? Steamed the oyster? Explored your love tunnel? Picked the peach?"

Mother of Gods above.

"No," I said, laughing at his ridiculous innuendos.

"Well, that's unfortunate. Though I'm positive Dash was happy about it." I knitted my brows together, not sure what he was inferring. "He gets to be the first." He shrugged as if the answer were obvious. *'But the next time I make you come, Ainsley, it will be on my tongue.'* His promise echoed in my ears, and warmth began to spread through my body like wildfire as I pictured his mouth between my legs. "And then what happened?" Felix asked, jolting me from my fantasies. By the smug look on his face, he knew exactly what I had been thinking about.

"I asked him to share a detailed example of a fantasy he had, and he opted to demonstrate rather than explain," I admitted, looking down as I bit my lip, thinking back to that night and how his hands felt as they slid up my thighs. I glanced at Felix to find a wide smile plastered across his face.

"Ainsley, you cheeky little minx!" he said, shaking his head in amazement. "Tell me there's more." I exhaled a long breath as I remembered the very reason I had nothing else to share about it.

"There would have been had we not been interrupted," I said, giving him a pointed look. Felix somehow smiled even wider as he gave an apologetic shrug. Something dawned on me at that moment. "Wait, you said Dash hadn't told you anything."

"He hadn't," Felix answered.

"But you were mad at me for not telling you about us," I explained. "So if neither of us had told you, how did you know that I had 'sexual gossip' about last night?"

"Oh, I knew the second I entered that room that something was going on between you two," he said. "Your hearts were beating out of your chest, and both of your emotions were running wild. I just couldn't figure out if something *had* transpired or if it was about to."

"So you decided to *stay*?" As I spoke, I felt a wave of anger and annoyance rush to the surface.

"Yeah, because what happened to me was far more important than either of you getting laid," he announced with zero shame. Metal dug into my hand, and I realized I had been clutching my fork; the prongs pointed directly at Felix. "Not to mention, I didn't want to have our Sanctuary tainted by your sexcapades."

"You are the absolute worst," I said, annoyed. I was close to removing his status as my best friend for this act of betrayal.

"No, I'm not," he mused, sliding his plate of food back in front of him. "Plus, you two deserve more than just a quickie on the couch for your first time together." I perked up at his words, the thoughtfulness behind them melting away my anger and frustration. I smiled weakly before picking up my fork and pushing around the remainder of food on my plate. Annette's fixed, pained expression surged into the forefront of my mind. I dropped my utensil, unable to finish my meal.

"So my attempts at a humorous distraction didn't work, did they?" he asked gently.

"Not really, no," I whispered. "But I appreciate that you tried."

"Do you want to talk about it?"

"I'm scared, Felix," I admitted. "It wasn't until today that I truly understood the danger that I'm in. If I hadn't gone looking for you, I wouldn't be here right now. Annette lost her life because I walked out of that room. How do I know the next casualty won't be Imogen, you, or Dash?"

"Because I won't let it, and neither will Dash. We'll add more guards and take more precautions. We'll figure out who is doing this, Ainsley." I knew Felix believed every word he told me, but I couldn't bring myself to feel the same. The more time that went on, the less confidence I had that we all would remain safe.

"Can we talk about something else?" I pleaded, and Felix nodded gently, no doubt able to feel the unease that was brewing inside me.

"Can I ask you a question?"

"Of course," I told him.

"With what happened between you and Dash last night," he began slowly. "Is it the same as it was with you and Logan?" By the look on his face, I knew he wasn't inquiring about the physicality of what Dash and I had done.

"No," I said immediately. "It's not like it was with Logan; that was purely just about sex. With Dash, it means so much more."

"Why?" he probed, setting his fork down as he stared at me. His amber eyes were soft, and a small, knowing smile began to spread across his beautiful face. I took a deep breath as I readied myself to say the words aloud for the first time.

"Because I'm in love with him." Felix's answering smile grew, and his eyes misted over, nothing but pure delight reflecting on his face.

"I know," he said, his voice thick with emotion and happiness. "I just wanted to hear you say it." Felix pushed away from the table and walked over, wrapping his strong arms around me from behind and pressing his lips to my cheek.

"You deserve to be happy," he whispered against my skin, holding me close, and I drank in his comforting spice and leather scent. Warm light spread through my body as he held me, and a sense of joy, longing, excitement, and pride filled me, though they weren't *my* emotions. Somehow, Felix had allowed me to feel his. I closed my eyes, allowing myself to drift through his essence, caressing every emotion he had as I explored.

After a few short seconds, he pulled away and walked back to his chair. He smiled as he sat, but something felt off. He seemed to be lost in his thoughts, and by the look on his face, there was sadness or confusion embedded within. I opened my mouth to ask what was going on in his mind, but before I could, he shook his head, already knowing my plan. Whatever it was, he wasn't ready to share it. I nodded my head, respecting his wishes. We spent the rest of the meal in a comforting silence until Felix causally announced he had someone waiting for him in his bed.

"So why are you down here with me?" I asked incredulously. Surely dinner with me wasn't nearly as exciting as what was waiting for him upstairs. He wiped the corner of his mouth with the white silk napkin and strode over, placing a kiss on the top of my head before he spoke.

"You'll always be my number one, sugar cube," he said, and the corner of my lips twitched. "Our Delicious Duo quality time is far more important than my need to... arrive." I rolled my eyes, not only at his attempt to refrain from a vulgar description, but at the pet name he dubbed our friendship. He walked backward toward the palace. "Oh, and tell him how you feel," Felix said with a wink before disappearing inside.

I wanted to tell Dash I was in love with him. I was ready to, and with how things had been going lately, I wasn't sure how many more chances I would get. With a long deep breath, I stood and began the journey back to my room, where I would wait for Dash to arrive.

35.

The hour was late, and my eyes, laced with exhaustion despite my nap earlier, began to droop. Dash was running later than I expected. It wasn't like him to set plans with me and not follow through, or at least send word. I knew he was looking forward to spending time alone together, and the fact that it was the middle of the night and I still hadn't heard anything from him worried me. The feeling was heavy and all-encompassing, like a boulder being dropped into the depths of the ocean. The only comfort I felt was that if something were indeed wrong with Dash, Felix would have wasted no time telling me. I took several deep breaths as I worked to calm my nerves. Climbing into bed, I grabbed a book from my side table to pass the time and clear my racing mind. I shook myself awake, determined to fight sleep and my tired eyes. I'd continue to wait for him.

"Good morning, Ainsley," Imogen announced as she flung open the armoire, the wood creaking with the motion. I sat up, startled as I looked around. Sure enough, the morning sun was bright as it illuminated my bed chamber. My eyes drifted to the armchair across the room, but it was empty, and the sheets next to me were crisp and untouched. My heart sank as I realized he hadn't come to me last night.

"Have you seen Dash?" I asked Imogen, and she looked up from her task, her forehead creasing as she did. My voice was coated in worry and uncertainty, and I knew she could detect it.

"I passed him in the hall this morning," she said tentatively. "Is everything okay?"

"I think so," I told her. "I just haven't seen or heard from him since yesterday afternoon."

"Oh," she said, relieved, and went back to selecting my dress. "He was probably just occupied with King Perceval. I'm sure they had a lot to discuss after what happened." There was truth in that statement. Finding another body and no culprit was starting to set the palace residents on edge. Though I felt comfort in knowing Dash was alive and well, I still felt like something wasn't right.

I didn't reply to her as I strode to the bathing room to prepare for the day, wanting nothing more than to head down to breakfast in hopes of seeing him. When I arrived on the terrace, Felix was there, bright-eyed and waiting, but no sign of Dash. My chest ached as I took in the spread, noticing that, once again, there was no place setting for him.

"So, how did last night go?" Felix said eagerly, straightening in his chair as I approached.

"It didn't," I replied, my facing falling with disappointment. "He never showed up." I sighed as I sank into my chair, sliding my plate of food away, my appetite nonexistent. Felix cocked his head to the side as he scrunched his brows together.

"Are you sure? I saw him enter his room, and I figured he was getting ready to head to yours."

"I waited for him most of the night, but at some point, I fell asleep," I admitted.

"Well, that's probably it," Felix said. "When I saw him, it was late. He probably found you sleeping and didn't want to wake you."

"Maybe," I shrugged. "But that's so unlike him. If he had come into my room and found me asleep, he would have taken up the armchair like he normally does or left a note, at the very least. This morning, when I woke, there was no sign that he was ever there."

"He may not have been in his right mind," Felix countered. "Yesterday was a lot to process, and he probably wasn't thinking clearly. The person he cares about was targeted *again,* and he hasn't been able to stop it. He hasn't been able to discover who is doing this. Every moment he's not with you, he's trying to figure this all out. If I know Dash—and I do—he isn't doing well right now." He made a good point, and I felt shame at feeling so insecure that I didn't stop and think about what Dash must be going through. "I won't complain if that means I get you to myself for another day," he added, and despite being upset, I smiled.

We spent our time just as we would any other day, walking the grounds and occupying our room in the library. Unsurprisingly, Dash didn't join us for lunch or dinner. I was resigned to giving him the time and space he needed though every part of my being ached at his absence. It was as though he took a part of me with him, and I felt cold and incomplete at the loss. Sleep evaded me most of the night, but when I found it, I envisioned grey, mangled corpses strewn on cold, damp floors.

A day passed. Then another. And by the fourth day, I felt as though I were coming undone at the seams. Every note I tried to send him went unanswered, and I didn't understand why. I couldn't sleep, couldn't eat, couldn't focus. My mind was plagued with haunting thoughts of concern for Dash. I missed him more than I could have hoped to put into words, and feeling so far apart though we were so close in proximity, was torturous. I just wanted to be there for him. I wanted to help him through the doubts and the darkness.

"So are you?" Felix's voice rang through my ears, and I jolted in my chair, dragging my gaze from the horizon to his eyes.

"What?" I asked, shaking my head to vanish the thoughts of helplessness and uncertainty.

"I said, are you excited about tomorrow?" he repeated, his hand outstretched to offer me the tea he had just poured. I reached for it, gripping the cup between my hands as I took a sip. It was weak and tasteless, save for a subtle hint of peppermint. "Am I terrible at making tea?" he asked, watching my reaction as I swallowed.

"No," I told him, and he arched a brow, calling me out on the lie. "Well, maybe a little, but it's the effort that matters." He smiled brightly. "What's tomorrow, and why should I be excited?" His face fell, and sadness morphed his features.

"It's your birthday."

"Oh," I said weakly. "I hadn't realized." With the stress surrounding the attacks and the situation with Dash following directly after, the days had all begun to blur. My highly anticipated twenty-first birthday would arrive tomorrow, and I hadn't been aware of it.

"I know you miss him—"

"It's more than that." I interrupted, meeting his curious stare. "Yes, I want him near, but more than that, I hate not being able to be there for him. Not being able to help him navigate his feelings or to even just sit with him. He has helped me through so much," I explained, "You both have, and it's hard not being allowed to reciprocate that. I wanted to be the person he shares his burdens with, and it hurts that I'm not." I fought the threat of tears. Felix sighed deeply as if he were lost for words, knowing nothing he could say would bring me peace or comfort. He stared at me a moment longer before deciding to speak.

"I haven't spoken to him either, but when I saw him the other day, I could feel him," he said, looking down. There was a slight note of dejection in his voice. "And what I could feel wasn't good. He was hurting, and lost, and confused. But more than anything else, he was angry. I miss him too, and it's difficult not to be able to help him through this." My heart fractured at learning Dash was experiencing so much torment within. Felix took a deep breath before continuing. "I know you want to be there for him, and so do I, but I think he wants to get through this on his own. I think he doesn't want you to see how broken or upset he is." I wasn't sure how to respond or how to feel.

I looked past Felix toward the garden beyond, needing to break from his intense stare as I processed his words. People casually strolled by, talking and giggling arm in arm. The weather today was perfect, warm but with a light summer breeze, indicating autumn would be on her way in the coming month. The air was filled with the scent of grass and jasmine, with a subtle hint of citrus and... salt. The second the aroma hit me, I heard a soft and low laugh in the distance. The sound was indistinguishable to anyone else, but to me, I'd know it anywhere.

My eyes found him a heartbeat later, my chest caving in at the sight. He stood tall and beautiful, his arms crossed over his sculpted chest and my favorite smile on his lips. His golden skin glistened in the sun, and his eyes were bold and bright as they stared down at Rosella and her friends. I swallowed thickly, trying to form words though all I wanted to do was cry.

"He seems to be doing just fine to me," I said, and in my peripheral vision, I could see Felix follow my gaze.

"Dash!" he yelled, waving his arms over his head in an attempt to get his friend's attention. I focused my stare on the cup I held, knowing that if Dash's eyes locked onto mine, the tears I was working to keep at bay would spill over. "What the Hell?" Felix whispered under his breath, and the sound of him reaching across the table for the fruit bowl echoed around us. A second later, a gentle thud resonated in the distance as if Felix had thrown something at a target. "That fucking prick," he said shortly after.

I couldn't take this anymore. I couldn't sit here and watch Dash be seemingly fine after ignoring me for days. I couldn't sit here and watch him smile and laugh with Rosella and her friends as if I meant nothing. I slid out of my chair and strode for the palace. A second later, Felix grabbed my wrist, halting my advance.

"Please, Felix," I whispered as a single tear streamed down my cheek. "I just want to go. I just want to be alone." He released me, and before he could respond, I hurried away, not bothering to stop until I reached my bedroom. I didn't come down for dinner that night.

I stared at my reflection, though I didn't recognize the girl who stared back. She looked exhausted and wan, her eyes duller and the red within brighter than its usual shade. Her face was pale and sullen; void of the joy present just a week prior. I couldn't say I was surprised by her appearance. She had barely eaten in days, and sleep had escaped her most evenings. Last night, she didn't even bother trying. She tossed and turned and cried until there was nothing left. She was confused and hurt and didn't understand how everything could be so perfect one second and so horrible the next.

I took a deep breath, smoothed out my blush pink dress, and headed for the door. The hallways were crowded with servants bustling about, preparing the palace for the evening festivities. Some carried bouquets of lilies and orchids, and others held sparkling crystal candelabras and silver platters as they hurried through the corridors. I reached the terrace, stopping to an abrupt halt on the threshold as I took in the sight before me.

"Happy twenty-first, my beautiful birthday dumpling!" Felix yelled, arms outstretched to showcase the table spread. There were dishes piled high with fruits, pastries, and every kind of dessert I could imagine. Scattered across the surface were several bouquets of blush pink peonies, a perfect match to my dress. In the very center of the table sat two boxes wrapped in lavender paper and tied with white satin ribbon. Felix ran for me as I approached, pulling me into an embrace as he swung me in a circle, kissing my cheek as he did. I smiled as he set me back down to my feet.

"Thank you," I told him, my heart feeling somewhat full for the first time in days.

"Shall we begin?" he asked, waving a hand toward the display on the table.

"Only if I can have dessert first."

"It's your birthday. You can have anything you want." It shouldn't have, but my face fell at his words. *Anything you want.* The only thing I wanted was for Dash to speak to me, but that wasn't likely to happen. "Dessert first, presents after." He led me to my usual seat, and when I lifted my plate to serve myself, he stopped me. "I get to do the honor," he said, taking the dish from my hands and piling it so full of sweets they began to spill over the sides, dropping to the iron table beneath. "What do you want to do today, dumpling?" He set the food in front of me and began to fix himself a plate.

"I'm not sure. Perhaps just go to the Sanctuary?" I asked, unsure if he would be okay with that option. I was tired after not sleeping last night, and the last thing I wanted to do was any physical activity like hiking or swimming. Lounging around all day with a book in my hand in a comfortable and quiet place seemed the ideal choice.

"Sounds perfect," he replied. "As long as we can include drinking."

"It's still morning," I said incredulously.

"Yes, but I want to know if your immortal healing has started to kick in," Felix explained. "I mean, I could always stab you to find out, but drinking seems more fun." Today wasn't just any typical birthday. It was the day that marked the end of my mortal life and began my immortal existence. "Do you feel any different?" he asked.

"I'm not sure," I said, wiggling my fingers in front of me. "Should I?" I checked myself over, not knowing what I was supposed to be looking for.

"Tell me what you see," Felix said, pointing his finger toward the woods in the distance. I looked past him, focusing on the large oak trees along the border. The leaves were a bright shade of green, and something was scurrying across the dark bark—a small animal, perhaps, though it was too far away to know for sure. I relayed to Felix my findings and turned to find him grinning at me.

"Your eyes are adjusting," he declared. "Yesterday, you wouldn't have been able to notice the animal at all. Give it a few more hours, and your vision will finish altering."

"Are there any other changes I can expect?" I asked. I knew precisely three things about immortal bodies: they had healing properties, perfect vision, and some possessed magic. Magic. The realization of today hit me, and I ran my thumb over my fingers as if I could somehow detect my powers that way. How would I even know I was given a Gift? Would it physically manifest randomly? Would I be able to feel it in my blood first? Maybe I wouldn't receive a Gift at all, like most immortals.

"All of your senses will change. You'll be able to see perfectly, and your sense of smell and taste will be heightened. You'll be physically stronger in some ways, and your hearing will also improve. Your body will learn to move quicker, though that change is subtle for normal immortals. If you possess magic in your blood, all of those changes will be even stronger."

"How will I know if I have a Gift?" I asked.

"It manifests differently in everyone, but usually, you'll feel the change. It may not be obvious that anything is different at first, but eventually, you'll be able to pick up on it." Placing my hands on my lap, I closed my eyes and focused on my body. I drifted through myself, checking each hidden alcove within, trying to detect any small change, but there was nothing. I felt just as I did yesterday. Just as I did nearly my whole life. I opened my eyes and gave Felix an exaggerated frown. "It's not always instant," he reassured. "It can take a little bit of time." I sighed disappointedly, and he laughed under his breath at my impatience.

"But you and Dash received your Gift while you were still children," I whined.

"We are a rare exception," Felix countered. "Not everyone can be *that* amazing." I threw a cherry pastry at this face.

"Am I too late?" a voice called, and I twisted to see Imogen striding across the terrace. The second she reached me, she planted a kiss on my head. "Happy birthday, Ainsley." She smiled down at me, her hazel eyes bright and beautiful.

"Just in time, actually," Felix replied, gesturing for her to take a seat. He reached over, taking my plate of half-eaten desserts away. I tried to finish what Felix had served, but my appetite wasn't quite what it used to be.

"Where were you this morning?" I asked. Imogen hadn't come to wake me up or help me get ready for the day, as she usually did, and I was disappointed that I hadn't gotten to see her. We had grown close over my stay here, and I cherished our talks and time spent together. She was the closest I had ever gotten to having a mother.

"I was busy helping Felix," she said, waving a hand over the spread along the table.

"You did all of this?" I asked, my heart warming at the sentiment and her wide smile as she nodded.

"Not *all* of it," Felix cut in. "I helped."

"No, you refused to listen to instructions and ate half of her sweets before they were finished cooling," Imogen said sternly, glowering at him. Felix rolled his eyes, and I laughed at their exchange. "Open your presents." She focused her attention back on me as she reached forward to grab the smaller of the two packages.

"You didn't have to get me anything," I told her, taking the lavender box from her slender fingers.

"Oh, stop," she said. "Just open it." I bit my lip nervously as I untied the white ribbon, letting it fall gracefully onto my lap. I removed the lid carefully, and in the corner of my eye, I could see Felix straining forward to take a peek. I reached inside, pulling out a pair of dangling earrings. They were gold and delicate, with a small marquise-cut amethyst gemstone that hung on the end of each one. "They were my mother's," she said, and my head snapped up at the declaration. She was watching me, her eyes glazed over and a warm smile on her lips. I began to shake my head.

"Imogen, I can't accept this." I moved to place the earrings back into their box, and her hand clasped over mine to stop the task.

"You can and you will," she said, her stare and words unwavering. "I want you to have them." The sentiment was too much, and the love in her eyes was overwhelming. I couldn't deny Imogen. All I could do was nod and lean forward to embrace her.

"Thank you," I whispered. "They're beautiful." She squeezed me tighter, stroking the back of my head as I spoke.

"Okay, okay, mine next!" Felix announced impatiently. When Imogen didn't release me, he threw a croissant at her, and I pulled away immediately, shocked by what he had done. He had a death wish. She slowly looked up from the croissant in her lap to meet Felix's eyes. They were hard and unyielding, like he felt no shame in his choice of actions.

"The only reason, child, that I am not going to murder you," she said, her voice as cold as the ice that now coated her fingers, "is because it is Ainsley's special day, and doing such would hurt her." By the cocky grin on his face and wickedness glinting in his eyes, that was the very reason he had chosen to act today of all days. Felix reached across the table, handing me his present while the two stared each other down, never breaking eye contact.

"Should I wait to open it until you both are done, or?" I asked, looking between them. Imogen's jaw was clenched as she glowered at Felix, the smirk he was giving not helping matters.

"Nope," he replied.

"Child," Imogen said under her breath before releasing his gaze and facing me. Felix chuckled, a sign of victory over the maiden, as he redirected his attention to me and the box between my hands.

"You two are ridiculous," I said, untying the ribbon.

"She started it," Felix replied, and before I could blink, he fell to the ground, the chair beneath him shattering like crystal. I stood, peeking over the table to see what happened, only to find a pile of ice shards all over the stone ground. I twisted to look at Imogen. Her back was perfectly straight, and she sat as though nothing was out of the ordinary. The only sign that something was amiss was that her hands were now under the iron table rather than in her lap like they had been a moment earlier. I arched a brow in question, and she simply shrugged.

"I said I wouldn't kill him," she explained sweetly. "I never said I wouldn't make him suffer." I couldn't help the laugh that burst through me. It was hearty and full and genuine. It was the first time I had laughed like that in days, and it felt good. I missed hearing that sound.

"Rude," Felix said, dusting ice from his pants.

"Yes, you were," Imogen remarked.

I sat back down, satisfied knowing Felix would be just fine, and went back to unwrapping his present in my lap. Inside the large purple box was a small thin rectangle. I picked it up and inspected it curiously. It seemed to be two pieces of glass fused with dried flower petals of different varieties in-between. At each end of the rectangle was an attached deep purple ribbon, long and slender.

"It's to mark your place in your books," Felix explained.

"Thank you," I said, meeting his amber eyes. "It's perfect."

"I know," he responded cockily, and I rolled my eyes.

"But why such a large box for such a small gift?" Imogen asked, confused. She wasn't wrong; the package itself took up my entire lap.

"Because her other gift is in my room," Felix said, winking.

"Gross," Imogen huffed, rising from her seat. "I have to get back to getting things ready for tonight." She pushed in her chair and leaned forward to kiss the top of my head. "Make sure you're in your room directly following lunch. I need time to get you ready for the ball," she instructed, and I nodded. She threw Felix one last death glare before heading back inside.

"Are you ready for your real present?" he asked with delight as he wiggled his eyebrows at me.

"The present you are referring to better not be a certain body part of yours," I told him flatly.

"You could only be so lucky, dumpling," he responded, rising and helping me to my feet before leading us through the palace to his room.

36.

Felix headed for his dresser as I strode for his mattress, wanting to sit down, but the bed was unmade, and the sheets were ruffled. By the looks of it, Felix hadn't been alone last night, nor had he used his bed solely for sleeping. I decided standing would be the safer option when a familiar object on the mattress caught my eye. I picked up Felix's beloved teaching stick, inspecting it curiously as I twisted to look at him.

"Felix," I asked, "why is this stick in your bed?" He looked up from his dresser to face me, and a sly half-smile appeared on his face as he arched a single brow, the look sinful.

"Do you really want to know?" he asked, scrunching his nose. I dropped the piece of wood immediately.

"No. No, I do not." I said, and Felix laughed as he went back to pulling open drawers, searching for his present. A thought crossed my mind, one I wasn't sure I should ask, but I was curious nonetheless. "Doesn't this ever get old?" I asked, causing Felix to bring his attention to me once more.

"Doesn't what get old?"

"This," I said, gesturing over to his unkempt bed.

"Sex will never get old," he replied as if the idea were ridiculous.

"I don't mean *sex*." I corrected. "I mean sex with someone new every time."

"If anything, I find it keeps the act fresh and exciting."

"Felix," I said, my face falling as I gave him a look that relayed I wasn't in the mood for humor. I wanted to have an honest conversation about the topic, and his attempts to deflect wouldn't stop me. "Wouldn't it mean more to be intimate with someone you cared about?" He didn't answer. "You're my best friend, and I want you to be happy. Can you honestly say that sex with random people every night makes you feel that way? I know you're having fun, but does it truly bring you joy?" He looked down at the stack of papers he had pulled from a drawer a moment prior but didn't speak. "I'm sorry if I've overstepped or made you upset. It's just that you're so loyal and thoughtful and caring to those you hold dear. You deserve to be with someone who treats you the same way. Someone who makes you feel loved and cherished and wanted." Felix's throat worked, and he closed his eyes as he inhaled deeply.

"Where was I born, Ainsley?" he asked. I was thrown by the question, not understanding what it had to do with our discussion.

"Ministro," I replied cautiously.

"And where do I reside now?"

"Caelum," I said, still trying to connect the dots. He was patient as I worked through his questions and their meaning, but I was coming up empty. I turned over each word like a mossy stone in a garden, yet found nothing underneath. When I was quiet for too long, he nodded to himself, accepting that I couldn't figure out this riddle on my own.

"Conjoining is punishable by death. You know this, Ainsley." Felix held magic from another kingdom, which meant he couldn't be involved with someone from Caelum. At least nothing more than the physical sense, and even that was risky should she get pregnant, though I'm sure Felix was taking the necessary precautions. "Finding someone to love... Having a family." He shook his head, opened his eyes, and brought them up to meet mine. There was pain and loss and heartbreak swirling within them. "It's not an option for me, no matter my desire. I'd never willingly go back to Ministro and raise a family in a place with such corruption and disdain for its people." I didn't blame him. I felt sick every time I thought back to Felix's story and how the king would decide if orphaned children should live or be *discarded*, as Felix had put it.

"But what if you got married and didn't have any biological children? If you married a man, that would be physically impossible anyway," I pointed out, desperately needing to find a solution for him.

"Yes, but they would not be permitted to marry *me*. Conjoining includes any legal union that involves two people from different kingdoms. No king wants their subjects to put the kingdom of their partner above the one they were born into. King Perceval would never allow one of his people to marry me in fear they would develop a stronger allegiance to me—to Ministro—than to him and Caelum."

"Okay, but there are Medicus here," I told him. "You could find love and be able to stay in Caelum." Felix's lip twitched in the corner, and his eyes softened as if he admired my attempt to help.

"There are," he agreed, taking steps to close the distance between us, the papers in his hands crinkling as he walked. "And most of them are fantastic lovers." He stopped in front of me and reached down to hold my hand. "I know what my options are, Ainsley, but I don't want to be resigned to settle simply because they happen to be from my home kingdom. I don't want to force a connection that isn't there. I know you're often not thrilled with my choice of partners, but spending my time with people that I know I have no chance of caring for makes this situation easier. I know I'll never have to feel the heartbreak of being with someone I could never truly have."

"I don't like this," I said because what else could I? There were no words I could express to take the sting off of the loneliness. None that would bring him comfort or peace. None that would right this wrong. He could already feel the anger, frustration, sadness, and hurt inside me, so voicing those thoughts made no sense. I didn't want to risk bringing forth those same emotions of his own by hearing me speak them aloud.

"I know," he replied, bringing my hand to his lips to kiss. "I know how much you care, Ainsley. It's part of the reason I want you to have this." He released me as he offered the stack of parchment he held.

"What is this?" I asked, flipping through the papers. They were covered in writing, the letters messy yet eloquent. Throughout the passages, there were several lines of dark black ink over the words, as if the author had changed their mind mid-sentence and decided to retract their thought.

"It's a story I wrote," he said softly, and my eyes moved to his. He gave a shy smile as he shrugged. "I've been working on it for years. No one knows about it, not even Dash. I wanted you to be the first to read it." My vision clouded with tears, and I flung myself at him, holding him close as I spoke.

"I'm honored, Felix," I whispered, my voice catching in my throat.

"And don't worry, it's a dirty book. Just how you like them," he said, squeezing me tight as I laughed.

"You know that I love to piss off Imogen," Felix said, grabbing the now-empty plate from my hands and setting it on the table in our Sanctuary. "It's my fifth favorite activity, but I like my balls too much to see her freeze them off for returning you late." I groaned as Felix pulled me to my feet. I had eaten as slowly as possible and tried desperately to convince Felix to skip the Ball with me the entire afternoon. I had promised to answer any five questions he had for me *and* to recite passages from his favorite dirty books aloud. He almost agreed until we were rudely interrupted by a servant coming to remind us that Imogen expected me directly following lunch. After what happened with Dash yesterday afternoon, Felix was thoughtful enough to arrange our meal to be served in the Sanctuary.

"I don't want to go tonight," I whined. "It's my birthday; I should be allowed to decline involvement."

"The event is happening *because* it's your birthday. You can't skip it, dumpling." Felix explained, dragging me across the room to the library entrance.

"I don't want to have to see everyone," I argued, though that statement was only partly true. I didn't want to have to see Dash. If yesterday indicated how tonight would go, I knew Rosella and her companions would surround him. There would be no running for me this time, no escaping the scene playing out before my eyes. I would have to endure watching him give her his attention, laughter, and smile. "Have you talked to him?" I asked, wanting to know the answer before I left.

"Yes and no," Felix admitted, locking the doors to the Sanctuary before escorting me through the library. "After you left yesterday, I stormed for him and sent his fan club away, wanting to know his problem." I was comforted knowing Felix had my back that afternoon, though I wouldn't have ever expected anything less.

"What did he say?"

"He said nothing was wrong, and when I called him on his shit, he left," he said, and I didn't miss the hurt in his tone. "He shut me out, and he's never done that. Not since that first day, we met as children. I wish I had better news, Ainsley, but I'm also at a loss this time." The sadness I had been feeling was starting to shift and mold into something more along the lines of anger. Anger that Felix had always been there for his friend and that Dash would shut him out and ignore him just easily as he had me.

"I'm sorry, Felix," I whispered as we stopped outside the library doors. "Is there anything I can do?"

"Yes," he said, and surprise flashed over my features. "Get drunk with me today and celebrate your birthday." I smiled widely as I nodded.

"I think I can manage that." Felix winked as he turned to walk down the corridor that led to his room.

"Oh, and don't stall on your way to your room. Allow me to keep my balls, please," he called over his shoulder, and I laughed.

I granted his wish, hurrying through the palace to get to Imogen as quickly as possible when a familiar scent hit me. I swiftly turned a corner to see Dash's back as he walked down the hall. I accelerated my pace, determined to catch up to him, to confront him once and for all.

"Dash," I called loudly, but he didn't turn. "*Dash*!" I yelled, but still, he kept walking. "Dashiell!" The fury in my voice was evident, and bystanders stopped to see what had caused my outburst. He stumbled but quickly righted himself. I halted my advance, waiting for him to turn, but he didn't. "Please," I croaked, and I hated the emotion that broke through more than anything. I hated that it seemed as if I were pleading and begging rather than calling him out from a place of rage. Which was greater? The anger or the hurt his actions had caused me. A moment later, he began walking again. I didn't follow this time.

"You look exquisite," Imogen declared, stepping back as she looked me up and down before bringing me to the full-length mirror across the room.

"You are truly an artist, Imogen," I replied. The gown she had selected for me was breathtaking. The neckline plunged deep and stopped a few inches above my navel, and the tulle covering my breasts was transparent though decorated with sparkling silver stones that looked like crystals or diamonds. They glittered as they weaved in intricate designs that looked like vines crawling down my body and stopping just past my waist, where the tulle had been cinched to show off my figure. It flared out slightly as the fabric fell to the floor, the color like porcelain in the moonlight. The gown was sleeveless, and the straps were thin as the glimmering stones crept over my shoulders and down the sides, exposing most of my back. Imogen had styled my hair in long simple waves with one side pinned loosely back with a matching diamond comb. The makeup applied was subtle, nothing more than light rouge on my cheeks and lips and a thin layer of neutral shadow across the lids of my eyes. The amethyst earrings she had given me this morning dangled delicately, and though she protested, saying they wouldn't match my dress, I refused to go without them. Even Dash's bracelet was clasped around my wrist.

A low whistle sounded from the door, and I turned to find Felix leaning casually against the door frame, his arms crossed over his chest. His silver hair was tied back in its usual style, though more groomed, with most strands that often fell pinned back. He wore fitted deep grey pants and a crisp white shirt with the sleeves rolled back as they usually were. His entire ensemble was tailored perfectly to him, showing off the muscles in his legs, chest, and arms.

"We match," I told him as I realized his pants and shirt were the same shades as my dress.

"Of course we do; you're my date tonight," he said, holding out his elbow for me to take.

"Does that mean you won't leave me when you find better entertainment for the evening?" I asked, striding for him, the high slit of my dress causing my bare leg to peek through as I walked.

"It's all about you tonight, dumpling. I'm yours for as long as you'll have me." I smiled up at him as I looped my arm with his.

"Have fun, you two," Imogen called as we departed the room. I tried to guilt-trip her into attending the festivities, but she said though she loved me dearly, she'd rather stab her eyes out than partake in a crowded function like the one happening downstairs.

"I read the first five chapters," I said as he escorted us through the palace. The halls were near empty, signifying that most guests had already arrived in the ballroom.

"And...?" he asked eagerly.

"I love it!" His face lit up with pride and excitement. "Marjorie is amazing, and I can't wait to learn more about him." I was almost positive Felix himself was the inspiration for the main character, Marjorie. He was charming, sarcastic, completely into himself, and everyone complimented his good looks and threw themselves at him. Though I would usually roll my eyes at such a character, Marjorie's undying love and loyalty for his friends and family made him worth reading about. "Abigail, on the other hand, needs to cut him a break. I understand Marjorie can be a lot to deal with sometimes, but she's entirely too mean to him!" He laughed at my explanation and winked. "Felix, it's captivating, and I was pissed when Imogen made me put it down to finish getting ready. I am *so* proud of you," I said as we reached the two large oak doors that led into the ballroom. His answering smile was bright and illuminated in happiness. My heartstrings tugged to see him like that.

"I can't wait to hear more of your thoughts," he said, leaning down to kiss my cheek. "But for now, are you ready?" He angled his head toward the massive doors, the boisterous celebration unfolding on the other side. I took a long deep breath and prepared myself for whatever lay waiting beyond.

"Yes," I told him. The doors opened on their own, and Felix and I crossed over the threshold.

The high ceiling above was fully draped in hanging purple wisteria, the sweet floral fragrance wafting through the room. Hundreds of glass orbs in the shape of teardrops floated beneath the florals and were filled with bright twinkling lights that cast dancing spots along the walls and floor. Several small round tables were blanketed in lilac-colored tablecloths and held the bouquets of lilies and orchids I had spied earlier this morning. The music that flowed through the room was soft yet expressive—not the kind you danced to, but instead, listened with intent and appreciation for its beauty. I stole a glance, scouring the crowd, most of their faces filled with smiles as they met my stare.

"You look lovely, my lady," a resident said as she approached, and I grinned, bowing my head in thanks.

"Perfection," another commented.

"You are simply divine," a man declared.

"Thank you," I told them, and as my gaze drifted over their shoulders, my eyes met his. My heart felt as though it had stopped beating. He was dressed like Felix, though his pants were black and his shirt a deep shade of blue that brought out the color of his eyes. His hair was partially damp as though he had just bathed, and his brows were knitted together like he was deep in thought. Dash's posture was straight, yet his body looked strained as if he were fighting the urge to move, his hand clenched tight at his side. Right next to Rosella. Her sinister smile was vicious, and her stance victorious as she stood next to her prince. I tore my stare away from the pair and brought it to Felix, who looked at me apologetically as the tears pricked the backs of my eyes. How could I think I could handle being here tonight? I was an idiot to assume I would be well enough to make it through this evening. I wanted to leave and didn't care if anyone had an issue with it.

37.

The melody shifted in the distance, though it was mostly drowned out by the pounding in my chest and panic in my veins. I didn't want to be here, couldn't be here.

"Dance with me," Felix said, and before I could protest, he began dragging me across the room to where couples were forming for the routine. Anxiety started to set in as I watched everyone take their positions, and the music began to play, my heart beating nearly as loud as the drums.

"I don't know the steps," I told him, trying to pull my hand from his, pleading for him to let me disappear from this room.

"It's an easy dance. You'll pick it up quickly," he told me, ignoring my protest.

"Felix, please." He halted his movements at the sound of my shaky voice and turned to face me fully. His liquid amber eyes poured into mine, searching for a reason behind my hesitation, though he already knew it. Without a single thought, I automatically turned toward Dash, who was still standing there. Still watching me. Still with Rosella. I turned to focus on my hands, not wanting to look at them anymore. Rage, sorrow, and hurt flooded through me like an unstoppable river, the current too quick and wild.

Felix slid a smooth hand under my chin and gently tilted my head to look at him. As I met his gaze, a tear managed to escape, but he quickly untangled our fingers and wiped it away before it could roll down my cheek. My face flushed with embarrassment and shame for allowing myself to fall for Dash. For allowing myself the ability to get hurt in the first place.

Seeing him with someone else, with Rosella of all people, was gut-wrenching, but I knew it wasn't entirely wrong of him. We flirted and teased, but we never openly acknowledged this... thing between us, whatever it was, or at least on the path to becoming. We never established rules or boundaries. We never even spoke about what we truly wanted from one another, what we wanted *with* one another. Still, no amount of salve in this realm could ease the sting of seeing him acknowledge her existence when these past few days, he tried so hard to forget mine.

It was an effort not to glance back over at him, but Felix's hand was firm upon my face as he studied me, his finger soft yet strong and determined, waiting on me. Giving me the time he knew that I needed to get control over my thoughts. Over the ache in my chest. I took several deep breaths, never breaking eye contact with him, before he leaned down several inches, closing the gap between us, and planted a soft kiss on my brow.

Felix whispered too low for prying ears to hear, "Tonight is your birthday Ainsley, and you deserve to be celebrated. More than that, you deserve to be happy. Just for tonight, let go of all the hurt, pain, and bullshit. It'll be there waiting for you tomorrow." I chewed on my lip as I glanced around the room. Couples were already beginning to sway in perfect synchronization as the dance started to take form, the men bowing deeply as their partners shifted the full skirts of their gowns from side to side. Felix was suddenly blocking my view as he stepped in front of me, hunching down even lower to meet me at eye level.

"Just for tonight, be happy," he said as he presented his open hand in invitation. "Now, Ainsley, my beautiful birthday dumpling, may I please give you the honor of dancing with me?" Despite the sadness I felt, I laughed softly under my breath. "There's my girl," Felix said, beaming ear to ear.

"Fine. I will dance with you, but first...." I decided to steal a page from Felix's book of dramatics and take two wine glasses from a couple walking by. I didn't give any thought to their objections as I shoved one into Felix's hand and emptied mine in one swallow. Felix's answering smile was dazzling as he finished his contents, squeezed my hand, and hurried me through the remainder of the crowd to take up our positions on the dance floor.

As Felix had predicted, I learned the steps rather quickly. The dance was simple, consisting of several turns and spins, but mostly just letting my partner lead when we came together. The routine was social, meaning I was spun to a new partner throughout the song. Felix hadn't warned me the first time it happened, and I panicked about being in someone else's arms. I immediately apologized to my new partner for being so unfamiliar with the dance as I stepped on his toes no less than three times, but he was kind and accepted gracefully. By my fourth partner switch, I had the steps memorized perfectly and caused no pain to those around me.

"Happy birthday, my lady," my current partner, Tommas, said. "You look lovely tonight."

"Thank you," I replied, laughing as he spun me around. I had spoken to him a handful of times before, and he always seemed nice enough.

"Are you enjoying yourself this evening?" he asked as the music faded out, the crowd rupturing with applause.

"Yes," I said immediately, not pausing to think about my answer, but it was true. Despite the hurt I had felt upon entering, allowing myself to get lost in the movements of the dance had taken my mind off of it.

"I'm so glad to hear it, my lady," he said. "Thank you for granting me the honor." He bowed and then disappeared through the sea of people as the music started up again.

"Another go around?" Felix asked, striding for me. "This one is faster-paced but still a good time."

"Absolutely," I told him, placing my palm in his as we took up our spots again.

I could barely keep up with this new routine, the steps so fast and complicated that my mind was dizzy as I tried to recall them. I was out of breath from dancing and laughing as I whirled and whirled, slamming into each new partner I had. I would have felt terrible about my lack of grace if it were not for the sound of their laughter meeting mine.

"I'm so sorry!" I yelled over the roaring crowd, their hysterics nearly drowning out the sound of the drums and strings that played.

"It's okay, my lady!" my partner said back. "It's tricky to learn, but if you can't keep up, just repeat each step twice in a row, and you'll stay in time to the beat!" He then twirled me to the next man waiting. Grateful for the advice, I did as instructed and repeated the steps, finally in sync with the music for the first time since the song had started.

"You're doing great, my lady!" he said and gave a bright, toothy smile, sweat glistening on his forehead from the exertion. My returning smile was one of gratitude as he held one hand around mine and the other on my side as we began the last set of steps before our time together ended. We shuffled around the dance floor, whirling together like tops from a children's game, laughing and drinking in the music. "Thank you for the honor," he said before twirling me out and away and into the waiting arms of my next partner. His scent and the searing touch of his hand against my skin burned me like a brand, and I knew instantly who held me now.

My heart dropped as his piercing ocean-blue eyes found mine. Without any words exchanged, without any hesitation, we fell immediately into step with the other dancers, our gazes never leaving one another. Through it all, Dash's face was hopeful yet filled with sorrow. It was calm yet conflicted. It was as if he wanted to speak, but the words constantly failed him, refusing to surface.

I wasn't sure how to feel. He had ignored me for days and was with Rosella all evening, yet he cut in and was dancing with me. My head spun at the whiplash. I had thought we were moving toward something together, that maybe he had been developing feelings for me as I had for him. But he refused to talk, let alone even look at me, and had pushed Felix away as well. We had been through so much, learned so much from each other, and I missed him desperately. My heart ached to be near him, hear his voice, and see his eyes always full of wonder. I didn't know if being with him right now would make everything better or worse.

At this point, the dance steps had become second nature, my body moving automatically to the music. Without glancing at the dancers next to me, I knew when to move forward and backward. When to curtsey and when to twirl. I knew I would be spun toward a new partner in just a few moments, and my chest tightened as I realized that the time between Dash and I would be ending far too soon. After days of silence and solitude, this was our first encounter, and it wasn't nearly enough time. I needed more time with him.

I took a deep breath as I prepared for him to let me go after one last spin, but he twirled me out and immediately back into him. He caught me as I stopped, his hand sliding down my exposed back and resting just above the base of my spine, pushing me in even closer to him until our bodies were pressed against one another. I stopped breathing entirely, and my mouth went dry at his touch, at our closeness. We began to move again, and for all I knew, we could have been the only ones in the room; there was no one and nothing but him. Nothing but the way his fingers felt splayed across my lower back. Nothing but the scent of lemongrass and sea salt. Nothing but the feel of his chest against mine. Nothing but the look of hunger and desire in his eyes. A look that I very well knew matched my own. Even though he had caused me pain, it didn't change the fact that I loved him. It didn't change that I wanted to be with him for just a few minutes before reality and anger would hit once again. I wanted to hear no words, just the sounds of the instruments and our beating hearts.

The tempo of the music increased, drums beating louder and louder, faster and faster now; the song and dance close to reaching their finale. The steps began to change, but Dash took the lead, spinning me around and around, sweeping me across the dance floor, his stare never once leaving mine, his attention focused solely on me. The instruments played loudly, reaching for the end, and with one final spin, Dash brought me into him tightly as the music stopped, and applause and cheers roared through the room. He held me against him as we rested our foreheads together, coming down from our high. Our faces were so close, and our breath mixed as we tried to control the pounding of our hearts. He tightened his grip on me, and I arched into him as he dragged his hand across my back, fingers pressing into my skin, claiming me. His other hand let go of mine and moved to my hair, holding me still as he brought his lips close, grazing gently. I held my breath, bracing for the promise of a kiss and needing to feel his mouth on mine, needing to taste him.

I felt his hand against my back ball into a fist as he whispered onto my mouth. "I'm sorry. I can't." He let me go and backed away through the crowd. I saw desperation and pain written on his face before he turned and fled from the room. The sudden absence of his body left mine feeling cold and out of place. I let out the breath I was holding and brought my trembling fingers to my lips, still warm from his. I felt nauseous, and my heart began pounding even harder, my breathing coming in quick bursts as I glanced around the room, finding Felix's eyes immediately. The concern on his face was overwhelming, causing my tears to flow.

Go, Felix mouthed before taking off through the room after Dash. Behind him, the king had been standing, watching us. He was deep in conversation with one of his advisors, but he had seen everything. The look on his face was one that I couldn't place. It was one of anger or maybe even pity. The instruments had started their next siren's call, and couples lined up for the dance. I needed to get out of this room and quickly. What the hell just happened? What could I possibly have done for him to run away like that? I gathered the skirt of my gown and rushed from the room, but before making it to the exit, someone slammed into me hard, knocking me to the ground. The contents of a goblet spilled all over me, covering me in dark red wine.

"Oh. I'm so sorry, my lady. I can be so clumsy sometimes," a shrill voice said. I got to my feet and pushed past Rosella as she laughed behind me, tears spilling from my eyes as I sprinted through the exit and didn't stop until I reached my bedroom.

I opened the door to find Imogen laying out my nightgown for the evening. As soon as she saw my face, she ran across the room, taking me into her arms and holding me as I fell to the ground hysterically sobbing.

I sat at the vanity, staring at my reflection, watching as Imogen combed through my wet hair. My face was red and blotchy, and my eyes were swollen from crying. It had taken her a solid hour of coaxing to get me into the bath. She had gently sponged my body clean as silent tears streamed down my face in a constant flow, their path stinging as they made their way over my raw cheeks. When she was finished, she helped me out of the tub, wrapping me in a thick velvet robe and sitting me at the vanity before she called for servants to bring up something for me to drink. Whatever her thoughts were upon seeing me tonight, she kept them to herself, never asking me to tell her what had happened.

"Come on, let us get into bed," Imogen said as a servant walked in with a tray carrying two mugs. I obliged wordlessly, crawling into the bed as she took the tray and walked to the other side. She threw back the blankets, climbed onto the mattress, and propped up the pillows behind her back as she leaned into the headboard, handing me one mug and keeping the other for herself.

I brought the beverage to my lips, drinking deeply, the rich, decadent flavor coating my mouth with sweetness. I eyed Imogen curiously, but she just smiled. "It's steamed chocolate. My mother would make it for me whenever I had a rough day, and it always made me feel better, even if it was just a little bit." I smiled warmly back at her as I took another sip.

"Do you see her often, your mother?"

She drank from her mug and shook her head. "Not nearly as often as I'd like, but she will be having her 800th birthday soon, so my brother, sister, and I will visit so that we may celebrate it with her."

"That sounds lovely," I said, staring at the cup between my fingers, my eyes lined with silver. She reached her hand up, smoothing my hair behind my ear.

"You do not have to talk about tonight if you are not ready to," she told me, her eyes soft and comforting. "But just know I am here to listen when you are." I couldn't stop the tears that flowed out at her kind words.

I took a deep shuddering breath as I put my mug down on the table next to me and turned to face Imogen fully. She then put her cup on the tray atop the bed and met me, grabbing my hands to hold tightly in hers. My lips trembled as I spoke. "I don't know what to do anymore. I thought everything was changing between us. One moment we are fine, and we are getting somewhere, and the next, he ignores me for days, and then tonight...." Imogen nodded as she listened, trying to follow the words that tumbled from my mouth. "Let me start at the beginning," I said, and she smiled gratefully.

I told her of how he had ignored my existence for days, not so much as glancing in my direction. I told her how hurt I was, how much I missed him, and how hard I had fallen for him. I told her of the events that had transpired tonight, of seeing him in close company with Rosella these past few days. I told her of my dancing with someone and how Dash suddenly appeared. About his refusal to let me go, holding me tightly against him, and then how fast he pulled away, running from the room. I told her about my brief encounter with Rosella, to which Imogen let loose a string of foul words under her breath that had me smiling.

When I had finished, Imogen let out a long sigh as she shook her head, and I waited eagerly for her response to everything I had said. "I'm so sorry to hear about all of this, especially tonight. Turning twenty-one is supposed to be a magical time full of happiness. It's supposed to be fun. I'm sorry that it hasn't been that way for you." I felt a lump in my throat, and I worked hard to keep the tears forming at bay, Imogen watching me closely. "Would you like me to be on your side, or would you like some motherly advice? Or, I can simply say nothing and just be here to lend an ear."

I eyed her before saying, "I'd like you to be on my side."

"Dash is a jackass who deserves to be drowned in that lake he loves so much," she said, and after a split second of stunned silence, we both erupted into a fit of deep and genuine laughter. The kind of laughter that makes you double over and gasp so hard for a single breath in fear that you will suffocate. We laughed and laughed for no less than ten minutes, choking out the words 'jackass' and 'drowned' repeatedly in between our wheezing.

When we finally started to come down from our high, I grabbed my steamed chocolate mug, took another sip, and held it against my chest. After a few moments of silence, save for a couple of quiet chuckles, I asked, "And if I wanted motherly advice?"

She was quiet for so long that I wasn't sure she would answer when she scooted closer, wrapping her arm around me. I rested my head against her shoulder as I took a deep breath, inhaling her scent. She smelled of cinnamon and honey, warm and comforting. "I have known Prince Dashiell since he was born. I was his mother's maiden until she tragically passed away to her next life."

"What was she like?" I interrupted.

Imogen smiled fondly as she remembered the queen. "She was beautiful and clever. She was always very kind and loyal to those important to her. She was smart and very headstrong, and you couldn't force her to do anything she didn't want to. You remind me a lot of her in that way," she said, and I felt my lips tug at the compliment.

"Calida loved her son more than anyone in this world, and every day she tried to instill in him those values that she held so tightly. It is a shame that she passed on when he was still so young, never able to fully mold him into the person she knew he could become." My heart ached as I remembered the story Felix had once told me of how much Dash had loved his mother and how hurt and lost he had been when she died. How he had wandered into the woods and stumbled upon his lake that fateful day.

"Although Dashiell inherited desirable traits from his mother, like her kindness, loyalty, and intelligence, he also received certain traits from his father. Like his pigheadedness and his inability to open up." I laughed softly under my breath. "I have watched Dashiell grow into the man he is now. I have watched him struggle to find himself and his place in this world, and I have watched him struggle with you, sweet girl." I pulled my head from her shoulder and sat up, meeting her hazel eyes. "You challenge him and push him, and he doesn't know what to do with that. You scare him, Ainsley. But I think losing you terrifies him the most, and he doesn't know how to cope with that thought. With the constant attacks, can you honestly blame him for trying to protect himself from feeling that loss again?"

I chewed on my lip as I let her words wash over me. I hadn't thought about what memories might have resurfaced for Dash, forcing him to repeatedly relive those feelings of pain and fear. I hadn't considered what might have been going through his mind as he saw death so close to my door numerous times.

"But fear isn't an excuse to treat me like shit," I countered, not caring that I swore in her presence. "If he needed time and space to process his emotions, he should have told me that. He should have cared and respected me enough to give me the courtesy of communicating rather than leave me to feel like I had done something wrong." I understood what Imogen was trying to relay, but it still didn't entitle Dash to inflict his pain upon me.

"I'm not saying he is going about all of this correctly. Gods above know that boy has the communication skills of a pack mule," she said, rolling her eyes. "I'm just saying, give him some time to work through this and work through what he is feeling." I nodded my head as she spoke. "Because, my darling, that boy cares deeply for you. That is a fact I do know." My eyes widened, urging her to continue, but she smiled and shook her head. "His feelings are his to express when he is ready to." She pulled me back against her shoulder and kissed the top of my head.

"Thank you, Imogen. For everything." I was so grateful that I had her in my life, the closest thing that I had ever gotten to a mother. It pained me to know that she had no children, that no one had been lucky enough to be able to call her that.

"Always, Ainsley. Always."

My eyes began feeling heavy, the events of the evening and the late hour finally getting to me. "Will you stay with me tonight?" I asked, not ready for her comforting presence to leave me.

"Only if you promise to get some sleep," she told me, and I nodded eagerly.

She grabbed a pillow from behind my back and set it on her lap, patting it twice, the feathers within visibly shifting. I curled my body up tightly against hers, resting my head on the pillow as she gently stroked my hair, my eyelids drooping closed. Imogen began humming softly, a beautiful lullaby. I let the melody fill me, soothing me as sleep finally came and swept me away.

38.

After dressing the next morning, I hurried downstairs, hoping to speak to Felix about what happened between him and Dash last night, but when I reached the terrace, I noticed the table had been set for only one. No one would be joining me, not even Felix, though I didn't know why. We had spent nearly every minute of the day together this past week, so it was out of the ordinary for him to miss a meal with me. Though I knew the likely reason for his absence was that he had duties to attend to, I couldn't help fearing that the cause was actually that the exchange between him and Dash didn't go well.

I lifted my cup of tea, sipping on the strong flavor of peppermint and citrus with a subtle hint of something new. Lavender perhaps? As I pondered the mystery note, I realized that it might not be new after all. I reached forward, grabbing a piece of melon and popping it into my mouth. The fruit was sweet and more flavorful than it had ever been before. Next, I selected a piece of cheese that was rich, nutty, salty, and melted on my tongue as I chewed. I looked around the space, the colors of the flowers in the garden more vivid than they were yesterday; the sounds of the songbirds in the distance were clear as they sang. The immortal senses Felix had told me about had fully taken form. I was elated at the development and upset that I had no one to share this moment with. I returned to my tea, not wanting to explore any more possible changes until I was with Felix.

Soft footsteps approached, and I whirled enthusiastically, ready to share the details of what I had learned with my best friend, only it wasn't him that strode for me.

"Good afternoon, Ainsley," Rosella called as she pulled out Dash's chair and took a seat. I was in no mood for her cruelty today, or any day for that matter. I closed my eyes and counted to five in my head, praying that she wouldn't be there when I opened them again. I hoped this was just a vile joke that my mind decided to play on itself because last night wasn't punishment enough. "Didn't get much sleep last night? You look positively awful." My lids fluttered open, and I stared at the cup between my hands, willing my blood to stay calm and my head to clear. "I can't say I blame you, though. It must have felt terrible when Prince Dashiell rejected you in front of his entire court." My head twisted to face her, and I accepted that keeping a lid on my temper was a lost cause.

"What the fuck do you want, Rosella." She grinned her evil smile at my outburst.

"I want to talk to you," She said as she shrugged and leaned back in her chair, the metal groaning with the movement.

"Say what you need to, and then leave me in peace," I said, crossing my arms over my chest. This conversation would go nowhere, and I needed it to be over as soon as possible.

"I think His Highness made his intentions with you painfully obvious last night." My heart threatened to fracture as I thought back to that moment. '*I'm sorry. I can't.*' I put the memory out of my mind, not needing to give Rosella any indication that her words had cut me as deep as she had hoped.

"Do you have a point?" I bit back.

"Yes. Stay away from him."

"I think you forgot the entire reason I'm here in the first place. We're engaged, so I don't think that's possible, but I thank you for the suggestion and your constant interest in the matter," I replied sweetly. Her lip curled in hatred, and I winked as I took a sip from my tea, just to piss her off some more.

"You'll be his wife in name only; he doesn't want you, and he's made that crystal clear," she replied.

"You have zero say in the relationship between Dash and myself. That's for us to decide, not you." She chuckled, and the sound was evil and conniving. For the life of me, I didn't know what Dash saw in her.

"You don't have a relationship. You've known him for a few short months; I've known him my entire life. After years of being with him, I know what he wants and needs." Her smile grew wide, and she leaned in close. "And trust me when I say this, I know exactly what he likes."

So she *had* been Dash's lover for years and wanted to ensure I knew that. Though I already figured that was the case, it didn't feel any better to hear it confirmed. I felt sick to my stomach, knowing his hands had been on her the same way he put them on me. I knew it wasn't fair to be upset about it, as I had a past lover in Logan, but it didn't stop the fury and jealousy from rearing their ugly heads as I pictured his mouth on every part of her body.

"Are we done here?" I gritted out, placing my cup on the table and rising to my feet.

"I suppose." She flashed her white teeth in my direction. "Do get some rest, my lady; you look like you need it." I turned on my heel and headed as far away from her as I could.

"We really shouldn't be this far out, my lady," my guard, Aleczander, said.

"I was told I had to stay within the palace grounds. The orchard is on the grounds, is it not?" I pointed out, not breaking my stride through the forest. After I left Rosella, I made my way to the Sanctuary, determined to drink the day away, but instead, I just got pissed that I couldn't get drunk. If there were any doubts of my immortality taking effect, the fact that six double-finger pours of alcohol later, I wasn't even the slightest bit altered was all the evidence of the transformation I needed. When I saw Felix again, I would have to have him teach me how to drink properly now that the rules of how my body processed the liquor had changed entirely. Once I had given up on that task, I figured a hike through the woods would be the next best thing.

"It's near the outskirts of the grounds," Dementri, my other guard, countered.

"But it's technically still a part of the estate," I responded, causing them both to groan. "You can head back to the palace if you don't want to come. I'll be fine on my own."

"You know we can't do that, my lady," Dementri said.

"I know," I said smugly. "So stop complaining, and come on." I shared my plan with them after leaving the kitchen with a satchel of food. They weren't exactly thrilled with my idea, but I didn't care. I needed to see the orchard for myself. I wanted to see this part of Dash's past without having to drudge up the memories within him. It also didn't help that we weren't exactly on speaking terms at the moment.

I tried my best to recall the directions the kitchen servants told me, but my proclivity for getting lost had the upper hand. Because neither one of my guards knew where the orchard was located, what I was instructed should only have been a half an hour's walk ended up taking the entire afternoon. By the time we arrived at the edge of the orchard, the sun was already making her descent back down. It was an isolated clearing surrounded by a sea of woods, quiet and secluded. Maybe that was why King Perceval had chosen it to be located here. It would have provided total privacy for him and his family during their picnics.

I strode forward, taking in the rows and rows of neatly lined trees, their fruit the brightest shades of red and green I had ever laid eyes on. I approached one, standing tall on my toes, as I plucked a ripe apple from its branch and studied it. The fruit was firm, and the slight citrus and earthy aroma made my mouth water. I bit into the flesh with a loud crunch, and the sweet juice dripped down my chin as I chewed. I picked another and tossed it to Aleczander.

"I'm not hungry, my lady," he replied flatly, not meeting my gaze.

"You're angry with me," I pointed out, taking another bite.

"No, I'm angry that we're so far from the palace. If King Perceval finds out—"

"King Perceval is the one who restricted me to the estate grounds. And as I've already pointed out, this orchard is on them."

Aleczander rolled his eyes at my response.

"We're not leaving until she commands us to take her back," Dementri told the guard, grabbing the apple from his hands and plopping himself down under the shade of a tree. "You might as well get comfortable." He took a bite of the apple, and I smiled as I walked away, determined to explore more of the orchard. "Fuck, this is good."

I wandered the eastern edge for an hour, inspecting the blackberry and raspberry bushes and several orange and lemon groves. I tried to picture Dash and his mother collecting the berries and citrus for a dessert she would teach him how to make, but I couldn't. Something about this place felt... off. Empty and abandoned, cold and uninviting. Maybe it was because I knew it held such pain for Dash that those feelings were manifesting in me today. Whatever it was, I just knew I didn't want to be here any longer, at least not without Dash present. I headed back for Aleczander and Dementri, the sky beginning to darken from the setting sun.

"I'm ready to head back," I said once I reached them. Aleczander opened his mouth to respond, but before any sound could escape, an onyx arrow with a trail of shadow shot straight through his throat.

39.

Before I could process what was happening, Dementri lunged for me, shoving me behind his back as his hands filled with light. No, not light—fire. A raging fire that grew larger and larger as it surrounded us, protecting us from the attack. Despite being encased in flame, the heat was bearable, with only a small amount of warmth radiating from it. Through the flames, I could see Aleczander's corpse on the ground, pooled in his dark blood. What the Hell just happened? The flame around us flickered as if Dementri was losing grip on his power, and I looked up to find sweat dripping down the side of his face. He wasn't going to be able to hold this for much longer.

Silhouettes on the other side of our shield began to take shape as the blaze surrounding us thinned and weakened, revealing six people. I swallowed the panic that rose, terrified that we wouldn't make it out of here alive. They killed Aleczander, and they would surely kill Dementri and me as well.

"You need to run, Ainsley!" he commanded, and my terror-stricken eyes met his with hesitation. "I can't hold them for much longer. You need to go now!" His fragile wall of fire flickered again, and I took that as my cue to flee. I twisted and bolted as fast as possible from the scene, praying to the Gods above that my legs would outmatch the pace of the men who were moments away from coming after me. An anguished groan reached my ears, and I glanced over my shoulder in time to see tendrils of shadow break through Dementri's defenses. He flung his hands out in one last attempt to use his magic, but the fireball he crafted missed the target completely. Instead, it went straight into the air, high above the tree line, and then fizzled out. Dementri collapsed to the ground. I pushed my legs harder as stampeding footfalls thudded behind me.

Thorns carved shallow fissures in my skin, and branches caught in my hair and dress, slowing my momentum, but I didn't stop. I couldn't stop. I strained my immortal ears to gauge the attackers' distance. The sounds of the boots behind me seemed quieter now like they had slowed their pursuit. No. Like there were fewer of them. I couldn't afford to divert my attention to check. I had to get back to the palace. I took a sharp left turn, leaping over a fallen trunk and hoping I was going in the right direction, when I spotted two massive oaks in the distance. I recognized them from our journey to the orchard and knew just beyond sat a small meadow with a view of the palace. Though the building was still far away, it was still visible. I could find my way back.

As I approached, two men stepped out from behind the trees, and I skidded to a halt. They had somehow made it in front of me, cutting me off from freedom. Terror crashed through me as my hand flew to my chest, gripping hard as if I could keep together the heart that was threatening to burst beneath. I gulped the air as if I were starved, but it wasn't enough. I felt like I was drowning on dry land, unable to breathe, unable to think. My knees trembled, and I began to sway like tall grass in a meadow on a windy afternoon, unable to stop the movement. I was trapped.

"We've been looking for you," an evil voice called out from the man straight ahead. The others caught up, surrounding me on all sides—six in total. They were thin and looked sickly, dressed in all black with darkness rippling from them, covering their faces in shadow.

Tenebrae.

I filled my lungs with air and let out the loudest scream I could, hoping it would reach someone. At once, shadows wrapped around my face, covering my mouth and transforming into fabric. My eyes grew wide, and I tried to break through the circle the men were forming around me, but tendrils wrapped around my middle, pulling me back and causing me to crash to the ground. Footsteps approached, and a thin, bony hand covered in deep scars wrapped itself through my hair, forming a fist. My eyes pricked with tears as I was yanked to my feet by my hair, my cries of pain muffled by the binding across my mouth.

"Where do you think you're running off to?" one of the men said as he strode for me. He was bigger than the others, but not by much, and his face was the only one not hidden in shadows. Clearly, he was the leader of this group and unafraid of revealing what he looked like. His long inky black hair was knotted and matted to his face, and his eyes were as dark as night. He was pale and so thin that his cheeks were hollow, the bones beneath the skin of his arms so prominent that you could see their outline. The man holding me stepped away, giving his leader ample room as he stopped before me, his dark eyes cold and dead as he stared at me.

"You haven't been an easy one to collect," the leader said, his face inches from mine. His teeth were yellow and stained with black, and his breath smelled rotting and sour. His face and body reeked and were covered with dirt as if he had been living in the woods for weeks. He probably had been. Sitting and waiting for the next opportunity to strike.

His nose brushed over my cheek and traveled to my hair as he inhaled deeply, drinking in my scent as if it were wine. Bile crept up the back of my throat, and I shook with disgust and fury as he brought his other hand up to the top of my head and stroked my hair. My blood pumped, and a roaring filled my ears like the sound of soft thunder in the distance. I took a deep breath as I called my anger to the surface, letting it rage and tear through me like a wild and unyielding fire. Using all of my immortal strength, I thrust up, striking him between the legs like Dash and Felix had taught me during our sparring lesson. The attacker fell to his knees, clutching himself as I took the opportunity to attempt to flee once more.

"You little bitch!" he gritted out, his voice rough and distorted from the pain. I had only made it a few steps before something slammed into me with a force as strong as stone, sending me flying through the air. My body collided with the trunk of a tree hard enough that I heard my bones snap. Burning agony cascaded through me as I crashed to the ground. Silenced sobs escaped my lips, and the binding across my mouth tasted of sweat and salt from the tears that had soaked into it. I tried to rise from the grass and dirt, no longer warm from the sun's heat, my fingers digging into the cold soil as I pushed up onto trembling elbows before falling again. "Pick her up," the leader commanded, rising to his feet.

The one with the scarred hands stepped forward, reaching for me, and with what little strength I had left, I lunged again, lifting my back from the ground as I clawed. My nails tore through the flesh on his arms, drawing blood as I scratched and hit and punched, fighting as Dash and Felix had taught me. Fighting for my life. I wouldn't go quietly as I was stolen to be enslaved and bred like a wild animal.

"Fuck!" he yelled before kicking me in the stomach repeatedly. A cracking sound reverberated through my frame, and my mouth filled with the metallic taste of blood. He pulled me to my feet and every part of my body burned in misery at the damage they had done. I stifled the sound of my cry as the tears continued to roll. "I want to listen to you beg for your life," he whispered as he pulled the fabric from my mouth and slammed my back against a tree, restraining me around the middle with his darkness once more. Blood spewed from my lips at the impact, and an excruciating scream climbed up my throat, searing on its way out. Too much damage was being done too quickly for my body to attempt to heal itself.

"Go fuck yourself," I hissed breathlessly as spots danced in my vision. Out of nothing but shadow and mist, a knife appeared in his scarred hands.

"We have our orders. We can't kill her," the leader said flatly, as if this whole situation bored him. He approached me, his eyes holding nothing but the promise of malice as he took the knife from his companion. "But he never said anything about roughing her up a bit. She'll heal.... Eventually." He pressed the knife to my throat, and I felt the expected sting of the blade as it pierced my skin, followed by the gentle warm drip of blood trailing down my neck. Thunder roared from the other side of the woods, the sound distant but distinct.

"There are no storm clouds," the scarred-hand man observed as he looked up toward the clear night sky. The leader reluctantly tore his gaze from me to look upwards as well. '*You are wild and unyielding and strong, Ainsley.*' Dash's words echoed in my mind, and as the leader returned his stare to me once again, he was met with my fist. He stumbled back a step, then spat blood onto the dirt at his feet. I wasn't going down without a fight. He returned, hitting me across the face so hard that my teeth rattled in my head. My vision became blurred, and my knees buckled, causing my body to sag in defeat against the restraints. A flash of lightning lit the sky, and thunder boomed closer. The men looked at one another at the sound, worry evident on their faces.

"We need to go. Now," someone from the crowd said. His voice was shaky and unsure—afraid. The leader looked at his men for just a moment before nodding.

"You two take the south path around," he commanded, pointing to two of the attackers. Without a word of acknowledgment, they sprinted into the woods. "You and I will take the north," he said to the scarred man. "And the two of you," he gestured to the remaining assailants, their eyes studying the space like they were anticipating an attack, "Take her down the eastern trail and meet us on the border." The leader and his accomplice began their retreat down the path he had chosen. "And if she gives you a hard time... Don't hold back." He disappeared behind the tree line, and the tie that had bound me vanished with him. No longer supported, I fell forward, my muscles and broken bones aching as I hit the ground.

The crash of thunder echoed again, this time even closer. My kidnappers shot each other terrified glances at the noise. They lunged for me, and I clawed back weakly, yelling as I did. I would fight and fight until my last breath. Pieces of my dress tore away during the struggle, leaving the cool night air to caress my exposed thigh and shoulders.

"Fuck this," one of them said as tendrils of shadow wrapped tightly around my wrists and ankles. "We'll drag her if we have to." Another strike of lightning and thunder. "Hurry," he said, panicked.

After another boom of thunder, a realization started to dawn on me. No storm clouds. Lightning. Dash. It was Dash. Tears flooded my eyes again, and though I knew I didn't have much strength left, I sucked in one last deep breath.

And let it out.

"DASH!" I screamed, and I knew it would be my last attempt. A binding flew over my mouth before I could finish the word, restricting the sound completely. I closed my eyes as a boot collided with my face, and a dull, crunching sound radiated through my head. The blood pounded in my ears, muffling the noises around me. All I could see were blurred silhouettes, and all I could feel was excruciating pain.

As I lay there, taking blow after torturous blow, the pain began to dissipate. I was becoming numb and cold. So very cold. Breathing was becoming harder as my lungs rattled with each sip of air I tried to take in. Darkness pulled at my mind, and my eyes began to droop, too heavy to hold open any longer. The men shouted as they assaulted me, but their voices were quieted by the rumble in my mind. It was as if they were far away, yet close. Clear, yet distorted. Every nuance of their tone suddenly changed. They became rushed and unnerved, and a faint gurgling sound filled the space.

Suddenly, I was being lifted into the air, my body internally groaning at the movement. They had beaten me and brought me to the brink of death just to keep me alive so that I would become enslaved. To be bred and beaten some more. Bile burned the back of my throat, but I paid no mind. Instead, I thought about Dash. I would never get to see those deep blue eyes again, never get to drown in the ocean churning within them. I would never again hear Felix's snarky comments or feel his warm embrace. An agony so great crept up, but it wasn't from my physical injuries.

I pushed all thoughts of them aside as I focused on maintaining a steady, shallow breath. I was being carried away to Tenebrae, and I would need my strength to survive.

40.

I drifted in and out of consciousness; for how long, I wasn't sure. Every inch of my body ached so badly that I couldn't move. I couldn't open my eyes. Part of me wondered if I had survived the attack or if this was just some in-between world I was stuck in. Horror struck as I understood that if I was currently alive, I was most likely in Tenebrae. A kingdom that wanted to torture me in the worst ways imaginable. Terror and panic began to surface, but then I heard a voice break through. *His* voice. It was a bright light that pulled me, called to me in that way that only he could. I fought with every ounce of strength I had left within my broken body to claw my way back to consciousness, his voice becoming louder and clearer as I climbed and climbed my way to the surface.

I became aware of my limbs. I could feel my toes, feel my fingers, feel my face, and... *fuck*. The agony was excruciating. Flashes of kicking and slapping and scratching pushed to the forefront of my mind as if I were right back in that orchard. I could once again feel the pain of my ribs cracking as I hit the ground. I could taste the blood from my busted lip. I could smell the sweat and dirt that covered the hands of the man who held a knife to my throat. I could hear the sound of fabric splitting as pieces of my dress were ripped away in the struggle.

A heaviness pressed onto my chest, curling around my heart in a vice-like grip. Immediately, I knew it was not to harm but to soothe, to comfort, to calm. Warmth spread through my body, and I wrapped myself in it. In him. Felix was here, I realized. I felt my fingers tightening as if being pressed together and registered that he was holding my hand. If he was with me, that meant he was alive and okay. I felt myself relax just slightly at the knowledge.

nt the summons sent out tonight," I heard Dash say. His voice was full of command, full of worry, and so far away. I begged my eyes to open, to just let me see a glimpse of him.

"His Majesty will not like that decision," someone said back, his tone short and clipped and one that I didn't recognize.

"While my father is away, Caelum is mine to rule." Anger and annoyance were evident in Dash's tone. "Tenebrae will answer for this, and I will not tell you again. Send out the summons." His voice was a low growl. The room felt like it thrummed and vibrated with power as he spoke. "The kings will be here in ten days, or they too will pay. We are not staying out of this anymore."

"With all due respect, Your Highness, I know your father well enough to know that—" Lightning cracked so loudly it was as though it struck within this very room. Maybe it had.

"Say one more fucking word, and I will make you drown in your own blood. I will drain every ounce of moisture from your body, leaving you as nothing more than a pile of shriveled-up flesh. And then I will freeze what is left of you and shatter it like glass into a million pieces. Do not test me when it comes to *her,*" The room shook, and sounds of rattling furniture filled the space. When Dash spoke again, his voice was as cold as death. "I don't give a shit who you are to my father. Right now, you serve me." A door slammed the moment the last word drifted from his mouth, a clear dismissal for whomever he was talking to. Never had I heard him that angry or scared.

I worked to open my eyes, to say his name, but the most I could manage was a small broken noise. One so quiet, I wasn't even sure he could hear it. The sounds of his quickening footsteps and my name on his lips told me that he had. A chair scraped across the tile on the other side of me, Felix no doubt rising from his position at my bedside. He squeezed my hand, and his magic gripped me tighter, willing my body to calm. I felt my heart steady, my breathing become easier, and the pain of my injuries slowly dull to a quiet ache. With my mind no longer focusing on the pain, I was able to hone my concentration on my need to see Dash.

My eyes fluttered open slowly as they tried to adjust to the sudden light after being kept behind tight lids for however long. Cool fingers brushed my face gently, carefully. So very carefully. As if I were fragile glass and he was afraid he would break me. It was as if he thought the touch would reopen the wounds that covered my body, but I knew it would be what healed them. What healed me.

"Ainsley," he whispered into the silence, his voice breaking on my name. I nearly crumbled right then and there at the pain that coated his voice. I willed my eyes to open wider, his blurry silhouette now coming into focus and shattering my heart entirely at the sight of his devastatingly handsome face so filled with such remorse, such dejection. At the tears of relief and sorrow that flooded his beautiful blue eyes, making them truly look as if he held an ocean within them.

"Dash," I tried and failed to say, only managing to get out the first sound and mouth the rest. He looked to Felix, who immediately dropped my hand and jogged out of the room, closing the door softly behind him.

"He's going to get you more tonic. It'll help with the pain," Dash explained.

"I—" I started but couldn't form the words yet again.

Dash leaned forward, resting his forehead ever so gently against mine as he held my face between his hands, brushing my cheeks softly. I inhaled the comforting scent of him. The scent that had become my home and held my heart. It took me until tonight to fully realize how in love with him I truly was.

"Shhhh." He kissed the tip of my nose, the only part of my face that felt uninjured. I leaned into the touch of his lips against my skin. "Don't try to speak yet. You need to rest." He leaned back, and I whimpered. Not at the pain but his sudden absence. He removed his hands from my face, bringing one down to hold mine and the other up to stroke my hair. I held his stare, the presence of him comforting enough that words weren't needed between us.

Felix returned a moment later, the groaning of the heavy wooden door announcing his arrival. A second set of footsteps walked with him, softer and at a quicker pace, as if they couldn't keep up with Felix's long strides. I listened intently as they approached, refusing to tear my gaze from Dash.

"How is she?" a woman's voice questioned, her tone dripping in that motherly worry only she could possess. Imogen. She stepped close behind Dash, coming into my peripheral view, and I reluctantly peeled my eyes from him to her, a single tear streaming down my cheek as I did. She brought her hand up, covering her mouth as tears welled in her eyes. She pushed past the Crowned Prince of Caelum to take his spot at my side, grabbing my hand as he released me and moved next to Felix.

"She's in pain," Felix said, answering Imogen's question. "I'm keeping most of it at bay the best I can, but these tonics will help. One of the Medicus will be up shortly to assess her."

"She's tried to speak a couple of times but is having difficulty. I told her not to try again for now," Dash added. Imogen reached her free hand toward them, palm open and waiting, never taking her eyes from me. Felix handed vials over to her at once.

"Sweetheart," she said, her voice so calm and reassuring as if I were no more than a sick child she was tending to. "I am going to need you to sit up a little bit so you can take these." She showed me the three vials in her hand, each liquid within a different color. I nodded my head before taking as deep a breath as I could to ready myself for the movement.

I had barely lifted myself onto my elbows when pain shot through my body. The agony was so great that it felt like my bones were being shattered into splinters, puncturing and shredding my insides. A piercing scream clawed its way free from deep within me, ripping through my throat and burning like fire on its way out. I fell back, my head hitting the pillow as three sets of hands were on me. The roaring in my ears muffled the rushed sounds of their voices, but I could detect the panic as they spoke quickly to one another or maybe to me. I couldn't tell, and I didn't care. I just wanted the pain to stop. Tears spilled from my eyes, passing over the cuts and scrapes upon my cheeks, stinging and irritating the damaged skin as they traveled to my chin and down my neck.

Strong, broad hands pressed onto my chest, and I blinked away the moisture to see Felix hovering over me, eyes closed in concentration. He wrapped his magic around me. Around every inch of my body, inside and out. His power was more unyielding than I had ever experienced before. I could feel my heart calm as it began to beat slowly. Too slowly. I lost all sensation in my legs, my arms, and my face, no longer able to feel any part of my body at all. Panic began to rise, and I felt my heartbeat slower still as if it were about to stop at any moment. Darkness as black as night and as mighty as a current inked into my mind reaching for me, trying to pull me under. I tried to fight, but its hold on me was too powerful as it curved around me, taking me with it.

41.

I sat huddled in a dark corner of my mind. A deep and unending cave, so hollow and empty. It was cold and quiet, yet comforting. I was alone here; no one could hurt or even reach me, except for the distant voices that echoed from within the never-ending cavern I dwelt in. The voices drifted in and out often, some I recognized and a few I did not. Some conversations I could follow and understand, but others... Others seemed to be about subjects or people or events that I couldn't quite fathom, their words incomprehensible. It was almost as if they were speaking in another language and talking about another time.

I gave up trying to decipher those and focused solely on the voices I knew. On Imogen and the soft humming that traveled through the cave at times. I cloaked myself in the symphony of notes that reached me, allowing her lullaby to soothe and comfort. I focused on Felix and the soft fluidity with which he spoke, as if he were reading a story. As if he wanted to take me far away from the trauma that I had endured and bring me to a new world of peace and joy, and love where nothing bad could happen. I only wished that I could fully make out the words rather than just the muffled tone of his voice. Like I was standing upon a high mountaintop, and he was shouting at me from a hollow valley below.

But my favorite voice was Dash's. He didn't speak frequently, but I knew whenever he was there, which was often. His scent would travel through the cavern, and I would bask in it. In his warmth, in his presence. I felt comforted just knowing that he was with me. When he did speak, his voice was like a song in my blood. One that I hoped would play infinitely. His voice came through the clearest, though I could only make out a single word or two, the most recognizable one being my name.

I wasn't sure how long I had been in the cave; it could have been hours, days, or weeks. My sense of time was distorted, completely lost. I was beginning to think there would never be an end to the solitude when a small iridescent light, no more significant than the glass orb Dash had given me weeks ago, floated at one end of the cave, drifting on a phantom wind. Suddenly, as if my mind had willed it, I was standing next to the light, following it as it traveled down the twisting dark tunnel. Voices rang through my ears, becoming louder and louder, clearer and clearer. It was two men having a conversation. No, by the tone in which they spoke, it was an argument. They were shouting at one another. I walked quicker, the glowing light moving faster to match my pace, to stay ahead of me.

"We have a plan for that!" one of the voices yelled, the echo bouncing off the walls around me.

"You have made the wrong decision, and by doing so, you put her in even more danger," the second voice countered sharply. I couldn't recognize who the voices belonged to. The sounds were too deep, too angry, too outright feral. I had to get closer in hopes that each step would start to unveil the owners.

"She almost died! That cannot go unpunished. We cannot let them get away with this!" the first voice replied with desperation and fury. I began to run, faster and faster, the magic light illuminating even brighter, growing in size with each stride of my legs.

"She almost died because you *were too weak to protect her, to keep her safe!"* the other man sneered, his voice now crystal clear in my head. King Perceval.

"Just like you were too weak to keep your mother from dying." I swallowed at his poisonous words, knowing how badly they would hurt his intended victim. Dash didn't reply. After a heartbeat of silence, the sound of thunderous boots descending flooded the cave, followed by a loud thud. A door closing, I realized.

"Don't you dare believe a single word out of his mouth," Felix said. He sounded so close it was as if he were standing right next to me in the dim light.

"He's not wrong," Dash replied, his voice so full of shame that it broke my heart. I ran quicker, needing to get to them. Needing to tell Dash that his father was wrong. What happened to me wasn't his fault, nor was his mother's fate. I hated the king. I hated the vicious lies he told. I hated the way he treated his only son.

"Yes, he is," Felix said forcefully, angrily, as if he were mad Dash would believe such things. My legs began to tire, and I realized that I could now feel them. I could feel my arms, my fingers. I could feel my heart beating thunderously in my chest. The gleaming light flickered, and I started to panic. I didn't know where I was going, but I knew I had to get there quickly before the illumination dimmed to nothing. Darkness started to creep along the walls, webbing in all directions like spilled ink upon parchment. I pushed myself harder, my aching limbs groaning in protest, the pain becoming unbearable again. I screamed for Dash and Felix, knowing they couldn't hear me. The darkness coiled itself around my body, pulling me back deeper and deeper into the cavern, the magic light going out altogether.

I settled into the same routine, listening to muffled voices, hoping to hear the ones I knew as I sat in the cold, quiet dark. Only this time, I had a purpose, watching the black tunnel for any sign of light. Waiting like a wolf in the night, ready to pounce, ready to attack. I had no idea how much time had passed, but I didn't care. I stayed vigilant. Eventually, it came—a tiny flicker of light in the form of a bright orange flame. I leapt to my feet and sprinted as fast as my body would allow, not thinking about the pain or anguish I was feeling. I ran and ran, and the flame grew bigger and bolder and hotter. The cave began to widen as I made my way through, the light so bright now that it hurt my eyes, the flame so hot that it began to burn. But I kept going. In my bones, I knew I was almost there. Just a little bit farther. If it meant finally reaching them, I could endure it.

Brightness blinded my vision as my eyes fluttered open. I worked to adjust to the light as I took in the room around me. Glancing at the open window, I noticed how the sun held her position in the sky, indicating it was midday. I had been propped up into a sitting position and looked over to find Imogen asleep on my right. She was clutching my hand, and her head leaned back against the armchair she sat in. I turned to see Dash on my left, fast asleep as well, his cheek resting upon the hand he held in his. My heart lightened at the sight of him.

I looked back at Imogen and squeezed her fingers. She awoke at once, releasing me and leaning forward to come closer. Before she could even speak, I brought a finger to my lips and tilted my chin towards Dash, not wanting to disturb him. She nodded her understanding before addressing me in a whisper-soft voice.

"How are you feeling?" She brought her hand up to cup my cheek. I pondered her question for a moment, checking over every inch of my body. Wiggling my fingers and toes, rolling my neck. Everything felt sore but manageable, with no sign of the excruciating pain I had been in earlier. I swallowed deeply as I focused on speaking.

"I'm okay. A little hungry," I admitted as my stomach growled. The words were horse and strained as if I hadn't spoken in weeks. I might not have, as I still had no idea how long it had been since the attack. Imogen smiled wide at my response, tears lining her eyes. My gaze wandered to Dash, watching his body gently rise and fall with each breath.

"He hasn't left your side these past four days," she whispered, and my heart constricted at her words. I glanced around the room, looking for the only other person I wanted to be there. "Felix is out right now, but he should be back any moment. I'll go fetch you something to eat and give the two of you some time in private."

"Thank you, Imogen."

I waited for the door to close behind her before I brushed the fingers of my free hand through Dash's silken hair, stroking softly. He stirred a little and then darted awake as if the realization of what was happening hit him suddenly. His eyes flew open and snapped to mine, looking completely exhausted. The purpling beneath them had told me he had barely slept since that night, and the shade of blue, usually so brilliant, had dulled.

"Hi," I whispered, giving him the best smile I could manage.

"Hi," he replied breathlessly as he huffed a soft laugh. "How are you feeling? Can I get you anything? Where's Imogen?" The questions poured from him as his attention turned to the empty chair on my right.

"I'm okay," I told him reassuringly. "And Imogen went to get me something to eat."

"You're hungry?" he asked as his eyes widened, and his face filled with an emotion that I couldn't quite place. I nodded, and Dash let out a sigh of relief. "Thank the fucking Gods. The Medicus told us that hunger would be one of the signs of recovery. It would mean that your body was no longer solely relying on the nutrients from the tonics you were being given," he explained. Dash shuddered as he took a deep breath, his eyes glazing over. "It would mean that you were going to be okay," he said softly and then quickly leaned forward, placing my face between his hands as his lips pressed against my forehead.

I wanted to melt into his touch, but my body stiffened, my mind recalling the last time we were this close. We were on a dance floor; our chests flushed together, and his fingers tangled in my hair. But then he pulled away, leaving me confused and empty in front of hundreds of people. Suddenly pain that had nothing to do with my injuries surged through my body, filling me as memories of the days leading up to my attack flooded my mind. Dash's cruel distance and the agony of my broken heart were all I could focus on. I placed my hand against his chest.

"No," I told him sternly, and his eyes widened in surprise, but he didn't fight me as I pushed him back. "You've ignored my existence for days, and yet now you're acting as if nothing happened." I turned my head away, trying to find the strength to stand my ground when everything inside urged me to go to him. To wrap my arms around his neck and breath in his scent until I was lost in the sweet oblivion of it all. Until nothing else mattered but the two of us together.

"I'm sorry," he said softly, shamefully, as his eyes searched fervently for a way within the fortress walls I was securing around myself.

"That's the best you can come up with?" I said flatly, not hiding the bite in my tone. I was determined to hold onto my anger like a lifeline.

"No, but I hoped it would be a start," he replied, sadness drowning out the words.

"I hoped many things too, yet here we are," I said, gesturing between us. He caused this. A grand chasm that had taken root and divided us so thoroughly. Its rocky edges had created sharp fissures in our foundation, and at this moment, I couldn't see a bridge in sight to connect what once was solid and intact.

"You're angry," he noted quietly, like he was reminding himself of this fact rather than pointing it out to me. His words had me twisting to look at him again, truly taking in his appearance for the first time. In addition to the obvious lack of sleep, his hair was disheveled, and there was stubble across his jaw. His skin was sallow, and his lips pale and chapped. He looked as if he were not just exhausted but ill.

"What would possibly give you that idea?" I demanded, my voice growing louder and more forceful, unable to help myself. My fury was a fire that demanded to be fed. He didn't dare attempt to answer my rhetorical question, and I had to at least give him credit for that. I searched around my jumbled thoughts, trying to pull forth precisely what I wanted to say to him. After days of frustration, hurt, and anger, I was ready to have this conversation regardless of how it would unfold or whether this was the right moment to have it.

"The last I had spoken to you, we were planning to stay the night together, and the next thing I knew, you were pretending that I didn't exist. The worst part about it was that I didn't know why, if it was something I had done to push you away." Dash reached for my hand but stopped halfway, deciding against the comfort he longed to give. I took a deep breath, steadying myself to continue. "Imogen suspected that the reason for your absence was the attacks in the palace. Perhaps the deaths and my proximity to them reminded you of the loss of your mother, and you needed to distance yourself from me to sort through those feelings. I wanted to be the person you leaned on and shared your fears and burdens with. But I understood that maybe that wasn't what you wanted. Knowing that was a possibility killed me, but I would have done anything Dash—given *anything*—to help you overcome those demons, even if that meant staying apart." His jaw clenched, and a wary expression painted his face. He balled his hands into fists in his lap but didn't speak, seeming to fight the desire to. His eyes misted over, and his throat worked as he broke his stare from mine, unable to look at me as he tried to hide whatever emotion was trying to break through to the surface. After a moment, he brought his attention back to me, nodding subtly to himself like he was readying for my next wave of attack.

"I thought you were struggling alone, barely holding yourself together, but then you suddenly appeared laughing with Rosella—right in front of me. Clearly intact and unaffected. I have never felt more like an idiot than I did at that moment. That is, until the night of my birthday." My voice broke on the last word, and I looked down, refusing to let him see me crumble. I swallowed the emotion like a bitter tonic and held my chin high again, looking him in the eyes with unwavering resilience. "I wanted to leave the room and not have to watch you with her. I didn't want to look at you after all the pain you caused. But then you had the fucking *audacity* to cut into that dance like you were meant to be there," I said viciously. Dash flinched at the tone and vulgarity of my words, but I didn't care. His pain and pride could wait. Tonight he would feel *my* suffering.

"Looking back, I hate myself for the thread of hope I held on to while I was in your arms. The way you clung to me, refusing to let me go, the way you looked at me; it was all so cruel in hindsight. All that just to leave me empty and alone in a sea of people, my heart shattered on that dance floor. I was fucking confused and mortified, Dash." His body tensed as if my words caused him physical pain. He didn't try to stifle his emotions this time, instead letting the tears brimming his eyes gently spill over, unable to contain them. My heart ached to watch his distress, and it took every ounce of willpower I had not to comfort him. Because despite the silence and the hurt and the bullshit, I loved him deeply. But for now, I had to protect my own heart. I had to put my feelings first because he certainly hadn't.

"Rosella sought me out the morning of the attack, needing to inform me about the relationship you held for years. Even though I assumed as much, I'm not going to say that I'm not disappointed you never told me yourself. And then she...." I looked away, tears burning the back of my eyes as I recalled our conversation that morning.

"And then she what?" Dash asked quietly. Shaking my head, I closed my eyes and quickly wiped away the traitorous tears that fell. "Tell me, Ainsley. Please."

The tender request wrapped around me like welcoming arms begging me to embrace them back. Letting out a deep breath, I nodded, facing him once more.

"And then she pointed out that I would be your wife in name only, reminding me that you made it crystal clear how much you didn't want me." His eyes widened, and his chest heaved quicker and quicker with each word.

"That isn't the case. I'm going through something, and I can't talk about it, but—"

"That isn't a good enough excuse. Not for what you put me through," I shot back.

"Ainsley, I—" he started, then immediately halted. He took a deep breath as he closed his eyes, and when he opened them again, they were bright though lined with tears once more. "Continue," he said delicately—a plea, not a command.

"What were you going to say?" I asked, but he shook his head, not wanting to divulge that information. "So another thing you're not telling me then," I pointed out.

"No," he said at once, begging me with his eyes to believe him. "You're angry with me right now, and I'm not going to explain or defend myself when there is no defense for how I made you feel. This isn't about me. I was a fucking dick to you, Ainsley, and you have every right to be furious and hurt by my actions. I refuse to invalidate or take away from that," he explained. "So, I will stand here and do the only thing I can. I will listen. And when you're finished, I will apologize and beg for your forgiveness." I tilted my head as I studied his features and replayed his words in my mind. It wasn't what I expected to hear, and I wasn't sure how I felt about it. But rather than ponder it any longer, I continued.

"I know we never discussed if this was more than just friendship, but I felt like it was. I hoped that it was. And though I feel like a fool for thinking you wanted me the same way I wanted you, more than anything, I'm hurt that you didn't trust me as a friend. I thought we had built this strong foundation and could be honest and open with one another about anything, but it seems like I was wrong to believe that.

"I understand that you may not be ready to discuss whatever it is that you're going through," I offered. "But what I expect is for you to respect me enough as a person—as your *friend*—to let me know that you need time and space rather than leave me confused and questioning everything between us simply because you're upset. I don't deserve to be treated the way you've treated me this past week, Dash." We stared at one another for a long moment, the silence between us painfully loud.

"I'm finished," I stated. I had said everything I needed to, and it felt like a weight had been lifted from my shoulders now that the words hung between us in the open air. It felt good to speak my mind and finally say my peace. "But I don't want to hear what you have to say. I want you to leave, Dash." I was too angry and bitter to care about his explanation, though I desperately wanted one. Not now. Not while my wrath poured off me like molten steel, forging me into something cold and lifeless. My words as sharp and deadly as a blade, poised to cut down anyone that got too close.

"We can come back," a voice said cautiously from across the room. I turned to find Imogen standing in the doorway with Felix on her heels. I wasn't sure how long they had been standing there, but it didn't matter. Whether they overheard our conversation or not, the tension in the room was palpable.

"No, that won't be necessary," I told her before bringing my attention back to Dash.

"Ainsley, I'm begging you, don't make me go. I don't want to leave you. Please let me take care of you. It kills me to see you hurt," he pleaded, and I looked at him incredulously.

"I am hurt *because* of you!" I yelled, and his face twisted as if I had physically struck him. His mouth dropped open before closing again, no words escaping. The agony in his eyes was so overwhelming that I wasn't sure I could take much longer of this. "I don't give a shit what you want, Dash. Get out," I said through a sob. He lunged for my hand, holding it tightly in his own.

"Ainsley, please," he begged, tears flowing down his cheeks like streams of raindrops on a window. He shook his head, refusing to accept this was what I wanted. It wasn't, but I knew it was what I needed. I ripped my hand from his grasp and then leaned forward to speak.

"I'm sorry. I can't," I told him, the words coming out as cruel as I intended. Dash's body went slack, his arms falling to his sides as he listened to me spew the very words he said to me before pulling away and abandoning me that night. After a moment he stood, though not as tall as he usually did; his shoulders hunched and his head hung low, utterly defeated. Without another word or glance at our company, he walked out of the room, quietly closing the door behind him.

The second the latch clicked, my hands flew to my face as sob after painful sob broke free from the iron prison I had caged them in. Two sets of hands found me just as quickly. I felt the mattress beneath me shift, and all at once, I was pulled onto Felix's lap. His strong arms wrapped around me as he cradled me against his chest, the warm scent of leather and spice filling my senses though it didn't offer the same comfort it usually did. Imogen's petite fingers stroked away the tears that ran like a persistent stampede, catching each delicate bead of moisture before they reached their final descent.

"Does love always hurt this much?" I asked through gasping breaths, my hysterics tumbling out of me like a treacherous landslide with no stop in sight.

"Yes," Imogen whispered as she reached down and squeezed my hand. "It can be torturous to be at odds with the one who holds your heart, but that's how you know it is real and true. The pain wouldn't be so great if it weren't." She leaned closer, sliding her hand under my chin and directing my stare to hers. Her hazel eyes shone bright and warm. "I know it hurts, Ainsley, but you did what was best for *you*. Your heart will mend in time, and when you're ready, and not a moment sooner, you will face him again."

"What if nothing has changed between us? What if the damage is too great?" I asked. Her lips spread into a knowing smile.

"My sweet girl, that boy cares for you far more than you realize. He will not give up. He will not stop until he has tried everything possible to make things right between you. I'd bet my life on it." Her declaration brought forth the first sliver of comfort I had felt in days. I held onto it like a precious gem, a priceless kernel of truth.

"And if I know Dash, which I do, he's sitting right outside your door," Felix added, and despite my heartache, I felt comfort knowing that he would remain so close.

42.

Imogen and Felix kept me company for the rest of the day, trying their hardest to keep my mind off Dash and the attack by teaching me new card games or telling stories. Felix even made Imogen laugh a few times, which she promptly tried to cover up by coughing. My maiden rose from the bed as moonlight began trickling through the windows.

"I'll bring you up a tray of food in case you get hungry through the night, but you should try to rest," she said, giving Felix a pointed look. He stood, preparing to be kicked out, when I grabbed his hand.

"Will you stay, please? I don't want to be alone." Felix looked at Imogen, and I followed his stare, pleading to her with my eyes to grant my request.

"Fine, but only if you promise to try and get some sleep," she proclaimed, and I nodded vehemently. Felix excitedly crawled under the blankets and snuggled up to me at once. "When I come back with your food, the two of you better be out cold," she warned as she opened my door. I watched her take a single step into the hall before glancing at the floor to the left, though I couldn't see what caught her attention. She turned to face me, smirking as she closed my door.

"I think she saw Dash," Felix said, dousing my curiosity.

"You think he's really still sitting there?" I asked. He got up and grabbed the spare pillow and blanket from the armchair Dash always slept in. He then strode out of the room and tossed the objects at the same spot Imogen had been fixed on.

"Thank you," Dash said quietly before Felix shut the door and returned to the bed.

"I told you," he said as he wrapped me in his arms. "He can't bear to be any farther apart from you than that." My heart both ached and lurched at the mention of him. It had only been hours since I told him to leave, and already, it felt like too long. I let the silence stretch between us, unsure of how to respond.

"What happened that night?" I asked, changing the subject. "How did you find me?" Felix was quiet for a minute before finally answering.

"I didn't," he said sadly. "I was listening to the commander give his daily report when I saw a flare go up. I hurried to the window to get a better look when I saw Dash sprinting into the woods," Felix closed his eyes tight like he could see the events unfold behind closed lids. "I started asking if anyone knew where you were or had seen you, but no one had. I immediately knew something was wrong, so I ordered the guards to go after Dash and the Medicus to be on standby. I didn't know if there was an impending attack, so I had every person within the palace go to the Grand Ballroom. I told them that before King Perceval left, he ordered a tally be conducted to ensure everyone was accounted for, though only a few guards knew the truth." He inhaled deeply. "I wanted to go after you the second I saw Dash take off. We might have been able to find them all if I had." He choked on the words as he said them.

"Felix, you had a duty to this kingdom. People here needed your protection and leadership should something have gone wrong. You kept the events quiet and the people safe. You did your job, and Dash got to me in time."

"I just can't believe we almost lost you," he said. His voice was strained, and his head hung with shame. I hated seeing him like this.

"What happened to me wasn't your fault. You know that, right?"

He nodded once. "It wasn't Dash's either," he said quietly, finally opening his eyes to look at me.

"Of course it wasn't," I reassured him.

"Then why did you tell him it was?"hHe asked, almost accusingly. I blinked away my shock and confusion as I wracked my mind around the conversation I had with Dash when I awoke. Felix told me he spoke to him earlier this evening when he left to retrieve dinner for us. Did Dash tell him I blamed him for my attack? Why would Dash lie about something like that?

"Felix, I would never blame him for what happened to me. You know that," I said, my voice thick with the emotion I felt building. "Why does he think that? What did he say? I wouldn't—"

"But you did," he interrupted. "I heard you say it too."

I stopped breathing, and the world spun around me.

"What did I say? Tell me," I ordered as my vision blurred with tears. Felix took a deep breath as he held my stare.

"It was when he was begging you not to make him go. When he said that it killed him to see you hurt." My thoughts traveled back, and I could see the conversation play out as clearly as if it were happening in front of me now.

"And I said that I was hurt *because* of him." Felix nodded, and tears rolled down my cheeks. "Oh Gods, Felix, no. I was referring to my heart, not my body. He thinks I blame him for the attack?" I grasped the blanket draped over me as I drank down greedy gulps of air, feeling as though I couldn't fill my lungs fast enough.

"Breathe, Ainsley," Felix instructed as he rubbed my back.

"He can't think that, Felix." I cried, trying desperately to catch my breath. "I can't let him think that." His father's words flooded my mind. *She almost died because YOU were too weak to protect her, to keep her safe!* I hated the king for what he said to Dash, and here I was, solidifying his greatest fears. "I need to see him, Felix. Right now," I demanded.

"Deep breaths first, and then I'll retrieve him," he offered. I opened my mouth to argue, but Felix shook his head. "If he sees you like this, he won't be able to hold himself together. It's hard enough for him to be away from you right now. Seeing you this upset will only make it worse for him." He was right. Dash and I weren't in the best place at the moment, but that didn't change how deeply we cared for one another. When I looked at him, I could see my pain was mirrored in his own, and I didn't want to add to that.

Finally, Felix determined I had calmed down enough to bring Dash in.

"Are you sure you're okay to be alone together?" Felix asked, and I nodded. Being alone with Dash was something I needed more than I wanted to admit. "Okay, I'll get him and then head down to the kitchens to sneak up some steamed chocolate." He kissed the top of my head before departing the room. Not a minute later, Dash entered cautiously.

"Felix said you wanted to speak with me," he said tentatively as he pressed his back against the closed door. He stood still as if he were afraid moving an inch would have me changing my mind about him being here. It wouldn't. If anything, having him here made me want to ask him never to leave again.

"Will you sit?" I asked, gesturing to the chair he had occupied earlier. Dash made his way over and slowly sat down. He reached for my hand as if on instinct before halting immediately, his cheeks instantly flushing with embarrassment.

"I'm sorry," he said before setting both hands on his lap. I smiled and waved off the apology because it wasn't needed. I wasn't offended or mad that he wanted to hold my hand. I craved his touch just as much as he desired mine. That's what made being angry at him so difficult. His presence had me wanting to act strictly on my need for him rather than my frustrations with his actions. "Before you begin, may I say something?" he asked.

"Of course." He took a long breath and held it for several seconds before releasing it slowly.

"Ainsley," he said as he leaned closer to look deep into my eyes. "I am so sorry for putting you through Hell. For making you doubt me and what we had built. For making you feel as though there was anyone who could ever hold my heart the way you do. I'm sorry for not being a better friend and for shutting you out completely when you would have never done that to me. I know how badly I fucked up, and if you need your space, I will give it to you, but please know that you mean the world to me, and I will be here waiting when you're ready. I will do anything and everything to make it up to you." Dash closed his eyes as tears spilled out. "I am not asking for your forgiveness. I don't expect it, and I know I don't deserve it. I wasn't there for you when you needed me, and I don't blame you if you want nothing to do with me—"

"Dash." I reached out and brushed the tears from his cheeks. "Look at me." He opened his eyes at my command, though I wasn't sure he saw me. The pain in his eyes and the desperation in his voice were almost too much to endure. He was afraid that he had lost me, but I knew the love I felt for him and the foundation we created together wasn't so weak that it would crumble over one argument. Looking at Dash, I didn't *want* to be mad; I just wanted the chance to work through this together.

"I want you to listen to me *very* carefully," I instructed. "I do not blame you at all for what happened to me." He let out a shaky breath as his lips trembled. I tightened my grip on his face. "My attack was not your fault in any way. And fuck your father for making you believe otherwise." Dash's eyes widened in disbelief, and I released my hold on him. "I overheard bits of that conversation while I was unconscious. I didn't hear much, but it was enough to tell me that your father was a dick." Dash let out a breathy laugh though his tears still fell. "None of this is your fault, Dash. It's mine." I admitted aloud for the first time.

It was a fact that haunted me since the moment that arrow went through Aleczander's throat. Dash leaned forward, taking my face between his hands. His blue eyes were suddenly hard and angry.

"No," he said, shaking his head. "Don't you ever say that again." Before I could stop myself, a sob broke from my throat.

"But it is. Aleczander and Dementri were killed because of me," I confessed. The bed shifted as Dash climbed onto it, pulling me to his chest. I didn't try to stop him or fight it. I wanted to be held and comforted. I wanted to be in his arms as my guilt ran wild and my world fell apart. "I tried to get away. I tried to fight, but...." My vision clouded with tears. "It wasn't enough. I didn't do enough," I cried, my body shaking as sob after sob broke free. Hands cupped my face, and gentle fingers brushed away the water from my eyes.

Dash called my name, but I was too in my head to care. Too ashamed of what I had done.

"Ainsley," he said again, gently grasping my chin to get my attention. I still didn't care. I was the reason my guards had been in the orchard. I was the reason they were dead. "Baby, look at me." The desperation and worry in his voice had my eyes fluttering up to his at once. He sighed in relief as he sat just inches from my face. "I want you to listen to me *very* carefully. You did everything you could have. You fought back, Ainsley, and doing so allowed me to get to you in time. You did enough. You did more than enough." I nodded but as much as I wished

I could believe his words, as much as I longed for them to bring me comfort, they couldn't. The truth of the matter was that I wasn't enough. Would I ever be? Was this ever going to stop? My heart grew heavy at the next confession I knew I needed to share with Dash.

"If I tell you something that has been on my mind, you can't get mad," I prefaced. He looked both skeptical and worried, but he agreed nonetheless. "A part of me feels like I can't do this anymore. Like I should just give up and let Tenebrae have me." Dash's jaw clenched, and his chest heaved rapidly like he struggled to control himself. "I'm constantly living in fear, Dash, and I don't want to anymore. It's not fear for *my* life. I'm terrified that something will happen to you or Felix or Imogen. I couldn't live with myself if you got hurt or killed because of me."

My heart raced, and my breath came in quick spurts as I felt my throat constrict with panic at the mere thought of their demise. Dash pulled me in tight, and I buried my face in his chest as the hysterics took over. His shirt muffled the sounds of my painful screams and broken sobs as his hand stroked my hair gently. "I can't do this anymore. They're never going to leave me alone. It's never going to stop. I just want it to stop," I cried out over and over again as he held me. "Please just make it stop," I begged through the tears as I clutched his shirt tightly in my fist. Dash rocked me back and forth, never loosening his grip on me as my body shook with violent tremors.

"It's okay, baby," he said as his lips pressed firmly to the top of my head. "It'll be okay. I won't let anyone ever hurt you again. I'll make it stop, I promise." His vow was unwavering, yet there was a deep sadness woven throughout the words.

An hour must have passed before I finally stopped shaking. Dash didn't release me or move from his spot on the bed, and I didn't ask him to. I needed him with me as I came undone, and I was grateful he stayed through it, though there was never a doubt in my mind that he would. A gentle knock sounded at the door, and we both looked up to see Felix poke his head through. His face drained of color as he looked at me, and I didn't want to know what he saw there. He strode across the room quickly, putting down the tray of food he must have intercepted from Imogen and throwing Dash an accusatory look as he reached me. I felt Dash shake his head against me, indicating to his friend that he was, in fact, not the reason I looked like complete shit. Felix climbed onto the bed, and I felt Dash's hold loosen as he shifted me into Felix's arms. It took me a moment to understand why he was giving me up, but then the memory of this afternoon flashed in my mind. Dash stood and stepped away as Felix laid us down, bringing me against his chest as he tucked us under the blankets. The pain in Dash's eyes at someone else comforting me the way he longed to had my heart breaking all over again.

"Is it okay if I check on you tomorrow?" Dash asked after a moment, the question filled with hope. I nodded, and he gave me a small, weak smile. Probably the best he could manage. "Goodnight," he whispered before retreating from the room.

"I could always—"

"No," I interrupted, already knowing what Felix was going to suggest. "I need to feel this." I closed my eyes and let the pain and heartache, and hope pull me away.

It was another two days before I was deemed healed enough to leave my bed. By the time I was finally allowed out of my room, I was practically as good as new, save for a small cut on my arm and a bruise along my side from the cracked rib that I sustained; the physical pain of everything was now nonexistent. The mental torment was a different story entirely. I found myself waking each night from the nightmares of reliving the event over and over again. Felix was always there to squeeze my hand, brush the hair from my sweat-soaked face, and remind me that it was just a dream. Dash was always at the door the second I awoke, waiting patiently for any direction on how he could help. He refused to go to his room and slept outside my door every night. Occasionally, I asked him to keep me company so Felix could get a few hours of uninterrupted sleep, allowing him to rest comfortably on the oversized armchair. It wasn't a bed, but it had to be better than the stone floor in the hall. Dash never once complained and was always willing to take any little bit of me I offered him.

Once I was free from bedrest, the three of us spent every day in the Sanctuary, and every night Felix and I slept there. I had no desire to return to my room and be filled with painful memories of waking up broken and bloody. The boys were both quick to accommodate my every request, especially Dash. Every morning, he crept into the Sanctuary to leave a full breakfast tray with my favorite foods next to my makeshift bed on the velvet couch. And every day, there was a single white rose, a mini chocolate tartlet, and a note that always read *'Good morning, beautiful.'*

After Felix and I finished breakfast, Dash would join us in the Sanctuary. He'd walk through the stacks pretending to be carefully choosing a title, though he never actually selected one. Sometimes he'd flip aimlessly through a book without reading anything written on its pages. More often than not, I would catch him staring at me from a distance, and the second I would twist toward him, he'd turn away. I had to admit, he was pretty cute. I couldn't pretend I wasn't flattered by his need to just be in the same room as me. Because honestly, I felt the same. I found myself perking up the moment I saw him walk into the Sanctuary. I even started waking up earlier so that I could pretend to be asleep when he showed up with breakfast every morning.

Slowly, my heart began to mend.

'Stay for breakfast tomorrow?' I wrote on the back of the note he left me that morning, hoping he would notice it when he came in. He didn't mention seeing the message, but the next morning, there he was; sitting in the armchair and sipping his coffee as he waited for Felix and me to wake up. Soon, we were standing next to each other as we joked with Felix and sitting near one another on the couch as we both read our books. And then, one afternoon, when our fingers brushed just barely, and I felt that electric current race through me from his touch, I knew we would be okay.

43.

"Can I ask you something?" Dash asked as I placed a book back into its spot on the shelf. I nodded as he handed me another title from the stack to put away. "I know your Primum Celebration is tomorrow night, but afterward, I was wondering if I could take you somewhere. Just you and I." I narrowed my eyes at him.

"Where?" I asked skeptically, and his answering smile was beautiful.

"Say yes, and you'll find out."

"Yes," I said, rolling my eyes as I went back to my work. I wasn't sure what he had planned, but I couldn't help wanting to skip my Primum Celebration altogether just to spend more time with him alone. We were so close to being how we once were, but there were still things preventing us from getting back there completely. Things I hadn't wanted to speak of until now. I peered around him to see Felix lounging on the couch, engrossed in his novel and in no hurry to interrupt us. Now was the time.

"I need to know about Rosella," I whispered though I knew Dash could hear me.

"What do you want to know?" he said immediately, sliding a book back into its place on the shelf.

"Everything."

He nodded, turning to face me fully.

"Rosella and I had an intimate relationship for years, much like you and Logan. It was strictly physical between us, though I knew she wanted more. We were involved with other people throughout the years, but we always found our way back to one another at different points." He leaned his back against a bookcase, crossing his arms over his chest as he watched me tentatively. "I never meant to keep that information from you, Ainsley. At your Welcome Feast, you told me that it was evident she and I had been lovers, so I assumed that you knew. Regardless, I should have made sure, and I am sorry I didn't."

"Did you have genuine feelings for each other?" I asked after a moment.

"No. Rosella and I enjoyed our time together, but she was never someone I could see myself with or even care for. We weren't serious, and it was nothing more than a physical encounter that occurred a few times a week. We never stayed through the night together, and what we had never went deeper than surface level. I didn't want it to. The relationship she was after was strictly about my crown and her status."

"When did you end it?" His eyes softened, his lips tugged in the corners, and my favorite grin spread across his face.

"I remember the first time that I saw you. I was with Felix in the garden venting about my unfair betrothal, and he said, 'Oh look, there's your bride now.' I followed his finger as he pointed up to your room, and there you were, standing by the open window. The most beautiful person I had ever seen." I felt my cheeks flush at the compliment. "It was as if you had heard him because right at that moment, you looked directly at us." Dash laughed as he recounted the memory. "And then you promptly flipped us off."

"You were being a prick," I said sharply as I smiled back.

"No, *Felix* was being a prick. I was an innocent bystander."

"Mmmhmm."

Dash's laugh was warm and boisterous as he shook his head. "As I was saying, smart-ass, after that *very* unladylike behavior, I strode over to Rosella and ended things between us."

"Why?" He didn't know me then. He had no reason to end things with her or anyone else he was involved with. Dash tilted his head as he furrowed his brows, not seeming to understand the question, or maybe he wasn't sure why I asked.

"Because you came into my life. Because even though I didn't know you yet, I knew that I wanted to." My heart squeezed at his confession.

"Well, that explains the death glares I received from her that day."

"I'm pretty sure those were directed at me," he said.

I snorted. "They weren't." Though I believed what Dash told me, it didn't change their exchanges whenever she was around. It didn't change that she constantly grabbed and touched him as if they were still lovers.

My thoughts must have been written on my face because he continued. "I'm not going to tell you that she hasn't propositioned me. That she hasn't invited me into her bed since then because she has." My mouth went dry, and jealousy rushed through me. I thought of her lips against his. I thought of his hands on *her*. I looked away as I struggled to bury those intrusive images down deep.

Dash's fingers slid under my chin, bringing my focus back to him. He spoke slowly and with a seriousness that told me I was to take his following words for fact above all others. "I swear to you, Ainsley, I have never taken her up on the offer. I have never so much as indulged her. I have told her numerous times to let it go. When you see me speaking to the other ladies, it's always because I'm stopped and never because I seek their attention. It's part of my duty as a prince to get to know my people, even if I would rather tell them to fuck off."

I thought back to the moment before we found Pecus and Josephine. *'Get the fuck away from me right now, Rosella,'* he had growled that day, clearly over her antics.

"I believe you about Rosella," I said, and I felt him relax beside me. "But I need to know more. Why did you ignore me?" Dash hooked a strand of hair behind my ear as his face became sullen.

"Because I wasn't ready to face you. I wasn't ready to look into your eyes and be unable to keep myself together. There are things I am dealing with, things that I'm not ready to share, though I'm trying to get to that point. I couldn't even confide in Felix, and I've always told him everything, Ainsley. There is no excuse for how I handled things. I should have told you I needed time, and I'm so incredibly sorry that I didn't," he explained. His voice was rough and raw like it was a struggle to say the words. "And right now, I fucking hate myself for what I did to you."

"I'm okay."

"No, you're not," he said. "You haven't been sleeping, your cheeks are red like you've cried for days, and your eyes are dull. The brown color is flat, and the red within is bright rather than its usual dark, bold shade. You're not okay, Ainsley, you're sad, and I'm ashamed for causing that pain." I swallowed as I processed his observation. Of course he was correct, but I wasn't aware that he could tell with just one look. "I just want to make you happy, see you smile, hear you laugh. I swear, I will continue to do everything in my power to set things right between us," he said, squeezing my hands gently as if to emphasize his declaration.

As always, his touch was electric, sending shocks of pleasure and longing through me. Dash's throat bobbed as if he, too, could feel the current pulsing between us. He pulled away, releasing one of my hands and bringing the other to his lips.

"Goodnight, Ainsley," he said, kissing the back of my hand gingerly before letting go. He turned to walk away, but before he could move a single step, I grabbed his shirt sleeve, stopping his retreat.

"Dash, wait," I said abruptly, and he whirled at once, his eyes bright with anticipation.

"Will you stay with me tonight?" I asked weakly. "You don't have to if you—"

"Yes," he said, nearly shouting the word. His chest heaved as if this request would tear him in two. As if I just offered him the world at his feet. "Yes," he replied again, softer, more assured.

I took a step forward, daring to do the one thing I had wanted to do for weeks now. I reached up and slid my arms around his neck, my fingers finding their way into the soft strands of hair at his nape. Dash went stiff as stone as I closed the distance between us, resting my head against his chest. I listened as his heart hammered beneath at a speed I didn't think possible. His scent curled around me, welcoming me home, and after the briefest of hesitations, he wrapped his strong arms around my body and buried his face into my hair.

"I've missed you," he whispered so low I wasn't sure I was meant to hear.

"I've missed you too," I said back, tightening my hold. Though we had been together every day since the attack, I knew what he meant. Because I ached for it too. The close proximity, the feel of his fingers brushing my skin, the way he held me as if he let go, I would drift away on an ever-changing current forever. We stood like that for several minutes before I finally pulled away. "Come on." I turned, interlacing our fingers together as I tugged him back to the couch to settle in for the night.

Felix glanced up from his book as we entered the seating area and gave a small sly smile as he took in our joined hands. He didn't comment, which was unlike him. He merely placed his book down and announced he would go and fetch more wine for the three of us. I tossed my pillow to one end of the oversized sofa and watched Dash throw his to the other.

"What are you doing?" I asked as he pulled two folded blankets from the empty armchair next to us. His brows scrunched in confusion as he glanced around and then back at me for clarification. I gave a pointed look to his pillow and then to the empty space next to me, and then to him. Understanding and joy washed over his features like a tidal wave. I swear I felt a shifting breeze in the room with how swiftly he moved, gathering his pillow and bringing it next to mine. Dash wasted no time crawling beside me, and we rolled to face each other. He watched as I deliberately scooted closer until we were nose to nose, determined not to let even the air between us keep us apart. His lips twitched and displayed my favorite grin.

"I've missed seeing that smile," I whispered. One hand slid to my waist while his other cradled the back of my head, holding me still against him.

"I've missed holding my girl," he replied, and my stomach fluttered at not only the endearment but the truth it held. I was his. Through the long walks filled with simple conversations, through the laughter and tears, through the joy and heartache. I was his. My hands moved to the back of his neck, and I pushed myself closer, feeling his chiseled muscles against me.

"Will you kiss me now?" I asked as I glanced at his full lips through lowered lashes. Dash's throat bobbed once. Twice.

"No," he said quietly, and my heart sank into the depths of my chest. His grip on me tightened as if reading my desire to retreat into myself. "Not because I don't want to. Trust me, I want that more than anything. But I know that if I kiss you right now, our friend will barge into this room not more than two seconds later. And I *will* kill him for it." I bit my lip as a bubble of laughter reached the surface. Dash smiled at the sound.

"I wouldn't object," I replied, daring him to reconsider his decision to wait. He moved his hand from my hair to cup my jaw and gently grazed his thumb over my bottom lip.

"When I kiss you, I want to take my time. I want it to be slow. Thorough. I want to steal your breath and make you weak. I want to fog every thought in your mind; erase every memory of anyone else. I want to do to you what you've done to me every second since I first laid eyes on you. What you've done to me by simply existing in my world, Ainsley." I swallowed hard, sure that my heart was about to burst open.

"If you're trying to convince me that this shouldn't happen right now, you're doing an awful job at it," I said breathlessly. Dash only smiled wider as the door to the Sanctuary creaked open.

"I told you," he said quietly, kissing the tip of my nose before pulling away and leaving me cold and empty. Felix's murder just jumped to the top of my to-do list.

44.

The night dragged on, and I gave up any hope that Felix would retire to his room, leaving Dash and me alone together again. I lay down, settling into the velvet softness of the couch as I closed my eyes, listening to them talk about everything from sports to history to sharing memories of when they were children wreaking havoc on the palace. Eventually, their words drifted like wisps of clouds through the sky, their voices becoming distant and sparse as sleep grabbed hold of me.

Later, warmth blanketed my body as a gentle and quiet groan pulled me from unconsciousness. I clung to the sounds around me, my eyes still too heavy with exhaustion to open.

"And how are *you* holding up?" Felix had asked. The tone of voice told me this was a serious conversation that I had wandered into—a far cry from the lighthearted stories of earlier this evening.

"You already know the answer to that," Dash replied, so close that his breath tickled my skin. My heart swelled, knowing he would be near tonight after the distance between us for the past couple of weeks.

"I want to *hear* it from you," Felix responded, not letting up. Dash heaved a sigh, clearly not wanting to answer his friend. Holding up how? What was Dash fighting against?

"As well as I can," he finally said.

"The nightmares?"

"Every night." Dash was having nightmares? Every night? My heart sank at his confession, knowing he had been suffering like this and that I wasn't aware.

"Dash—"

"How is *she* holding up?" he interrupted, determined to take the spotlight off himself. Felix didn't answer at first, and I wasn't sure he was going to with how long the quiet hummed between them.

"She's struggling," he said softly. The words were strained, like they were painful for him to voice aloud. "She's trying her best, but... It's hard to feel her fear, to watch her suffer, and not help ease that burden for her. To not take away that pain." Dash exhaled loudly like Felix's words had cut into his own heart.

"Why won't you?"

"As I did with you," Felix began, "I gave her my word that I wouldn't do anything unless she asked for help." Dash groaned at his explanation, the sound a medley of frustration, annoyance, and overwhelming understanding. "Our girl is strong-willed."

"She certainly is," Dash replied as his fingers gently grazed my face, tucking a loose strand of hair behind my ear. I melted into the touch, and his hand withdrew from me too quickly.

"She does better when you're around," Felix added. It was true. Whenever Dash was near, the haunting events of the orchard began to dissipate, to evaporate like smoke on the wind. Whenever he would look at me, whenever I would hear his voice, parts of me started to heal. The love I felt for him was miraculously putting me back together, despite the strain in our relationship.

Dash didn't respond. Instead, he tugged the blanket he had draped over me higher, letting it fall just below my chin. "Do you...." Felix asked, not finishing his question.

"Once again, you know the answer to that." My interest was piqued.

"And once again, I want to *hear* it from you," he replied. A minute passed, and the only sound was Felix getting comfortable on the couch across from us. Another minute went by. And then another. Sleep tugged at me again as if the silence between them was a lullaby beckoning me. Dash's hand returned to my face as he tenderly stroked my cheek, pulling me from the clutches of slumber once again.

"Good," Felix said into the deafening stillness.

Dash must have answered his question with a gesture or look because he had not uttered a single word aloud. I found myself a little annoyed at that fact. I wanted nothing more than to know what Felix's query was and how Dash had answered. I supposed it was fair that I would never know, seeing as I was unabashedly eavesdropping, after all.

"You know, if Rosella finds out—" Felix warned.

"I know," Dash cut in. His tone was clipped and dripping with annoyance, but I didn't understand why. What did she have to do with this? We discussed Rosella, and I believed Dash regarding his lack of feelings for her. But still, why would Felix mention her? The room was silent for a few moments once more.

"Tell Ainsley," Felix instructed. Yeah, Dash, tell me. Wait, tell me what? What didn't I know? Maybe Felix was referring to his unfinished question. Dash let out a long breath before answering.

"I will. When the time is right." *When the time is right.* What did that even mean? More time passed as I waited with bated breath, hoping Dash would elaborate. Felix shifted again, and I could tell their conversation was nearing its end if it hadn't already reached it.

Warm lips pressed to my cheek. "Goodnight, beautiful," Dash whispered. My heart leaped into my throat, and butterflies swarmed within my stomach as he settled in, interlacing his fingers through mine. I nuzzled into him, letting out a soft moan of comfort as I did. "I didn't mean to wake you," he said softly. I felt him shift onto his back as he pulled me with him, positioning my head on his chest.

"I don't mind," I replied sleepily. A soft laugh and then another kiss. This time on my forehead.

"This is the first time I get to hold you through the night." His grip on me tightened at once, and I inhaled deeply, savoring the moment.

"Just promise me it won't be the last."

"I promise," he whispered. I let sleep take me then. I let it sweep me up and carry me away on a gentle breeze of lemongrass and sea salt.

The following day was spent swimming in the lake and lounging in the tall grass of the meadow, allowing the warm summer sun to dry our clothes. We stared up at the clouds, telling stories as they shifted shapes while passing overhead, letting our fears and worries drift away with them.

Dash had received word while I was still on bed rest that all five kings had agreed to the meeting, including the King of Tenebrae, who had been accused of orchestrating the entire attack. Dash and Felix assured me they took every precaution to keep my identity secret. They were still trying to figure out if I was targeted because Tenebrae knew who I truly was or simply because I was engaged to the Crowned Prince. After all, as the future Princess of Caelum, I was the perfect person to use to send a message to King Perceval. The fact that Cordelia had also almost been kidnapped had everyone believing it to be the latter. I wasn't sure if I did too, but I trusted Dash and Felix with my life, knowing they'd never willingly put me in danger. The kings were set to arrive in two days, and there was no telling how everything would play out. Would war against Tenebrae be declared? Would it end their constant pursuit of power or merely fuel their fire?

"Just because I'm not manipulating your emotions doesn't mean I don't feel them." Felix's voice cut through my thoughts. I turned from Dash, who had fallen asleep next to me, to face my best friend. Felix was on his side, head propped up on his elbow. His silver hair was still damp from our swim, and his amber eyes were piercing as they bore into mine. "Talk to me." I shifted closer, mirroring his posture as I considered what I wanted to say.

"I'm afraid that the visit won't go well," I whispered, not wanting to wake Dash. "The two of you are acting as if you aren't worried, which tells me things are more dire than you're letting on." He narrowed his eyes. "I know you both, Felix. You're keeping up appearances for my sake, and I wish you wouldn't." Felix was quiet for just a moment before nodding to himself.

"What do you want to know?" he asked.

"If the King of Tenebrae admits he was behind the attacks, he'd be actively declaring war against Ministro and Caelum. I'm not versed in politics, but that doesn't seem like a smart decision." I said; not exactly a question, but I hoped Felix would respond nonetheless.

"King Evander of Tenebrae wouldn't declare war unless he had allies. There have been rumors for decades of his kingdom allying itself with continents outside of Disparya," he said.

"Wouldn't that be considered treason? Requesting outside help to attack your own continent and the kingdoms within it? Why has no one stopped them?"

"There hasn't been any proof, just whispers. If he declares war, he draws that line in the sand and shows his hand. If that happens, your attempted kidnapping would just be the start of a much greater battle." I swallowed as a shiver snaked down my spine. What was done to Cordelia and me would only be the beginning.

"And if he denies it?" I asked tentatively.

"If King Evander denies any involvement, which I think he will do, then a couple of things will happen," Felix said, holding up his hand as he counted off his fingers. "One, the five kingdoms, including Tenebrae, would work together to uncover who is truly at fault. And two, every move Tenebrae makes in the future would be thoroughly watched."

"No one trusts them to tell the truth?"

"No," he said plainly. "You saw firsthand the kind of people that hail from that kingdom, Ainsley. Would you trust their word?" I shook my head. Regardless of the King of Tenebrae's answer, the future of Disparya had been permanently altered. "I don't want you to worry, but I'm not going to lie to you about what's happening. Accusing a king of attacking another kingdom—of treason—isn't something that's been done in centuries and has repercussions."

"Is that why the King of Ministro didn't call for the meeting after the attack on Cordelia?" I asked, though I already knew the answer.

"Yes," Felix said. "Without proof, it's a dangerous accusation that could effectively end the peace in Disparya, pinning kingdom against kingdom."

You have made the wrong decision, and by doing so, you put her in even more danger. The words King Perceval had spoken to Dash rang through my mind.

Dash had called for this meeting after finding me beaten and barely alive, making the decision while he was filled with terror and fury. Was it the wrong call?

"Do you support Dash's choice?" I asked.

"Yes," Felix answered immediately. "It's a risk, but something is pulling me to believe that these attacks won't stop until Tenebrae is formally accused." I pulled at my fingers as anxiety spooled around me like thread. "You'll be kept safely in your room, out of sight of everyone while the meeting takes place," Felix added, his voice patient and understanding. "We've got you, lemon drop." I offered a weak smile but knew he could see right through it.

I rolled onto my back and focused my attention on the bright blue expanse above. The fluffy clouds that had once floated by now stretched thin like foam on the sea. I wasn't sure what to make of everything Felix had shared, but I trusted his opinion fully. If he believed that Dash made the right call, then so did I. Soon, we would find out for sure.

45.

Imogen had outdone herself yet again with her artistry, dressing me in a long high-slitted velvet gown. The dress clasped at my nape and crisscrossed in front of my neck, with a diamond-shaped cut out that plunged from my throat to just above my navel, leaving much of my bare skin on display. The shade of the gown was a deep and rich emerald that Imogen explained was to represent both Caelum and my new life as an immortal.

I left my room just as the sky changed into a pink hue and walked alone through the grounds, save for the guards that followed, as I journeyed to the location the Primum Celebration would be taking place tonight. Dash and Felix disappeared shortly after we returned from the lake, and I hadn't seen them since. The party was to be held outside, under the stars, as a way to honor the Gods and the Gifts they had chosen to bless Caelum with. I pushed through the tree line and entered the large clearing; the same one Dash had arranged my first birthday celebration to take place at.

Throughout the meadow were several medium-sized triangular pyres with fire blazing through them. Embers swirled above in a synchronized dance, and I watched as Ingesians twisted their fingers, causing the sparks to shift and change in shape, earning applause from the observing crowd. The trees along the clearing border were wholly wrapped in ice, their leaves as clear as glass and glistening in the moonlight. Tonight wasn't just about celebrating my immortality; it was a way for the people of the palace to showcase their given Gifts as well. The music that played was faster paced, the song merry and jubilant as dancers spun themselves around the undulating grass of the clearing.

I smiled as I watched the scene play out and the happiness on the faces of the guests as they enjoyed their evening of food, magic, and celebration. Water and fire wielders crafted animals in their elements high above the crowd, using their magic to make them chase after one another. People clapped and laughed at the show, encouraging more and more displays of abilities. I turned from them, peering through the horde of residents in pursuit of Dash and Felix, but instead found Rosella.

She was dressed exquisitely in a luxurious gold gown that set her apart from everyone else. Heads turned as she parted the sea of people and made her way to an untouched tree. Rosella pressed her hand to the wood, and ice weaved its way over the bark. But she didn't cover the tree entirely in ice the way the other Unda had. Instead, she was a sculpture, and her magic was her chisel as she carved swirling spirals into the wood. She twirled her fingers through the air, moving her tools from the base of the trunk to the very top and covering every branch in between. When she finished, she filled the intricate cracks with water and froze them solid. Her work was a masterpiece, and when the ice melted, her beautiful creation would remain—forever carved into the wood.

There was a pang in my chest at my lack of a Gift, feeling like even though this party was meant for me, I didn't belong there. Other than my immortality, I had nothing to show. No fire, no water, no weather-altering magic. I wrapped my arms around myself, hating the emptiness that lay within my heart and the jealousy that watched with envious eyes at the wonders around me.

Tiny, joyful giggles caught my attention, and my eyes settled on an Unda playing a game with a small group of children. They stood in a circle, and as the magic wielder closed his eyes, the children tossed a small ball of water around their perimeter faster and faster. I walked over, getting as close as possible without intruding upon their fun. I wasn't sure of the point of the activity until I saw the Unda open his eyes, and the ball of water burst in the hands of the child that had not gotten rid of it in time. Now thoroughly drenched, she broke from the circle, removing herself from the game.

"I always lose," she said quietly to herself, squeezing the fabric of her dress to release excess water. I bent down to meet her at eye level, wanting to say something to comfort the child, but before I could, a deep soothing voice spoke from behind me.

"On the contrary." My heart stuttered a beat, and every nerve within me fired off at once like lighting coursing its way through my body, jolting me alert and in search of him. "I think you are actually the winner," Dash said, coming into view beside me as he crouched low to meet the girl's eyes.

"How?" she pouted, and her bottom lip stuck out.

"Because, while everyone else is standing around, you get to have this," Dash said as he pulled his hand from behind his back to showcase a small chocolate tartlet. The girl's eyes widened, and her beautiful face spread into a grin as she wrapped her tiny hand around the dessert.

"My mother says I'm not to eat treats before dinner," she explained, though it sounded like she was trying to reason with herself rather than us.

"It'll be our little secret," he whispered, bringing his finger to his lips. "Now run along, Lyra, before anyone sees you." She gave him a conspiratorial wink, and I couldn't help but smile at their exchange. She made it all of two steps before whirling around once more.

"But what if my mother catches me?" she asked.

"Then tell her it is a gift from the prince and princess," I told her. I felt Dash's eyes on me, and I was pretty sure he stopped breathing at my willing use of my future title. Lyra curtsied before running off into the crowd, clutching her tartlet like it was a precious stone she was tasked to keep safe.

Lips pressed firmly against my temple as Dash's voice caressed my skin as intimately as his kiss.

"You look beautiful, princess," he said, sliding a hand around my waist. I twisted to face him, wrapping my arms around his neck as I pressed my body flush to his. I gazed into his dark blue eyes, watching as embers from the flames reflected within them like tiny fireflies fluttering in the night. "Dance with me?"

"Always," I replied, beaming ear to ear.

The music had transformed into a slow, haunting melody, and though others danced eloquently around us, all I wanted to do was sway gently in his arms. Though Dash held me tight through it all, he never quite closed the gap between us. It was as if he were unsure what I would be comfortable with. Unsure how to maneuver our relationship after everything. I was reminded of how things were when we were first becoming friends. He kept his distance, never pressuring me to move faster than I was ready for, and this felt so much like that time. I smiled as I remembered how innocent and beautiful it was when we were learning the ins and outs of one another. Since then, we had come so far, though we still had much to learn and work through. I supposed that's what a relationship was— a never-ending path of evolution and growth.

"Have you seen Felix?" I asked as he spun me out and back into him. I pushed myself against his chest, refusing to let him continuously allow space between us. He smiled as he gripped me tighter.

"I'm sure he's around here somewhere," he said, looking over my shoulder to spot his friend. "Would you like to try and find him?" I thought about that request for a moment before shaking my head. I wanted to be here with him. Felix would find us if he wanted to. Dash grinned.

"Good. Because I want you to myself for a little while longer."

"Just a little while?" I teased.

"Okay, a long while, but I'll take whatever I can get."

"I think I can arrange that, prince," I said before reaching up on my toes and kissing his cheek.

We laughed through the night, dancing together as song after song played until we were out of breath and needed refreshments. The second we made our way from the path of dancers, guests rushed toward us. The ladies complimented my dress and jewelry, and Dash nodded along absentmindedly to the men speaking to him, all while never taking his eyes off of me or dropping the smile from his face. I bit my lip as I stared at him, only half-listening to someone asking me about my earrings.

"Are you ready to get out of here?" he asked the moment the last guest left our vicinity. My eyes widened, and I nodded my head with excitement.

"And go where?" I asked, popping a grape into my mouth.

"To your surprise," he said as we both turned to see another group of residents striding for us. I groaned automatically, knowing we would be interrupted once more. All I wanted was to be alone with him, unbothered by company.

"How are we supposed to sneak away?"

"I have a plan. You get the wine, and I'll grab the chocolate tartlets and—"

"Why can't *you* grab the wine, and *I* grab the tartlets?" I objected.

"Because I know you. You will have eaten them before we've arrived." He arched a brow, daring me to argue.

"Fine." I couldn't blame him for taking the precaution. He probably wasn't wrong.

"Meet me at the south end of the clearing in five minutes." He kissed my cheek before greeting the approaching crowd, and I used the distraction to slip away to the wine fountain.

Five minutes felt like an hour as I paced back and forth, waiting for him to arrive, sticking to the shadows so I wouldn't be seen. Finally, he emerged from the crowd, looking handsome as ever, with a plate stacked full of chocolate tartlets. "Come on," he whispered urgently, taking my hand in his as he led us through the woods and away from the celebration.

46.

"Happy birthday, beautiful," he said as we stepped into our meadow by the lake.

"Dash," I said breathlessly as my hand flew to my heart, tears instantly pricking my eyes. The field was littered with hundreds of candles illuminating the dandelions growing throughout, and white rose petals were sprinkled upon the grass leading to the meadow's center. The floral path ended at a blanket with a private feast for two strewn across, the silver dishes glinting in stark moonlight above. "I don't know what to say," I whispered, fearing my heart was about to explode. Dash gave me a dazzling smile as he pulled me down the trail of flowers to our picnic.

"Do you like it?" he asked shyly as we sat on the cashmere blanket, and my eyes widened in shock. How could he think I didn't?

"It's amazing," I told him, biting my lip nervously. "You did all of this?" He surveyed the surroundings and nodded.

"I came back out here the second we got back to the palace. I wanted it to be perfect. I wanted to show you how much you mean to me."

"I love it, Dash," I said, curling against him. He pulled me close, holding me tight as he kissed my forehead. I pressed into his touch, into his warmth. It was like finding home after being lost for so long. Embarrassingly, my stomach growled, ruining the intimate moment and causing Dash to chuckle.

"Hungry?" he asked knowingly.

"Maybe a little," I admitted and held out my hand for the tartlets he had swiped before leaving my Primum Celebration.

"Promise me you'll eat actual food after this," he whined, placing the dessert in my hand before tending to the meal he had packed.

"I make no such vow," I said, biting deeply into the tartlet. He rolled his eyes but dropped it, knowing it would be a losing argument.

After I finished two tartlets and the meal of chicken and vegetables he had packed, we cuddled together on the blanket, staring up at the stars above. Dash pointed to the sky, telling tales of what each constellation represented and why the Gods had created them. A faint sound pulled my attention away from his story, and I sat up, searching for the source of the noise, when I noticed two eloquent birds sitting at the water's edge. Excitement rushed through me, and I grabbed a dinner roll as I jumped up and headed for the shoreline, determined to feed them.

"Ainsley, I wouldn't do that," Dash warned, rising to his feet.

"Oh, relax, it's fine," I told him, cautiously approaching the geese, their feathers shining brightly in the light of the moon. Their necks craned toward me as they heard my near-silent steps in the grass. The larger of the two rustled its feathers in warning, and I halted my advance, extending a hand to toss a piece of bread over to it. Before releasing the food from my fingers, the bird let out a loud honking sound, stretching its wings wide and heading straight for me. I screamed in panic as I dropped the bread and ran for Dash, the bird now so close I could feel the wind from its flight. I dove onto the ground, the soft blades of the meadow softening my fall. Rolling onto my back, I raised my arms to cover my face from the oncoming attack. I squinted through my shield in time to see a wall of water appear overhead, deterring the geese from swooping down on me and sending them flying up and back toward the lake. The water stayed suspended in the air for a few moments as if frozen in time before finally falling to the ground, drenching me completely. I screamed at the temperature, so cold it felt like ice shooting through my veins.

"I figured you needed to cool down before you made another dumbass decision," Dash said, struggling hard to keep in the laughter building within him. I stood up, my feet squishing in mud from the sodden ground beneath me as I wrung out the excess water from my hair and soaked dress. Dash stood a few feet away, hands resting firmly on his hips, amusement dancing in his eyes. "I did try to warn you, you know."

I gave him a sweet smile that said *go fuck yourself,* as I picked up a handful of cold, wet dirt and threw it, smacking him directly in the chest. Dash's mouth dropped open as he looked down at the mud smeared all over his crisp white shirt. Slowly, he picked his head up, a wicked smile spreading across his face as he glared at me.

"I suggest you run," he said carefully. Mischievous intent played in his magnificent eyes as he bent down and grabbed a fistful of mud. Horror flashed through my mind, and I turned, sprinting as fast as I could away.

I made it all of ten feet before he caught me and wrapped his arms around my stomach. He pulled me against him, keeping me in place as he transferred the mud from his clothes to the back of my dress. Dash reached around to wipe the cold dirt from his hand across my cheek, down my neck, and throughout my hair. I squealed as I tried to break free from his embrace, but he held me tightly, coating me in the disgusting mud, as he laughed.

"I surrender!" I screamed, still trying to squeeze out of his grasp. At my declaration, Dash loosened his hold. I took the opportunity to twist myself around in his arms as I removed some mud from my cheek and smeared it onto his face.

"You little liar!" He laughed as he tightened his grip on me again, his face moving to my neck as he nuzzled against it, rubbing the mud from his cheek there. I laughed as his stubble tickled my skin, and my hands moved to his shoulders as I tried to push him away to no avail.

"Okay, really, this time! I promise!" I pleaded breathlessly. Dash pulled his face away from my neck but kept his hold on me, his hands sliding down to hold my waist, my body firmly pressed against his. He looked down at me with a broad smile, his cheek still covered in dirt, his face flushed from laughter. His hand came up to cup my face, and his skin was warm and soft as I felt him smear some of the dirt with his thumb. Suddenly, his features became serious as he gazed at me, and I felt my heart stop at the change.

"You are so beautiful, Ainsley," he whispered. I was sure I wasn't breathing as he slowly leaned forward, closing the distance between us.

His eyes flickered to my mouth for just a second, making his intention clear and needing to know this would be okay. I gave a subtle nod, and he placed his lips against mine, kissing me slowly, thoroughly. The world as I knew it froze. Every ounce of my being burned with the taste of him as I savored his kiss. I didn't need food or water, or air to survive. I only needed him. His tongue swept over mine with the barest of touch as if sampling what I had to offer. With every movement of his mouth, every stroke of his tongue, I melted into him like molten magma, my body blazing and liquid as I molded myself around his touch. My head was unclear, my breath stolen, and my knees ready to buckle beneath me as he stripped me bare with his longing kiss.

Dash broke our embrace too soon, and I whimpered as I felt his absence from my lips. His forehead rested on mine as I glanced down, staring at his mouth. That mouth that I wanted so badly back against mine. He smiled as he said, "I have wanted to do that for so long."

"Me too," I shivered, and he ran his hands over my arms, trying to warm me. "You made me wet," I told him. His fingers instantly stilled, and his eyes widened. "My dress," I clarified quickly. "You made my dress wet." My hands flew to my face, my cheeks already burning with mortification at what I had just said. Dash laughed softly under his breath at my embarrassment as he put a couple of feet of distance between us.

"You already know I can help with that," he said. The way his eyes sparkled, I wasn't sure if he was referring to my dress or something else. He held up his hand, concentrating as his fingers twisted slowly through the air as if he was holding and inspecting some small invisible object. All at once, I begin to feel a force tugging me ever so slightly toward him. I looked down at my dress to see tiny water droplets pulled from the emerald fabric and drift aimlessly through the air.

We were now standing under a natural chandelier, the water sparkling like crystal in the moonlight. I reached a finger out, and as soon as I touched the droplet, it simply floated in the opposite direction rather than coating my skin in wetness. I marveled at the movement, and all at once, the droplets burst into nothing more than mist as they fell through the air, settling upon the grass below. I beamed up at Dash in wonder of him, and the beauty of his magic. I brushed a loose strand of mist-covered hair from his brow, his eyes softening at the touch of my hand.

"You're amazing," I told him, reaching up on my toes to kiss him. His mouth parted for me, and I took the invitation to slip my tongue over his, exploring him. Fire ripped through my body once again at his taste, at the way his hands gripped my waist firmly as if he was struggling to restrain himself. I pulled back just barely and brushed away some of the still-present dirt covering his face. "Do you want to go for a swim?" I asked against his lips, and Dash smiled widely as he nodded his answer before grabbing my hand and leading me toward the moonlit lake.

He halted as we reached the shore and turned around, giving me privacy to undress. I unclasped my gown and draped it over the low-hanging branch of a nearby oak tree, now donned in nothing but my undergarments. Looking over my shoulder, I spotted Dash leaning against the trunk, arms crossed, back still facing me, waiting to hear the sounds of the lake indicating that I was completely submerged before he dared to turn around. I smiled at his chivalry and decided at that moment to strip off my undergarments as well, laying them next to my gown before making my way into the warm water. I swam out until my toes could barely touch the sandy lake floor beneath and twisted around to face him, the water lapping over my body in small ripples.

Once I began treading in place, Dash turned around and took one step before stopping dead in his tracks. I followed his gaze to the entirety of my wardrobe hanging over the branch. His eyes slipped straight to mine, and I raised a single brow before turning around in the water, giving him his privacy. Giving him the decision of whether or not to accept the invitation I had extended.

I dipped my head beneath the surface, scrubbing away the mud that coated me as I waited for him, praying that I didn't just make a fool of myself. Once clean, I swam backward until I could once again touch the seafloor. I felt Dash's presence before I heard his near-silent approach, and I wasn't sure if it was just him or the magic that flowed in his veins that caused him to be so stealthy in his element. I turned around to find him standing a few feet away, the water only rising to his chest, his face and hands now clean from any dirt. Water droplets beaded on his hair as he ran a wet hand through it, his abdominal muscles flexing as he did, his body perfectly sculpted and toned. I swallowed loudly as I tore my eyes from him, only to see that he had hung all his clothes next to mine. I tried to fight the fire that I could feel coursing inside me and resisted the urge to wrap my legs around him and run my hands over his chest.

"So," I started, "we kissed."

I watched as Dash fought the smile that tried to take form. "We did."

I looked down as I brushed my hands over the water's surface, enjoying how the ripples felt beneath as I sorted through how I wanted to word this conversation. I could feel Dash's eyes watching me curiously, cautiously. "It doesn't...." I looked up, meeting his gaze. "It doesn't have to be more than just that if you don't want." His face fell, and his brows furrowed. "We never exactly discussed what we wanted from one another. If you wish for things with us to be as they were with you and Rosella, I want you to know that's okay. We've already been forced into an engagement; I don't want to force anything else on you that—"

"Ainsley," Dash interrupted as his cool fingers interlocked with mine beneath the water. His eyes were soft and thoughtful, as if he had so much he needed to say. "It pains me to know that you think I don't want this to be more than that—that I don't want everything with you." I opened my mouth and closed it, struggling to come up with a response. "I should have told you this long ago, but I *want* you, Ainsley. I want to be with you in every way possible." I held his stare for a moment as I let his declaration wash over me, nothing but honestly shining within his deep-sea eyes. My heart swelled at his confession, at the words I had longed to hear from him.

"Okay," I said as I moved closer, almost closing the distance between us completely, my hands releasing his to wrap around his neck. My heart pounded at the fact that there were virtually no barriers between us now, save for a few inches of water separating our naked bodies. Dash's free hands moved down to grip my waist, and he swallowed as if he, too, had just come to the same realization. He leaned down, brushing his lips back and forth softly over mine.

"Okay," he repeated. Dash kissed the side of my mouth, nose, and cheeks, setting my skin ablaze with each pass of his lips on me. He moved to my chin and began planting kisses down my neck as my body became liquid in his hands. Once his lips finally reached my mouth, I was open and ready for him, and Dash wasted no time sliding in his tongue and flicking it against the roof of my mouth.

"I want to be with you too, Dash," I whispered once he had retreated. Whatever leash of restraint I had been holding on myself disappeared as I crushed my naked body against his, wrapping my legs around his middle as I kissed him back hard. We were all tongue and teeth and passion as our hands roved over each other's bodies like we couldn't get enough of the other. My fingers dug into his shoulder as I felt him harden against my stomach and his size alone had me aching, craving. I writhed against him, needing to feel every inch he had to offer and eliciting a deep groan from him as I did. He licked up the length of my throat, and I felt my release building at just the touch of his tongue against my skin. I raked my nails down his back, determined to mark him in the same way his tattoo had.

Dash's mouth claimed mine as he palmed my breast, his calloused fingers brushing over their sensitive peaks. I gasped at the touch, and he let out a growl of approval into my mouth as he flicked my nipple. I couldn't take it anymore. I was about to combust, and I needed to feel him. I needed to feel *all* of him. I lifted myself higher, positioning his length exactly where I needed it. Dash's hands slid down my body to hold my backside, squeezing tightly. Just one quick motion and he would be inside of me.

He pulled his face back from mine to look into my eyes, needing to see the reassurance there. He needed to see that this was what I wanted as well before we crossed that final line. I grinned widely as I nodded, and Dash's answering smile was as devastatingly beautiful as always. He brought his lips to mine, kissing tenderly as he slid slowly in, both of us releasing a breathy moan. He eased himself gently out and back in, allowing me to adjust to him, each time filling me more and more. Dash gripped my hips, lifting me as he withdrew himself to the tip one last time. My hands dug into his hair, and I groaned as he pulled me back down in another slow, torturous descent that finally filled me entirely. I needed more of him. I needed him to go faster. To go deeper. I needed him to give me everything that he had to offer.

"Are you okay?" he asked.

"Yes," I whispered as I clung to him.

"Are you sure? I can stop."

I took his face between my hands, his skin hot beneath my fingers as I rested my forehead against his and shook my head. "Never let me go," I breathed.

My words were Dash's undoing. He claimed my mouth with his as he slid out and back in, each movement hard and deliberate as he slammed into me, as desperate for me as I was for him. I tore my lips from his and moved to his neck, tasting his hot skin mixed with the lake's crisp, cool water. Dash tipped his head back, groaning at each pass of my tongue on him, the sound vibrating against my lips. I withdrew my mouth, pulling back to study his face. His cheeks were flush, his lips were swollen, and his eyes were glazed over and hazy from lust. I relished in knowing that I was the reason he looked so undone. So *hungry*. I bit my lip at the thought, and Dash's breathing became heavy, his chest rising and falling in slow, steady movements as his eyes flickered to my mouth. When he lifted his gaze again, his eyes were darker somehow, wanton. I wondered what thoughts and images had been going through his mind as he stared at me.

My breathing quickened, my insides knotted, and a delectable heat spread through my veins as I thought of every desire I had for him in my head. As I thought of every place I wanted his hands. Every place I wanted his mouth. My toes curled, and my legs tightened around his middle as if I could fuse our bodies. Dash raised a hand, running his thumb slowly over my lower lip like we had all the time in the world. Like he was contemplating what he wanted to do next. He slid his fingers under my chin, his grip soft but firm as he pulled my face to his, parting my mouth with his own, and we began to move against one another once more. He kissed me deeply, thoroughly, as if I intoxicated him. As if he was marking me as his own. As if he needed me to survive. I began to completely unravel at each stroke of his tongue, each thrust of him inside of me. There was no one and nothing in this world except for us, except for this moment in time.

Dash ran a hand through my hair, cradling the back of my head to keep my lips firmly against his as he explored my mouth. The fingers of his free hand pressed into my skin as he dragged them down my back from the top of my neck to the base of my spine. It felt as though his touch would forever be imprinted upon my body, and I delighted in his claim on me as I traced the stiff muscles of his arms, his shoulders, his back. I wanted to make him mine in the same way he made me his. Whether he realized it or not, I was his from this point forward. I didn't want to deny or fight what I felt for him any longer. I didn't want to push it away.

I just wanted to be.

My hips undulated in time to his, matching him movement for movement as gentle waves collided against our backs, our bodies becoming one with the lake around us. Dash held me tight against him, and I felt like I was being wrapped in the arms of an ocean. As if he was a mighty current pulling me under and drowning me in the quiet in and deep. I stopped fighting and willingly gave in, going under as the devotion I felt for him crashed into me.

"Ainsley," he said, and a tingling sensation shot through my body like lightning at the sound of my name on his lips. I felt my release quickly building once more, and I knew by the dark look in his eyes and how he gripped me so firmly that he was close. I wanted to go together as one. I ran my fingers through his hair, tugging tightly as I called out his name, no more than a broken whisper—a plea.

We moved quicker and deeper against one another, taking and giving everything we had, our breathing uneven as we both gasped for air, pushing towards our climax. Dash buried his face into my chest as he yelled out my name, his voice rumbling through my body, sending me entirely over the edge. My vision blurred, and I had no sense of up or down or right or wrong. I had no grip on reality. I had no knowledge of even my own name as I barreled into my release, my legs clenching hard around him as if he were the only thing holding me to this world.

All I knew was him.

47.

Neither of us spoke as we came down from our high, holding each other as we worked to even our breathing, our breath mixing, and our bodies moving as one. After a few moments, Dash's chest ceased heaving against mine, and his fingers began to draw long, idle strokes along my spine, caressing gently. I pulled back to look at him, and his eyes were full of a kind of devotion and longing I had never seen before. He brought his hand up to cup my jaw, and the water slowly ran down his arms and dripped back into the lake with a soft patter.

"I have wanted to do that for so long," I whispered, and Dash let out a breathless laugh at my use of his words.

"Me too," he chimed, pressing his lips against mine. Somehow, my feelings for Dash had grown exponentially in the few minutes that had passed. The desire and need for him were more substantial and prolific than they'd ever been before. "How are you feeling?" he asked, tilting his head back to look up at me.

"Satisfied?" I said, not sure if that was what he was concerned about. He laughed and shook his head.

"Although I'm thrilled to hear that, I was referring to your immortality." His hands trailed down my body and landed on my waist as he lifted me and removed himself. I whimpered at the sudden emptiness I felt, already craving him again. "Being intimate for the first time after becoming immortal can be overwhelming. I want to make sure you're okay."

"I am," I told him. "More than okay." Dash narrowed his eyes, and I kissed the tip of his nose, dismissing his skepticism.

"How are you adjusting to it?" he asked, seeming to accept my answer.

"My senses have fully altered, but I'm still getting used to everything else." He arched a brow in question. "I'm having trouble controlling my speed sometimes. It's like my mind is moving faster than my body is. This afternoon, I reached for a book, and my hand closed around the air before I grabbed it, like my brain was already two steps ahead." He nodded in understanding.

"That's your instincts and reflexes taking form. It can be tricky to master at first but will eventually become like second nature. Remember when I caught you as you fell off the desk while we played Wyvern Pit? It was thanks to my super awesome reflexes." He winked, and I rolled my eyes at his cockiness.

"Do I seem any different to you?" I asked, batting my lashes and turning my head from left to right to give him a complete look. He smiled and pressed kisses to my cheeks before settling on my lips.

"Nope. You seem like my same old Ainsley. Stubborn and fierce and beautiful. The bearer of the most captivating eyes I've ever seen." A faint rumble caught my attention, and I pulled away to see tiny ripples spread throughout the lake as storm clouds brewed in the distance. I glanced back at Dash to see him with a shy smile and an apologetic look.

"Is this you?" I asked, scanning our surroundings.

"Yes. I'm having a hard time restraining it," he admitted. I had never seen his magic come forth without him actively calling to it.

"Is it always a struggle?" He raised a brow, not understanding my question. "During sex, I mean. Is it always hard to control it?"

"No," he said immediately. "I've never had an issue. I never once had to give it a second thought until tonight." There was a slight smile on his lips. "I'm surprised you didn't notice the waves earlier."

"I was a bit distracted," I said, tightening my hold around his neck and giving a flirtatious wink. "Why do you think you're having difficulty restraining it suddenly?" His face grew soft, and his grin widened.

"I have a theory."

"And that is?" I probed. He leaned in, kissing me deeply before he spoke, the gesture searching as if he could find the answer between my lips.

"My magic calls whenever we're close, and I think that's because I'm drawn to you. I believe that since my Gift is a part of my blood, of who I am, it feels connected to you because I do. I think it plays off of my emotions and as they grow stronger, so does the need for it to be released. It's trying to break free because of how I feel about you." He tucked a strand of hair behind my ear as he drowned me with his eyes. "It's trying to break free because I am in love with you." My eyes widened.

"I love you, Ainsley," he whispered as he took my face between his hands. "What I feel for you is the kind of love that I know only comes once in a lifetime. When you look at me, I see my forever. When you look at me, I have never felt so happy, so free, and so alive." My heart constricted in my chest, and my breathing turned shallow and ragged, my lips trembling beneath his. All thoughts in my mind were consigned to oblivion. I swallowed hard, unable to think, unable to form a single word.

I kissed him hard, as if the world were about to disappear, and we only had moments left together. Dash's hands tangled in my hair, holding me still as his tongue slipped over mine, claiming me. My body heated, and my blood sang with the taste of him, with the declaration that now hung between us. Dash pulled back, breaking the embrace that had us gasping for air. He leaned forward, resting his forehead against mine as he tried to catch his breath and gather some inkling of control. I gave up on my attempt at the exact moment our lips first met. Minutes had passed when he lowered his head, brushing his lips against mine in a featherlight touch, nothing more than a ghost of a kiss. He then moved to my jaw, followed by my neck, and my legs constricted around his middle, already wanting more.

"I want to apologize," he said, though he sounded seductive rather than re-morseful.

"For?" I asked breathlessly as my chin tilted toward the sky, and Dash licked up the column of my throat.

"For breaking a promise." His mouth moved up my neck, and his teeth tugged gently on my ear. My toes curled, and my nails dug into his shoulders with growing feral need. "I told you the next time I made you come," he whispered.

"It would be on my tongue." My stomach knotted, and I clenched around him. He claimed my mouth, and his hold on my head was gentle but possessive.

"Trust me, I don't mind," I said against his mouth and reached down between us to grab him, finding he was already hard and ready for me. Dash's head dropped to my chest as he let out a growl against my skin, the sound deep and guttural, as I began stroking slowly, savoring the luxurious feel of him.

"Regardless of your forgiveness on the matter," he began, and I hissed as his teeth grazed my nipple, pain and pleasure mixing as one. "I very much want to rectify that wrongdoing." I released my hold, gliding my thumb over his tip before letting go.

"So, what's stopping you?" I challenged just as I had on the night we played Ten Questions. The only difference was no one would be stopping us now. The entire Kingdom of Caelum could come to find us buried in each other, and I wouldn't give two shits. Every time we had gotten close to one another intimately, we had been interrupted, and I would sooner set this land on fire than allow it to happen again. Dash smiled devilishly, and the sound of water shifting filled the space. I twisted in his arms to see the lake slowly parting a path as he moved to the shoreline. "Show off."

"Oh, you have no idea," he said, and I couldn't help but feel like that was a promise for what was to come.

Dash laid me on the blanket and hovered above as he kissed me softly, love shining in his eyes. Carefully, he pulled away, and his gaze roamed over my body as if assessing every inch. "You're beautiful," he whispered as he gently caressed from the base of my throat, over my breast, and down to my waist with the back of his fingers. "I want to try something." He held up his hand before us, and I watched as tiny ice crystals coated his fingers.

"You don't have to," I told him as I recalled our earlier conversation.

"I want to, Ainsley," he said. "I love you and want to share every part of myself with you, including this." He carefully pressed his fingers to my skin and trailed them down my chest, leaving a line of cold water in their wake. The temperature was frigid, causing my skin to prickle as he circled my breast. I gasped as he reached my nipple, and his mouth was on me next, his hot tongue flicking over it, instantly thawing what his fingers had done. The mix of ice and heat was delicious, and my mind swam at the constant switch of extremes. His ice-covered fingers stroked down my body as his tongue followed closely behind until he was primed between my legs. I propped myself on my elbows, watching as he swirled his cold thumb around my most sensitive part, my breathing becoming labored with his finger's movement.

"Please," I whimpered. He removed his hand and stared down at me as his chest heaved and his jaw clenched like he was restricting himself. He dipped his head, but his eyes locked on mine as he dragged his tongue up my center. I fell to my back, moaning at the delicious feel of his mouth on me.

"Fuck," Dash growled in pleasure as he licked his way along, exploring me. His hands grabbed my hips holding me in place as his tongue slipped inside. Every nerve in my body seemed to sing to life as he worked me, the sensation more than I could bear. The feel of his fingers the night we played Ten Questions was bliss, but his mouth... *My Gods,* his mouth was euphoric. A pleasure so great, it would bring about my complete and total ruin.

"Dash," I croaked, but he didn't stop. He plunged his fingers in and out of me as he licked and kissed and sucked the spot that had me screaming and begging for release. I fisted the blanket beneath me as if it would stop me from falling off the edge of ecstasy. Suddenly, Dash pulled away altogether, and I glanced down to find his dark eyes watching me, his lips gleaming with my wetness, and his breathing coming in tortured gasps. "Why did you stop?" I whined, needing his mouth back on me.

"I've wanted you for so long," he said in between quickened inhales, "I'm trying very hard to make this last. I'm trying very hard to restrain myself."

"Don't," I begged, and it was all he needed to hear. He gripped my waist tightly with one hand, fingers digging in as he dipped his head back down and unleashed himself on me. Thunder rumbled beyond the horizon as his fingers thrust inside me relentlessly, causing the pressure in my core to build and my inner walls to clamp around him. His tongue swirled and flicked. He moved with purpose, a feral need. As if he had been starved his entire life. He devoured me as if he needed to in order to survive.

"Fuck yes," he said against me. "Let go, baby." My legs began to tremble, and my heart raced as a roaring fire spread throughout my body, obliterating my focus on anything except that raging heat. My back arched off the ground, and my fingers clutched the blanket as I began to barrel into my release. "Good girl," he said, and I fully came undone at his praise, screaming his name as I climaxed hard around him.

I shook from each wave of pleasure that crashed over me, and Dash held me firm, kissing and licking me through it all. When my body finally relaxed and settled back upon the blanket, he lifted his head and kissed up the length of my body, stopping at my breast as he took one into his mouth, flicking my nipple with his tongue. I moved one hand to his hair, tugging gently, and my other hand reached between us to stroke him as I guided him to my entrance. Dash groaned at my touch and moved his mouth to my neck as he plunged inside me, taking what I had given him. He was unrelenting in his claim, pounding into me repeatedly, making that pressure in my spine build once more at the feel of him.

A flash of light caught my eye, and I turned my head to look out at the lake scene. Waves were beginning to form, crashing into each other from all directions, and beyond the shoreline at the opposite end, thunder rumbled, and lightning struck. Dash had followed my line of sight, and I turned back to see him twisting to me once more and closing his eyes in concentration. I took his face between my hands, and his lids fluttered open to find me shaking my head.

"No," I breathed. "Let go, Dash. I want all of you." His stare flickered to the water and then back to me as if debating. "I can handle it, Dash. Give it to me." A deep-sounding growl came from the base of his throat as he released his hold on himself. He hooked an arm under my leg as he positioned me in a way to allow him to go deeper, hitting my back wall. I dragged my nails down his back at the new sensation, and I watched as Dash's magic was unleashed into the world.

Dark clouds formed over us, and thunder roared as lighting came down over the body of water, striking over and over again. The wind howled, and the surf crashed violently into the rocks along the shoreline. The lake came to life, the water rough and chaotic as waves slammed into each other hard from the storm that unfolded all around us. The scene was wild and dangerous though I never felt safer than in that moment with him.

Dash's lips collided with mine, his kiss forceful and longing. I met his tongue stroke for stroke, sliding my fingers through his hair as I held him. When he pulled back, we could see our frosted breath as ice trails webbed from our blanket in all directions. His deep ocean eyes fixated on mine, and he slowed his movements. His brows knitted as if we were reading some emotion in my eyes that he couldn't place. My heart constricted as I thought of the words he had confessed to me minutes before, and the fingers from my free hand reached up, cupping his cheek, the skin hot beneath my touch. I took a deep breath before breaking the silence between us.

"I love you, Dashiell." He stopped moving entirely, stopped breathing, it seemed like. He just stared at me, relief and elation washing over his face. "I am in love with you." He let out a shuddering breath before leaning down to place his lips gently on mine, the kiss tender and soft. It wasn't one of passion or desire; it was fueled by love and happiness. Dash tangled his hand in my hair, holding me tight against him as he began to move again, the burning in my blood quickly returning.

"I love you," he said against my mouth, and the desire in his voice was my undoing as I completely fell apart at the seams, climaxing with the declaration of love on my lips. The world around me crumbled away as my head swam with pleasure. Dash found his release as he held my body, still shaking from its ecstasy against his. There was no going back now. Things had shifted between us permanently, and I gladly welcomed the change.

48.

Dash's soft lips pressed into my shoulder as he clasped my dress. I leaned into the touch, unsure if I would ever get enough of feeling his hands or mouth on me. Once we finished putting our clothes back on, he laid out the blanket under the oversized oak tree, and we settled in for the night, deciding not to end our evening together just yet.

I reached into our picnic basket and pulled out the small bowl of raspberries I had spied earlier, before placing them on Dash's lap. He stared at the fruit incredulously for a moment before his face finally broke into a knowing smile.

"You did a *really* good job," I told him, and he threw his head back in laughter. I wanted to get lost in the sound forever. He leaned down, kissing my forehead as he shifted and pulled something from his pocket.

"I want to give you your birthday present," Dash said as he held out a small deep blue box.

"The only thing I want is you," I told him, lifting my face to kiss his cheek.

"You already have me," he replied, handing me the present. "Plus, I want you to have this." I opened the lid and laughed the second I saw what it contained. "I figured it couldn't hurt to try again." I pulled out the delicate gold necklace with the peridot gemstone he had left for me the morning after my Welcome Feast. I smiled widely as I handed him the piece of jewelry, moving my hair away from my neck so he could secure it. His fingers ran gently over the clasp as he kissed just above my spine. "It was my mother's," he said, and I whirled immediately. My face filled with horror, and my hands flew over my mouth as I shook my head, denying his claim.

"This was your mother's?" He nodded, a small, crooked grin forming. "This was your mother's, and I literally *threw* it at you?" He nodded again, his smile more pronounced as he watched my terror play out. "Oh my Gods, I'm such an asshole!" I buried my face in my hands, mortified at what I had done. Dash laughed loudly as he pulled me against him, his scent cocooning and calming me.

"You didn't know," he reasoned, kissing the top of my head, and I groaned loudly.

"That doesn't make it any better," I said, my voice muffled. "I'm so sorry, Dash," I whined as I thought back to the look on his face after shoving the necklace into his pocket. There was an emotion he had shown that I couldn't figure out at the time, but now I knew it for what it was—heartbreak.

"Don't apologize. I was a dick, and you were angry; the necklace's history shouldn't change that." He removed my hands from my face so I had to stare into his eyes.

"I love you," he said as he parted my lips with his, and I melted against him. "Lay with me," Dash whispered into the night. He set his back against the tree's trunk, and I curled into his side, basking in his heat.

"I love you," I whispered back, and he pressed a kiss to the top of my hair as I stared up at the stars that peeked through the canopy of leaves.

The scent of lemongrass and sea salt guided me to consciousness as Dash's broad chest beneath my cheek rose and fell with each breath. His fingers gently caressed the arm draped across his stomach, each stroke sending a tingle down to my very core. Memories of last night flooded my mind. Images of Dash's lips on mine, his hands and mouth on my body, claiming me and taking everything I had given him. My cheeks flushed, and my breasts ached at the reminder. I shifted, pressing myself further into him, trying to fuse our bodies as one.

Soft, smooth lips pressed against my head. He knew I was awake.

"Good morning," he said into my hair. I moved from his chest and propped myself onto my elbow, my long golden-brown curls spilling over to one side, the red within pronounced as the morning sun shone.

"Good morning," I replied, studying his face. His cheeks were a light shade of pink, his lips swollen, the evidence of our night together, and the corner of his mouth lifted just barely. I stared into his eyes, so tender and yet so haunted, the dark shadows underneath coming into focus. He looked exhausted, as if he hadn't had a single night of peace in days. "Did you sleep at all?"

His face went slack, and he tipped his head back, his gaze focusing on the sky as he said, "No." The word was clipped and filled with sorrow. A moment of silence passed between us before he continued. "We should head back; the guards will start looking for us soon." His tone was off-putting, and I could tell there was something on his mind that he didn't want to tell me. Did he think last night was a mistake? My heart began to crack at the thought, and a broken noise escaped me before I could garner control of myself. I felt Dash's eyes on me immediately as I looked away, trying to steel my nerves enough to ask the question that was eating at my mind, at my heart.

I didn't have the bravado to meet his stare as I asked, "Do you regret...." I trailed off, unable to continue, when Dash shifted from beside me, sitting up completely and leaning his back against the giant oak tree behind us. He gave me his full attention, eyes widening at my words and pain flashing over his features. I hated myself for even thinking it, but I had to ask; I had to know. I took a deep breath before forcing myself to continue as a lump grew in my throat. "Do you regret what happened last night between us?" His eyes filled with shock, and his mouth dropped open, but no words came out. "It's okay if you—" Before I could finish, Dash slid his long legs under him and leaned forward on his knees, taking my face between his strong hands as his eyes poured into mine.

"No, Ainsley! Gods no, I could never regret—" the words were rushed, flowing out of him as if they were desperate to flood the space between us. He lowered his forehead to mine, stroking my cheeks with his thumbs. I breathed deeply, drinking in his intoxicating scent in greedy gulps. "Last night was perfect, Ainsley." He leaned back just enough to study me. "I meant every word I said. I love you, and

I want to be with you. Last night was the single greatest night of my existence." He pressed his lips to mine as if he could transfer the truth that way.

"Then what is it? I know something is wrong, Dash, just... Just talk to me. Please." He was quiet for a long while as his eyes studied my face, searching like he was debating what to tell me. He took a long deep breath.

"I'm still struggling with everything I've been dealing with, still trying to understand and navigate it, but I promise you, Ainsley... I promise you this has nothing to do with what happened last night. Please know that." His words were pleading and desperate. I exhaled, and his eyes searched my face, trying to find any hint of anger or sadness, but it wasn't there. He didn't shut me out when I asked, and that's all I had wanted. "Come here." He pulled me onto his lap, one arm wrapped around my body, the other on the back of my head, caressing my hair in long strokes as I buried my face in his chest. His warm cheek pressed onto my forehead, holding me firm to him as if, at any moment, I would slip away. We sat there for an eternity, nothing but the sounds of our breathing and pounding hearts. I was content never to move from this spot. To never have to leave his embrace. Dash removed his hand from my back and slid it to my chin, tilting my head ever so slightly to look at him, those blue eyes swallowing me whole. "How are *you* feeling?" he asked. I shrugged noncommittally.

"I've had better nights," I said, my tone coated in unsatisfied boredom. Dash flipped me so quickly that I almost didn't register the movement.

"Is that so, smart-ass?" he asked, trailing kisses down my neck as he hiked up my dress. I didn't answer. I lost all ability to speak as Dash's fingers worked their way up my thighs and settled right where I wanted them.

49.

The trek back to the palace was quiet, neither of us saying much. Though Dash's mind was still being tormented by whatever he was dealing with, he never missed the opportunity to squeeze my hand or kiss me. He never missed the chance to show me physically how much he loved me and how he wanted me near.

"I'm sorry," Dash announced as we walked. "I didn't mean to ruin our morning; I'm just in my head about things."

"Are you concerned about the meeting tomorrow?" I asked, but he shook his head. Well, at least that made one of us.

"Is it about those men in the woods? The ones you…." I dared to ask.

"No," he said without a thought. "They were the first lives I'd ever taken, and I know that I should feel changed or altered after, but they hurt you, Ainsley. They beat you until you were barely alive, and then they were going to kidnap you. The only thing I regret about their murder was that I didn't drag it out to make them suffer as they should have for what they did to you." I didn't flinch or shy away from his confession but instead felt comforted knowing that he was okay with what he'd done. More than that, *I* was okay with it.

"Is it about your father?" I tried again, and he stilled. I remembered the words I had heard King Perceval say the night I had drifted in and out of consciousness following the attack. I hated him for what he said to his son, to blame him for what Tenebrae had done to me and for the death of his mother.

"Amongst other subjects, yes, my father is involved in my struggles." The way his jaw was clenched, I didn't want to ask him to elaborate further. He would tell me when he was ready.

We cleared the final thicket of trees and made our way onto the sprawling lawn that led up to the terrace. I stopped before we reached the steps and tugged on Dash's arm. "I know you don't want to discuss the details of what you're going through." He looked away from me uncomfortably, staring out to the gardens beyond us. I reached for his chin, gently bringing his face back to mine. "But when you are ready to talk, if you ever are, I will be here to listen." I pushed myself onto my toes, reaching my face up as high as possible to meet his lips, kissing him softly. He leaned forward, sending me flat-footed once more as he deepened the embrace, his fingers twining in my hair.

"Thank you," he said as he broke it off, and I smiled lovingly at him. The sound of footsteps on stone approaching had us glancing up to find Felix walking toward us.

"Hey! Where did you sneak off to last night? Or should I say, whose bed did you sneak out of this morning?" I asked Felix, throwing him a wink. But his eyes were cold and hard as he glared at Dash, who glared right back; neither seemed to be breathing.

"Ainsley, I need to have a moment with Dashiell. Alone," Felix replied harshly, not taking his eyes off the man next to me. My heart stumbled as I ran through Felix's words. *Dashiell*. He had never once used Dash's full name in the months that I had been here. The tone he used was so unlike him as well. I looked at Dash, who was now staring at the space between them, his eyes sorrowful, his head slightly drooped. I rubbed my thumb along the back of his hand in a comforting stroke.

He turned to me, giving a small encouraging smile, and nodded. "It's okay," he whispered. "Go ahead inside. I'll find you shortly." He leaned forward again, kissing my forehead before I made my way up the steps. I stopped once I reached Felix, who still had not taken his eyes off Dash. I gently touched his arm, dragging my hand down to clasp his, and squeezed tightly.

"Felix," I said quietly. The fury in his eyes made the amber look like molten steel, and the rage surrounding him was palpable. "Felix," I said again. He was reluctant for a moment but then pulled his gaze from Dash to me. I had never seen him furious, and it terrified me. Taking a deep breath, I addressed him again.

"I will go inside if you want privacy, but I need to ask you something before I do." His eyes narrowed as he waited for me to continue. "Are you okay?" Silence. I brought my hand up and cupped his cheek, rubbing my thumb softly over his skin as I tried to comfort him in the only way I knew how to. "I don't need to know about what happened; that's between the two of you. I just need to know that *you* are okay." After a few quiet moments, he pulled me into a tight embrace.

"I'm not right now, but I will be," he whispered, letting go as I nodded. I threw Dash one last glance as he mouthed, '*I love you*' before I headed inside the palace and up to my room, leaving them to themselves. I prayed to the Gods above that they would be in one piece or at least still alive when I saw them again. As I hurried through the corridor, muffled shouts and hushed tempers erupted from outside, and I quickened my pace, trying to leave them to their spat.

When I reached my room, Imogen was there, arms crossed, as she peered out of the window overlooking the gardens.

"It's not polite to eavesdrop," I said as I strode over to her and looked out the window.

"It doesn't count as eavesdropping if you're too high to make out the words. Not to mention, they put up a silencing shield as well," she said, justifying her actions as we watched Dash drag a hand through his light brown hair while shaking his head. Felix then placed a comforting hand on his friend's shoulder. "At least things seem to be calming down now."

"How bad was it before?" The halls were filled with people getting the palace in order for the kings' arrival tomorrow, so it took twice as long as usual for me to make it upstairs to my room.

Imogen let out a low whistle. "Those boys have been best friends since they were children. The times I've seen them spat can only be counted on one hand, but I've never witnessed them like this. Whatever happened, it had to have been serious." I continued to watch as Dash spoke and Felix paced back and forth in front of him, looking torn and conflicted. Imogen eyed me sidelong, and I raised my brows at her.

"What?" I demanded, knowing she was insinuating something.

"Could this be in regards to *you*?"

"In regards to *me,* how?" I asked flatly.

"You and Felix are close." She shrugged. "I wouldn't be surprised if he—"

"Absolutely not. It is not like that at all between us," I quickly said, rolling my eyes at the ridiculous idea. She pursed her lips. "It's really not!"

"Okay, okay, fine. I'll leave it," she said, throwing her hands up defensively and going back to observing the boys below.

"Dash was pretty torn up the morning about what he's been going through. Though I don't know exactly what that entails, I do know part of it has to do with King Perceval. Could Felix be upset about that?"

Imogen nodded along thoughtfully. "It's quite possible. Felix has always been too good for this place; Prince Dashiell too. The king's views are different than theirs, and they struggle with that. The prince often gets caught between his best friend and pleasing his father. King Perceval likely said something to his son that Felix disagrees with."

"That sounds like a horrible position for Dash to be in," I told her.

"I'm sure it is," she replied sadly, and just then, Dash tilted his head toward the window. Imogen and I immediately dropped to the floor, ducking beneath the opening. That was definitely going to leave a bruise on my knees.

"Do you think they saw us?" I whispered, and Imogen gave me a mischievous look.

"There's only one way to find out," she said, smiling. We sat up slowly and tried to inconspicuously peek over the window, only to find Dash and Felix staring up at us, arms crossed, the look of disappointment and amusement clear on their beautiful faces. I waved tentatively back, and they shook their heads, laughing as they made their way back inside the palace together, Felix's arm draped over Dash's shoulders. I smiled widely, knowing that they were okay or at least working through their issues.

"So, where we you all night?" Imogen asked, gesturing to my untouched bed.

"Didn't you once tell me that gossiping was for busybodies?" I asked her with a pointed look.

"That only applies to everyone except myself." I laughed softly as I strolled over to her, pulling her to sit next to me on the bed as I dove into last night's story. I told Imogen about the dancing, the meadow, and the declarations of love, though I made sure to leave out the more explicit details of our union, allowing her to connect the dots without giving a descriptive visual. "I am glad to see that everything worked out and that you are happy," she said once I finished.

"So am I," I told her as a soft knock rapped on my open door. We both turned at the sound to find Dash standing in the doorway.

"Am I interrupting?" he asked.

"Not at all, Your Highness," Imogen replied, standing from the bed and bringing me up with her. She smiled before heading toward the door, stopping in front of Dash, her hand reaching up to cup his cheek. "Your mother would have adored her," she whispered to him. Dash's stare widened, and his eyes misted over at the mention of his mother. "Treat her well," she added, and Dash nodded at once as Imogen looked back toward me before finally departing from the room.

Dash stood there silently, looking down at his hands as he fumbled with his fingers. "Is everything okay between you and Felix?" I asked as I walked over to him.

"I think so," he said quietly, giving me his full attention, wonder shining in his brilliant eyes as he gazed at me. I pressed myself into him, wrapping my arms around his neck, my fingers finding their way into his hair.

"Good," I told him. "Do you want to tell me about it?" He shook his head just barely.

"I'm not ready right now, but someday, I promise." He pressed his forehead to mine. If time were what he needed, I would gladly grant it.

"Well, in that case, I can think of a few other things we could do to pass the time. They don't include talking," I replied, and a smile spread across his face.

"Oh, is that so?" he asked, and I shrugged coyly.

Dash swept me into his arms, eliciting a squeal from me as he kicked the door shut behind us. He carried me over to the bed, setting me down gently as my lips crashed into his. I let the kiss burn through me, allowing myself to get lost in him and the love that blossomed so beautifully between us.

50.

We never made it down for lunch, or even dinner, for that matter. We spent the entire day in my bed, talking and laughing and tangling ourselves together, and somehow it still didn't feel like enough of him.

Between our lovemaking, we had serious conversations about the past couple of weeks in an effort to move forward and heal. Dash had answered every question I had asked him and had been patient and listened as I vented and cried, holding me tight as I did. He explained what his conversations with Rosella entailed, most of which were her trying to worm her way into his bed once again, and he shared what he had done each day we were apart. He was either in the War Room with his father or locked in his bed chamber, refusing to see or speak to anyone, except for the time he was with Rosella and her friends. That day, he came down to meet with one of King Perceval's advisors but was stopped by the group of ladies.

When I asked why he didn't just walk away, he told me it was because he could sense my presence, and though he wasn't ready to face me, he wanted to feel me for just a moment. He explained that he hadn't expected us to be on the terrace that late in the afternoon, or he would have never come downstairs. He also claimed he never expected Felix to throw an apple at him for the first time since they were children, though our friend's actions didn't surprise me.

We had finally reached the discussion of my birthday celebration, and though I had no desire ever to recount the events of that night, I knew that to put it behind us, I had to.

"I tried to get out of going, but it was no use, so I planned to stay hidden in the back, hoping it would be enough not to disturb your night," Dash began. "You deserved to have an amazing birthday for the first time in your life, and I didn't want to get in the way. But then I saw you, and your eyes locked onto mine. It was like everything I had felt that week melted away and became nonexistent. I had to fight the urge to run to you, to sweep you into my arms and tell you that I was sorry and that I loved you." I closed my eyes as he spoke and tried to keep my composure as I listened.

"I watched you from a distance, dancing and smiling the night away, enjoying yourself completely. I shifted closer, and when I heard the sound of your laughter, something in me just snapped. I moved before I couldn't even process the decision I had made. With you in my arms, it felt like home, like none of the bullshit mattered, and I would be able to get through anything because I had you. But then the music stopped, and you looked at me like you missed me and wanted me as much as I did you. My heart shattered. I could see the pain I had caused in your eyes, and I knew I was still broken and torn up and couldn't do what...." He stopped, and I opened my eyes to find him dragging his hands over his face, unable to continue. So I didn't force him to.

Dash cradled me in his arms as I cried, describing that night from my point of view. I shared how he had made me feel and how my heart had broken at that moment, standing there cold, empty, and alone. It took a long time for me to settle the sobs, and Dash held me through it all, rocking me gently as he wiped away my tears.

Warm lips brushed along my forehead, pulling me from sleep. "I love you," Dash whispered as he placed a kiss on my skin. "I love you," he repeated against my cheek, kissing me yet again. "I love you." He moved to my other cheek. "I love you. I love you. I love you," he repeated over and over and over, leaving soft kisses between each declaration across my face. His touch sent shivers down my spine, setting my blood on fire.

"So you've said," I replied sleepily, my eyes fluttering open to find his.

"And I will keep saying it," he told me softly, brushing my hair from my face and tucking the loose strands behind my ear as he always did. "It still doesn't feel real to me."

"What do you mean?" I asked, shifting on my pillow to fully look at him. Dash pulled the blankets up higher over my bare shoulders, and I sank into the warmth of the furs. I hadn't even been aware that I was cold, but somehow he had.

Dash shook his head, struggling to pull the words from his mind. Explaining what he was thinking and how he was feeling had never been something that came easily for him, and my heart ached to know that after what we had gone through, he was trying. For me, he would always try.

"I mean that I never expected this to happen between us." I raised a brow at him in speculation. We were betrothed for my entire life; how could he not think this was possible? "Don't get me wrong, I had hoped it would—Gods, did I hope it would—but I never thought it would actually happen." Dash read the confusion on my face and my silent request for him to elaborate.

"When you came here, Ainsley, you were so angry, and you wanted nothing to do with this place with the people here." My heart sank deep within my chest, and a lump began to form as I remembered those first few days. "I tried to talk to you and get to know you, but every time I did, it always seemed to make things worse, and it always ended in disaster. I didn't know what to do, and it killed me because..." he trailed off, eyes searching my face as he continued to fight and claw for the words he needed to express. "Because I knew I was in love with you from the first moment I saw you, Ainsley. I can't explain how I knew, but I did. It was as if my world had stopped, and there was nothing in it but you. It was the first time I ever even remotely believed in fate or destiny. I wanted to be close to you, aching to be around you every second of the day, but you didn't feel the same." I felt the gentle slide of a tear rolling down my cheek.

"I used to pace outside your door at night like an idiot, trying to work up the courage to knock and concoct some ridiculous excuse to see you or hear your voice. Just for a minute. On the day of your Welcome Feast, I made sure we were alone at breakfast because I knew that would be the only chance I had to get you to speak to me." I swallowed hard as I remembered the conversation that morning. "You wanted nothing to do with me, and I felt so broken at that moment. As I looked into your eyes, I knew there wasn't anything I could say to convince you to give me a chance, so I left, hoping I could come up with the words to reach you that night instead." He let out a deep breath, and I closed my eyes, forcing my mind to travel back to the evening that ended with me crying on my bedroom floor until dawn broke through the windows.

"When you walked into that ballroom, my heart stopped. It was as if all the air from my lungs had been taken from me, and I was content never to breathe again. You looked so beautiful and full of wonder, and I couldn't stop asking myself why the Gods had chosen to bless me by bringing you into my life." A small smile tugged at the corner of his mouth as he reminisced. "But then the room got quiet, and everyone's eyes fell upon you. You seemed so terrified and helpless at that moment, and I knew I had to get to you." I thought back to how Dash had appeared at my side that night and held out his hand for me to take. "The entire night, I couldn't take my eyes off you, and wherever you went, I did. It's like my body knew it had to be near you. You have this power over me, Ainsley; that's the best way that I can think to describe it." I knew what he meant. For weeks, I felt this constant pull that gravitated me toward Dash.

"I thought you kept staring at me because you were embarrassed that you had to marry me, or that you hated me, or that you were wondering how to get out of the betrothal, or that you were trying to make me jealous of Rosella. I had a lot of thoughts running through my mind that night," I told him, laughing softly at exactly how little I had known.

Sadness flowed through Dash's eyes like he didn't understand how I could ever believe he had felt that way. "I was staring because I was in complete awe of you. With Rosella that night, I can only remember being pissed off that she wouldn't leave me alone; she kept interrupting my thoughts and appearing next to me whenever I'd go to find you. I finally told her to fuck off and went after you when you slipped onto the balcony." He closed his eyes, and shame washed over his features. "And that conversation is one I'll regret for the rest of my life."

I didn't want to go there and think about the words that he had said to me; the words that had made me crumble so wholly that night. Dash took a deep breath before continuing. "I was so nervous about being alone with you after that morning. Watching you stand out there, you looked so at peace for the first time since you had arrived, and I convinced myself that I should tell you how I felt.

Not that I was in love with you, but that I wanted the chance to get to know you, but of course, I fucked that up. Before I could tell you what was in my heart, you asked about Rosella. A part of me had hoped it may have been out of jealousy, like the thought of me with someone else didn't sit well with you. But then you gave me not only your permission but also your blessing to be with her or with anyone else that I wanted. Even if you didn't say the words aloud, I knew what you meant; anyone *but* you. Hearing that you didn't care if I took someone else into my bed, into my life, crushed me, and I lashed out. I was hurting and stupid, and I don't even know why I fucking said those things to you, Ainsley. They were so far from the truth. I tried to go after you when you ran, but when I reached your door, I could hear you on the other side. A piece of me died as I listened to you cry." Tears began rolling down his face, and I wiped them away softly, rubbing my thumb along his cheek.

"I sat there outside your door all night until Imogen arrived for you the next morning. I gave her the necklace to give to you because I knew you didn't want to see me. Then, I went straight to breakfast to wait for you. I can't even tell you half of the shit Felix said to me because I was so out of it. You had consumed every thought in my mind." Dash laid his head back against the white pillow, so bright in the moonlight that crept into the room, and stared up at the ceiling. I could feel the pain radiating from him, and I wanted nothing more than to make that vanish.

"You don't have to continue," I tried to reassure him.

"Yes, I do." I reached for the hand resting on his chest and brought it to my lips, kissing him gently. "And then you showed up, and my heart broke seeing you. You tried to cover it up, but I could still see the pain in your eyes. You looked so drained and exhausted, and then you started talking about that fucking Logan guy and your time together, and I lost it. The thought of you being in someone else's arms, of someone's else hands on you...." Dash took a deep breath, composing himself as if trying to banish the thought from his mind. "You had a life before me, and I had no right to feel the jealousy that I did. I knew you were talking about it to prove a point, but I couldn't handle it; I had to get out of there. And then the look on your face when you threw that necklace back at me. I knew at that moment any possibility of us being more was gone, and there was no one to blame for that but myself."

"I had no idea you had felt that way," I replied, and he smiled weakly as he shook his head, his story not yet finished.

"After you and Felix left, I decided I was done trying to be more to you. I decided that if friendship were the most you would allow me to have, I would gladly take it. I decided that the only thing I needed was to be in your life in any way you would have me. I would love you silently for the rest of my life, forever quietly yours. And even though we were to be married, it didn't have to go farther than a political alliance; it didn't have to cross a line you didn't want. I would simply marry my friend, and I would be happy with that. Because even if it meant that I could never have you the way I desired, I would still have you in my life."

Dash's gaze drifted past me, and he smiled at whatever he found there. I followed his stare to my nightstand and the roses strewn across the wooden top. Buds that were fresh and crisp mixed with those wilted and withered. Even though their brief life had ended, their once bright white flesh now worn and brown, I wouldn't let Imogen clear them out. Every rose Dash had ever given me had stayed there on that nightstand. "You kept them," he said.

"Every single one," I replied, turning my attention back to him.

He clamped his lips and narrowed his eyes at me as if trying to assess whether or not he wanted to tell me more. As if he had another secret, he wasn't sure he wanted to divulge.

"Tell me," I said as I playfully smacked his shoulder, the ink from his tattoo barely visible in the darkness. Dash chuckled a shallow breathy laugh as he nodded his head, content to share.

"Once I had decided that I would be solely your friend, I couldn't very well share with you how I truly felt, so I gave you those." He jerked his chin to the flowers. "A rose for each time I wanted to tell you how completely in love with you I was but couldn't. It was my way of telling you without ever being able to say it aloud." My chest tightened at his confession, and I felt like a part of me had always known their true meaning. Maybe that's why I refused to get rid of them even after their time had passed.

"I was content with how everything was between us, resigned to being your friend, but then something changed. I don't know what exactly, but we started to get closer. You started to let me in, let me get to know you, and my feelings for you only grew more each day. Every little bit you gave me became forever imprinted upon my heart. You were the first thought I had every morning, the last before I went to sleep, and every thought in between." Dash turned back onto his side to face me, his eyes slightly glazed over and shining with love and devotion. "And though I still wasn't sure you would ever want more from me, I held on to that hope because of these moments... These moments, you'd look at me as if you were wondering the same thing. There were so many times when I wanted to wrap you in my arms and feel your lips on mine. There were so many times that I wanted to hold you through the night, but I promised myself I wouldn't try until you uttered the words first or gave me some indication that you felt the same. It was a struggle for me at times to be so close to you and not be able to have you in the way that I wanted. The day at the lake after the ice slide, I almost lost control completely. Feeling your touch on me as you traced my tattoo...."

Dash swallowed as he shook his head, thinking back to that day, "It took every ounce of willpower I had not to give in to the desire to grab you and kiss you; to tell you how much I loved and wanted you. And when you pulled away from me, I thought that I must have crossed a line, and I was furious at myself for making you feel uncomfortable when you had already expressed that you didn't want me. I was pissed at myself for letting my feelings get in the way. Then when you recited the same words you gave me at your Welcome Feast about me being free to...." He didn't finish the line, and I was thankful for that. I didn't want to hear the words I had spewed at him. "I realized it was coming from a place of anger, but I didn't know why until Rosella appeared, and I could see the pain in your eyes as she mentioned the day I had last used *Solstice*. I wasn't sure if you were jealous or if it was merely because you hated her, but I knew I couldn't let you think anything was happening between her and me. I had to at least let you know that there was no one else I was interested in. Even if we remained just friends throughout our union, I wouldn't be pursuing anyone else. I didn't want to pressure you, and I didn't want to break what we had built. I was content to forever love you in secret, although I broke that rule once."

"What?" I asked, thinking back to the times we had together. He never once expressed his love for me until last night.

"After you were attacked in the woods, I was out of my mind. I had never felt such rage and terror. I thought I had lost you, Ainsley." My body stiffened as I remembered the attacker's hands on me and how the knife felt as it was held to my throat. I swallowed my fear and focused instead on Dash and his story. "When I was carrying you back to the palace, I talked to you. I was begging you to be okay, to stay with me. I kissed your head and told you that I loved you. I know you didn't hear me, but I promised myself I would never say those words aloud until I knew you wanted to hear them. Not even Felix could get me to say them, though he tried."

"Dash, I..." I didn't know what to say or where to even begin.

"Everything was so different before. And now..." he trailed off, unable to continue. His ocean eyes poured into mine, pulling me beneath their current.

"And now I'm yours," I finished for him. Dash leaned forward, resting his forehead against mine as he breathed me in.

"And I'm yours. Forever. For eternity. For as long as I exist, I will *always* be yours."

His words were my undoing. I wrapped my arms around his neck, pulling him against me as I pressed my lips softly to his. His mouth parted for me, and I took the opening to deepen our kiss, his hands grasping my face, his fingers tangling in my hair. He kissed me like he was still trying to convince himself that I was real. The love I felt for him crashed into me like waves breaking against rock. I'd surrender to it. I'd let this ocean sweep me under its current and drown me. For eternity.

51.

The sun had yet to rise when Dash woke me with a breakfast tray in bed and urged me to eat quickly. There was a smile on his face and excitement in his eyes like I had never seen, which sent butterflies swarming in my stomach.

"Come with me," he said as he led us to one of the large rose bushes on the grounds and plucked a single white rose from the leaves. Dash twirled the stem between his fingers, but he didn't offer it to me as he stared down at the flower. I waited patiently as I could tell his mind was working, arranging the thoughts he had into words. Finally, he loosed a breath and brought his gaze to mine, a question written in his eyes.

"I know we are still learning about each other and are both still growing into who we want to become. I know that you didn't ask for this life—for me, for any of it—and it hasn't been easy. You have been through so much in the months you've been here, and I can't comprehend how you must feel." He rubbed his thumb over the back of my hand as he smiled down at me. "You allowing me to get to know you, you becoming my best friend, and you loving me has been the greatest honor of my life, Ainsley. I know we weren't given a say about how we started, and we don't have one regarding our marriage, but...." He stepped closer, holding the flower between us. "But I want the decision of what our relationship means to us to be our choice. I know we're technically already engaged, and we'll be married eventually despite what we decide, but I want to say this." He took a deep breath and swallowed.

"Ainsley, I love you, and I want a life with you. Not one of politics, but one of our choosing. Regardless of what others have already decided, I choose you to be my wife. I choose you to love and cherish every day. I choose you to protect with my life and with everything that I am. I choose to do everything I can to make you feel safe and loved." He extended the rose for me to take as he spoke his final words. "I am asking if you will do the honor of choosing me to be your husband." Tears spilled from my eyes, and my heart caught in my throat. I leapt into him, throwing my arms around the person I loved deeply and wanted nothing more than to share my life with. "Is that a yes?" he asked, squeezing me tight.

"Meh," I said through the sobs, and Dash laughed, lifting me from the ground as he kissed me passionately, tasting our devotion mixed with tears as he held me. I grabbed the rose from his hand as he placed me back down on the grass. "Yes, Dash. I choose you." He grabbed my face, rubbing away the tears of happiness that streamed down my cheeks.

"Your Highness!" a breathless guard said as he rushed us, interrupting our intimate moment. Dash released me at once, and the look on his face had the blood from mine draining. His eyes were wide and worried, yet there was also a look of cold authority within them. Dash looked like a royal, like a warrior. Like he was ready to attack and defend against any threat that came his way. "Both the King of Venator and the King of Agnitio have arrived. His Majesty sent us to alert you at once." Dash went stiff, and his jaw clenched tight. I couldn't read his thoughts, but I could tell his mind was working.

"What? It's barely past dawn," he said, glancing at the spot in the pink sky where the sun would eventually crest the mountains. The worry was heavy in his voice. The kings weren't set to arrive until mid-afternoon. They were early. Too early. But why?

"Where are they now?" Dash demanded.

"They are in the Grand Hall with your father," Felix announced, coming up behind the guards. "And their companions are sweeping the main corridors for any threats." Dash looked at his friend, a question written on his face. Felix shook his head in answer.

"We won't be able to get her back to her room without being seen," Felix told him.

"The Sanctuary?" Dash asked after a moment, but Felix shook his head once more.

"We'd have to go through the Royal Corridor. It's too risky."

"The escape tunnels?"

"Barricaded after the attacks," Felix replied.

"Fuck," Dash gritted out as he dragged a hand through his hair. He turned toward the palace, eyes narrowing as they darted across the exterior, the gears in his mind shifting as he tried to formulate a plan. I pressed myself against his chest, wrapping my arms around his middle as I stared up at him, hoping that whatever comfort my touch could offer would be enough to calm him. His blue eyes found mine, softening slightly as they took me in. Dash took a deep breath, and his lips curled in the corners as he stared down at me, hooking a loose strand of hair behind my ear. "The western corridor?" he asked, his gaze never tearing from mine.

"That could work," Felix agreed after a moment. "It isn't being occupied right now and has the most direct route back to her room. We can move her in the night." Dash nodded before leaning forward and pressing a kiss to my forehead.

"Thank you," he whispered against my skin as if I had done something useful. He pulled back, and I arched onto my toes to kiss his cheek, his answering smile sending my heart racing and stomach flipping. "We need to go now," he said, and I nodded, following him and Felix as they led the way through the grounds.

The halls were quiet, and the people were sparse as we cautiously scurried into the palace from the western entrance. It was the one part of the estate people didn't regularly venture to, often used to house visitors when large celebrations were underway. Because the kings and their companions would be staying in the Royal Wing and Royal Corridor, there would be no reason for anyone to travel to this side of the palace.

"Shit," Dash whispered, halting our advance as he spun to face Felix. "It's Tallis. Take her the long way; I'll meet you there." Felix wasted no time grabbing my hand and pulling me quickly around the corner we had just come.

"Prince Dashiell! How nice it is to see you," a voice called the second we were out of sight.

We hurried our way through the corridors. Felix checked around each bend before venturing into the open, not wanting to stumble upon any unwanted guests again. Finally, we stopped in front of a large set of oak doors at the end of a long hall. He twisted the knob and poked his head through, making sure it was empty before pulling me along.

"Who is Tallis?" I asked once Felix had shut us inside.

"The King of Agnitio." He began walking the perimeter of the room, looking behind doors and curtains to ensure we were alone.

"If he isn't from Tenebrae, what would it matter if we were seen?"

"King Tallis may not be from Tenebrae, but at this time, we don't know which, if any, of the other kingdoms have aligned themselves with their cause. It's safer to stay completely out of sight until everyone has gone." Felix said as he dropped to the floor to look under the bed. I supposed that made sense. Until we knew who was on our side, it was better not to trust anyone at all.

"Why do I have to wait until the middle of the night to return to my room? Can't I slip out once the meeting begins?" None of the kings trusted each other, so it was a requirement that everyone who came to the palace was to be in attendance at the meeting. This helped ease their minds that there wouldn't be any conspiring behind their backs. Felix stood and placed his hands on either side of my shoulders as he looked deep into my eyes.

"We didn't want to tell you this," he began, and I raised a brow, my chest already rising and falling at a quicker pace from anticipation, "but there's a chance that this whole meeting is a trap."

"*What*?" I yelled furiously.

"We didn't tell you because we knew this would be your response." I opened my mouth to argue. "And before you open your mouth to argue, just know that the chance is very, very minuscule. Almost nonexistent, really." The door opened, and we both glanced up to find Dash entering quietly.

"A trap? Seriously?" I snapped, stomping over to him. He gave Felix a pointed look before addressing me.

"We didn't say anything because—"

"Because you knew this would be my response," I finished, twisting my head to glare at Felix.

"Because," he said, resting his hands on my waist and pulling me close, "we didn't want to worry you. When royalty is gathered in one place like this, there is always a chance it's a trap." He gripped my chin with his thumb and forefinger as he guided my face to his. "If I truly believed that danger would come of this, I would have sent you away from the palace." He leaned forward, pressing a kiss to the tip of my nose.

"But just in case we're wrong, you can't leave this room until we come to get you," Felix added, and Dash gave a small apologetic smile. He seemed to hate this as much as I did.

"Ministro's arrival was announced while I was speaking with Tallis," Dash told him. "Tenebrae is all that is left."

Felix nodded and headed for the door. "I'll come to retrieve you once they arrive," he said, peeking his head into the hallway and slipping out.

"I hate that you have to go." I wrapped my arms around Dash's neck, my fingers twirling a lock of his hair as I held him. The unease I felt at being apart during a time like this was overwhelming. My thoughts constantly bounced back and forth between every possible scenario of how the meeting could go. "If this is a trap, and something happens to you...." I couldn't finish the thought.

"I thought you wanted a fearless prince," he countered. I rolled my eyes, and that perfect cocky grin appeared.

"What I want is for you to come back to me alive and well," I said flatly. "I don't like being apart."

"Trust me, I'd much rather be here with you," Dash said as he bent and, in a quick motion, swept me off my feet, carrying me over to the large bed at the back of the room. He set me down delicately and pulled me to his chest. I curled into his warmth and let out a long sigh. "What's wrong?" He asked, stroking my back.

"I have this overwhelming feeling that I shouldn't be in this room right now. I should be in that meeting with you, and I know you're going to say it's too dangerous, but—"

"Because it is," he stated. "No one knows Tenebrae's true plans, and I'm not going to dangle you in front of them like a prize and pray to the Gods that they don't take you."

"Why would they attempt something like that in a room full of witnesses, Dash?" I bit back, annoyed that he wasn't seeing my side.

"Why would I risk it?" he rebutted. I loosed an agitated breath and looked away. He wasn't going to give in. We sat in frustrated silence, the tension between us high and heavy, but we never pulled away from one another. The need to be close overpowered the discontent and desire to be right. His lips pressed gently to my cheek. "I love you," he whispered. I turned to look at him again, and he presented a small smile—a peace offering. A white flag. I pressed my lips to his in acceptance, and he sighed as he squeezed me tighter. "I know you hate having to stay here, Ainsley, but know it's not done maliciously. I'm not trying to keep you out of the conversation, and I will fill you in on everything that happens, but I can't have you in that room. It's too—"

"Dangerous," I finished for him.

"Yes," he replied. "Cordelia will not be attending the meeting either. Her father ordered her to stay in Ministro."

"I just want to help," I admitted, hating how weak and pathetic I must sound. Dash's fingers traced my lips before he leaned down and kissed me softly.

"I know you do, and I love you even more for it."

The door creaked open, announcing Felix's return. His face seemed paler, and his features fell with an emotion I couldn't read. With slow deliberateness, he walked towards us, his posture straight and his chest rising and falling too quickly. Felix, usually calm and collected, was on edge, and that made me even more anxious for this day to be over.

"They're all here," he announced, but there was something off in how he said the words. Something that told me he wasn't telling us everything.

"What's wrong?" I asked, climbing down from the bed, Dash following close behind. Felix glanced at me, holding my gaze longer than necessary. His brow furrowed a little, the movement almost unnoticeable. Before I could comment, he quickly turned his attention to Dash.

"Something feels wrong, but I can't place what," he explained, his eyes shifting to me again. There was a curiosity, a question within them, and for the life of me, I didn't understand why. "I don't think this will be a civil or easy meeting."

"Do you think Tenebrae is planning something?" I questioned, holding Felix's stare. His eyes narrowed as he shook his head. There was so much more he wasn't saying. Was it to not frighten me?

"I don't think Tenebrae will declare war today, but there's more going on with them than we know," Felix said, moving his gaze to Dash. "I could feel their anger and unease the second I laid eyes on King Evander and his companions."

"Maybe they just aren't happy about getting caught," Dash offered.

"No, it's not that," Felix replied, crossing his arms over his chest as he contemplated how to explain what his Gift showed him. "There was an arrogance and confidence about them too. There was excitement medlied with cruelty like they were planning and plotting the second they entered the palace." My blood went cold at Felix's observation.

"So it *is* a trap," I said weakly, my hands trembling at my sides.

"No," Felix countered immediately. "I don't think it is, but we need to keep a close eye on them while they're here." Dash loosed a breath, worry radiating off of him in gentle waves. "Everyone is assembled and waiting. I told your father I would retrieve you so we could begin." Dash nodded as he turned to me, his eyes bright and searching as he scanned my face. I threw my arms around his neck and offered him the best smile I could, though I knew it was anything but reassuring.

"I'll be okay," I whispered, reaching up on my toes to press a kiss to his lips.

"I need you to listen to me," he said seriously. "You cannot leave this room. You cannot be seen. You cannot let anyone know who you are to Caelum and who you are to me. If something goes wrong and you're found, you must lie, Ainsley." He reached up to hold my face between his hands. "If you have to lie, make sure your words are as close to the truth as possible; it's more believable that way. Do you understand?" I swallowed the lump that had formed in my throat and nodded.

"Yes," I said softly as I stared up at him. He smiled, but it didn't reach his eyes as he released me, stepping away.

"We'll be back as soon as we can," Dash said as Felix pulled me into an embrace.

"Don't let anything happen to him," I whispered as he hugged me.

"Never," he replied, giving me his famous wink as he and Dash left, the latch clicking in place as they locked me in.

I felt the anxiety rise the moment they left and fought the urge to go after them. Every instinct in my body screamed at me to leave this room and step into the hall, but I knew I couldn't. I gave Dash and Felix my word that I'd stay put, so I'd honor that.

Unable to sit still, I paced the room for the first hour. I spent my time doing everything to take my mind off their absence, off the fear and worry that plagued my thoughts. There were two hundred and twenty-two flower prints on the curtains that hung tall over the open windows. There were seventeen sets of magic candles, their flame emitting no heat as they burned. Twelve pillows, three rugs, two dressers, four windows, and six vases that each held seven tulips.

I was just about to count the different shades of green in the room when hushed, distant voices reached me. I rushed to the door, pressing my ear against the wood as I strained to hear the conversation taking place in the hall. The entire reason that Dash and Felix chose this location to keep me hidden was that no one ever ventured down this corridor. Panic flowed through me as the voices outside the door began getting louder, growing nearer and nearer. *'You cannot be seen,'* Dash had warned me. My heart sank deep as the door handle rattled.

"It's locked," one of the voices said, and I breathed a sigh of relief, thanking the Gods above for this small mercy.

"Well, it's a good thing I have the key then, isn't it?" the other voice answered.

Fuck.

I whirled around, searching for somewhere to hide, when I spotted a door on the room's eastern wall. I ran for it, not caring what lay behind, as the sound of a lock clicking free roared in my ears just as I slid inside. Pressing my ear to the door, I tried to listen to their conversation, their voices muffled and distant. Who were they, and why were they here? My heart dropped into my stomach as a deep, satin voice called from behind.

"Why hello there, love."

52.

Startled, I spun around, my hands flying to my mouth to muffle the sound that escaped me. Sitting in an oversized chair across the room lounged a man, his eyes a deep, haunting grey, striking even from this distance. He leaned forward, interlacing his tanned fingers and resting his elbows on his knees. His head tilted as he studied me, his short black hair—slightly unkempt—shifting with the movement. I quickly glanced around, unsure of what to do or where to look.

"Can I help you with something?" the stranger asked curiously, his lips curling up at the corner, his voice as soft and smooth as silk. Something about how he spoke and the way he moved made me believe that he wasn't much older than myself or Dash. In actuality, he could be hundreds of years old, and there would be no way of knowing unless he told me.

I opened my mouth, but nothing came out. I struggled with what to say, what lie to come up with, my mind racing so fast I had no hope of slowing it down. He mistook my lack of words for one of confusion at his question. He opened his hands, gesturing around the open space in front of us. "You're in my room," he said, stating the obvious.

The words tumbled out of me faster than I would have liked. "I'm sorry. No one was supposed to be— Wait," I said, my brows scrunching together as I took a tentative step forward. "What are *you* doing here?"

Surprise flashed over the stranger's features, and he straightened just a fraction. My heart hammered in my chest, but I took another step closer. "You're supposed to be in that meeting," I said carefully, my eyes narrowing at him. The agreed-upon terms were that each king was to bring his queen and up to three trusted advisors, all of which were required to be in that room. No one was to leave, and no one extra was to be brought along. Felix had come to tell Dash that everyone had arrived and was present. He would never have lied about that. He would never put me in that kind of danger, so why were two people now occupying the room I had been placed in? Why was this stranger here with me now? My breathing quickened as my mind ran rampant. Was this the trap? Were Dash and Felix in danger this very second? Something like anger glinted in his eyes for just a second and then disappeared.

He stood slowly, eyeing me suspiciously. "And how do *you* know of that meeting?" he asked as he approached me. *Shit.* No one was supposed to know of that meeting except me and those in that room. Even the servants had all been told a lie. Everyone had been informed that the kings and queens of Disparya had all come to offer gifts and their congratulations on the pending union between Dash and myself.

Both Dash and Felix had done everything possible to keep the details surrounding my attack a secret. Only those involved that night knew the truth. Everyone in the palace was under the impression that I had fallen off my horse while out riding. The cuts and scrapes covering my body backed up the false narrative. As a sign of good faith and respect for those involved, the kings had all agreed to keep the details of the meeting and accusations secret. The fact that I had just mentioned it betrayed that.

Everything in my head screamed at me to back away, but my instincts told me to stay, to stand my ground. I felt this odd sense of calm and understanding I couldn't place. Was he an Empathi?

"Servants gossip," I said entirely too quickly. A half-smirk formed upon the stranger's lips as he shook his head, calling me out on the lie. *If you have to lie, make sure it is as close to the truth as possible.* "I overheard My lady and his Royal Highness discussing it."

"And who are you to have the privilege to overhear such an important conversation? Does King Perceval have a spy amongst his Court?"

"No!" I blurted, and the stranger chuckled under his breath. "A servant," I ground out, fixing my mistake.

He stepped closer, now only inches from me. He was tall. Taller than Dash, maybe even taller than Felix. His charcoal eyes poured into me as his hand reached down, grabbing mine to hold up between us. He examined my open palm, his fingers caressing it softly. My heart quickened at the foreign touch, and I worked to calm my breathing, to not be afraid.

"Your hands are much too soft, so you clearly don't work on the grounds or in the kitchens," he observed, curiosity glinting in those deep eyes. I withdrew my hand from him, bringing it back to my side as I lifted my chin in defiance.

"I am the future princess's personal maiden," I spat out, and he smiled wider at my sharp tone.

"I see," he said quickly, nodding his head, clearly not believing a word coming out of my mouth. His whole presence exuded arrogance and smugness. I felt my temper rise as I watched him take a small step backward, crossing his arms over his chest and taunting me with his questions and responses. He was a cat playing with its meal before he devoured it. I swallowed hard, preparing for whatever more he had to say. "I don't recall the servants of Caelum being so well dressed," he said, looking me up and down.

"It was a present from my lady," I said flatly. This interrogation was getting old.

"Mmmhm," he said, amused and nodding once again as he began to walk, circling me. I stood still, not daring to move a muscle, even though everything in me wanted to punch him, my hands balling into fists at my side. "She seems quite generous, the future princess."

"She is," I replied, the words short and clipped.

"And you are her personal maiden?" he questioned, still circling like a vulture getting ready to attack.

"That *is* what I said, isn't it?" I remarked, lifting my chin higher, fire blazing in my eyes.

"And who is it that I have the pleasure of speaking to now?" A lump caught in my throat, and I froze, refusing to say another word. The stranger stopped in front of me, his eyes now hard as he raised an eyebrow and leaned in closer. "Your name," he said coldly, a command, his patience ending. *Make sure it is as close to the truth as possible;* the words echoed in my head.

"Imogen," I replied, forcing my voice to sound calm and confident. He watched me curiously as if debating with himself how to proceed. I wasn't sure if he believed me, but his response immediately told me he did not.

"And if I give King Perceval that name," he mused, sounding bored, "and demand retribution for one of his servants knowing about the *very* secret meeting currently taking place," a smirk appeared, "would it be you that I would see brought before us, or another?" I stopped breathing altogether, and my hands began to tremble. I couldn't allow Imogen to pay for my loose tongue. I clenched my jaw as I tried to devise a way out of the mess I had created.

"And what if I tell King Perceval that another kingdom broke the agreement and brought someone who did not attend the meeting?" I questioned. The stranger's dark eyes widened with excitement.

"I like this game," he said, smiling wickedly. So that's what this was to him; a game. "But tell me, why would King Perceval take *your* word for it? You're just a simple servant, after all."

"And you are?" I said, fishing for a name, a title, anything to give me a clue as to who he was or why he was here.

"Not," he replied simply. "So, Imogen, is it?" He had me, and the sparkle in his eyes told me he knew it.

"Ainsley," I said tightly in defeat. Dash had informed me that they would give the kings a false name to protect me further. When conversing with the other kingdoms, they had always referred to me as 'the lady' or 'the future princess.' My real name had no meaning to this stranger. He had no way of knowing that the subject of the meeting was standing before him now. If he presented King Perceval with my actual name, it would be me that was brought before the king and this man, and I knew that the retribution would not be paid for with my life. The same courtesy I could not guarantee for Imogen.

"Ainsley," he repeated like a caress. As if he was savoring the way the word tasted, trying to detect the lie there. After a moment, he smiled again. "Now, was that so hard?" I looked back toward the door, straining to hear. The voices beyond suddenly laughed softly. I wanted desperately to leave, but I couldn't risk being seen by anyone else. I was trapped with this stranger for now.

"Another gift from your lady?" he asked, glancing down, and I followed his stare to my wrist and the bracelet dangling between my fingers. I hadn't been aware I was clutching it.

"No," I told him.

"Oh? So a lover then," he declared, eyeing it curiously. I didn't deem a reply as I clasped my hands behind my back, taking them away from his view. I wouldn't let him pry into what Dash and I were. The stranger frowned slightly at that. I was tired of being on the receiving end of this interrogation.

"Where are you from?" I asked bravely.

His brows scrunched together as he said, "How do you know I'm not from Caelum?"

"You're not," I replied. Everything about this person screamed foreigner, from the way he looked to the casualty in which he spoke. I didn't know enough about the other kingdoms to place him, and Dash and Felix had explained that, unlike in Caelum, most powers within Disparya could not be physically seen. There was no way for me to know for sure where this stranger hailed from.

"Maybe you'd like to come to see for yourself," he replied flirtatiously as he winked.

I tilted my head to the side and replied sweetly, "Maybe I wouldn't." He laughed, and my anger grew at the melodic sound. "Why are you here?" I snarled, my tone impatient and cold. If he was here to hurt me or Dash and Felix, I needed to know.

"Because of the super secret meeting," he whispered dramatically, tapping his finger on the tip of my nose. I swatted his hand away and lunged my knee high, determined to make him fall to the ground. But the stranger was too fast, blocking the movement with ease. He clicked his tongue as he shook his head in disappointment. "Well, aren't you feisty?"

"Tell me why you're here," I gritted out.

"I did, love. You can choose to either believe it or not." He began circling once more. "Now, it's your turn to tell me why *you're* here."

"This is my home," I said, annoyed.

"Is it?" he asked skeptically.

"What is that supposed to mean?" The stranger's lips lifted, and then he shook his head as if dismissing the thought.

"If this truly *is* your home, why are you sneaking about as if you are somewhere you don't belong? Court procedures change a bit from kingdom to kingdom, but it is commonly accepted that servants move about the palaces as they please." I looked away, trying to collect myself and come up with my next lie. He was right, of course. There were no restrictions on where servants could journey within this palace. They were as free to wander as the residents were. Strong, calloused fingers slid under my chin, directing my focus back to the stranger's face. My heart stuttered, and I stopped breathing at the contact. I jerked my chin away, wanting to be free of the intimate touch. He took a step back before continuing. "You, however, slipped into this room at the first sound of a disturbance; clearly, because you were somewhere, you shouldn't have been. Why?"

"I'm not telling you anything." I crossed my arms over my chest as I glowered at him. He rolled his grey eyes before sighing deeply.

"Well, that's not very fun," he said absentmindedly. The stranger walked over to the door I had come through, placing his ear upon the wood to listen. "Perhaps I'll just go and ask King Perceval to tell me more about this lovely woman named Ainsley that I encountered." He turned to face me then, a cocky grin on his lips. The tight leash I had kept on my anger vanished completely, and my blood burned like fire. I strode for the stranger, and his eyes widened a fraction from shock at my audacity.

"Do you want to know what I think?" I said, stopping inches from him. The heat from his body radiated off of him and coiled itself around me like a flame.

"Desperately." He arched a brow, and intrigue swirled in his eyes.

"I think," I said, lifting my chin higher, "that you won't say shit."

"Is that right?"

"I'm not supposed to be here, but neither are you. Mentioning to King Perceval that you saw me only hurts yourself and whatever kingdom you're from." I smirked as I tilted my head, studying him. "Not to mention breaking an agreement of this magnitude would be considered treason, would it not?"

"Looks like you're learning how to play, love," he said, flashing his perfectly white teeth.

"This isn't a game," I said, staring into his grey eyes. "And I'm not your *love*." The stranger laughed at that, and the sound pulled forth an emotion I couldn't precisely place. Annoyance, perhaps. He stepped closer and leaned in, his eyes studying me, storm clouds billowing within them. We stood there for minutes, neither of us breaking our stare as we sized the other up. Finally, the man smiled as he whispered, his face so close to mine that his breath caressed my skin.

"I think you're in the clear." My brows furrowed, not quite understanding his meaning. He angled his chin to the door.

I listened hard, and sure enough, the two male voices had stopped completely. I turned from him and immediately headed for the door. Taking a deep breath, I reached for the handle, twisting quietly as I peeked my head through to the next room to ensure they had indeed gone. The space was empty, thank the Gods. Before I pushed my way through, the stranger called out from behind me.

"Oh, Ainsley?" I turned, throwing him a glance over my shoulder. One hand slid into his pants pocket as the other picked at his nails, a smile plastered wide on his face. "It was simply enchanting to meet you." I didn't dare respond as I made my way through the door, closing it behind me.

53.

I paced the room again for what felt like hours, debating what to do. Should I leave and risk being seen, or should I stay and risk the men coming back and being seen? Either way, I could be caught. Sighing, I rested my back against the tapestry on the far wall as I weighed my options when a faint clicking sound from behind echoed in my ears. I turned around, sliding the hanging fabric out of the way, to see a slight crack within the stone—a hidden door. I pushed hard, and it groaned with the movement. Apparently, not all of the tunnels had been barricaded.

After grabbing a magic candle from the dresser, I eased my way into the hidden path, not closing the door completely in case I needed to find my way out. The tunnel was dark and damp, with hanging spiderwebs and the sounds of tiny scurrying feet. When was the last time anyone had been in here? I moved cautiously, running my hands along the stone walls as I went to look for any fissures within, indicating another secret door. Finally, after an hour of nothing but a twisting pathway, a crack in the wall appeared. I pushed gently, not wanting to bring attention to the door from the outside in case people were around, though the area sounded quiet. I poked my head out and found myself in the alcove at the end of my bedroom corridor. Was this the tunnel used when Josephine and Annette were killed? I made to slip out when soft, muffled voices drifted to me from within the passageway. I should have turned away and shut the door behind me. Instead, my curiosity got the best of me.

I followed the sounds, unsure who the participants were and only recognizing that many were involved in the conversation. With how the voices increased in volume and intensity, it was a conversation that couldn't be deemed pleasant or cordial. King Perceval's loud and commanding chuckle bounced off the stone walls around me. *Holy shit*. I was standing on the other side of the meeting. A cool breeze wrapped around my calf, and I glanced down to see a small hole in the stone. I dropped to the dirty floor at once. Far too many rocks obstructed the view inside the room, but I could hear more clearly if I placed my ear against it. King Perceval laughed again, the sound menacing and agitated as if he were insulted rather than joyful.

"That is a fucking lie," a voice gritted out. Dash.

"Is it?" someone asked. I didn't recognize him, but his voice was deep and sultry, and terrifying. It demanded both respect and fear. "Tread carefully, young prince. You are accusing us of treason with no proof." The hairs on my arm stood erect. This voice must have belonged to King Evander of Tenebrae.

"*I* am the proof!" Dash yelled, and the sound of a chair sliding roared in my ears. He must have stood in his fury. "I was there the night she was attacked. I fought the kidnappers *you* sent to retrieve her. I saw the magic they possessed. I —"

"*You* killed those men before anyone else could identify them. You ended their lives before anyone else could confirm their magic was from Tenebrae," King Evander interrupted. "Bring forth the future princess so she may tell her side of what happened that night. King Tallis will be able to use his Gift, and if she is truthful, we will know."

"He can use it on me." Dash countered, and King Evander laughed.

"I do not trust you, boy. As a royal, you've had the training to help deflect every kingdom's Gifts. We all have. But, since you refuse to bring her out, I take it your princess has not."

"The answer is no," Dash growled, retaking his seat. "I will not put the woman I love in more danger by putting her before you."

"How convenient," King Evander replied. "From here, it looks as though you are wrongly accusing us so you can start a war between our kingdoms."

"This kind of treason isn't something I would put past Tenebrae. I stand with Prince Dashiell. King Evander and his court should stand trial for these acts," a new voice added.

"Father, we surely cannot charge someone with such a crime without solid proof," a soft and kind voice pleaded.

"You are here to observe, Jahier, not speak. I will hear no more interruptions from you," his father demanded.

"Though you may not want to listen to what your son has to say, Prince Jahier is correct," someone else interrupted, and I recognized this voice from the hallway earlier. King Tallis. "We cannot carry out a trial without proof, and we are getting nowhere with these discussions. The King of Tenebrae and his company have already denied their involvement with the attacks. We have established that Princess Cordelia's story cannot be corroborated, and you, Prince Dashiell, refuse to have your fiancé present for this meeting, though she is the reason you called us here in the first place. It seems we are at an impasse, yet we are talking of declarations of war."

"My great kings," King Perceval announced as if trying to defuse the growing need for blood. "Disparya is in a period of peace. I do not believe anyone present wants to end that. My son is rash and called this meeting prematurely. He thought with his heart rather than his head. I know that no king in this room would ever commit treason upon our great continent. Let us continue this discourse peacefully as we try to locate the real culprit behind these attacks." The room filled with mumbled agreements, and soon discussions broke out over rumored rebel groups scattered throughout the lands. I noted that King Evander didn't speak again, seeming to want nothing to do with the conversation. Dash also didn't utter a single word after his father's speech.

Another hour ticked by as I listened to the kings of Disparya discuss people and places I had never heard of. No one could agree on who was behind the attacks and what their motivation for pinning it on Tenebrae would be other than causing unrest between the kingdoms. We were no closer to figuring out who was truly behind this than we were at the start, though I could tell by the snide comments tossed out that many of the kings still believed King Evander was at fault.

"We have been at this for hours. Let us take a break and reconvene over dinner. Perhaps some time away from the subject will shed light on what we have yet to see," King Tallis suggested.

"Wise words, King Tallis. My servants will show you all to your rooms. You are free to rest or wander. My home is yours during your stay," King Perceval said. Murmured thanks and hushed conversations filled the space.

"We are leaving," King Evander announced, and the sound of him and his company rising filled my ears.

"The meeting is to take place over these two days. It is not over yet," King Perceval countered, annoyance thick in his voice.

"It is for us," King Evander responded.

Agitated voices flooded the meeting room, and accusations of planned attacks were thrown at King Evander.

"Of course, you would dismiss yourself early. All so you can attack our kingdoms while we are away!" someone yelled.

"King Harbin, we do not know if that's why—" King Tallis began.

"You are awfully quick to defend his traitorous schemes, Tallis!" King Harbin countered.

"This is getting out of hand," Prince Jahier tried.

"I said enough from you, boy!" his father exclaimed. Angry and undistinguishable shouts stretched across the space and reverberated off the stone walls surrounding me as everyone in the room held their own arguments.

"You are not leaving this room until we finish this, King Evander," Dash's voice broke through above the rest. I clung to the sound like a raft saving me from the current of furious disagreements that tried to pull me below the surface.

"I would be more concerned about the safety of your princess instead of who stays for this pointless meeting," King Evander replied, cold and calculated. "You wanted a war, young prince." He paused as if he were surveying the chaos around him. "It seems like you got one."

"Is that a threat?" Dash growled, and thunder, loud and all-encompassing boomed so hard it shook the entire palace. Screams and panicked footsteps were all I could hear as tendrils of shadow snaked through the small hole I had been listening through. I shuffled away from the opening and got to my feet, sprinting as fast as possible from the meeting room. In a few short moments, I reached the alcove. Not caring if anyone saw me, I pushed through the door and ran for my own bedroom, locking the door behind me.

Beyond my room, the halls were overflowing with commotion. Gentle strides and quiet conversations were replaced with quick footfalls and rushed voices, panic evident in the residents. My heart hammered, and I listened to gasps and shouts as the building shook and small pieces of stone fell from the ceiling. My door opened, and two guards rushed to my side after securing the lock again.

"What is going on?" I yelled over the crash of lightning outside my room.

"We aren't entirely sure, my lady. But we are here to protect you. It'll be alright." I wasn't worried for my safety. Dash and Felix were in that room. They were in danger.

"Let me go speak with the kings. Maybe I can end this," I tried though I knew the answer before I spoke the words.

"Absolutely not," my guard said immediately. All of a sudden, my room went completely dark. I turned toward the windows to see the exterior wrapped in shadow so black it looked like it was the middle of the night. Screams erupted from the palace halls as we were thrown into total darkness. Then all at once, it disappeared as if it were never there. The sun shone bright, and the palace ceased rumbling. My entire body trembled as we waited with bated breath for the next wave. Five minutes passed, then ten, then twenty. Nothing happened.

A pounding sounded at my door, and my heart dropped into my stomach. My guards took a protective stance as their flames twisted around their fingers.

"Open this door now!" Dash commanded, and my guards hurried to unlock it. I ran and flung myself at him before he could take two steps inside the room.

"Go see your commander and await further orders," Felix told the guards as he appeared, as well. Once they were gone, Dash's hands grasped my face as he pulled me back. "Where were you? We told you to stay put. Someone could have—" He stopped abruptly, eyeing the dirt on my dress, hands, and face. "Ainsley, what happened?" he asked, his hand now stroking my hair, his face full of concern.

"Someone came into the room," I told him, and Dash's eyes flew to Felix, sheer panic reflecting in them.

"Tell us everything that happened. And quickly," Dash said as he led me to the bed to sit down, Felix following close behind.

I recounted to them the events of this morning. I told them of the two men that entered and how I fled to the adjacent room before I was seen. I told them of the mysterious stranger who had been sitting there and our curious conversation. I left out the parts detailing how close he had gotten to me because Dash looked furious enough, and I didn't want to add fuel to his already burning fire.

"This stranger you spoke to, did you recognize him at all?" Felix asked curiously.

"No. He didn't seem to be from Caelum."

"Did he use magic? Did he give you an idea of where he could be from?" Dash cut in, kneeling in front of me.

"No, and no. At least no magic that I could see," I replied. "But maybe something I could feel?"

"You felt something?" Dash asked.

"I'm not sure," I answered honestly. "I was terrified and angry, but there was also this sense of calm."

"Like Felix's magic?" he asked. I stood then, pacing a few steps as I recounted what I had felt.

"Not the same, but it felt similar," I answered. Dash looked at his friend.

"Could it be someone from Ministro?" he asked. Felix bobbed his head back and forth as he contemplated that.

"It's possible, and it's certainly something King Harbin would do," Felix answered. "Though Ministro and Caelum are close allies, his daughter was just attacked. He wouldn't want to take any chances he didn't have to. Positioning people through the palace while the meeting took place to ensure there were no surprises would be a smart move on his part. What did he look like?"

"He was tall with tan skin and dark black hair."

"Any tattoos?" Dash asked.

"None that I could see," I told him. "He was also annoyingly flirtatious."

"Brandle," Felix and Dash said in unison as they locked eyes.

"Who?"

"Brandle is one of the Princes of Ministro," Dash explained. "He's King Harbin's oldest son, though not by blood."

"And a total prick," Felix added. "It would make sense why King Harbin hadn't chosen him to participate in the meeting." Dash stalked for me, sliding his arms around my waist as I gazed up at him.

"Yeah, because the fucker was too busy hitting on my fiancé," Dash retorted, the words dripping in jealousy like venom off the fangs of a snake. His grip around me grew strong and possessive. I had never seen him envious before, and my heart fluttered, knowing it was over me.

"Are you worried about a little competition?" I asked, arching a brow.

"Do I have reason to be?" he replied, eyes narrowing as he waited for my answer.

"I don't know," I shrugged. "Brandle *was* attractive," I told him, though I hadn't noticed if this was the case. A muscle feathered in his jaw, and I clenched my lips together to keep from smiling.

"He is *not* attractive," he said stubbornly.

"Oh, he most certainly is," Felix added from across the room. "If he weren't such a tool, I would have let him have it time and time again." A low rumble reverberated in Dash's throat as he rolled his eyes. I stood on my toes as I whispered in his ear.

"As for if you have competition, I'll let you know for sure after tonight." I sank back to my normal height to see Dash's eyes bright and eager.

His fingers dug into my sides, and my blood pumped with need and desire for him as warmth spread over my entire body from anticipation.

"I'm still right fucking here, you two. It's rude to dirty talk with company present," Felix complained. "Unless, of course, you want me to join in."

"Fuck off, Felix." Dash and I said as one.

"Fine," he whined. "Anyway, back to the events at hand. The men that came into the room, you didn't recognize their voices?"

"No, neither of theirs." My fingers pressed against my temples, gently massaging a headache that had begun to form. I wanted to change the subject and find out about their morning instead. "Tell me about the meeting. What happened?

Did Tenebrae admit to it?" Though I eavesdropped on most of it, I wanted to know what I had missed.

"Of course not," Dash replied, shaking his head. "King Evander was quiet most of the time, just seeming to observe the dynamic of the conversation rather than be a willing participant. He let his advisors do most of the talking."

"So he didn't deny it?" I asked.

"Oh, he denied it, alright," Felix said as if alluding to something. I raised my brows at him in a silent demand to continue. "The very second the meeting started, he went on and on about how outraged he was that Tenebrae would be accused of such a thing. How dragging him here was a waste of his time when there was no evidence against him or his kingdom." I looked toward Dash, who was nodding along.

"After that outburst, he sat down and refused to say another word, only allowing his companions to answer for him for the rest of the meeting," Dash added.

"Do you believe him?" I questioned, Dash's face growing serious.

"I don't know for certain, but I don't think so. Tenebrae is not a good place, Ainsley. There's a reason it's known as the Dark Kingdom, one that I'm sure doesn't have to do solely with their Gifts." *Illusions. Shadows. Fear.* I recalled the words they had told me days ago, and a shiver went down my spine.

"There wasn't a shred of evidence to be shown?" Dash sighed loudly, scrubbing his face with his hands, a gesture I'd learned meant he was frustrated.

"Because most of your attackers got away, and I killed the two that hadn't, there is no proof they possessed Tenebrae's Gifts." He was shaking his head, unable to meet my eyes. "The advisors from Tenebrae accused me of falsifying the entire story to declare war on their kingdom." My heart hammered in my chest as mighty as a drum as I listened.

"But Cordelia—"

"Was found beaten and tied up, but alone," Dash interrupted. "There was no hard proof that Tenebrae was the one who attacked, though Cordelia saw their magic firsthand, just as I had."

"That's total bullshit," I spat. I wanted to yell, to scream. To march across the palace and demand an audience with the kings. "Let me try and talk to them. Maybe if I explain what happened that night—"

"No," he said over my words. "I will not risk your safety, Ainsley. It's not an option. We will figure out another way to go about this." Dash's stare was still transfixed on the spot across the room as he worked on composing himself and swallowing down that anger and frustration I knew was building inside of him. I stepped away, knowing he needed time to work through his feelings and that even my touch couldn't bring him solace.

"I still don't understand how they were able to get in, though," Felix said. "I know we locked that door."

"One of them had a key," I told him. I watched as Felix's eyes went wide and shot to Dash, who was already staring back. "What is it?" I asked, demanding to be let in on whatever their silent conversation meant. Dash reached into his pocket and pulled out a small metal object.

"I have the only key," he said, still looking at Felix.

"But I heard the lock click. I heard them say they had a key and then enter the room, Dash." Felix raised an eyebrow, and the prince nodded. "Will you two please let me into your Godsdamn conversation! I am just as much a part of this are you both are!" I said angrily.

"Felix thinks you're right about a spy amongst us, one who dwells within the walls of this palace," Dash answered.

"It makes sense how those men were able to find you in the woods. Someone must have known where you were and shared your whereabouts," Felix added. The passageway.

"There's a passageway," I said at once, remembering how I had gotten back here in the first place. "It led from that room to an alcove at the end of this corridor. It looks completely forgotten about. I think that's how they've been getting so close to my room."

"Too much has happened for it to be considered coincidence anymore," Dash finished and walked over, taking my trembling hands into his. Someone was feeding information about me to others outside of the palace. I didn't know who I could trust outside of Dash and Felix anymore. I shuddered to think that Imogen had betrayed me. No. She wouldn't do that. I refused to allow myself to go there.

"But the men that showed up didn't seem like they were looking for me. They..." I stumbled for the words, my eyes darting back and forth between Felix and Dash. "They seemed like they were just having a casual conversation. They were even laughing at one point."

"They might not have been looking for you, but that doesn't change the fact that they had a key to that room. And that means they probably have keys to other rooms, including yours," Felix said, shaking his head as he dragged a hand through his silver hair, strands falling loose from the tie that kept them back. The thought of someone unwelcome, someone who wished me harm, coming into my room sent my stomach roiling, and I sucked in a deep breath.

"Hey," Dash said gently, and I took my eyes off Felix's concerned demeanor and moved them to him. His face was worried but calm at the same time. "We will find them, Ainsley. Whoever is doing this, we will find them." I nodded my head barely, trying to convince myself of his words. "Felix, call for an immediate search of every resident's quarters. Do it quickly, and do not give them time to try and hide anything. Once that is complete, confine them to their rooms and search the entire palace. I want those keys found and the culprits brought forward." Felix nodded at Dash's orders and rushed from the room. I focused on my breathing, willing it to calm, willing my stomach to settle, and my nerves to ease.

"Ainsley," Dash said, his fingers brushing back a loose strand of hair from my face and hooking it behind my ear. "The kings and queens of Disparya have already started to depart the palace. Only a few remain but will be leaving at any moment." My mind instantly traveled to moments ago when it felt like the entire building was under attack.

"The palace was shaking. It was loud and then went dark and—"

"I know," he soothed, stroking the back of my head.

"Dash, what happened?" I asked shakily.

"The meeting didn't go well. It was rough initially, and then tempers seemed to even out, but things took a turn once Tenebrae decided to leave early." I gave a pointed look, demanding he explain what exactly took place. "No one was happy with King Evander's choice to depart the meeting early. Some feared it was a strategic move to attack their kingdoms while they were empty of their sovereigns. Arguments broke out amongst the crowd, and then King Evander made a threat to your life. That's when I lost control," Dash admitted as he tensed beside me. "I issued the first attack, but his shield deflected it. Then everything went dark, but for only a second, and when the shadows cleared, he was on the other side of the room, positioned by the exit. No one knew how he had gotten there so quickly, and it caused even more unrest. Members of the advisors present also started issuing attacks on him."

"Did they manage to hit him?" I asked though something deep within my bones told me he was unhurt. If the King of Tenebrae had been successfully taken down, the kings would have had no reason to flee back to their homes so soon.

"No," he said more to himself than to me. "He and his company were too skilled and rehearsed. Like they planned on a fight being the outcome and were prepared for it. Somehow they wrapped the palace in shadow and took advantage of the darkness, managing to escape before the shadows cleared."

"So what now?" I asked tentatively.

"Regarding Tenebrae, I don't know," he said, his blue eyes shining like the sea. "But right now, I have to go and talk to my father about your encounter with Brandle and the situation with the keys."

"How long is that going to take?" I asked, not wanting to be away from him yet again today.

"I'm not sure, honestly. It depends on how he wants to go about this all."

"Fine." I huffed like a child throwing a temper tantrum, and Dash smiled at my antics. "I'll see you tonight, though?" His smile widened, and he nodded eagerly.

"I'm looking forward to it," he said, backing away and heading down the hall. Once he was fully out of view, I closed my door and locked it, though I wasn't sure what good that would do anymore. If someone had a key, there was nothing I could do to stop them from coming in. I walked over to the window at the far end of the room that overlooked the front gates and watched as ornate carriages and horses began their trek from the palace back to wherever they came from.

From the corner of my eye, I spotted a man staring up at me from where he stood next to a large stallion with a golden saddle. The horse's coat was as white as snow and as bright in color as the man's hair, so stark against his deep olive skin. I flinched under his piercing gaze, and he smiled, placing a hand over his heart and bowing deeply. I wasn't sure what to make of this gesture, this odd, distanced encounter. Did he know that I was the future princess, or was his bow just one of chivalry? Before I could give it more thought, he mounted his steed and rode away, disappearing through the front gate. Could he have been one of the people that had entered the room this morning?

I crawled into bed, curling up under the thick blankets, desperate for a nap after today's events. I wasn't sure when Felix or Dash would come and let me know it was safe to leave, but I could guess it wouldn't be for several hours, giving me plenty of time for some much-needed rest. I willed my mind to calm, to help me escape from everything I had experienced. To bring me dreams of meadows and lakes, dreams of Dash and Felix. But the only images that flooded my thoughts as I slept were mysterious male voices, dark shadows, and deep grey eyes.

54.

I extended my arms beneath my pillow; the warmth of the morning sun coming in from the windows stretched across my bare back. I opened my eyes to see Dash awake next to me, watching me intently, his eyes bright and bold in the sunlight. When he and Felix returned last night, they shared that the keys and culprits still had not been discovered. Not exactly the best news.

"Why are you staring at me?" I asked, hiding my face with my hands but peeking at him through my fingers to see a sleepy smile spread.

"I enjoy watching you sleep. You look peaceful."

"What I'm hearing is that you prefer it when I'm not speaking."

Dash chuckled softly. "Well, I mean, that *is* an added benefit." I reached my hands out, pushing against his toned chest, but he merely grabbed my wrists with ease, pinning me against him as he nuzzled his face into my neck. "I'm only kidding," he said, planting tender kisses along my throat, cheek, and forehead before settling on my lips. I melted into his body as his fingers trailed my back in long gentle strokes. I would never get enough of being wrapped in his arms, of being his. My heart ached at the possibility of him being taken away from me, at the prospect of King Perceval deciding against Dash and I being together.

"Ainsley," he said slowly onto my mouth, fingers twinning into my hair.

"Hmmm," I said back, deepening our kiss.

"Is there ever a time when your mind isn't running wild with thoughts?"

"It's not," I told him, pushing myself closer, my arms snaking around his neck as I pulled him on top of me. Dash withdrew his face from mine, studying me, a single eyebrow raised as he shook his head slowly.

"I know you, beautiful. And I know when your mind is elsewhere. Just tell me what you're thinking." I closed my eyes, sighing. I didn't want to get into this now, but I knew he wouldn't let it go. Even if he didn't pressure me to talk about it, he would still worry and fear the worst.

"It's been nearly two weeks, Dash." He furrowed his brow, not understanding my meaning. "It's been almost two weeks since my birthday, and there has been no sign of my power. Nothing." Understanding washed over him, and he sat back on his knees, pulling me onto mine to face him.

"It can sometimes take a little while."

"A few days, maybe, but it's not supposed to take this long. As far as the research I've done about it, it never has." I had snuck away to the library when Dash and Felix were deep in conversation at dinner last night and consulted with the librarians about the history of magic wielders in Caelum. There were detailed records of each resident of the palace and when they received their Gift within the archives. Most people's powers had manifested on or just after their twenty-first birthday, with the longest wait time of only three days. Only a select few, mostly royalty, had received their Gift younger than twenty-one, Dash being one of them. I looked toward the door as I chewed the inside of my cheek. "What if — What if I have no magic?" Dash's hand gripped my chin, bringing my face back toward him, his eyes soft and loving.

"Would that be the worst thing?" he asked softly, carefully, as if he didn't want to upset me with his question. "Sometimes it feels like magic is more of a burden than a blessing. Would it be so bad if you were free of that trouble?"

I sat there for a few moments contemplating how to answer, trying to figure out how to explain what I was so afraid of and what I wanted. Dash patiently waited as he dragged his thumb over the back of my hand in a comforting caress.

"I never really cared before — if I had magic or not. I had resented even the possibility of it for years, especially after being told of my betrothal to you." I smiled at the memory of how I tried everything to get out of the arrangement, only to find myself in love and blissfully happy months later. "Based on the whole reason that you and I were thrown together in the first place, I just assumed it would happen, and now that it hasn't...." I trailed off.

Dash leaned forward, resting his forehead against mine as he said, "You know I'll love you no matter what, right? Magic or no."

"I know, Dash, but I worry that your father won't care about that." He sat back and cocked his head.

"What do you mean?"

"I mean that our parents entered into this arrangement with the common thought that I would have something to offer you and this kingdom. I fear now that it's evident that is no longer the case, your father will find you someone who can. I can't say that I would blame him." I blinked back the tears that were starting to form. The thought of him being with someone else, loving someone else, was unbearable. I had given him all of me, body and heart, and it terrified me to know that may never be enough. I knew it would be for Dash, but I wasn't sure about his father. "Not to mention, with the possibility of war on the table, I may be more trouble than I'm worth. Why would anyone risk the lives of their people to fight for someone who offers nothing? If that is the case, your father would be wise to replace me and let Tenebrae do as they wish."

"No," he said, and I watched as he clenched his jaw tight. "I would never let that happen, Ainsley. Ever," he said, holding my face between his hands. "You are the only person I want. Forever. You have my whole heart, and I will do everything I can to make you happy, to take care of you—everything in my power to protect you at any cost. You are my entire life now. Why do you think I'd willingly let you go?"

"You may not have a choice, Dash."

"I do have a choice. You are my choice, and I will always fight for us. It's always been you, Ainsley," he said as he leaned forward to brush his lips tenderly against mine. "So please, stop worrying about my father. I love you, and that's all that matters. I promise." I wrapped my arms around his neck and kissed him deeply, his mouth parting for me.

"I love you, Dash," I told him as I fell backward onto the bed, pulling him down to entangle ourselves together once more.

"You know, you're making it very hard for me to keep my promise to you," Dash said, standing from the bed as he buttoned his shirt. "Part of taking care of you means ensuring you have food in your system, which is becoming increasingly difficult when you insist on staying beneath the sheets together all day."

I strode for his side of the bed and turned my back to him, sliding my hair out of the way, a silent request for him to fasten my dress and maybe a tiny temptation to get him back into bed. "Are you saying that you object to our activities?" I asked, leaning into his touch. Dash quickly clasped the gown and spun me around to face him.

"Nice try, but I know what you're doing, temptress," he said as he flicked my nose.

I sighed deeply. "It was worth a try but fine; food first, fun later," I said, winking. Dash smiled mischievously as he dragged me out of the room where Felix was waiting, leaning against a marble pillar, arms crossed and looking bored.

"Hey, Felix!" I said as I hurried over to him.

"I'm sorry. Do I know you?" he replied, looking confused.

I rolled my eyes as I pressed myself into him. "Shut up and hug me," I said, and Felix wrapped his arms around me, squeezing tightly as he spun me around despite my shouts of protest.

"Days ago, I had two best friends, and now I have none. I'm feeling very neglected."

"When are you not?" Dash added.

"True," Felix replied. "But not the point. I miss you both, and I'm desperate for attention, so how about we remedy this? Lunch like the good ole days?"

"Felix, we literally had dinner together last night and have spent every day with one another," I said, confused.

"Yes, but the two of you always run off and lock yourselves away all night, and I get bored."

"If we say yes to lunch, will you stop being so dramatic?" Dash asked, and Felix agreed at once. "Fine, but I have to speak to my father first and then grab fresh clothes."

"Yes, yes, the walk of shame, I am familiar. Okay, so we'll meet outside your room in an hour?" Dash nodded as he pulled me in close for a kiss. "Don't worry, I'll take good care of our girl while you're busy," Felix said, shoving Dash away. Once he was entirely out of view, Felix turned to me. "Ainsley, my little dewdrop, how have you been since yesterday?"

"I've been alright," I said, smiling at him, although thoughts of the king's meeting kept me up most of the night.

Felix didn't wait for one full heartbeat before replying. "No, you haven't. Fess up, dewdrop, and tell me what's going on. Oh, and don't try lying—Dash may fall for that shit, but I won't." I always forgot how perceptive Felix was and just how well he knew me.

I looped my arm through his as he led us through the halls, laying everything in my mind out for him. I told him how worried I was that the king would change his mind about Dash and me because I had nothing to offer him or Caelum. I shared my fears that King Perceval would offer me up to Tenebrae once he realized I wasn't worth the headache. I told him how desperately I wanted a Gift of my own and had only just come to realize it. And I shared how I couldn't explain that to Dash after seeing the pity and sadness in his eyes this morning. Felix silently listened, offering no words of wisdom, no sage advice, just a friendly ear. He had always been so attuned to what I needed. Partially due to his magic but primarily due to our close friendship.

When I finished rambling, Felix took a deep breath before stopping our walk and pulling me in front of him, holding my hands in his. "I'm so sorry this has been haunting you. I don't like to see you in pain of any kind."

"I know. Thank you for listening and for always being here for me."

"Always, Ainsley," he said, pressing a kiss to my hair. "And for what it's worth, I think it'll be okay. I think you'll get your Gift."

"What makes you say that?" I asked.

Felix smiled as he replied. "It's just a feeling, and I know you. You'll stop at nothing to get what you want. It's one of the many, many things that I simply adore about you."

"I wish it were as simple as that."

"So do I," he replied, throwing his arm around my shoulders as we began walking again. "Now, let us go find our third wheel."

We strolled slowly to Dash's room, savoring our "Delicious Duo time," as Felix so lovingly called it. I pushed back Dash's door as we strode in, laughing at Felix's story about his latest conquest, when my eyes found Dash standing at the back of the room, his arms crossed and looking distraught. I followed his gaze across the vast space to find Rosella. In his bed. Completely naked.

55.

My heart leapt into my throat as I saw her sprawled across his bed, her body bare save for a sheet covering the parts of her I was certain nearly everyone in the palace had already seen. Her devious smile spread as she met my eyes.

"Dash, darling, send her away so we can get back to what we were just in the middle of starting," Rosella said, dragging her fingers up her exposed thigh seductively. She glared at me with an eyebrow raised, a challenge to object. Since my stay here, when it came to Rosella and him, I had ignored her antics, never confronting her or staking my claim over him. I knew Dash had ended their triste once I arrived at the palace, but clearly, nothing would stop her from going after the crown she wanted. "The bed is getting so cold without you," she told him, sticking out her bottom lip in a desperate pout.

"Go fuck yourself, Rosella." Dash snapped, his tone dripping with disdain, and she giggled.

"Now, why would I go and do that," she started, fingers trailing higher up her legs, dipping below the sheet, "when you always do it *so* well." I could hear Dash's heart pounding beneath his chest as I turned toward him, his eyes wide with rage and worry as he looked at me.

"Ainsley, nothing happened, I swear—" The words rushed out of him like an avalanche cascading quickly down a mountainside. I held up my hand to silence him, glancing back at Rosella, so arrogant in her demeanor, hoping that she was about to witness the end of Dash and me. The end to her only threat.

"Rosella," I said, calm and composed. "I'm only going to say this once. Get the *fuck* out of my fiancé's bed." Her eyes grew larger at my tone, but she did nothing more than prop her head under her elbow to get herself more comfortable.

Well, okay, then—we were going to do this now.

I strode over to Dash, brushing a soft kiss on his lips. It wasn't to throw in Rosella's face—though her witnessing our affection was an added benefit—but rather to remind Dash that I loved and trusted him. "Take Felix with you down to the terrace. I'll meet you both for lunch shortly. I just need to have a quick word with our mutual friend here first." Dash was unnervingly still as his eyes shifted between Rosella and me, debating whether to leave me alone with her. "I'll be gentle," I whispered as his eyes finally settled on only me. A barely noticeable smile dragged up at the corner as he kissed my forehead before striding over to Felix and grabbing the sleeve of his jacket to drag him out of the room.

"But I want to watch!" I heard Felix say as Dash closed the door behind him, leaving us completely to ourselves.

I stalked over to the bed and traced my fingers along the blankets as I walked, the fur soft beneath my touch.

"I understand that you and Dash had a special kind of *friendship* in the past and that *friendship* ended upon my arrival." She watched as I sat down to face her, crossing my legs and placing my hands on my lap. "I also understand that despite his many, *many* protests, it still has not stopped you from pursuing him." Rosella's jaw clenched tightly, and her eyes raged with a simmering fury, the room growing colder around us.

"Why do you care? You don't even want the crown," she retorted, looking me over as disgust weaved over her beautiful face.

She was trying my patience. "The crown, no, but what I *do* want is Dash. So here is what's going to happen," I explained, straightening my posture. "You're going to leave him alone for good. As pathetic as they have been, your advances are not welcome. He does not want you, Rosella, and he's made that *painfully obvious*." Her lip curled as she bared her teeth at my using her own words against her.

She sat up snarling, inches from my face. "Who are *you* to tell *me* what to do?"

"Well, for one, I am your future queen."

Rosella snorted a snide, evil sound, filled with as much hate and contempt for me as she was. "You will never be my queen. You are nothing, and you have nothing." My eyes narrowed, and she tilted her head slightly, a cruel smile spreading across her face. "Don't you know? The palace talks and rumors have been flying lately. It's been, what? A couple of weeks since your birthday, and yet," she waved a hand up and down, gesturing over my body, "No powers seem to grace you." My blood went cold. I wasn't aware that everyone had been watching me so intently, waiting to see what Gift I would be given. "You should know by now that a woman's worth is tied to what she has to offer. I've worked for years to covet him. The title of princess was to be mine until you came along and ruined everything," A part of me would feel sorry for her if she wasn't currently naked in the bed of the man I loved. "And for what? You are worth *nothing*. What could you possibly give him now?"

I shook my head as I tried to garner control of myself and keep the hole in my heart stitched up, but it threatened to rip open. "Dash and I love each other, and if a lack of magic doesn't matter to him, it doesn't matter to me."

She laughed under her breath, pity coating the sound. "Maybe for now, but he will grow tired of you. Prince Dashiell needs someone that can give him what you can't." Hoarfrost covered the tips of her fingers, and I found it fitting that her magic was as cold as her heart seemed to be. "And eventually, he'll decide to find someone who will."

My blood simmered, and I felt like I was on fire as anger flowed through my entire body, filling every crack and crevice within. I shifted closer as my breathing came in hard and heavy, my chest heaving with the fury that had built up. I felt a force, unlike any other, rage within me. Something flashed in Rosella's eyes as she looked into mine, and it wasn't the usual defiance that was always present with her—it was something that looked oddly like fear.

I was done trying to reason with her. "I have put up with you for months. With your insults. With your snide remarks. With your cruel glances," I said viciously as Rosella began backing herself across the bed as I inched closer with each declaration. I let the rage take control, imagining I was as brave, strong, and deadly as the vipers Dash loved to compare me to. I allowed the venom of the words to coat my tongue before I spat them out. "Dash and I will be married, and whether you like it or not, I will be your ruler."

I reached forward, taking a lock of her golden hair between my fingers, the strands soft and luxurious. "But sweet Rosella, I don't have to be a queen to make your life miserable," I said with deadly calm. "Dash and I are together, and I know he feels about you the same way I do. Would you like to know what that is?" I dropped her hair, and she flinched. "It's that you are increasingly becoming a problem to be dealt with, and neither of us has the desire nor the patience to put up with you any longer." The blood drained from her face as she listened, her body still as stone. "You will leave Dash and me alone because if you don't...." Rosella was now at the edge of the bed, her chest moving quickly, her eyes filled with terror. "I will come for you and make your life a living Hell." My final vow caused her to fall backward off the bed with a loud thud as she hit the tile floor. She scrambled to her feet, gathered her dress quickly, and sprinted from the room, still naked. If Dash could fight for us, so could I, and I would. Every single day.

I had barely made it into the hallway when Dash sprinted for me, his hands finding my face as he looked me over for any sign of ill will from the vicious woman I had just been with.

"It had been a while, so I came back looking for you and passed Rosella running through the hall without any clothes," he said, still checking me. "I thought she might have done something to you."

I covered the hands that held my cheeks. "I'm okay, Dash, really. She didn't touch me."

"Ainsley, I promise you, nothing would have ever happened between us. I came out of my bathing room, and she was in my bed. I tried to get her to leave, but—"

"Dash, stop. Even when I first saw her there, it was never a thought that crossed my mind. I trust you completely," I told him and kissed his lips gently as he breathed a sigh of relief. "But I'm just letting you know we aren't staying in your room until we change those sheets."

"I'll tell my maiden to burn them," he said, laughing softly. "I'm sorry you had to deal with her. I had a feeling that she might try and pull some shit if she found out how I felt about you, but I hoped that she had better sense than to try. What happened between you both back there?"

"I'll explain on our way to lunch. I'm sure Felix is about to combust at any moment now for having to wait." Dash laughed as he nodded and interlaced our fingers to tug me toward the terrace. "Guess what?" He looked down at me as we walked, waiting for me to continue. "I felt something."

His brows furrowed. "What do you mean?"

"When I was threatening Rosella—" Dash's eyes grew wide, and his features tightened, begging me to explain what I meant by that, but I continued. "Something coursed through me. I don't know exactly what it was or if it was even magic related."

"What did it feel like?" His tone was serious, concerned.

"I'm not sure how to describe it. It was like fire and a storm raging at the same time. It was burning hot but also frigid. It felt strong and heavy, and... *Powerful.*"

"Have you ever experienced anything like it before?"

"I don't think so, but perhaps? Maybe once, when I was a child, but I never thought anything of it. It's not something I've ever focused on, and I have only started looking for any signs of magic recently. Maybe the situation with Rosella sparked something in me. What does your Gift feel like for you?"

We stopped walking, and Dash closed his eyes as he focused, his breathing steady as he held his hands up, and I watched as water coated his fingers. The droplets then transformed into delicate clear crystals of ice, and sunlight from the open windows refracted off of them, sending rainbows glinting upon the walls. "It feels calm and soothing as it washes over me." The frozen water disappeared as he opened his eyes, staring thoughtfully into the distance.

"What is it?" I asked, worry thick in my voice.

"Nothing," he said, bringing his attention back to me. "I just... I just don't want you to get your hopes up. You were so convinced this morning that you weren't given a Gift, and if this leads to nothing, I don't want you to be upset or hurt. I don't want you to feel lesser than you are, Ainsley."

"I know, Dash. I know you'll love me either way, but it's not going to stop me from hoping, and it's not going to stop me from wanting magic of my own." He nodded his head in understanding and kissed my cheek. "If I had a Gift, then maybe I would have been strong enough to protect myself from what happened in the orchard. If I had magic, perhaps I could ensure that it would never happen again." Dash stiffened, and I knew it was because I had brought up that night and allowed those worries to resurface. Though he was sparse on the details of his struggles, he divulged that they surrounded his fears of me being hurt and his inability to protect me.

"You know I will do everything to ensure your safety, right? I won't ever let anything like that happen to you again." I smiled reassuringly, knowing he meant every word, but it didn't change my desires. "Come on, let's go eat," he said as we picked up our pace again. "And tell me again exactly what it felt like."

I had just finished explaining to Dash, for the third time, what had happened with Rosella, and the feeling that rushed through me, when we finally reached the lunch table to find Felix practically bouncing out of his seat.

"You both ignore my existence every night, and then you keep me waiting on the story of the year?" Felix quipped, looking at Dash, whose focus was now on his plate, already piled high with fruits, cheeses, and meats; no doubt Felix's doing as an attempt to hurry us along so he could hear the gossip sooner rather than later.

Dash pulled out my chair for me to sit down and then grabbed a handful of raspberries from the fruit tray, adding them to my plate. I grinned like a fool as I looked up at him.

"You did an amazing job handling her. I'm proud of you," he explained, leaning down to brush his lips softly over mine.

"So her reward is fruit?" Felix asked, confused.

"Don't worry about it," he replied, smiling down at me before announcing that he would fetch us the drinks Felix had forgotten in our spread. The second he left, I dove into my story.

"I wish I could have seen Rosella's face when you kicked her out, or Hell, even her bare ass." I threw an apple across the table at him, narrowly missing his face. "It sounds like you had quite an eventful morning, Dewdrop," he said, laughing.

"Is that right? How so?" a voice said from behind us. We turned toward the sound and quickly made to stand. "It's alright; you may stay seated," King Perceval called as he walked toward us.

"It's nothing, your Majesty. Just gossip," I said as he reached the table.

"Ahh yes, I seem to remember hearing the servants talk about how someone was running through the halls this morning crying and *unclothed*." The king gave me a pointed look. "Your doing, I suspect?"

I looked down at my plate, mortified. I wasn't sure how much trouble I was about to be in, especially if the king himself felt the need to come and see me. "I'm sorry, Your Majesty."

King Perceval chuckled loudly. "My Gods, don't be my dear; it was quite entertaining." I glanced back up, surprised at his response. "Sometimes people need to be reminded of what isn't theirs. You protected what belongs to you, and there's no shame in that." There was something off-putting about his choice of words and tone of voice. His gaze dragged up and down me slowly, lingering entirely too long. I looked at my friend to find him glaring at the king. Felix's stare was hard and tense—uncomfortable.

"Thank you, Your Majesty," I said carefully, trying to break the blatant tension. King Perceval brought his eyes back to mine as he gave a smile that didn't reach his eyes. Dash finally returned, a teapot and wine goblets in hand, his face growing weary as he took in the three of us. He approached slowly, placing the contents he carried onto the table and returning to my side. His hands rested on my shoulders, gently stroking me as he tried to calm my nerves. Dash was clearly as distressed as Felix and me.

"Such a lovely couple," The king said, eyeing us. "Which is the reason I have come to speak with you. Dashiell, I was giving thought to our earlier conversation about Ainsley here," the king said as he gestured to me. I looked up at Dash, his glare frozen on his father and his jaw clenched. "My dear," he said, addressing me now, and I brought my attention back to his dark green eyes, the color like emeralds in the night. "My son has informed me of your fears regarding the longevity of your union." My mouth went dry and a lump formed in my throat. "It has come to my attention that you lack any... How do I put this delicately? Talent. You have nothing to offer him and, thus, are worried about your place here at the palace and my son's side. Rightfully so, I would add." I prepared for the panic to rise, for my breathing to quicken, but it didn't. My heart beat slow and steady, and I realized that Felix was using his power to keep me calm and grounded. I said a silent prayer to the Gods above for this friend in my life.

After another moment, King Perceval continued, "I could announce to Tenebrae that their efforts are futile as you do not possess magic, though I would be willing to bet my life that they would not believe me. If anything, I feel that would only make them want you more, thinking me a liar. I could simply dissolve this union between you and my son to show King Evander that you are useless to me." My stomach knotted, and I was sure I would be sick. "However, even though that may be what is easiest, I promised your father that I would care for you as my own, and I will honor that vow. You may not have anything to offer my son in the way of magic, but you are a part of this family now and will be protected as such." He stepped around the table toward Dash and me and stopped just before us. "With that said, I have decided to move your wedding date to two days from now."

"What?" I choked out. I was prepared to be told to leave, that I would never be with Dash, not that we would be wed months or even years sooner than expected.

"Is this not what you want? Are you not happy with Dashiell?" he asked though he didn't seem genuinely concerned. "Based on servants' gossip, it would seem that you have been *very* pleased with him every morning and night these past few days."

"Father," Dash cut in, the word short and clipped, anger wrapping around it.

The king laughed under his breath without humor. "I'm only joking, son."

I felt Dash's hands tense on my shoulders, and I spoke before he had the chance to respond. "Yes, I am happy and in love with him, but I'm not sure I understand the urge to marry us so suddenly. I appreciate your commitment to my father and am grateful for your loyalty to your word, but I'm confused. As you said, I have nothing to offer your son, so why not marry him to someone who does while still allowing me to stay in the palace?"

"Because it is the best way to keep you safe. Right now, you are only a lady with no power, engaged to the Crowned Prince; but with you wed, you will officially be a royal. Your life will mean more to this kingdom and Disparya as Dashiell's wife rather than just his fiancé. We would have cause to challenge Tenebrae if they tried to take you again."

"But Cordelia is a princess, and no retribution was demanded for her attack. Why would it be any different for me?" I argued.

"Because I am not Harbin," King Perceval said forcefully. "I am not weak. I do not shy from confrontation or war the way he does." His face grew redder, and his lip twitched in agitation and my constant questions. He must have read the fear on my face because his following words were soft and precise. "What I mean to say, my dear, is that I protect my family. I could not ask the kings to go to war over a simple lady, but I can demand that they do over the future Queen of Caelum. You will be better protected once your union is official." I swallowed thickly as I reached up to squeeze Dash's hand, still gripped on my shoulder.

"I understand, Your Majesty," I replied weakly.

King Perceval smiled widely, flashing his too-white teeth, the gesture anything but comforting. "You belong in our family Ainsley, and as I told you earlier, there is no shame in protecting what belongs to you." I wasn't sure Dash was breathing. I wasn't sure any of us were at this point. The king brought his piercing eyes to his son. "You will be married in two days, Dashiell. Do not forget what we discussed," he said, his tone cold and demanding. Dash's grip tightened automatically on my shoulders, a protective instinct. The king turned on his heel and headed for the palace entrance calling over his shoulder to no one in particular, "You're welcome." And then he was gone.

I slumped my shoulders and let out the breath I had been holding as I turned my attention to Felix. His face was drained of all color, and his stare was blank, probably coming down from the struggle of keeping my emotions at bay. "Thank you for having my back, Felix." He nodded but didn't meet my eyes, too focused on an empty spot in front of him. I reached for the tea Dash had brought me and drank deeply, willing the hot liquid to soothe my nerves, but instead winced at the bitter taste. Felix finally glanced up, watching me place the cup with shaky hands back onto the table with a soft clatter.

"Did I make it wrong?" Dash asked, reaching for my drink. "I tried remembering how you did it that night in the kitchen."

I smiled up at him and shook my head. "No, it's fine. It's just a little stronger than I tend to like."

"I'm sorry," he replied, kissing my cheek. "I'll go fetch some sugar for you."

"Thank you," I said, watching him leave again. Once he was out of view, I turned back to Felix, who had also watched after Dash. The look in his eye told me something was wrong. "What's going on?" He didn't answer as he stared at the palace entrance. "Felix?"

"What?" he asked as if he hadn't heard my question, bringing his amber eyes to me at last.

"What is it?"

"Nothing. I'm fine. Everything is fine."

"*Fess up, dewdrop, and tell me what's going on. Oh, and don't try lying—Dash may fall for that shit, but I won't.*" I mocked, but he didn't so much as crack a smile. He just watched me. I slid out of my chair and hurried around the table. I knelt in front of him, taking his hands into my own. "Felix, talk to me. What's wrong?" My voice cracked on the words. It was terrible to see him so withdrawn and unnerved. I thought about what it would be like to have his Gift. I wanted to wrap my very essence around him and soothe his nerves, mind, and heart, as he had done so many times for me. I desired to be able to steady his breathing and calm him, but wishing for what wasn't possible was of no use. I would provide the only thing I could— my unyielding support and friendship. I would never understand how the Kingdom of Ministro, a place known for its horrible practices and bloodthirsty power-grabbing, could produce such a pure-hearted soul like Felix.

He squeezed my hands and gave me a weak smile. "I'm feeling very uneasy about everything that just happened here."

"So am I," I agreed.

"And I really do not like how the king looks at you." His jaw clenched so hard that I could hear his teeth grind together.

"You caught that, did you?" I said flatly, both embarrassed and disgusted.

"It was kind of hard to miss."

"Well, hopefully, getting married puts an end to it."

Felix brought his stare to me, his brows pulling together. "How are you feeling about that?"

I sighed deeply. "I don't know," I answered honestly. "I love Dash more than anything, and I want to marry him; I just...." I chewed on my cheek as I fumbled for the words. "I can't help but feel like King Perceval is playing some twisted game and will use my lack of magic against me any chance he can." Felix nodded thoughtfully as he listened. "I can't figure out the 'why' of it all, though. Is it because he actually hates me and enjoys degrading me whenever possible, or is it a strategy to use on Dash? Will he be so blatant in his disdain, or even his lust, that Dash will push me away to protect me from his father, giving the king the very thing he wants— Dash with someone who has something to offer him?" I rubbed my temples as a headache started to form from the stress.

"You know what I think?" Felix asked after a minute of silence.

"What's that?"

"I think we'll need something a Hell of a lot stronger today than your tea, dewdrop," he said, rising to his feet and bringing me up with him.

"I think you're correct," I replied, smiling as Dash returned, teacup and sugar in hand.

"No need. We're going for the hard stuff today," Felix told him, throwing an arm around both Dash and me as we walked to the library in search of the good liquor.

56.

"I'm going to bed," I slurred, gripping the arm of the couch as the room spun around me. We drank more liquor than I thought possible as Dash and Felix instructed me on the best way to get drunk as an immortal. Dash stood, draping his arm over my shoulder as he readied himself to leave.

"You're not going anywhere," Felix demanded, and we froze.

"But I'm exhausted and entirely too intoxicated," I whined, hiccuping on the last word, and Dash giggled beside me, just as drunk as I was.

"Oh, you can go to bed, dewdrop. But you…" he said, pointing a finger at his friend, "aren't going anywhere." I looked up at Dash to find him scrunching his face at Felix in confusion. "I haven't seen you in days, and I want attention," he explained as Dash rolled his eyes.

"I've been with you every day. Besides, you're letting *her* leave," he countered. "We're all friends, so she should be forced to stay if I have to." My jaw dropped open as I glared at him. He flashed an innocent and loving smile, but I shook my head, already planning how to punish him for selling me out.

"I like her more than you," Felix said, shrugging. "And also, she's the bride and gets whatever she wants."

"She wants me to come to bed with her," Dash replied.

"Actually, I want you to spend time with your friend," I corrected as I smiled sweetly at my fiancé, thrilled that I didn't have to wait long to make him pay for his betrayal. Though I desired nothing more than to curl up with him in bed, Felix's request tugged on my heartstrings. I could relinquish Dash to him for just one night.

"See!" Felix exclaimed. Dash turned to me as he pouted, but I shrugged.

"You brought this on yourself," I told him innocently.

"Fine. I'll walk you back to your room," he grumbled, defeated.

"You will do no such thing!" Felix demanded. "I will escort dewdrop to her chamber, and you will sit your ass down on that couch and wait for me to return." Dash threw his head back and groaned loudly. "If you walk her back, we both know you won't return."

Felix had a point, and we all knew it.

"Am I allowed to at least say goodnight to her, or does that break some fucking stupid ass rule you've implemented?" Felix bobbled his head back and forth as he considered Dash's request.

"I'll allow it," he said, heading towards a stack of books across the room to give us some privacy. "But make it quick." I couldn't help the wide drunken smile on my face at their juvenile exchange. Dash stuck out his bottom lip as he pulled me against him, taking my face between his hands.

"I'll make sure to have a spot made up for you at the foot of the bed. Maybe next time you won't try and sell me out," I said, pushing myself higher to kiss the tip of his nose before slinking down to rest my head on his chest. A laugh rumbled through him, vibrating against me and an answering smile filled my face.

"If that's what you want," he said sarcastically as he squeezed me tighter, his lips pressing against the top of my head. "I suppose that is an appropriate punishment." I laughed as I pulled back to gaze up at him.

"You think sleeping at the end of the bed is your punishment?" His eyes widened a fraction. "Oh, no, no, no, my sweet, fearless prince, I have something else in mind," I said as I kissed him gently. "You get to stay at the end of the bed and watch me do things to myself, unable to participate." Dash swallowed loudly.

"When you say *unable to participate*...."

"I mean not a single kiss, touch, or taste. Not one," I whispered against his lips. Dash inhaled sharply.

"Baby, let's talk about this," he replied eagerly. "Let's not make a rash decision. Surely we can arrange something else. Anything else." I bounced my head back and forth as if considering, and Dash's features filled with such hope. Slowly, I shook my head as I smiled up at him. His face fell into the crook of my neck. "I'm begging you, don't do this," he pleaded, kissing along the length of my throat, letting his tongue flick over my skin as he went. My Gods, he was persuasive.

"I'm going to have to deny your request. I like the idea of watching you suffer too much." Dash groaned loudly, palming my breast and kissing me harder. No doubt getting his fill before I took it all away tonight.

"Fine," he growled, righting himself. "I deserve it."

"I love you," I teased.

"Do you?" Dash questioned flatly.

"I'm sorry, do you want your punishment to be for two nights?" I arched a brow at him and gave a look that dared him to test me. He quickly shook his head before taking my face between his hands and planting kisses all over.

"I love you, my beautiful, intelligent, hilarious, fierce, *forgiving,* and *merciful* fiancé," Dash claimed as his lips brushed over mine.

"Much better," I announced before snuggling back against his chest. "Don't be too long, or I'll get started without you," I said, winking. Dash released a low rumble in his throat as he crashed his lips to mine. I melted into him as his tongue slipped over mine, tasting of mint and bitter liquor. My toes curled as I pressed my body harder against him, needing more than he gave. I was about to change my mind and call off Felix's plan just as a hand tugged me away from Dash, breaking our embrace.

"Goodnight!" I yelled as Felix dragged me through the Sanctuary.

"I love you," Dash replied as he plopped himself back onto the velvet couch just as Felix slammed the door behind us.

"It's not very nice to interfere with my sex life," I told Felix as we stumbled through the corridors, now virtually empty due to the late hour.

"Well, maybe I'd like to sleep through the night for once and not be jolted awake due to thunder roaring and lightning striking every hour." I snorted as I giggled. After I commanded him to let go that first night, Dash hadn't tried to restrain his power while we were intimate, often causing vicious storms to appear, though we were usually too distracted even to notice. It wasn't until I took him in my mouth for the first time and saw that the room was covered in ice after he had finished that I suggested leashing his magic just a little bit. 'That *was* me attempting to restrain it,' Dash had said breathlessly, and his lack of control over himself had me lowering my mouth to him again.

"You're just jealous that you can't let the entire palace know how good the sex you're having is," I said, nudging him with my hip. He howled in laughter but nodded his head.

"That's the fucking truth," he admitted. "But I do get to feel exactly what I'm doing."

"What do you mean?" I asked curiously. Though Felix and I had discussed sexual exploits in the past, he had never shared what, if anything, his magic could do in that way.

"You know how I can feel heightened emotions?" he asked. "Well, those emotions are extra intense during sex. I can instantly tell when I've hit my partner's very special spot." He winked, and I found myself jealous of the use of his Gift. I thought about what it would be like with Dash. Though there were always physical indicators that he enjoyed what I was doing or was close to release, I wondered what it would be like to wrap myself around him from the inside and feel his heart racing and his body clenching tight as I worked him.

"You lucky bastard."

"How else do you think I got so good?"

"I wouldn't know about your skills in that area," I reminded him.

"Oh, please," he scoffed. "You could take just one look at me and know I'm fucking phenomenal in bed." We both laughed hard as we turned a corner to the hallway that led to my bedroom, and I halted as I saw Rosella at the far end. Her eyes went wide as she looked at me, and her face paled as she began retreating, walking backward through the corridor. I stalked for her, Felix following close behind.

"Do I need to make good on my threat?" I yelled, tripping over myself as I quickened my pace. "Because I'll fight you right here and now!" The declaration was jumbled and slammed together as if they were all one word, evidence that I was completely inebriated.

"No, my lady!" Rosella yelled as she sprinted down the hall, fleeing as fast as possible. I chased after her, the hallway swaying with each stride of my legs.

"I will make your life a living *hell*!" I called, reminding her of my promise as Felix's arms wrapped around me, lifting me from the ground. I flailed my arms around as I spoke and watched her slam into stone as she rounded a corner, disappearing from view. He set me down, and I turned to face him, his eyes wide and face amused. "That's gonna leave a bruise," I said, pointing a thumb over my shoulder at the wall Rosella had collided with. Felix and I snorted before falling to the floor in hysterics. My stomach cramped from the laughter, and my lungs burned for air. My actions may have been entirely immature and fueled by alcohol, but that didn't change how good it felt to see Rosella terrified of *me* for once.

"You are *so* wasted," he said through his cackling as tears streamed down his face. I closed one eye and pinched my fingers together.

"Just a little bit." Felix shook his head as he calmed down, still beaming ear to ear. He stood and scooped me into his arms to carry me the rest of the journey to my room. Once we entered, he walked over to my bed and set me down gently before tucking me in.

"Sleep tight, dewdrop. I promise I won't keep Dash long," he said.

"Thank you," I told him. "For everything today." His smile was soft, but his eyes seemed sad, though that could have just been my drunken state focusing on things that weren't there. He placed a kiss on my forehead before heading out of the room.

I hadn't realized I had fallen asleep until Dash's lips were on my neck, planting soft wet kisses on my collarbone.

"You're back," I whispered sleepily, my eyes fluttering open and my fingers finding their way into his hair.

"Nothing can keep me from you," he said, bringing his mouth to mine. "Not even an overbearing best friend determined to ruin our sex life." I laughed softly as I kissed him back. "You said something about starting without me?" he asked, pulling back so I could see the devilish thoughts behind his blue eyes. I shrugged and arched a brow as a wicked grin tugged at his lips.

"You may have started, but did you finish?" I gave a smile that matched his own as I shook my head.

"Good, because I'm starving," he growled before removing my dress and working his way down my body. I didn't bother to stop him, forgetting all about his promised punishment.

57.

The door to my bedroom swung open, a loud bang echoing through the room as it slammed into the wall behind, jerking both Dash and me from sleep. I squinted into the dimness, trying to see the culprit as Dash leaped from the bed. The room instantly dropped in temperature as ice coated his hands, ready to defend me against any unwelcome visitor.

"Good morning, lovebirds," Felix called as he stepped further into the room carrying a breakfast tray; the pastel lights of dawn creeping through the window illuminated his features. I breathed a heavy sigh of relief as I pulled the sheets higher, covering my bare chest.

"Mother's fucking tits, Felix," Dash said as he climbed back into bed, throwing the blanket over himself. "You scared the living shit out of us.

Felix rolled his eyes. "Oh, Dash, you're so dramatic." He approached the bed, set the tray down, and sat on the edge.

"Says the one who just barged in here at the crack of dawn," Dash countered, laying back and throwing a pillow over his face. "Go away and let us sleep." My hands flew to my temples as my head began to pound vigorously. We drank so much yesterday that I wasn't sure how any of us were even alive right now.

"How are you perfectly fine this morning?" I asked him, my stomach twisting, sending a bout of nausea weaving through me as I thought back to last night, the smell of alcohol fresh in my mind.

"Ahhh," Felix said triumphantly, "For one, I am not an amateur, and two—" he reached into his pocket, pulling out two small vials with bright green liquid swishing inside. He handed one to me and tossed the other onto Dash's muscled chest. He curled his fingers around the bottle and gave a thumbs up in Felix's direction.

"What is this?" I asked, eyeing the contents suspiciously.

"It's a special tonic to get rid of the hangover," Dash said, his voice muffled.

"Cheers to that!" I replied, popping the lid and swallowing the liquid, its bitter taste threatening to come back up.

"We created it ourselves," Felix announced proudly. "It took a while to perfect it, but it never failed us once we did. All those nights of drunken foolery with no hangover afterward." An arrogant smile was displayed on his face in self-satisfaction.

"And how often did you two need this?" I asked.

"Do not answer that. It's a trap!" Dash yelled into the fabric. I pushed his side hard, and he threw his pillow at me, but I deflected, causing it to ricochet and smack Felix right in the face. "Well, that works too," Dash said, laughing as he propped himself up to a sitting position, head resting against the headboard.

"Here I am, trying to help, and instead of you two being appreciative, I'm getting assaulted. I'm appalled at this behavior," Felix said dramatically.

"I am very appreciative. And also curious how long it took you to make such an amazing concoction," I said, shaking the now-empty vial.

"Nope," Dash cut in immediately as he shook his head at me before turning to address Felix. "She's fishing for information about the good old days we used to have before she arrived." I squinted my eyes at him. Dash leaned over, placing a kiss on my cheek. "It's not going to work, beautiful," he whispered, and I gave him a sarcastic smile.

"I'll get it out of Felix eventually," I offered confidently as we turned our attention to him.

"Well, she's not wrong," Felix said as he shrugged. "But for now, it's time for the other reason I'm here. Your father asked to see you this morning before breakfast... in the Council Room."

Dash let out a loud and long groan.

"What's so bad about that?" I asked.

"Every time King Perceval asks to see us in the Council Room, he keeps us there for hours," Felix explained.

"There's always some strategy or lesson he tries to teach, and it takes him the entire day just to get to the fucking point," Dash said, shaking his head and looking pissed.

"With the wedding tomorrow, it might just be about that," Felix offered.

"Or about more shit about Tenebrae," Dash countered. "After what happened at the meeting, the past couple of days have been too quiet. It doesn't feel right."

"I know, but let's hope that this request has nothing to do with them," Felix said. "I'll be back in ten minutes, and you better be ready by then."

Once Felix left the room, I turned to Dash. He stuck out his bottom lip, pouting as he placed his head across my lap. I stroked his hair, laughing softly at his little temper tantrum.

"I just want to stay here with you," he whined. "Those meetings are insufferable."

"My poor little Crowned Prince," I said mockingly. "It's probably just about tomorrow." My heart began to race as I thought about that. The wedding. The Entwining Ceremony. My fingers stilled in his hair. Sensing my distress, Dash quickly sat up to face me.

"Talk to me," he said, his voice full of worry.

"I don't understand how it will work when I don't have a Gift to give." Dash's face grew solemn, and he cupped my jaw as he pressed his lips against mine, demanding entry with his tongue. I opened willingly for him as he kissed me passionately like the act could take away his sadness. When he was finished, he stared deep into my eyes as if he saw straight to my soul.

"I know you hate that part of the ritual. I know how much you don't want to give that piece of yourself away, but the ceremony isn't solely about what magic is given; it's about the promise the participants make." My brows knitted as he held me, silently requesting him to elaborate. "The Entwining Ceremony does just that; it entwines two people together, creating a deep and permanent connection. The attachment that happens when the ceremony is complete is instantaneous, and for the rest of their existence, they will protect and stand by one another. To be Entwined with another person is to give yourself to them and make them yours in every way. It's a vow sealed by magic that cannot be broken in cases other than death."

"And your parents were Entwined?" I asked, though I already knew the answer.

"Yes." There was a hint of anger behind the word, and I hoped the curiosity in my features would be enough for him to explain. "She wasn't happy with my father. He loved her, but it was obvious she did not feel the same. She was not only married to a king but forced to stand next to him for eternity with no chance of breaking free."

"But you said it creates a deep connection."

"It does, but a connection doesn't equate to love, Ainsley. It is a string and path to each other, but it doesn't mean there will be feelings of passion and desire present. Love is its own kind of magic, one that cannot be forced." I swallowed as I wrapped my mind around his words.

"My parents never had what we have. I love you, Ainsley, and I want to Entwine my life with yours. I want to give you every part of me and protect you for the rest of our existence." As Dash explained the Entwining Ceremony, I realized I had been utterly wrong in my assumptions. Though I still believed that taking a sliver of someone's magic who didn't want to give it was wrong, and though I still thought that forcing someone into a permanent vow without their consent was wrong, I understood the beauty in the ritual for two people who wanted to participate willingly.

"What happens in the ceremony if there is no magic to offer?"

"I would assume everything would be conducted the same way, and just the transferring of the Gift would be left out," he answered. "Are you nervous?"

"A little bit," I replied honestly, and his face fell slightly. "But I'm also excited, Dash. I want to be your wife." I had been so scared of Entwining myself to him, but now, after what we had built and the love we shared, I wanted to. I wanted to feel that connection grow more profound than we could ever have thought possible. As I lost myself in the deep blue shade of his eyes, I realized that if I *had* possessed magic, I would have wanted to offer him some. Not to make him more powerful, though I knew it would, but because of how I felt. He had always shared every part of himself with me, including his Gift.

My mind journeyed back to when he had created a ball of water by pushing his power through me, allowing me to hold it in my hands. I thought of the way I had felt as the tingling of his magic shot through my veins. It was beyond words. And every time we were intimate, he granted his power the ability to come forth. With each rake of my nails down his back or thrust of my tongue in his mouth, he allowed me to manipulate it, causing lighting to strike or frost to appear. I didn't control magic, but I controlled its wielder, and that was a power in itself. I would want him to experience the same. Whenever he accessed that piece I had given, I would know he felt my love for him.

He leaned over and kissed me tenderly. "Wife," he mused against me. "I like the way that sounds." His lips moved to my neck, and I shivered. "And I would very much like to be with my soon-to-be wife for the remainder of our morning together," he said, his hand sliding down my waist as his mouth traveled to my collarbone.

"Felix only gave us ten minutes," I said breathlessly as I molded my body to his.

Dash smiled devilishly. "All I need is two," he said as he grabbed my legs, pulling me down flat onto my back and throwing the blankets over us.

"I thought we established that you only required one." He growled at my sass before plunging deep.

We had barely finished when Felix came busting through the door again without a courtesy knock. "It seems that I have impeccable timing," he observed as Dash finished clasping his pants. I didn't bother attempting to get dressed, as I thoroughly planned to lounge in bed all day.

"I really hate you right now," Dash told his friend as he took my face into his hands for one last kiss. A low growl escaped from the bottom of his throat as I kissed him harder, and Felix let out a loud gagging sound from behind us. I smiled as I broke off our embrace. "I love you," he said as he finally stepped back and made his way for the door.

"I love you," I replied.

"I promise I'll take care of our little tartlet while you're apart," Felix added.

Dash gave a long-exaggerated wave to both of us as he replied, "I'll meet up with you two later." And then disappeared into the hall.

Felix released a long sigh before turning and heading to the armoire, throwing it open wide and rifling through its contents. "Looking for something in particular?" I asked, wrapping the sheet around myself as I stepped out of bed and walked over to him.

"Your riding clothes," he told me, and my face lit up.

"We're going riding today?" Felix's answering smile had me bouncing in place.

"Yes, and you're taking Nox. Consider it an early wedding present."

"Felix, I would throw my arms around you right now, but I am completely naked under this sheet."

"Ainsley, I'm flattered by the proposition, truly," he said, placing his hands on my shoulders. "But I'm just not into you like that." I punched him hard in the stomach. His muscles, like rocks beneath, told me that I probably did more damage to myself than to him.

He pushed an outfit and a pair of boots into my arms. "Go get dressed and do it quickly. We need to leave immediately in case Dash comes back." I looked up at him curiously.

"But you said that he would probably be gone for hours."

"Yeah, I did say that. But I may have lied a little bit." My eyes widened in surprise. "His father never asked for him. I told King Perceval that Dash was the one who wanted to meet him in the Council Room to go over some strategies he had in mind."

"What? Why?" I asked incredulously, as my mouth hung open.

"Because I wanted to kidnap you. He always gets you, and you're getting married tomorrow, and I wanted to have some Delicious Duo time before that. This was the only way I could make that happen."

I smiled at the sentiment, and if I was entirely honest with myself, I missed spending time with just Felix, and I could use someone to talk to about the wedding and ceremony.

I shook my head disapprovingly at him. "He will kill you when he realizes what you did." Something like sadness flashed briefly in his eyes. I wondered if it was because he had lied to his friend and set him up for a miserable morning while we were off on some adventure.

"I know," he said quietly, and something in his tone broke my heart a little.

I sighed loudly in defeat. "Give me two minutes," I said as I hurried to the bathing room, and Felix's lips spread into a wide smile. I dressed quickly, tying my hair back as I emerged to find Imogen standing next to Felix, a hand on his back as she spoke softly to him. I cleared my throat, announcing myself, and they both looked up at me. Was there something going on between them that I hadn't noticed before?

"Well, isn't it nice to see you up bright and early for once," Imogen said by way of greeting.

"Am I interrupting something?" I asked, gesturing between the two of them.

"I was just telling Felix here that I packed a breakfast for you both and had it sent down to the far stables, so you have something to eat on your journey."

"Thank you, Imogen," Felix said kindly, leaning into the maiden. She nodded and then stretched her arms out toward me. I obliged the request, throwing my arms around the person who had come to mean so much to me. She squeezed tightly and held me for a few silent moments before clearing her throat.

"You two better head out, you have a big day tomorrow, and you'll need an early rest," she said, kissing my head before setting me straight and heading over to make the bed.

"Come on," Felix said, leading me from the room.

"Bye, Imogen!" I called out, and she waved a hand over her shoulder as she straightened the blankets across the bed, not deeming to reply.

58.

"Here," Felix said, tossing an apple to me as we rode through the woods. It took us less than five minutes to hurry through the palace, making it to the far stables. Nox and Aura were already saddled and ready for us, with a basket of food, courtesy of Imogen, on the ground outside their stall.

"Where are we going?" I asked as I bit into the fruit, juice dripping down my chin. He hadn't said where he was taking us, just that the journey would take a few hours. The sun was climbing higher in the sky, the heat a constant blaze indicating it was close to midday, so we had to be getting close. Felix ignored my question to ask one of his own.

"Are you happy?" he said.

"What?" I replied, not understanding where this was possibly coming from. Had I been giving false signs that I wasn't? He repeated his question. "Yes," I told him. "Why—"

"And you love Dash?" he interrupted as if he somehow doubted that fact, and hurt spread through me.

"Yes, Felix," I said, forcing my voice to lose all curiosity and pain and to instead be filled with reassurance. "I love Dash." He nodded, seemingly pleased with whatever clarification that answer gave him.

"Do you regret coming to the palace?" he continued, and my heart dropped at his line of questioning, my eyes beginning to prick with tears. Did he genuinely believe this to be the case? Was there doubt in his mind that I wanted to be here and loved Dash?

"I know I made things difficult for everyone when I first arrived, but...." I thought for a moment before continuing. "But coming here to the palace led me to Dash. It led me to *you*, Felix. How could I possibly regret that?"

"And if you had a choice in the matter?" he asked.

"What?" I wasn't sure what he could mean by that.

"If you had been given a choice to either come to the palace or choose a different life... A life of your own, a life where you and you alone designed your destiny. Which would you choose?"

"Felix, why are you asking me this?" I asked, navigating Nox forward to take her place next to Aura. He didn't answer, focusing his attention on the path before us rather than on me. "Is this some sort of test to ensure that I'm good enough for your best friend?" I pressed. My stomach began to tighten, and I felt as though I would be sick.

Felix chuckled under his breath, but the sound seemed empty and anything but humored. "Something like that," he replied, still refusing to meet my eyes. Panic began to creep up as I replayed his words in my mind. Things between us had been different since the night of my birthday, though I couldn't pinpoint precisely why. The was a slight change, but enough for me to notice it. He was quieter and more withdrawn from me than he'd ever been. And now, with his line of questioning, I was starting to worry.

I focused on breathing, willing my nerves to calm and my stomach to settle. I focused on the sound of our mare's hooves gently trotting against the dirt path, willing the roaring in my ears to quiet. I focused on the cool late summer breeze blowing through my hair and against my skin, willing the sweat I felt bead against my brow to dissipate. I took a deep breath, my head spinning with the nausea I was working to keep at bay.

"I don't get to choose, Felix. The path for my life was decided before I was born, and you know this, so pretending it wasn't is pointless. I have made the best out of the situation I was forced into, and I found love and happiness by the grace of the Gods above. The only choice I had been given was the one you gave me." He looked at me now, his head tilting a little in question. "You offered me your hand and friendship," I said, smiling at him. "And taking you up on that offer was the best choice I could have ever made." His bright amber eyes shone, silver beginning to line them.

"I love you, my Angsty Ainsley," he said, a single tear rolling down his face.

"I love you, Felix."

"Arguably more than Dash?" he asked, a playful smirk creeping upon his face.

"Arguably more than Dash," I agreed, winking at him as I strode forward, taking the lead. "But if you tell him that, I'll deny it," I called over my shoulder. He laughed loudly, and the sound of Aura's pace quickening as he moved to catch up, followed.

We trotted along for another hour before Felix led us off the dusty dirt road and through a small opening in the woods. "Are we almost there?" I asked breathlessly, my stomach never quite settling after Felix's barrage of queries.

"It's just up ahead, straight through the trees," he replied, dismounting Aura and guiding her on the lead. I climbed down from Nox and fed her an apple before following after Felix, pushing my way through the broken, hanging branches and stepping out onto a small field atop a cliff. I halted abruptly as I looked out before me, never seeing a sight quite as beautiful as this.

As far as the eye could see, sprawling green hills and plains were spotted with crystal blue lakes. Where the bright blue sky met the land were mountains that looked no larger than small mounds from this distance. They were rocky yet deep green, and dark blue lines snaked at the base—rivers, I realized. Shades of purples and blues and reds and oranges peppered the land, the wildflowers in full bloom despite autumn being right around the corner.

"It's the best view of Caelum that I've ever come across. And that little speck over there—" Felix said, coming close and pointing to a tiny white dot barely visible. "Is the palace."

"Felix, this is…." I trailed off, completely lost for words as I took in the scene.

"Dash has the lake," he said, nodding, surveying the land before him, "This is my little haven. I come here when everything gets to be too much." He took a breath and let it out slowly. "I've never shared it with anyone before. Not even Dash." My eyes flew to Felix to find him already staring at me, and my hand reached up, resting on my quickening heart as tears began to fill my eyes.

"I'm honored that you feel safe enough to share this with me," I told him, a lump forming in my throat. Felix cared about his friends fiercely, but he always used humor as a way to connect. For him to share a piece of himself that he had kept private for years meant more to me than I could ever hope to put into words.

"I'm honored to have someone to share it with, especially because that person is you," he said, wrapping an arm around my shoulder, pulling me into him, and planting a kiss on my head. My heart began pounding harder, my stomach tightening at the embrace.

"Ainsley, are you alright?" Felix asked, pulling back to look at me. Whatever he must have seen on my face gave him his answer, and his hands immediately moved to my cheeks, my forehead. "You're burning up," he said worriedly.

A bout of nausea hit me hard and fast, like a rockslide cascading down the face of a mountain, and I turned from him as I emptied the contents of my stomach into the grass. Felix grabbed my hair at once, pulling it back from my face as I heaved and heaved until nothing was left within me.

"I'm sorry," I told him. "I've been nauseous for a little while now. I thought it was from your interrogation back there, but obviously, it's not."

Felix eyed me up and down, a look of concern flashing over him. "You're not...." I waited for him to continue, but he just stared at me.

"I'm not what?" I said, unscrewing the lid and taking a sip of water from my canteen to rinse my mouth.

"You're not...." Felix began again, and I followed his glance to the hand clenching my roiling stomach.

"*Pregnant*?! Gods, no!" I yelled. "Dash and I had sex for the first time just a few days ago, and I'm pretty sure pregnancy doesn't work that fast. Not to mention, I've been on a contraceptive tonic since I was seventeen, Felix. Once I told my caregivers that I sullied my virtue, they put me on one to ensure I wouldn't welcome any unwanted children before being sent to the palace. And though I was desperate to find a way out, I wasn't *that* desperate." I took another sip of water. "Imogen has kept me on it since my arrival."

Relief flooded his face, and he let out a long sigh, shaking his head. I found myself laughing softly at his concern.

"Speaking of tonics," I continued, "Clearly, the one you and Dash created is terrible."

Felix gasped in mock horror. "I am utterly offended!"

"I have a hangover worse than Hell itself, so obviously, it didn't even work," I countered, giving him a sidelong and disappointed look. Felix rolled his eyes at me before striding over to Aura and riffling through a small pouch attached to her saddle. He returned to me and handed over another small vial; this time, the contents were a bright yellow liquid, a far more appealing color than the green substance he had me drinking this morning.

"Is this another Dash and Felix invention? Because if so, I will have to very politely decline," I told him, breathing deeply as my stomach began to churn again.

"It'll help with what you're feeling right now." I opened my mouth to protest, but Felix continued. "And before you protest, I did not make it; Imogen did." I eyed him suspiciously, not sure I believed his tale. "I swear it. She wouldn't let me take you out here without a full satchel of supplies to keep you alive and well." I thought back to my maiden and her constant concern for my well-being. Dash had told me that when he brought me to my room after the attack in the woods, she refused to leave my side for days, and my heart warmed to think about what her motherly warnings to Felix this morning contained. I opened the bottle and swallowed the contents, the flavor of berries and peppermint going down smoothly.

"Atta girl," he said as he took the vial from me and patted me on the head. I swatted him away feebly and turned back to the view.

"Why haven't you shared this with anyone?" I asked, trying to wrap my head around the fact that he had kept this a secret all these years. Felix sat down next to me but was quiet for several minutes as he tried to find his words. I waited patiently, giving him the time he needed, taking small sips of water to ease my sickness, and listening to the birds in the distance.

"Like you, I was shipped off here with no say. I was to just accept that Caelum would be my home forever or as long as I was welcome here." He leaned forward, resting his forearms on his propped knees and spinning a single blade of grass between his long fingers. "Being up here," he gestured around us, "makes me feel bigger than this place. It makes me feel bigger than the things that were decided for me. And as for keeping it a secret, I did so because it was something I had a say in. A choice in. A choice no one would decide for or take away from me." Felix shrugged, bringing his eyes to me, and they were warm and full of hope. "It seems small and ridiculous when I speak it all aloud, but—"

"No," I interrupted. "No, Felix. It's so very monumental." I put my hand on his and squeezed gently, the movement harder than it should be with my body feeling weak. "I'm so grateful that you shared this all with me, but more than that, I'm so grateful that you had a place for yourself all this time," I said, trying hard to focus on the words. Felix's eyes narrowed at me, and his hand moved to my forehead.

"Your temperature seems to have gone down a bit, but how are you feeling?"

"Exhausted," I told him slowly, and he rose, helping me to my feet.

"Come on," he said, throwing my arm around him. "There's a stream right through these trees. We'll get you some fresh water and rest there for a while."

The short walk only took a few minutes, but I was winded by the time Felix set me down by the water.

"I feel like I've ruined our Delicious Duo day," I told him as he handed me my now-refilled canteen. I drank deeply, letting the cold spring water fill my veins. Felix rested a hand on my cheek and shook his head.

"As long as we're together, it's considered a perfect Delicious Duo day." I opened my mouth to object when the faint sound of branches snapping in the distance drew my attention. My eyes flickered to Aura and Nox, sprawled out in the grass sunbathing, the source of the noise not from their doing. Another snapping sound and my gaze flew to Felix, still crouched in front of me, his amber eyes hard, stare serious. He slowly brought his index finger to his lips, instructing me to be as silent as possible as his free hand slid to the dagger he kept sheathed at his hip. I swallowed deeply as another wave of nausea hit me, and my head spun at the sickness coursing through my body at the worst possible moment.

The sound of near-silent footsteps approached, almost entirely concealed by the babbling of the stream, and I watched as a tall, dark figure pushed his way through the small opening of trees, flanked by a man and woman. My eyes grew wide with terror as Felix stood, whirling around quickly and taking a defensive stance in front of me. He held the dagger across his body, ready to attack and protect.

The man in the middle—the leader, it seemed—held out his hands, halting his companions from advancing any further. His head tilted slightly as he studied the sight before him, his turquoise eyes sliding to me in curiosity, so bright against the deep golden ebony of his skin. He threw a sidelong glance at the strangers with him and gave them a shallow nod, an order given. His companions began to move farther out, circling wide and scanning the tree lines as they did. They were surrounding us. Our only hope of escape was the stream that lay behind our backs. Darkness began rippling off the leader's body as if he had been cloaked in the night itself.

Fuck. Tenebrae.

Dash had mentioned citizens of Tenebrae had been spotted on our southeastern border, but we were to the north, and how they had found us here in this secluded location, I didn't know. My vision blurred as I tried to rise on shaky legs, my balance so off-kilter that I had nearly fallen onto the rocks along the stream in my attempt. Felix twisted around as I stumbled, catching me in time and wrapping an arm around my middle as he helped me stand, but the distraction cost us. The leader took the opportunity at my misfortune to close the distance between us, now only feet away, his arms outstretched as if he was ready to grab me and drag me off to his kingdom.

Felix's eyes grew cold as a feral snarl ripped from his throat, a warning. A sound that said *back the fuck off*. He was a knight protecting his queen. The leader lowered his arm as he looked at the woman, slowly making her way closer, her features so much like his that they must be related, siblings perhaps. He jerked his chin towards Felix, and she unsheathed the sword strapped down her spine, a smaller dagger already in her hand as she approached. Felix's grip on me tightened as he angled his weapon, ready to take on this warrior, prepared to defend me until his last breath. Not a single word had been uttered between either party, yet all intentions had been made clear. The intruders from Tenebrae would be taking me with them, and Felix would give his life to ensure that wouldn't happen.

The woman smiled slyly as a sword dripping in shadows appeared at Felix's throat from behind. She had been a mere distraction as the leader's male companion crept up silently to disarm him. My heart thundered in my chest as realization hit. I had watched Dash and Felix spar on multiple occasions, and never once had Dash ever been able to surprise him; his mind was always too quick, always one step ahead. For Felix not to have anticipated an attack that seemed so obvious in hindsight, he must have been genuinely terrified and so set on finding a way to get us out of here that he missed a move that could cost us our very lives. I understood Felix enough to know that he was screaming within his head at his mistake, and by the look in his eyes, he was hurting over it.

"Let her go and back up... slowly," the second man said. His shoulder-length russet brown hair was half tied back, revealing a scar that stretched from his eyebrow to ear. Felix didn't dare move a single inch. "Now." He ground out, his sword pressing harder against Felix's throat, causing a single drop of deep red blood to spill, and his eyes flickered to me, the color a deep gold. My heart clenched at the sight of any harm coming to my best friend, and I pushed myself from his body, my arms raised in surrender as I slowly stepped farther away.

"You can have me, but let him go unharmed," I spat at the leader, his eyes narrowing as I spoke. There was a faint smile tugging at the corner of his mouth as if he was amused that I would be bold enough to make a demand when they had the high ground here. His gaze slid to his gold-eyed companion, and he nodded once. The man's sword instantly disappeared into shadows scattered upon the wind, and he disarmed Felix before grabbing his hands to restrain them behind his back. I stifled my relief that Felix was no longer in immediate danger as I stared down the leader. I needed him to come for me. I needed to get him closer. If I could get him next to me, I could use the dagger I had sheathed on my hip, currently concealed by my riding coat. It was the dagger Imogen always made me swear to carry whenever I stepped foot outside the palace after what happened in the orchard.

The leader made his way toward me, and my breathing quickened in anticipation as I ran through all the possible scenarios of how to catch him off guard. I scanned through every fighting technique Felix and Dash had taught me as I pondered how to get us out of there safely. The odds weren't in our favor, but I had to try. Even if the possibility of me leaving this clearing free was nonexistent, Felix still had a chance. If I could cause enough of a distraction, he could take on the man with the scar and then flee to safety. My gaze slid to Felix, finding his face pale, eyes wide as if he could read every thought in my mind. He shook his head slowly, urging me not to attempt something so reckless.

The leader grabbed my left hand to pin it behind my back as another wave of nausea and dizziness hit me like a tidal wave. It was now or never. I reached beneath my coat with my free hand and snatched the dagger as I twirled around, bringing the blade down hard to stab the leader in his leg. But he was too quick, as if he had anticipated my every intention. He grabbed my wrist and twisted, the pain shooting through my hand, causing the dagger to fall to the ground a foot away. I spun into the man to face him, ignoring the agony from his hold on me and the sickness that ran rampant. I thrust my knee up like Felix had taught me, hoping to catch him in the area he claimed to be a man's weakest spot. Once again, the leader was ready and waiting. He released my wrist and shoved my leg back to the ground with a slight push, the movement sending me staggering back as spots began to fill my vision, and the world beneath my feet felt as though it was trembling. Breathing was becoming difficult, and I wasn't sure how much longer I would last. The leader's smile was even wider now, and I felt my blood heat. He was messing with me as a predator would with its prey.

My stomach cramped with excruciating pain so great that I doubled over, screaming and gasping for breath.

"Ainsley!" Felix's voice shot above the roaring in my ears.

The leader moved for me again, his hand grazing my arm as I pulled away, stumbling backward as a reflection caught my eye. The sunlight glinting off the discarded dagger in the grass was a beacon calling me, and my eyes flickered to Felix, knowing that this very well could be the last time I saw him.

"You have to get out of here, Felix." He shook his head, begging me not to do this, not to hand myself over to Tenebrae. "Please," I whispered. I would sacrifice my life for my friend if it meant he had a chance to get away unharmed. If it meant Dash wouldn't have to lose both of us. My heart began to shatter.

"No!" Felix bellowed, but it was too late. I lunged for the dagger just as the world spun around me, my vision blurring completely. I was falling. I had no sense of up or down, day or night. "Ainsley!" I heard Felix yell just as I was engulfed in darkness. Consciousness left me entirely.

59.

The sensation of chilled air brushed over my skin, bringing forth a shiver, the cold dragging me to consciousness and awakening my senses. I fought the rise of panic that began to surface as I remembered the encounter with Tenebrae, but my mind struggled to fill in the gaps. I focused on my breathing, steadying my heart as I tried to piece together the puzzle of events that had unfolded earlier. Flashes surged into view of Felix's terror-stricken eyes, a dagger glinting in the grass, my hands lunging in front of me, and then being enveloped in darkness with screams drifting through like a mighty wind.

I squeezed my eyes tighter as I relinquished the memories and instead brought my attention to what I could detect of my surroundings, though I still didn't dare to open my eyes. Voices were speaking in low indistinguishable whispers, and the words were muffled and drowned out by a ringing in my ears, most likely from hitting the ground hard. I couldn't make out what they were saying or if the owners were men, women, or even children. The breeze that caressed my body made me believe I was still outside, but the plush fabric underneath me indicated otherwise. It was as though I was lying on furniture like a bed or a couch. I slowly inched my fingers, trying to explore further without identifying that I was awake. The cushions were luxurious beneath my touch, feeling warm and like velvet, just like the couch in the Sanctuary. The voices became more apparent with each second that passed, the high-pitched sound in my ears lessening and replaced by a pounding in my head. My heart raced as I realized the voices belonged to two males. Had I made it home? Had Felix managed to get me out of there and bring me to the Sanctuary?

A laugh rumbled, echoing off the walls and bouncing to me, but the nuance in the voice wasn't anything like Dash or Felix, and I began to worry.

"I say we start with torture," one of the men said. His voice was as clear as if he were standing next to me now, and there was something familiar about it. I realized I had been wrong. I wasn't home, nor would I ever make it back there. The second voice responded, but it was nothing more than a whisper that I couldn't understand. "But that's the best part about the healing; we can slice an immortal up, their blood will fix them, and then we start again." A soft chuckle filled the room, the sound smooth and dawdling like melting snow in the winter. I felt my face pale, and my body began to tremble in fear at their cruel plans for me.

"Something tells me she'll put up a fight, but you can try," the other man responded, and my heart stopped beating. I knew that voice. "We can always find out when she stops pretending to be asleep." I swallowed deeply, steeling my nerves as I opened my eyes and sat up, ready to face what was before me. I had indeed been lying on a velvet couch, the color a deep burnt rust, and was facing a large open window, the source of the chill. It was night, and the horizon was so dark that I couldn't make out anything other than the altitude. Judging by the slight illumination of mountains from the moonlight, our current location seemed to be elevated.

I stood as I took a deep breath, ready to face my kidnappers. The room was massive and covered in black marble, with high ceilings and tall pillars lining the space. The wall at my back and the one directly across from me held several grand windows spread out, and placed between each opening were couches and armchairs in that same burnt rust shade. The one I had personally been lying on seemed to have been dragged in front of the open window to torture me with the freezing temperature of the night air. The sound of a throat clearing pulled me from my observations, and I gazed at the two men on the other side of the room as they watched me curiously.

The turquoise-eyed leader from the stream this afternoon looked at me with curiosity and intrigue. He leaned in close and spoke too low for me to hear to none other than Brandle, the same person who had trapped me in a room with him the day the kings had their meeting in Caelum. I stalked for them, making each step loud and deliberate though pain crashed through me at each stride of my legs. My footsteps echoed in my head, and my stomach knotted at the still-present sickness. Imogen's tonic had either worn off, or its effects were too weak to soothe the virus within.

"You!" I sneered, stopping a healthy distance from Brandle, not wanting to get too close, knowing that I had lost my dagger earlier. He looked the same as he had that afternoon, his grey eyes just as piercing and his short dark hair unkempt. He was dressed in all black, his shirt unbuttoned slightly, and his sleeves rolled to his elbows, showing off his toned forearms.

"Me," he replied, and a cocky grin crept up his face. I wanted to punch him, but there were more pressing issues, so I turned my attention to the leader instead.

"Where is Felix?" I demanded, but he didn't answer. "Did you let him go?" Again, no answer. "What did you do to my friend!" I yelled, the fury breaking through and causing my mind to swim with dizziness once more. I reached over and grabbed a tall round table for support, not realizing I had been standing next to it. My fingers dug into the wood as I sipped on the air around, willing my senses to settle. Nausea circled, and my vision danced with spots as I held the table, waiting for the torment to cease. The leader had drifted closer, almost unnoticeable, but I caught it. "Where is Felix," I gritted out, and my head and sight became clearer with each inhale. The leader turned, and I followed his gaze to Brandle, whose stare was blank and jaw clenched tight. "I said, where is Felix?" I demanded, releasing the furniture and straightening, my chin angled high in defiance. Brandle's cold grey eyes were hard and filled with rage as he studied me.

"Marceline," Brandle said, and the patter of footsteps sounded. I turned to see the woman from earlier striding for them.

"Ainsley here wants to see her friend," he said, not taking his eyes from me. "Bring him." She didn't move; instead, bringing her stare to the leader.

"Van," the leader warned, though I wasn't sure why. Where did I know his voice from?

"She wants to see him, Olivier," Brandle replied, anger caressing the words like silk. Why did his companions not want me to see Felix? Would it be his mangled corpse brought before me? Did they feel that it was beneath them to have to drag a body through this place so I could set my eyes on him? I didn't want to let my thoughts travel to images of Felix, lifeless and drained of color. "So bring him." Darkness began to swirl across his exposed skin like ribbons of spilled ink on parchment. I saw the woman bow her head from the corner of my eye before retreating from the room. My chest heaved as I began connecting the dots from the information I was just presented. Marceline bowed. Olivier called him 'Van.' The tattoos on his arms and chest were like shifting shadows. My eyes darted past him to see a great throne upon a dais.

"You're not Brandle," I whispered, terrified, hitting the table as I tried to inch away. His smile was present once more, and his eyes were bright as he shook his head slowly. "You're King Evander." He moved for me, and my back pressed hard into the wood, too paralyzed with fear to flee. He halted a few feet away and dragged his stare up and down my body, inspecting his newest possession. His eyes stopped as they reached the bracelet clasped around my wrist, and his face flashed with disgust so quickly that I almost missed it. I covered the delicate chain and gemstone, blocking them from his view as if I could protect Dash by doing so. As if it would keep Dash hidden and unharmed. "What do you want?" I demanded, though I already knew.

"You," he replied, the answer sounding rushed and calculated.

"No."

He shrugged as if my response didn't matter and began to pace, sliding a hand in his pocket like he had all the time in the world to fuck with me. He wanted me to be fearful and anxious at the anticipation of what was to come. This was where the torture started. He was correct about one thing; I would put up a fight.

"You've wasted your time and resources, and your assailants were killed for nothing." He tilted his head to the side as he listened with intrigue.

I smiled widely, knowing he had no idea that his efforts to kidnap me were futile. "Your plan to enslave me," I stepped closer, chanting the words in my mind that Dash had spoken to me the night he gave me the bracelet. *You are wild and unyielding and strong, Ainsley.* "Your plan to bred me like a fucking animal," I spat, and his dark eyes burned with unrelenting indignation, "is completely pointless," I finished, stopping my advance a foot from him. His eyes narrowed, but his face was unreadable. "You see," I began when it was clear he didn't understand my meaning. "I have no magic. I was given no Gift from the Gods, so your efforts to use me for your advantage were all in vain."

A grin appeared, and a breathy laugh escaped him.

"Oh, love, I think you are mistaken." He removed his hand from his pocket and crossed his arms over his chest. "I believe you have tremendous power running through your veins." He closed the gap between us, leaning down as he spoke. "So much can be done with such magic," he whispered, and I swallowed the lump that had formed in my throat.

"You're wrong," I replied weakly, unable to keep the tremor from my voice. His eyes slipped back down my hand, and he grabbed my wrist. The movement was purposeful and angry but gentle.

"Tell me," he said, running his fingers over the flame gemstone. "Why has King Perceval moved up your wedding date?" I didn't answer; I couldn't. Not because I didn't want to but because I wasn't sure of the true reason. It had never made sense to me that he chose to advance our union simply out of the kindness of his heart, but I was never able to come up with another motive. I had thought that he would use me in some way to manipulate Dash but for what gain? What would marrying his son to a powerless immortal do for him? I had hoped his choice was to earn favor with his son for being a shit father to him his whole life. "You would participate in the Entwining Ceremony, would you not?"

"Do you have a point, or will you continue asking questions to which you already seem to know the answer?" I snapped, my patience for this game of his ending.

"I always have a point, love. Could it be because King Perceval recognizes the prize he has attained and wants you for himself?" Did he think that I was to marry King Perceval?

"I am marrying Dash, not the king," I corrected.

"While that point is valid, you're suggesting that the King of Caelum doesn't have a plan for you."

"And you don't?" I argued.

"Oh, I most certainly do, but let's stay on topic for now." He took a step back, crossing his arms over his chest as he began to pace again. "Here's what I believe: you are powerful, Ainsley. King Perceval knows it, and I know it. The King of Caelum has done a fantastic job of keeping you hidden from me for such a long time, despite my efforts to find you. Your magic—"

"I don't have magic," I interrupted, annoyed that he kept bringing this up. The outburst cost me, causing my stomach to cramp and pain to rupture. I winced as I gasped for breath, clutching my middle as King Evander watched impassively.

"You do," he drawled. "And I very much want to explore what you have to offer." The words were a promise or a threat, but either way, I was terrified. "As I was saying," he continued, "I believe that King Perceval planned to take your Gift for his son during your beautiful Entwining Ceremony."

"I don't have—" He raised an index finger, reminding me not to argue that I didn't possess magic. "If I did have a Gift, I would have willingly offered it to Dash during the ceremony, so your point is moot." I wanted to share a piece of me with him, and it hurt that I couldn't.

"A sliver, though, correct?" I looked at him, confused. "You would have offered him a small amount of your magic," he clarified.

"Yes." I wasn't sure where he was going with this.

"But not all of it," he said. It wasn't a question but an observation.

"What?"

"You wouldn't have willingly surrendered all of your magic to him, right?" His words rocked me. I hadn't even known that was a possibility. I shook my head.

"What are you getting at, Evander?" I quipped and didn't care that I left out his title. I wouldn't give him that respect after he kidnapped me and planned to use me for himself. His eyes brightened, and his body perked at the defiance— another game to him.

"Well, Ainsley," he mocked. "I have it on good authority that your king and dearly beloved planned to drain you of your magic entirely, leaving you without an ounce for yourself."

I laughed. Hard. This was the most ludicrous notion I had ever heard. No power had ever manifested for me other than an odd and intense feeling when

I had threatened Rosella. If I had a Gift, I would have willingly given part of it to Dash, making him stronger. It's not like I ever had a say in my own life. I was sent to the palace to marry the prince and relinquish part of my potential power to him regardless of whether I wanted to, so why would King Perceval go through an elaborate rouse and keep the fact that I had magic hidden from me? He could have just told me that I was powerful and that he would be transferring all of my magic to his son. I wouldn't have been able to do anything about it, so keeping it a secret made no sense. Unless he did it to keep Dash in the dark, knowing he would never have gone through with his plan. That was the only way this theory could be valid.

"And I believe King Perceval will be furious to know that I got to his Holy Grail first," he added.

"You're insane."

"Am I?" Evander questioned, arching a brow.

"Even if you're right," I started, "Even if that were King Perceval's plan, Dash would have never let it happen."

"Are you sure about that?" he asked, glancing back down at my wrist.

"Yes," I ground out, angry that he would insinuate Dash would ever do something to hurt me like that. "He doesn't know what his father has planned."

"He does," a voice called from behind, and I whirled to find Felix standing in the middle of the large room with Marceline and the golden-eyed man from the stream standing against the far wall, watching us. My eyes darted up and down his body, looking for any sign of distress or injury as I rushed for him. He was unbound and looked to be unharmed, though his posture seemed heavy with exhaustion. I made it all of two steps before I halted abruptly as the weight of his words sank into me. *He does.* I shook my head at him, not believing his lies. We were in Tenebrae; this had to be an illusion, a trick.

"No," I breathed. Felix's eyes were wide and red-rimmed, his face sullen and pale. He closed his eyes, and his throat worked as he opened his mouth to speak, but nothing came forth. "You're lying. Dash wouldn't—" I couldn't finish the sentence as his eyes flew open and tears began to spill out. "Why are you lying, Felix?" I said, my voice breaking on words as my vision clouded with tears. "He wouldn't." My chest ached with a pressure so forceful it felt as though I were being torn apart from the inside out. "Felix, why are you lying?" The question came out as a sob, and I knew he was being honest as I looked to see him so broken and ashamed. "Oh Gods," I whispered as my chest heaved hard, and I doubled over, resting my hands on my thighs as I struggled to breathe, gasping through the pain of my heart shattering.

"Ainsley," Felix said quietly, but I couldn't look at him. "Please."

"Has he known the entire time?" I managed, straightening as I scrubbed the moisture from my eyes, though my lips still trembled and my body shook from the betrayal. Felix shook his head as his tears continued to stream. "How long?" I demanded.

"The day Annette's body was found." A whimper broke through, and I covered my mouth to hide the sound, though it was no use. He had known for weeks. I twisted, gripping the table for support as my world ripped open and crumbled before my eyes. That was why he didn't come that night. That was why he had ignored me for days. He had found out that he would steal my magic from me. The magic that he knew I wanted.

"How long have you known?" Silence hung between us for minutes before I looked up to see Felix staring at the floor before him, unable to meet my eyes. "I said, how long have you *known*?" I demanded, raising my voice.

"Ainsley," he said, choking on my name.

"Tell me." Felix took a deep, shuddering breath as his amber eyes, dull and misty, found mine. He took a step closer, trying to reach me. "Stay away from me," I spat, and he halted immediately.

"Since the night of your birthday." I bent and emptied whatever remained in my stomach on the tile floor. I screamed from the pain of the sickness in my body and the agony of my broken heart. It felt like shards of glass were being stabbed through the organ, cutting away strips with every confession. Felix rushed for me, but I held out my hand to stop him.

"*Stay the fuck away from me!*" I yelled, and he stumbled back as if I had struck him, his hand flying over his chest, grasping hard as if he were in pain. The irony of it all was the pain he could feel was mine, the pain he helped cause. I righted myself again, my frame shaking hard with fury and anguish. "When you went after him that night," I realized as my mind shifted through the events of that evening.

"Yes."

"What else have you kept from me?" I asked, the anger rising and boiling my blood like fire. "I'm twenty-one, Felix, so why hasn't my magic manifested?" I wasn't sure he would know the answer to that, and some part of me prayed that he didn't. I wanted so badly to believe that he didn't purposefully keep the truth hidden from me after I had poured my heart out to him about my desire to have magic of my own. Felix let out a long breath, giving me my answer.

"The tea," he admitted. "You were being drugged with the tea." I felt sick as I recounted the memories I had with the beverage, from drinking it after being ill as a child until Dash served it to me the other morning. Fucking Gods.

"You seem to know a lot. Did you know who I was that day?" Felix stared at me and his brows knitted together in confusion. He opened his mouth but quickly closed it as Evander answered my question.

"I had no idea that the future Princess of Caelum stood before me, but what a delightful surprise it was to find out," Evander said, and I felt his presence next to me as if he moved closer as he spoke. Felix's eyes grew wide in shock.

"He was who you spoke to?" Felix asked incredulously, shaking his head. "No. You were in the meeting; I saw you there."

"Did you, though?" Evander asked slyly.

"But—"

"Why, Felix?" I cut in, changing the subject. I couldn't care less about Evander's motives at the moment. My focus was on the liar standing in front of me. Felix's gaze shifted back to me, and his face fell like looking at me pained him. Good. "Why didn't you tell me."

"When I confronted Dash the night of your party, he told me he was planning to tell you. I stayed away the following day because I didn't know what to do."

"The argument you had with Dash the morning after my Primum Celebration," I said, understanding washing over me.

"Yes," Felix said, nodding. "I could tell something happened between you two, and I knew he hadn't said anything yet. I was pissed he had let it go that far without you knowing the truth, and he swore that he would tell you if he couldn't find a way out of it. And then the king moved up your Entwining Ceremony, and you still didn't know, and Dash—"

"I don't give a shit about what Dash told you he would do," I snapped bitterly. Evander was suddenly at my side. I turned my head to see him studying Felix curiously as tendrils of smoke snaked around his fingers, waiting and ready to be released into the world.

"Ainsley," Felix said as he rushed toward me.

"No!" I yelled, not wanting to hear his excuses, and he stopped his advance. "No," I cried and clutched the table as the pain of my broken heart coursed through me once more. My chest was caving in, and my insides felt like they were being shredded apart, sending a scream ripping through my throat. I wanted to curl up on the floor and waste away to nothing. Everything I had come to know and love had been a lie. Felix shook his head as he came for me again, determined to reach me. "I said stay away!" I screamed, and black shadows surged from behind me, slithering like snakes as they slammed into Felix, knocking him into the stone wall with great force. I didn't know why Evander unleashed his magic, but I was grateful he did. Thankful that he restrained Felix and stopped him from reaching me before I was ready.

"Please," Felix said as tears spilled from his eyes. He wasn't begging for Evander to release him; he was begging for my forgiveness, and I wasn't sure I'd ever be able to grant it.

"Tell me why," I cried.

"Dash said—"

"No, Felix!" I yelled, frustrated and hurt. "I don't care about what Dash said. Why didn't *you* tell me." He shook his head as he opened and closed his mouth, unable to come up with a response. "You were my best friend, and I trusted you. I trusted you to have my back, to protect me, and instead, you made me out to be a fucking fool! *'We don't keep secrets from each other, Ainsley.'* Remember that?" I said, mocking his words.

"I'm so sorry," he sobbed, and the dark hold on him tightened.

"How could you!?" I yelled as angry tears poured from my eyes. Felix had meant everything to me. He was my first friend and the person I told everything to. Our relationship was deep and genuine, and beautiful in a way that was different from what Dash and I had. Felix understood me and what my life had been like. We were the same; both stripped of our choices and made to walk a path others had deemed for us. He knew how that felt and how much I craved a choice in my own destiny. And he watched quietly as the king plotted and planned to steal the last shred of me that was my own. He had a hand in the deception by not telling me the truth. Felix shook his head, unable to say another word.

"I suggest you answer her," Evander added viciously as the shadows made their way around Felix's neck.

"Please, Ainsley," he said as he hung his head in shame. The words were barely distinguishable as his emotions caught in his throat.

"How could you, Felix!" I screamed as a searing pain tore through me again, but I didn't falter this time. I stood straight and let the agony take me.

"I think that's enough," Evander said, but he didn't call his magic back. Instead, Felix rose, back sliding up the wall a few feet. By 'enough,' did he mean he would kill him? I was furious, but that didn't mean I wanted Felix to die. He opened his mouth to speak, but Evander did first. "That's enough," he said again, and his hold on Felix constricted.

I felt Evander move to my side, and I looked up to see him watching me, his arms crossed tight over his chest. I met his cold grey eyes as they held my stare for just a moment before dipping to the space in front of me. I followed his line of sight to find my hands extended with dark shadows spooling from my fingers and weaving their way through the room before colliding with Felix. My chest heaved, and panic crashed over me as I observed the magic I had expelled. Felix grunted in pain, and I redirected my attention to find the shadows pressing into him so hard the stone wall was cracking. I didn't know what to do or how to stop. My wide terror-stricken eyes shot to Evander, and he stepped forward without hesitation, waving a hand through the darkness and causing it to vanish instantly. Felix slid to the ground, gasping for breath just as Marceline grabbed his arm, dragging him from the room.

Evander closed in, and I could see him watching me stare at my trembling hands as I desperately tried to breathe; the panic so great I felt as though I were suffocating. My eyes found his, and a cocky grin curved on his lips as he leaned forward, his face only inches from mine.

"Welcome home, love."

What. The. *Fuck*.

Acknowledgments

Well, damn. I did it. I wrote a freaking *book*. It feels beyond cliche to say, 'I couldn't have done it without you all,' but it's the truth. So many people have had a hand in making this dream of mine a reality that I don't think I could name you all. But I'm going to try.

To the fantastic authors I've met through Booktok: I would still be crying in a puddle on the ground if it wasn't for your guidance on everything self-publishing. Thank you for holding my hand and explaining everything like I'm five.

To my INCREDIBLE Beta Readers: Allison, Alyssa, Amanda, Ashley N, Ashley S, Brittany, Jade, Maddie, Maggie, Mary, Rebecca, Sarah, Shaye, and Skye. Thank you for all of your comments, concerns, and suggestions. This book would not have become what it is now if it wasn't for you all.

To Chelsea and Kayla: Thank you so much for reading my very chaotic first chapters when this was all starting and giving your thoughts and input. This book would literally not have the opening it does if it wasn't for you both.

To Melanie: I'm not sure whether to call you an Alpha or a Beta... or something in-between. But thank you for your excitement over this project and passion for my characters and world.

To Lexy: Thank you for FaceTiming me for hours as we chaotically assigned birthdays to my characters while laughing our asses off. If it weren't for you, Felix wouldn't have the birthday that he does. I'm sorry, I mean Ghost Honey.

To Dom and Rachel: My amazingly hilarious and sexy AF DemiAlpha Readers. My Found Family. My Wingspan Clan. I'm not sure what I did to deserve the world bringing us together, but damn I'm glad it did. Thank you for all the cookies, merch, love, laughter, support, zoom calls, and IG voice memos. Thank you for letting me read the Ten Questions chapter on zoom the day I wrote it. I'll never forget that. I love both of you to the moon and back. P.s. The crust is the top.

To my wonderful husband, Kenny: The support and love you've given me for the past year as I've worked on this project has meant everything. Thank you for all you've done and for keeping our tiny humans alive as I chased this goal.

And finally, to Kodie: My platonic soulmate. I don't think it's possible to convey just how much you mean to me, but once again, I shall try. This book... would, without a doubt, not have happened if it wasn't for you. Thank you for being the best Alpha Reader I could have ever had. Thank you for loving this story, this world, and these characters as if they were your own. Thank you for your input and edits. Thank you for the suggestions you'd write, just to make another note a paragraph later to disregard it. Thank you for loving and supporting me almost as much as you do Felix. Thank you for our shower FaceTime calls (relax, people, it wasn't like that) and for listening to me vent and cry and lose my damn mind over this book. Thank you for constantly pushing me and never letting me give up. Thank you for fighting for my story when I didn't want to anymore. Most of all, thank you for sliding into my DMs on November 12th, 2021, and giving me the gift of your friendship. I'll love you forever.

Lightning Source UK Ltd.
Milton Keynes UK
UKHW011316130123
415295UK00005B/471